I0823601

FALLEN GODS

FALLEN GODS

#1 *NEW YORK TIMES* BESTSELLING AUTHOR

RACHEL VAN DYKEN

RED TOWER BOOKS™

Entangled Publishing, LLC
644 Shrewsbury Commons Ave., STE 181
Shrewsbury, PA 17361
rights@entangledpublishing.com

Red Tower Books is an imprint of Entangled Publishing, LLC.

Visit our website at www.entangledpublishing.com.

Cover and edge design by LJ Anderson
Jacket design by Liz Wayant
Cover images by soulscience/CG Trader and Juggernaut69/GettyImages
Edge image by Pobytov/GettyImages
Case design by Elizabeth Turner Stokes
Case image by Nadia Murash/Shutterstock
Endpaper original illustration by Kateryna Vitkovska
Interior design by Britt Marczak

HC ISBN 978-1-64937-467-7
Ebook ISBN 978-1-64937-657-2

Printed in the United States of America
First Edition December 2025

10 9 8 7 6 5 4 3 2 1

ENJOY THESE OTHER SERIES BY RACHEL VAN DYKEN

EAGLE ELITE

New Adult Mafia Romance

Elite
Elect
Entice
Elicit
Enamor
Enchant
Bang Bang
Enforce
Ember
Elude
Enrapture
RIP: A Bratva Brotherhood Novel
Empire
A Very Mafia Christmas
Enrage
Eulogy
Envy
Debase: A Bratva Brotherhood Novel
Dissolution
A Two Twirl Christmas
Exposed

THE CONSEQUENCES

New Adult Romantic Comedies

The Consequence of Loving Colton
The Consequence of Revenge
The Consequence of Seduction
The Consequence of Rejection

THE DARK ONES SAGA

Adult Supernatural Romance

Dark Origins
The Dark Ones
Untouchable Darkness
Dark Surrender
Darkest Temptation
Darkest Sinner
Darkest Power
Darkest Need
Darkest Descent

THE BET

New Adult Romantic Comedies

The Bet
The Wager
The Love Strategy
Love Hazard

RED CARD

New Adult Sports Romance

Risky Play
Kickin' It

To my Grandpa Gjengstø (Jacobsen): who knew that all the books you gave me on Norse mythology would pay off. I have you to thank for my Norwegian heritage. Love you so much, Grandpa, thank you for the many stories, and while you are no longer here to see me write mine, I know you're proud. Shine bright in Helheim.

In *Fallen Gods*, myths walk among mortals…and scheme for domination. As such, the story features elements that might not be suitable for all readers, including injury, blood, death, drowning, physical abuse, alcohol use, graphic language, perilous situations, and sexual activity on the page, from tender kisses to angry sex. Grief, loss of family, and war are discussed. Readers who may be sensitive to these elements, please take note.

Welcome to Endir University, where the gods spark
chaos and runes rise from the mist. Grab a syllabus.
It's going to be one hell of an orientation week.

Author's Note

I grew up on Norse mythology. My grandpa was always telling me stories and handing me books, and while I didn't see him much when I was little, I could count on the books while he traveled. Some of them are now missing pages, and others I've kept specifically for my own kids.

I was always asking him questions, and he'd exaggerate about Gods in Asgard. He was a larger-than-life character, and had you told me when I was little that he was Odin, I would have been like, *yes, my world is complete and that makes total sense*! He's also the one who told my dad that his firstborn should be named Torbald. My sister ended up not inheriting that name, but we were finally able to make his dream come true when we named my oldest son Thor. Don't worry—in my own story, we have plenty of Mjölnirs around the house (all real if you ask my ten-year-old, shhhh).

Mythology has always been a passion, but it really does hit different when it's something that ties to your childhood and family. While *Fallen Gods* does deal with Norse mythology and was extensively researched, please know that I did take creative license with a lot of subjects. I wanted to create a what-if story that takes the reader on a journey they've never been on before. Everything has meaning, after all.

Enjoy my version of the Gods and Giants, and be warned—you do have to pick a side.

HUGS
RVD

Prologue

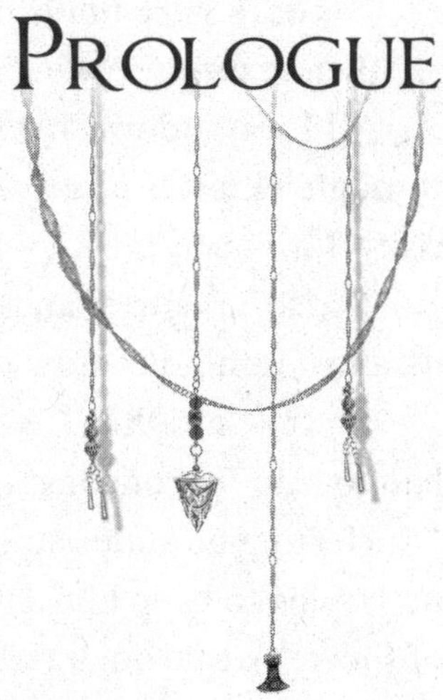

REY

"Would you?" I whisper, hating the tremor in my voice. We're stopped in the middle of campus, a cool breeze brushing against my heated cheeks giving me the courage to ask again. "Would you run away with me, knowing that the world would eventually end? Knowing that the world would *burn*?"

Weeks ago, I never would have thought we'd have a conversation like this. Now the air between us is cold enough that his breath fogs in front of him in a frosty haze. In another life, I would have thought it poetic. Now, it just reminds me exactly what he is.

A Giant.

Ruthless.

Powerful.

A God in his own right.

Aric shifts his weight, and silence stretches between us like a chasm neither of us can cross.

Maybe I never should have let go with him. Not after knowing what was really behind the war between the Gods and the Giants. Now it just feels like the end.

"You're hesitating." I can barely get the sentence out.

His dark gaze holds mine, and his jaw clenches.

"I can't promise you," he finally says. "Not until we end this."

All I wanted was for him to say yes. I wouldn't have made him go through with it. I just wanted to know that he was *willing* to take the risk—for *me.*

The soft rustle of ancient leaves threads through the space between us, a low reminder of where we stand…and what's at stake.

"So that's it, then? We're doing this." Heat burns my cheeks, but I had to ask. Just one last time.

His tongue slides across his bottom lip, then his jaw tightens—like he's trying to keep himself from saying too much. As a few errant flakes of snow float through the air, his eyes remain locked on mine.

I shake my head. One of us needs to be strong enough for this.

"I don't need the cold," I say and feel even more pathetic. "I don't want it."

"But I still need your warmth," he adds, and I know he means it. But it's no longer enough. Snow dusts his broad shoulders, the same shoulders that have carried so much.

"One of us is going to die." I finally say the words out loud.

And deep in my soul, I know.

It's going to be me.

Chapter One

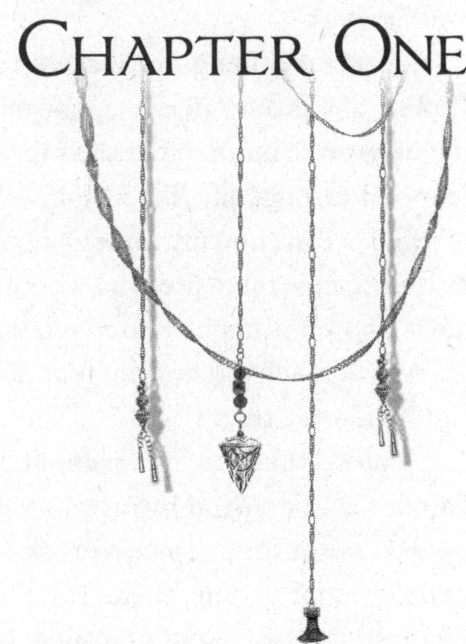

REY

One week earlier...

The note in my hand is so crumpled and damp with sweat that I'm sure the ink is etched into my skin like a brand. But that's not what gets me.

Despite the way he treated her, I've never seen my stepmother cry. Not once. In all my years with her, Laufey's been a fortress—unshaken, unreadable. Through his abuse, through her sickness, through everything.

Until today. My eighteenth birthday.

At first, I thought it was because of what my father finally asked me to do—that one "favor" I always knew was coming but prayed never would. Until of course it finally did.

But this? It feels heavier.

Like she's been holding in something massive for years, saving her tears for this very moment.

Today, Laufey finally broke.

Between sobs, she begs, "Please, Rey. Don't do this. We can find another way."

I can't meet her gaze. She was the only safe space I had other than Rowen. She protected me, and now it's my time to protect her. She may not be my real mother, but she's the only one I've ever known. And her tears cut through me like a blade.

I glance around my father's opulent home and, for the first time in my entire miserable life, wish I could stay. But I can't. Father has given me a mission—and promised me the world if I succeed.

My stomach pitches, but fear doesn't matter. Can't. Not if it means setting Laufey free.

"I know what you dream about, Rey. One day being away from me," Father says, unmoved by his wife's hysterics. "I know it eats you alive."

His words dig deep into my skin like an ache I can't get rid of, and I don't bother to deny them. Instead, I turn to hold his dark gaze, and I let just the tiniest hint of a spine bring my shoulders higher.

An icy smile spreads across his face, and my gaze shifts. White hair pulled back into his signature low ponytail. Patch covering his right eye. Three-piece navy suit accented by a sharp walking cane. Gold adornments draping from his tie. One a hammer, the other the head of his enemy.

He's a riot at parties.

Father glances at his bodyguard leaning against the darkened doorway to my left and nods. Without a word, Rowen moves to collect Laufey. He's just a few years older than me and taller than Father, his shoulders seemingly twice as wide, his demeanor youthful and strong. And yet, he's always appeared the weaker man. Maybe that's because he obeys Father's every whim without question.

I get it. I feel just as small in his shadow.

My stomach twists as Rowen wraps an arm around Laufey's waist and hauls her up. She collapses against his broad chest as he leads her down the hallway to her private rooms.

Father ignores them both.

"You have one week to find Thor's hammer." His voice is sharp, heavy. "Remove anyone who stands in your way. Destroy them all for what they took from us, Rey. The Eriksons, every last one. But don't be quick about it." His voice draws into a low command. "Make them suffer."

"How do you know Aric has it?" Sigurd's more powerful. Why wouldn't the Giants keep it with him?

"I know." He raises his voice. I try not to flinch. "Because his parents hid it. Last mistake I ever made." He clenches his jaw. "Your job isn't to ask questions. It's to do what I ask."

I nod in agreement. That's all anyone can do around this man if they hope to keep their head. I don't know why I thought asking him would help at all. At least he didn't say it was all my fault.

It would have been nice to ask Laufey for intel before starting this mission, since she's a Giant herself, but my father would never allow it. She fears his anger so much, she's left the room any time I've so much as mentioned the Eriksons. Even thinking about what Father might do to her in my absence has my stomach turning.

I almost flinch when he leans in and brushes a hand down my cheek, kisses me on my forehead. A soft brush devoid of comfort. "I'm proud. You know that, right? Out of all my children…you are the most worthy."

I know he's trying to compliment me, but it feels more like a curse.

Stepping back, he drops his hand. "Rowen will have the car brought around in a minute. Gather your things and let's be off. I've waited too long for this moment and do not relish further delay." With that, he walks away, his cane slapping against the marble floor in a rhythm that dares me to follow.

I grit my teeth, shove the crumpled note from Laufey deep into my jeans pocket. I haven't read it yet, but I don't need to. I'm sure it's begging me to give up this mission. Pointless.

Reaching down, I grab my new rucksack, then throw it over my shoulder. Father's right. Might as well get this over with as quickly as possible.

Within minutes, we're both settled in the back seat of a sleek black Mercedes sedan, Rowen expertly taking the turn that will lead us onto the highway out of Bellevue, Washington—toward the town of Everett, Endir University, and my freshman year.

I stare at the rain pelting the windshield, the wiper blades whooshing back and forth. Someone nearby lays on their horn, and I want to rage at them: they don't know how good they have it. I *wish* my worst day was encountering a bad driver.

But pain is pain—it doesn't care about rank. It just exists. And knowing someone, somewhere, carried more of it than I did...that's the only thing that got me through the last two years.

I'm in this mess because of who my father is—what he's capable of and what's been done on both sides of this war. Some might say it's because I was born special.

They'd be wrong.

In fact, the real reason I'm here is because of how *not* special I am. Or at least, how unimpressive one person in particular found me.

My heart races as a flash of warm brown eyes crosses my mind. No, not warm. I run my finger across the faint scars on my knuckles and focus on the traffic.

Rowen's knowing gaze meets mine in the rearview mirror, then flicks away. Typical. I stare at his thick blond waves brushing his shoulders, like staring at something solid will help me forget how splintered we are underneath.

I don't remember when exactly Rowen became my closest friend. He just was—one day not there, the next day orbiting my life like a second moon. He moved in three years ago, probably right after graduating high school, but we never talked about hobbies or birthdays or any of the things normal people compare to feel less alone. Sharing space under my father's roof was enough. Trauma bonds faster than time.

And now, after today, I'll likely never see him again.

My heart sinks to the bottom of my stomach as beside me, my father snaps open a newspaper, like phones and social media don't exist. Every few seconds, he clears his throat and adjusts his tie with his right hand—the one with the tattoos that tell the world exactly who he is, *if* they're privileged enough to know what the runes mean on all five of his murderous fingers.

Even to a casual observer, the markings look dark and menacing. Because of course they do. He likes the attention.

At the end of the day, I know what sort of hand those tattoos belong to. One of authority, terror, and power. I wonder what it says about me that my first daydreams were about cutting his fingers off.

Taking away his pride and joy. One. By. One.

I sigh again and look out the window, digging into my pocket to clutch the piece of paper there, crinkling it tighter and tighter.

We dodge through traffic. It feels like we're going faster and faster. Too fast. I wonder if it would be better if we had an accident. Would it change anything? Probably not.

Legends don't die.

And that's exactly what my family is—legendary.

I know who we are. I know our bloodline. It's been hammered into me since birth. Which is how I also know my father's never going to give up. Not when I'm the only person in the position to get him what he wants.

A fact I *know* he resents, because my father is neither patient nor kind, and having to give up even a smidgen of control, to rely on someone else to obtain his goal, well, that's the definition of hell for him.

I smile at the thought. Maybe I'm not the only one who's furious with this outcome. Maybe that's my birthday gift—him needing *me*.

I shamefully take it.

I push aside the anger that he would risk my life in order to regain what was taken from us—what they *stole* from us—and cling to this one silly concept. That I'm needed by Odin himself.

He didn't even know where the Eriksons were keeping Mjölnir until last year. Which is when I became the final chess piece and his only option.

He needs me. But he doesn't need the people I love, which is why I'm sitting in this car.

"You have exactly one week. It's all the time we have left." My father finally speaks, his voice a low, rasping growl, edged with anger. Always.

I don't flinch. Not outwardly. But inside? A storm rages. "I understand."

I keep my eyes on the rain, watching as it streaks along the window in erratic patterns. It's the only steady thing in a life drowning in chaos. The water beats down relentlessly, ruthlessly, but it will stop, will have its end. All things must.

The car winds up the steep mountain road, taking us deeper into the heart of the evergreen forest. My father used to tell me stories about the forests and the cold within, always warning me that an early frost never meant the beginning of something but the agonizing end of it, that it meant the Gods were stirring, screaming for vengeance.

I shiver and try to keep my hands still in my lap, take a soothing breath. I finally have a purpose—diabolical as it may be—and I can't fail. I stare out at the towering pine trees, the rugged landscape shrouded by an eerie fog. Yet even through the driving rain, the fairy-tale mist curls among the trees, weaving over green moss and a brush of frost, and I realize: it's beautiful here. Peaceful.

Better than Bellevue, at least.

I hate the filth, the bustle of the city.

I hate even more what my last name means there.

The forest thickens as we near Lake Stevens, home to the Eriksons—the family I'll be forced to orbit at Endir, since they founded the university that will become my new prison.

And of course their oldest son, Aric, will be there, too. Because it's not enough that he's the only person who knows where Thor's hammer is. No, my life is a Gods-fueled soap opera: complete with family drama, revenge plots, and even a former fiancé.

If you can count a betrothal that barely lasted an afternoon.

Just thinking of Aric has my stomach twisting. It's been years, but the thought of seeing him again still knots something deep in my chest. Avoiding him will be impossible. Pretending he doesn't exist will have to do.

We stop at a red light in Everett.

My father lets out a frustrated grumble, as if the light is purposefully slowing our journey, as if it has stakes in this game. He fails to understand that the world no longer runs according to his ancient Rolex.

A black Land Rover Defender pulls up next to us, engine roaring, and I'm jealous of the power behind that accelerator. The windows are down, and though I barely get a glance inside the vehicle, I can fully appreciate the loud music annoying the hell out of my father, along with the muscular arm resting partially out the window.

I smirk as he shifts in his seat and lets out a grunt under his breath. It's the little things.

I've learned to count my small victories where I can find them.

The minute the light turns green, the car cuts us off and speeds ahead. We follow in the same direction while my father starts a monologue about respect and kids these days. I've heard it a million times. It has zero impact.

I know we're close when the sound of Father folding his newspaper fills the car. With each crisp snick of the paper, my body tenses.

And then he turns. I know he turns, not because I see it but because the musky smell of the earth follows. I squeeze my eyes shut for one brief second and then shift toward him.

The car pulls to a stop, but I don't dare look away from him. It would be too disobedient, and if I want to get out of this car, I need to show him I know my place. The newspaper is lying forgotten on his right thigh.

His hand curls around the head of the golden raven adorning the top of his ever-present cane, and he taps a tattooed thumb over it, the heavy gold ring on his hand banging out an insistent rhythm. I know he does this on purpose; he wants to draw attention. I might be one of the few people in this world who knows the power that cane holds. It's a relic of our world, concealing a sword of Asgardian steel. It's part of him. It never leaves his side.

"I don't think I need to remind you how important this is, Rey." His free hand reaches for his jeweled, braided white beard. With each stroke, his anxiety surely lessens while mine ratchets up. "You know, I didn't want children, at least not…" He makes a face. "You."

And just like that, we're back to reminding me of my worth.

For as much as he needs me, he never fails to remind me of my place.

Me. A nobody compared to him.

Just like Laufey, just like Rowen, just like every other person in his life, I've never been good enough. I'm just his weak bastard—his words, not mine. "I understand, sir."

Most children are born being told to shine.

I was born being told to stay dim.

But it's my turn to shine now. I've been given no choice.

He nods. "Yet you've done well despite my wife's best efforts to encourage the opposite of my training. And now you've got seven days. One week to prove that I was wrong about your worth." He reaches for my chin. My lips tremble at the gesture. *Don't cry. Don't flinch.* "Everyone will adore you. After all, they can't help it, can they?" He grins, and there's nothing but malice in his smile.

Because he's right—they *will* adore me; they have no other choice. They're drawn to my Aethercall. A sort of glamour, old as the blood in my veins. People don't *choose* to notice me. They just do.

It's fitting that the only gift my father has ever given me is a curse.

"Thank you," I whisper, hating myself all over again. "For the honor of serving you."

His nostrils flare. He leans in and whispers in my ear, "You forgot the last part."

I don't shake.

I don't yell.

I'm numb.

I lick my lips and say, "Odinfather."

"Good girl. Now go hunt."

Chapter Two

REY

As we pull to a stop in front of the school, Father doesn't reach for the handle. He waits, as always, for Rowen to open the door for him. Valet. Guard. Pet. Whatever role he's assigned today.

I adjust my long black coat and put on my black Celine sunglasses, like they're the only armor I need to walk into the enemy camp.

The notorious Erikson family has its legacy stamped all over campus. They even have a family sculpture in front of the student center featured on the brochure that came with my acceptance letter. The founder, Sigurd, holding both of his grandsons in a huddle, Aric and Reeve gazing adoringly into their grandfather's beaming smile.

I've met the youngest brother, Reeve, a handful of times over the years at various social events. Enough times to know I'd rather jump off a cliff than fake a friendship with him.

His older brother, though—Aric didn't bother with pretending.

He rarely spoke unless forced, and even then it was usually a grunt or a sharp glance meant to dissect every inch of your confidence.

Except for that one time.

The moment I've since convinced myself didn't count. A lapse. A weakness. One I couldn't afford then and sure as hell can't afford now.

They're opposites. Reeve talks until you beg him to stop. Aric barely exists in the room—until you realize you can't stop wondering what his voice might actually sound like saying your name.

And then there's his achingly beautiful face.

Jawline like it was carved from granite. The kind of dark, wavy hair stylists try to manufacture for cologne campaigns—except on him, it just falls, effortless while expensive, across his forehead.

"Listen to me carefully, Rey." Father doesn't raise his voice now. "Find the hammer or don't come back."

"I understand," I say, nodding. I'd say anything to end this goodbye.

He already spent all night drilling the plan into me:

Find the hammer.

Kill anyone who gets in the way.

Bring it home.

He made it all sound achingly simple. And maybe it will be, because I grew up knowing exactly what we were.

The Eriksons didn't.

They clung to power out of instinct, circling my family for decades without ever understanding why. As far as they knew, it was all business—territorial tension, inherited wealth, fractured alliances.

But the truth was older. Blood-soaked. Divine.

Odin's final act at the end of the war between Gods and Giants wasn't conquest. It was erasure.

He wiped their memories.

All of them.

Everyone but himself, of course.

And the few he *needed* to remember.

Rowen.

Laufey.

Or those like me who were graced by Odin with the knowledge.

For us, truth is a leash.

Odin never lets us forget what we are—he just dangles our freedom like a promise he never intends to keep.

"If you don't, it's not just you who will suffer." He reaches out and flicks the strap of the blue rucksack he gave me this morning that's nestled between us on the seat. "This has everything you'll need. Study the information well and remember who suffers if you do not."

My throat tightens, and all I can do is nod this time.

If Aric gets in my way, he won't see it coming. He won't even feel the knife slip between his ribs until it's too late. Until I've taken everything from him.

I'll do it because my father's right. He's always right about the world and our enemies in it.

Maybe deep down, I'm not much different than the man who sired me—ruthless, willing to do whatever it takes to get what I want.

For a fleeting moment, shame tightens its grip around my throat, regret following like it always does, but I can do this.

I *have* to do this.

I crinkle Laufey's note in my hand until my fingers ache, then leave it in my pocket. Now isn't the time to break down. I keep telling myself I have one job and that's all I'm allowed to focus on. Because there's no backing out of this.

As if on cue, Rowen opens the car door.

"Good girl," Father repeats and climbs out of the car.

I pick up the rucksack, but Rowen's already there—he swings my door open and takes it from my hand like it weighs nothing. His eyes catch mine for half a second, but it's enough. Enough to see the resignation. The shame. The quiet kind of defeat that doesn't scream—it just *sits* in your chest and rots.

I give him a half smile anyway. A lie with teeth. It's fine. Everything's fine.

My father once told me Rowen's family has been serving ours for generations—like that makes it noble. Like inherited chains are some kind of legacy. We were walking the beach, waves chewing at the shore, and I'd asked how long their penance would last.

He bent down, scooped up a handful of sand, and said, "When this is gone."

"From your hand?" I'd asked.

"From the world."

And that was that. Life sentence without appeal. Loyalty carved from bone.

He'd dusted his hands on his pants and walked away, stabbing his cane into the sand with every step—sharp, deliberate, like he wanted the beach to remember it.

And that was it. Conversation over.

I knew in that moment that it was the same for me, for Laufey, for anyone in my father's circle. We'd never be free of him unless he chose to release us.

And Rowen? He just accepts it as his fate because he feels like he failed and has the scars to prove it.

From the stories I've been told since childhood, it wasn't always this way. Where did it all go wrong? When did it become about who held the most power? The most wealth? When did our world get so corrupt? I've never asked.

I don't think I'm scared of the answer anymore. Not really. What scares me now is knowing it won't matter. Not after everything. The truth won't save anyone. Least of all me.

Rowen's already at the open trunk, waiting. I follow, footsteps too steady, breath too measured.

Other cars begin pulling into the lot now. Some parents with tear-streaked cheeks, others fumbling with luggage and half-hearted hugs. All of it too loud, too *normal*. Maybe that's why my father suddenly leans forward and wraps an arm around my shoulders—like he's playing at being human.

I freeze. His warmth presses against me, unfamiliar and uninvited. It feels like wearing someone else's skin.

One pat on the back. Then he pulls away and flashes that too-white grin that never reaches his eyes. "I shall try to miss you, daughter."

Now *that* sounds more like the college send-off I expected from Odinfather.

He turns without another word and climbs back into the car. The door shuts with a soft snick, but it hits like a death sentence. Final. I feel it settle in my chest.

Rowen lifts my other bags and my one large trunk from the car without looking at me. Without looking at anything, really.

As we step onto the sidewalk, the window rolls down just enough for my father to urge, "Ticktock, Rowen."

And then the glass slides up again.

"Stay safe," I say to Rowen as he settles my luggage on the ground. I can't help the crack in my voice or the feeling that I'm walking into an empty grave, one my father dug for me. "This is where we part ways. Stay alive. Don't text."

I hate being cruel to him, but it's easier to cut ties now before I get in too deep. I know myself. I'll want to pull him down into the depths with me, and in a moment of weakness—a cardinal sin in this family—I'll ask him to save me.

And Rowen will. He always will. And then he'll pay the price for it, the same way he did last time. When everything was taken from him.

Rowen scratches the scars that run the length of his right arm, and though he doesn't respond, I can see what his silence is costing him in the grimace tightening his jaw. I focus on those scars. Though I can't possibly fathom what he's been through, I understand enough to know he gave his all and had the most precious thing that made him *him* stripped away.

That's as much as he's been willing to share. To this day, I have no idea what he lost. I just know the guilt he feels over it must be massive for him to work for my father without killing him in his sleep.

My stomach drops as Rowen pales, realizing what he's been doing. His blond hair shifts in the breeze, and his eyes meet mine. He's effortlessly beautiful and the perfect example of what actual sacrifice looks like. He's given himself to our family for life, and he still won't tell me what my father did to earn such loyalty.

Tears burn my eyes.

He's always been my anchor. And now…I need to force him to live a life where we can't rely on each other any longer.

His eyes focus on the blue bag, full of my father's secrets. I know what he's thinking. *Run. Run away*. But that's not an option. My father, his…people, they're relentless. Ruthless.

And then there's my stepmother.

I'm afraid my father's going to ask us what's taking so long, so I quickly grab my bags from the sidewalk and the handle to my trunk. I nod toward Rowen. It's the best I can do. "It's been great."

It's been sad.

It's been the seventh circle of hell, actually, and now I'm walking into another circle without him by my side.

His eyes are so big, it feels like they're going to swallow me whole. "You'll be back. Right?"

For the first time since my father pulled me aside a few weeks ago, I want to cry. I'd felt almost happy, getting ready to attend Seattle University as a psych major. I'd allowed myself to feel excitement for the first time, over new beginnings, over possibly being truly free. From him, from the intense studies, the martial arts, the endless training—and then he'd forced me to accept a sudden offer to attend Endir instead.

I was heartbroken.

At first, I'd assumed the last two years of training and torture, beatings when I failed, a meal when I didn't, were all designed to punish me for being rejected by an Erikson. My humiliation needed penance. I'd assumed even the curse of my Aethercall was given so my father would never feel the bruise of anyone rejecting me again. How wrong I had been on all counts.

But these are pointless thoughts now. I am here, and I have a job to do.

So I conjure up a semi-chipper tone and offer Rowen a half smile. "Of course. I could never leave my best friend."

Rowen doesn't smile back. "See you on the other side, then?"

I'm not a fool. Neither is he.

He knows the risks and has the scars to prove what happens when things don't go to plan.

I choke out my next words. "The other side. I've heard it's not so bad." Death might actually be the only escape for both of us.

He swallows, then his smile is so big, so convincing. "They probably, at the very least, have heart-attack-level greasy fries."

Gods, what I would've given to have sat next to him during the drive here, listening to his dry jokes and getting all of my fears off my chest. Honestly, just sitting next to him would have made me feel better.

"I love fries," I finally say.

"I'll make sure they're extra crispy when I see you again."

I smooth an invisible wrinkle from my cashmere sweater, desperate to stretch this moment until it breaks. The only words left are "good luck" and "don't die," but luck's never been mine, and an early death is the likeliest ending for us both.

"You'll be bored without me," I finally say.

Rowen lifts his hand but then drops it, fingers balling into a fist at his side like he wants to cup my face but knows he shouldn't. "You know I will, because I'm impatient."

"Aren't we all?" I tease.

The horn honks, making us both jolt. The fact that my father managed to reach toward the front and honk means he's beyond irritated.

Rowen inclines his head. "To the other side, where there is no war." He lifts his hand to the right side of his face, then brings it down his cheek until he hits his chest, flipping it over in an ancient offering of the Gods. "No war with *them*."

Mouth dry, I whisper, "Only life for us."

"Only life," he whispers. "Hunt well, daughter of—"

I shake my head.

I don't need his damning words cast into the world. I don't think I can bear the weight of them. Everything already feels heavy. Everything already feels *wrong*.

Maybe because it is.

"Everything will be fine," I say.

I hate that I lie so easily now.

I hate that I actually want to believe the lie even more.

Chapter Three

ARIC

My jaw aches from clenching it, and I drag a hand over the day-old scruff, as if I can rub the tension out. I should go for a run. Shower. Shave. Pretend I'm ready for the onslaught of new and returning students about to flood campus.

I stay where I am.

I've been standing at this window, staring down at the loop in front of Endir's gates, long enough for my breath to fog the glass.

Watching. Waiting.

For *her*.

The absolute last person I ever wanted to see again.

Two years ago, that day on the beach, I made the mistake of doing her a kindness. She went straight to her father. And by the end of the week, my parents were dead.

I hoped she rotted in hell.

When I saw her name on the enrollment list last week, I froze. My brother, Reeve, was reading the roster over my shoulder, and I knew the moment he saw her name, too, because he took a few steps away like I was going to throw something.

Which only pissed me off more. I'm not violent. Usually.

My grandfather is a cunning bastard. Nothing happens on this campus without his permission. So if she was coming here, he'd allowed it to happen. He *wanted* it to happen. Only question is, why?

I brace one arm across the window casing and continue to wait. There was no point pushing the old man for answers. He'd give them only when they served him. For now, I just needed one look at the woman responsible for ripping my family apart. One look to confirm I feel absolutely nothing for her except hatred.

Then, like I'd summoned her myself, a long black car glides to a stop. And Rey Stjerne steps out, rain catching in the dark shine of her hair.

I only get a brief look at her before she turns away from me—but it's enough.

The last time I saw her, she had wild, dark curls, ripped jeans, and an oversize NYU sweatshirt with a mustard stain on the sleeve. Odd, the things that stick.

Now? Everything's different. Sleek bun, hair yanked back so tight it looks painful. Wide sunglasses. A mouth set in a line that makes her look carved from ice. Long black coat, dark-wash wide-legged jeans, high-heeled boots, soft gray sweater. Every piece deliberate, calculated.

I let out a long breath, the tension in my jaw easing for the first time in more than a week. This version of her will be easy to hate.

I continue to watch as the trunk closes, Rey and her father hugging before he heads back into his car. Then she and her driver walk over to stand on the sidewalk. Too close.

I reach up and clear the fog from the glass again, imagine I can hear her voice in the air, drifting through my second-floor window. Even though we haven't seen each other in years, I'd never forget a voice like Rey's.

It's a complete and total contradiction, soft and airy when it shouldn't be and extremely sharp when it needs to be. The kind of voice that slices through you like a knife, cutting you to ribbons but making you thankful for the pain—until you realize it's too late and you're already bleeding out.

I shudder. I may not survive this semester.

I don't even know why I keep watching them. I shouldn't care, and I really don't. I'm just curious.

From up here, she looks smaller than I remembered. Almost fragile.

She's angled slightly away from her driver, like she's already halfway gone. He says something, but she doesn't laugh. Doesn't smile, either. Just nods once and keeps her hands in her coat pockets.

Other students are starting to arrive—parents dragging suitcases, hugging too long, laughing and snapping family photos on their phones. But she doesn't move like them. Doesn't carry that awkward, wide-eyed energy everyone else has. She's composed. Still. Like she's going to a funeral instead of her first day of college.

The driver shifts closer. She doesn't flinch. She doesn't lean in, either.

Instead, she lifts her head slightly, scanning the buildings. Her gaze never reaches this window, but I take a step back anyway.

Not because I'm hiding.

Just habit.

Everything about her stance is the same as I remember—guarded, purposeful, almost cruel. She's a monster dressed up like an angel.

I don't look at Rey as she passes closer. My father always told me not to stare at storms—especially the ones that wear a human face.

I learned that too late.

The last time I ignored the warning signs, it cost me everything. My parents are a memory now—scattered in ash and silence.

And the man responsible for that silence raised her.

I exhale, long and slow, until my shoulders relax, then look down at my phone. It's only day one, and she's already affecting me this harshly. Maybe she'll ignore me the way I plan on ignoring her.

Why the hell is she at Endir? Her of all people? The daughter of the antichrist?

I hate her father.

I hate *her*.

I despise everything their family stands for and everything they did to hurt mine. Haven't they already done enough? Now they have to infiltrate the only peace I have left?

She turns, and the sunlight streaming through a cloud behind her casts her in an otherworldly glow. She glances up and, in an instant, she's looking right at me. Right through me. But no, I already took a step back. She can't actually see me.

I'm going to give her a wide berth and pray she does the same for me. I've worked hard for the peace this place gives me. I'm not about to surrender it now.

One thing's for sure. Rey Stjerne can burn in hell.

And maybe she will.

If I keep my distance. If I can stay in control.

Although, with my heart hammering like it already knows what's coming, neither feels likely right now.

CHAPTER FOUR

REY

My father's car fades into the distance, but I don't look back. I keep my eyes shut to center myself. I'm equipped for this. The air shifts, subtle but undeniable, and I can feel the charge beneath the surface. There's a storm coming.

I open my eyes when a group of students walks past me. I need to get moving before more rain hits.

I grab my bags and start toward the dorms. I haul the trunk behind me, its wheels dragging over the stone like it resents being here as much as I do.

Just then, a breeze kicks up, lifting strands of hair across my face. The lake on my left doesn't ripple. Doesn't move at all.

I follow the shoreline with my gaze and finally take in the campus buildings, really *see* them—and what stares back doesn't belong in this world.

Endir's campus rises out of the landscape like it was never built—just *unearthed*. It's a mixture of buildings from the eighties scattered in between older-looking ones that aren't even dated. Most of the questionable buildings are carved from some unnamable black stone, slick with age and myth, rumored to be the last thing the Gods or

Giants shaped before the world tore itself apart. Behind them, the mountains loom, massive and unyielding, like sentinels keeping watch over something too old to name and too dangerous to forget.

My father says the oldest structure can't be carbon-dated, but considering the source, I file that under maybe true, maybe propaganda. Either way, it doesn't matter. The place feels ancient in a way that makes my skin itch.

This isn't a normal campus.

And most of the students walking across it aren't normal, either—even if they think they are.

A few, like Aric, are here for reasons they'll never understand. The rest? For the most part, trust-fund humans pretending their bloodlines didn't buy them a seat at something holy.

I walk along the stone pathway with my bags and almost trip when a wheel gets stuck in a groove. Looking down, I see that etched into one of the small cobblestones is a mark shaped like the rune Thurisaz. Wow, fantastic. I'm only a few minutes in and already I'm greeted by the rune that represents destruction.

My father always said there were twenty-six runes, each with different meanings and abilities. Humans, of course, are only aware of twenty-four of them. Regardless of the number, though, I'm really not a fan of running into this specific one.

It's not like I needed a reminder of how dangerous this is.

I can't help glancing around to see if I've triggered some sort of waiting trap, but no. Just another cool breeze hitting my skin greets me. Thank the Gods.

Is this how the entire semester is going to be? Wondering what's safe and what's not? Always looking over my shoulder, doubting everyone and everything? I didn't expect even the air to taste different here, but it does. My father said the bag he gave me had all the information I'd need to complete my mission. Yet I'm only a few minutes in and already thinking he exaggerated.

Maybe that's why he didn't step foot on campus.

I wonder.

Is this school protected from him? From us?

I sidestep the rune and shake my head. I didn't think to ask my father, but the question gnaws at me now. I grip my bags tighter, reach for my trunk's handle, and start walking again toward the door to the dorms. Students are everywhere, smiling under the bright signs welcoming them to Endir like it's going to somehow change their lives.

I'd laugh if my sense of humor still existed.

A lanky redhead bumps into me, and he pauses to mutter, "Oh, sorry."

His eyes roam up and down my body. Nope. Not today.

I'd like to think that I'm good at keeping my emotions in check, so I merely tilt my head and do what I do best—I charm him. "Don't worry about it. I wasn't watching where I was going."

His brown eyes widen. "Oh, um, right, okay. But I really am sorry. What's your name? Are you new?"

I smile. "I'm sure I'll see you around."

He frowns like he's confused about where he is. "Right, yeah. I'll just be more careful while walking."

"It's a dangerous sport."

He laughs and then turns around and immediately trips over his feet.

My father says it's a gift that people momentarily forget themselves around me, but I always want to ask him how *he'd* feel if he never knew if people genuinely liked him. Of course, he always knows. In what world would they have anything but fear?

"Already making friends?" A familiar voice sounds from behind me. "What's next? Adopting a puppy so you look approachable, only so you can abandon it later?"

Great.

I don't even have to turn. "Reeve."

Aric's tabloid prince of a brother, born for headlines and allergic to responsibility. The kind of guy who makes parties feel like war zones and somehow always walks away untouched. He isn't dangerous in the traditional sense—he just doesn't care who gets burned as long as he stays entertained.

I turn to face him as though I have all the time in the world. His light brown hair is in such disarray, I wonder if it's just directionally challenged the same way Reeve is. His green eyes zero in on me, and I can't help but notice the taunting edge to his smile. He's begging me for a verbal fight; I can feel it in my soul.

He's waiting for my answer, so I get in his face. "Boo."

He chuckles. "Nice try. But nothing's more terrifying than graduating and getting a real job." He shoves a hand into his front pocket, his other gripping an iPad, and rocks back on his heels. "You grew into your ears. Good for you."

I shake my head. "And you've sadly failed to grow out of that mouth of yours."

His grin only widens as if to prove my point. "No complaints."

"Well, this has been fun, but I need to get moved in. Orientation starts tomorrow. It was nice, though; we should do this again sometime." I flip my fingers in a careless wave, then sidestep him, dragging my bags with me.

When a whistle goes off, I stop walking and turn. *You've got to be kidding me*. "They gave you a fucking whistle?"

"Life isn't fair, I know. It was the only way I'd volunteer to help the new students move in." He puts it between his full lips again in a taunt.

I glare. "Blow. I dare you."

He takes the whistle out immediately. "Weird. Normally it's the other way around with this sexy banter, but okay, if you really want me to—"

I groan. "I don't have time for this."

Reeve grins and holds up his iPad. "Then let's get started. Here you are on the list… Welcome to your first year of college, 'Rey Stjerne.'"

So it's going to be like this. Great. "You say my name like a curse."

"Yup."

"Yours isn't any better."

"Pretty sure it is." He snorts, then taps his iPad screen and begins reading. "At Endir University, we believe the world is our students' oyster. Your freshman year will take you as far as you are willing to invest in yourself and your future. Note the godlike mountain range, the beautiful forest surrounding the campus, the majestic Lake Stevens—"

He pauses to look up at me again. "Do I really have to read this to you? It's going to be a long day already, and knowing you, this will just make you angrier."

Well, at least he has some self-preservation. "Please stop."

"Aw." He presses a hand to his chest and winks at me. "You learned how to say please. It *has* been a while."

"And you learned to read. We've both grown up, made amazing improvements in life. There's no goal too small, right?"

"Have I ever mentioned how charming you are? No? Well, I'm so glad your murderous father spent a shit ton of money to buy your way into Endir, when there are plenty of schools far, far, far away from us." He sighs. "How sad, though, that you took a spot here, meaning some poor innocent college student is sitting at home wondering why their straight A's and volunteer service at the local pet shelter weren't enough."

Somewhere deep down, my stomach bottoms out. I've never thought of that before. But I can only smirk. "Life's hard. They'll save a puppy and get over it."

"You're a monster."

"I'm worse." I channel all my pain into my voice, which comes out as a growl, and I'm not mad about it.

He says nothing. Maybe his silence is my answer, like he actually knows what sort of person my father has turned me into. But of course he doesn't.

Reeve looks up at the daunting building we're standing in front of. "If you're nice for the next five minutes, I might help you carry those bags upstairs." He snaps his fingers. "And before I forget, we recommend that all students leave their windows open at night. Fresh air lets the school's many ghosts escape so they don't hurt you." He taps his chin. "Hmm...maybe keep *your* windows shut."

I take a steady breath. Dear Gods, I'd forgotten how annoying Reeve can be. "Good thing I don't believe in ghosts."

He shrugs, gaze flicking away from mine. "Yeah, well, spend a night here and you just might."

An athletic guy with warm brown skin jogs past us in an Endir hoodie, flicking Reeve on the shoulder in greeting. "Party's on."

"Wouldn't miss it," Reeve fires back, holding up his hand for a quick high five before the guy disappears into the crowd. The whole exchange lasted maybe two seconds, but it's seamless—like Reeve has done this a hundred times before.

He turns back to me with the same easy grin, as if the interruption hadn't happened at all.

I bite the inside of my cheek, annoyed for no reason that he has friends and a life—and I don't. "Scared of *ghosts*, Reeve?" I taunt.

"Concerned." He nods, his gaze catching mine again. "Maybe this is where I give you *all* the warnings we give newcomers on campus who are too curious for their own good. That includes you, by the way."

"I figured. All right, let's hear the scary things. Get 'em off your chest and make it fast. I'm already bored."

"You really are lovely."

"Likewise."

"I was being sarcastic."

"Likewise."

Reeve rolls his eyes. "All right, keep up. Rule number one, don't go near the lake after midnight. Sounds weird and superstitious, but there have been many dares to do just that." He shrugs as though any resulting misfortune was their own. "We aren't sure if it's because the lake is so dark that once they jump in, they get confused which way is up, but, point is, most don't survive a midnight swim."

"Awesome." I'm a decent swimmer, but my fear of drowning pretty much guarantees I won't be wading into any creepy lakes.

He ignores me. "Moving on, rule number two. Don't enter the Hall of Ormir without being invited by someone. Basically, the state has lauded it as a historical landmark, so we want to keep it that way even if it's creepier than shit."

"Got it, creepier than shit, Hall of Ormir, get on a tour." I nod. "Isn't Ormir another name for Ymir? The original Giant in Norse mythology?" I wait for him to flinch or give me a hint that he knows more than he should.

Father always enjoyed sharing how he was responsible for putting every God and Giant to sleep, hiding their memories to temporarily end the war, as though he were a savior or something. But it doesn't hurt to test his bragging, to see if everyone really is unaware. I can't imagine forgetting who and what I am—although, oddly enough, the idea warms my chest.

"Pay attention, Rey. We're only sharing useful facts today." He offers me another insufferable wink, and I resist the urge to kick him in the shin. "The next rule, and I know this will be hard for someone of your refined breeding to resist, but please don't drink the lake water. People say it has magic properties, but it doesn't. It's just quite toxic, and in every single scenario where someone has drank the water, they've had to be committed for at least three days in a catatonic state while also shitting their pants from all the bacteria. Zero out of zero, do not recommend. Actually, I changed my mind: go chug, little daughter of Odin. I'll wait."

My spine locks. Just for a second, my stomach tries to crawl into my chest.

He can't know who my father is. Not *really*. He already passed my earlier test…

"What does my being Odin's daughter have to do with anything?"

Reeve blinks once. Twice. Then lets out a snort. "You're not seriously going to stand there and pretend your dad isn't the most notorious mob boss on the West Coast, right? I'm sure he's already sent three guys swimming with cinderblocks today—and that's before lunch." He gestures vaguely in the air. "No doubt you inherited his same…joie de vivre."

Relief hits me so hard, I almost feel a little dizzy, and a giggle escapes the back of my throat. "Time will tell, I suppose."

He barks out a laugh. "Can I just say I missed our cheerful conversations, little mobster daughter?"

"Hey, my father has legitimate businesses." Total lie.

The air shifts.

Reeve's smile vanishes like it was never real—just something he put on for show. His posture doesn't change, but the temperature does. Like a room with the heat suddenly cut.

He leans in, voice low. "Your hands reek of the blood he's spilled."

I don't flinch. Don't look away. "As do yours from your family's crimes, Erikson." I lift my chin. "Now, any other pithy advice before you carry this heavy bag up those stairs like a good little boy?"

"Only one more left," he mutters.

He glances around, making sure no one's close enough to hear, then leans in again. His green eyes sharpen—like frost forming over something that used to burn. "Stay very, very far away from Aric. Time has *not* made the heart grow fonder."

Then he straightens, grabs the handle of my trunk, and hauls it toward the dorm without another word.

I follow slowly, eyes lifting to the building carved against the side of a mountain—massive, shadowed, half eaten by the trees. It doesn't look built. It looks grown. Claimed. Like it's always been waiting.

Just like me.

I cross the threshold.

No turning back now.

Chapter Five

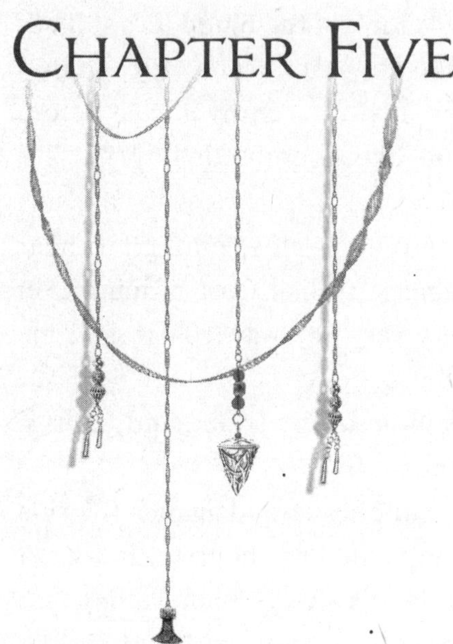

REY

My palms sweat, clinging to the strap of my rucksack, and I try to look casual as Reeve walks me past the wide double exterior doors into the interior foyer. Where another set of locked doors awaits. I start to dig into my bag for the key card that came with my syllabus, but Reeve is already tapping his against the black box by the door. It blinks green, unlocking with a cheerful beep that contrasts sharply with his deadpan expression.

As I pass through, I notice a carving above the electronic lock that looks a lot like the rune Algiz. Interesting choice.

"Curfew's midnight on weekdays. Weekends? Just don't get caught out after two." He winks like he's doing me a favor. "Your RA's a real hard-ass."

He pauses, eyes dancing.

"It's me, by the way. Didn't want the suspense to kill you."

Then he jerks his chin toward the corner above the door.

"Oh—and there are cameras. Everywhere. So try to commit your crimes indoors."

I nod, pulling my sunglasses off and hooking them onto the collar of my gray sweater. "I'm only here for one thing, Reeve. But note taken.

I'll definitely murder you where you sleep if you get in my way."

And with that, I walk through the door, letting it shut swiftly behind us.

"I have to admit, I'm still curious why you're here when your father could just conveniently bury a body to open up a spot at Harvard or Yale instead. I mean, isn't that just a typical business lunch on a Tuesday for him?"

I swallow the bile in my throat. Reeve is not wrong, but it irritates me anyway. The enemy should never be right. I grit my teeth while he hits the elevator button to go up.

"My family doesn't work that way." Lie. Total lie. *I* may not work that way, but my father has spent the last few years torturing person after person in the dark underworld of the mafia in order to gain the intel I'm holding.

"Mobster." He coughs.

"Tycoon." I snarl defensively.

He raises a hand. "Does 'crime syndicate' sound friendlier? Asking for a friend."

I roll my eyes as the elevator doors open. "You're one of the most annoying people on the actual planet and I barely know—"

I run right into a wall.

Not a wall.

A person.

A very warm, tall person.

I exhale and stumble back.

It's *him.*

I should not be fixating on the fact that he smells so good, like the outdoors combined with the sea and fresh rain. Crisp and cool, like water itself.

He has no reaction. He's unfeeling. His expression is as cold as his body is warm. He finally looks down at me and tilts his head. I try to keep my face impassive.

I can tell from the twitch that begins in his jaw and the narrowing of his eyes that he recognizes me. How could he forget the girl he so openly and blatantly rejected? The world freaking knew about our little alliance gone wrong. Most teens' rejections circle around their friends and family—mine made the local news. *Bad Blood? Broken betrothal between business moguls Eriksons and Stjernes.*

I meet his unblinking eyes—dark brown, like wet bark or bitter coffee—and wait. No response, none whatsoever. Except for that little tick, tick, tick that's going in his jaw. Still, I may as well be the paint on the wall behind me for all he acknowledges me.

My heartrate kicks up. It shouldn't. But it's a traitorous bastard.

So I wait.

Aric says nothing. His expression gives away nothing.

He looks at me like *I'm* nothing.

He looms over me, easily six foot six, maybe taller. His presence is completely overwhelming. Electric. His gaze is sharp, analytical, like he's already decided that I'm not worth his time. Or worse, that maybe I am.

His wavy jet-black hair falls over broad shoulders, the kind of effortless perfection that shouldn't exist outside of a dream—or a nightmare. His full lips are so devastatingly tempting, it doesn't matter if he's about to throw me a compliment or stab me with a dagger.

High cheekbones and eyes the color of the earth after rain—dark, rich, and impossible to escape once you're in too deep—make him into something almost inhuman, a force of nature wrapped in fury. And those arched eyebrows? I doubt they've ever had the audacity to lift in anything close to amusement.

He's angry, a lightning storm bottled tight, and the worst part is, he has no clue why.

Confusion flickers across his face for half a second, a micro-expression of hesitation, before his jaw sets like iron.

And now he's leaning in closer. My pulse spikes, betraying me.

Finally, he leans down as if to get on my level. His sneer has me almost taking a step backward. "So are you lost or just looking to get burned again?"

CHAPTER SIX

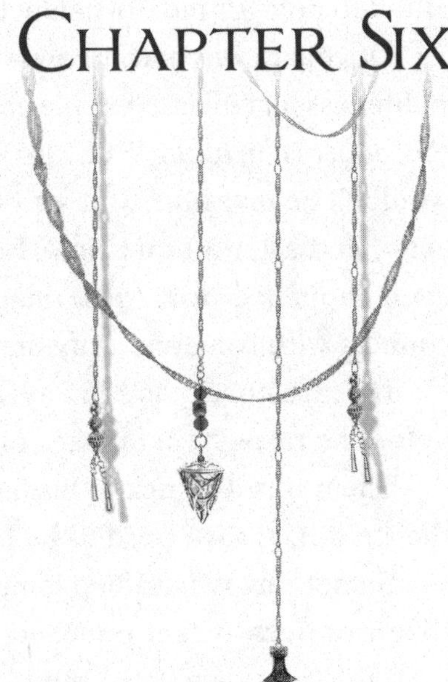

REY

I watch him. I don't flinch. I don't react. I am, after all, the one who's going to take him down.

Besides, Father taught me it's smarter to observe than engage, even as Aric's words slice through me. No hint of softness from the guy I met on the beach, the guy who gave me actual hope for something different. He's unfeeling. But what more could I expect from Aric than an absolutely soul-altering chill?

I force a smile.

I show teeth.

He can try to intimidate me, but I know exactly who I am and what I'm capable of.

"She's with me, unfortunately," Reeve drawls, barely looking up from his iPad. "Just checking her in. Due diligence, graduation requirements, blah blah blah."

Reeve's tone is a complete contrast to the warning he gave me earlier. No anger here, just boredom.

Aric grunts and shoulders past me. Damn, he's strong. Then again, of course he is. Honestly, nothing should surprise me about him anymore.

"Nice to see you again as well," I offer, my voice too bright. Shit.

He's already got me off-balance.

Of course, we both know we need to keep up some semblance of politeness just in case people are watching, which I can guarantee they are, popcorn in hand. With two rich heirs to their parents' thrones, who wouldn't be invested? But we haven't said a word to each other in two years, and after all that time, I can't help a part of me wondering if it even happened or if I just imagined the whole thing, so desperate to connect with someone. Anyone. Even an Erikson.

He turns back, and his burnished eyes linger a moment too long before he rasps, "That makes one of us."

There it is. The tick in his jaw. That flicker of something raw under the ice. Ah, always good to be reminded that you mean nothing.

Something twists deep in my chest—sharp and cold and shameful. Like I've been sucker punched and have to pretend it didn't hurt.

I don't know why I bothered hoping Aric was different. He's not like me. He's like *him*. The kind of person who wounds carelessly—until the knife is buried too deep for you to even scream.

Knowing he's capable of that kind of cruelty will only make it easier when he ends up on the other side of my blade. This man is only out for himself; the rest of the world can burn. Unlucky for him, I was raised to handle men exactly like that. Another of my father's gifts.

Reeve breaks the silence by dragging my bag onto the elevator, louder than necessary. I follow without giving Aric a backward glance.

"Good talk!" Reeve calls to his brother as the elevator doors slide shut.

My stomach flutters a bit. Which makes no sense. Aric's just proven exactly what kind of an ass he is. And yet…

One thing *is* clear. If I'm going to be successful in this mission, I need to kill every flicker of emotion…and inconvenient attraction… Aric inspires in me. *Still.*

"At least his moods have gotten better," I mutter.

Reeve ignores me and stares down at the iPad. "Room 209, and yes, my brother has perfected the fine art of assholery. Also, he has no soul." He taps the screen. "And unfortunately for you…" He makes a face. "You're right next door."

"To what?"

Please say the bathroom.

A balcony.

The laundry room.

I need at least one place of solitude.

Reeve hits the second-floor button and smiles at his own reflection in the shiny elevator doors. "Him."

Chapter Seven

REY

Tension builds in my shoulders as I wait for Reeve to step out of the elevator first. I keep my expression neutral, forcing myself to take in my surroundings like I actually care about whatever hallway decor they have going on.

My stomach drops.

Son of a bitch.

Legends humans call "Norse" line the dorm walls like a shrine to revisionist history...but the truth is older than language. These weren't myths. They were beings. And they weren't born from story—*they* birthed the stories.

I almost punch the wall when I see the centerpiece of it all: Odinfather, flanked by Thor, regal and untouchable.

Worshipped.

Revered.

Ah, yes. So benevolent. A father for the ages.

My father was clearly behind this. I'd bet money that part of his generous "donations" to the university went into this ridiculous display. Back when he was interested in peace with the Eriksons.

A reminder? Possibly.

A warning? Absolutely.

This isn't just mythology. It's history—*our* history.

The faces decorating these walls belong to murderers, conquerors, deceivers. They turned Giants into monsters, turned themselves into Gods, rewrote the past until even those who lived through it began to doubt what truly happened, a truth my father has yet to fully reveal to me.

He says the past is too painful. I call bullshit.

My father wants me to be reminded of the pain he will inflict on me: the way he expects me to inflict it on those who set off this war.

I shouldn't be surprised. Every breath I take here is another reminder of what's at stake—and what I can potentially lose if I don't fall in line.

He may as well have pumped the scent of blood through the dorm.

My fingers twitch at my sides with the need to hit something. Instead, I swallow the absolute fury in my soul.

Reeve spreads his arms wide. "Looks like you've already noticed, but every floor has a theme. We chose this one after we watched that really sick movie about—"

"Don't care," I interrupt, even though I'm grateful for the distraction from the gravity of my situation. "Also." I point at the *Thor* poster, where he looks ridiculous, holding a giant hammer, golden braids running down his back. "He had red hair."

We continue down the hall. I point at another picture and try not to flinch. "And Odin? He didn't lose his eye right away. He willingly dropped it into Mímisbrunnr—Mimir's Well—in exchange for wisdom of the past, present, and—yay for the world—" I gulp. Ha, true story. "The future."

Reeve's smile falters. Just for a second. What did I say?

"So you're a comic book nerd? Or—God, please tell me you're not a lit major. Those parties are always the worst."

"Just because some of us can read doesn't mean we can't let our hair down, too."

"Oh, lit majors know how to party," he says, shaking his head. "They just can't hold their liquor. Nothing kills a vibe like someone quoting Yeats before puking on your shoes."

I snort despite myself. In another life, I might've liked Reeve. There's something almost enviable about the way he doesn't take anything seriously.

He looks up at the poster of Odin on his throne, face unreadable.

A chill slides down my spine—and not the kind that inspires reverence. The kind that tells you to run before the God on the wall decides you're prey.

"I wonder," he muses.

"What?"

He shrugs. "Just saying, after gaining so much wisdom, if I knew all the secrets of the world, I don't think I'd bother trying to save it."

A deep, cold feeling twists in my stomach, instantly making me feel sick. "Why is that?"

"Because." Reeve points for us to keep walking. "Knowing the secrets of the world means you want to save it from itself. But saving the world often enough while getting zip in return does nothing but make you bitter. It wakes you up and makes you realize the truth."

"What's the truth?"

"You should have always let it burn." Reeve stops in front of a door with *Rey* written on the hanging white board in bubble letters, and he hands me a black packet. "Get your shit settled. Today's likely the last day you'll have entirely to yourself for a while." He taps something on his iPad, then, as if moving through a list of items, continues. "All your meals are taken care of and will be at the dining hall, but they only serve until eleven at night, so make sure you don't take a nap and forget. You'll need your strength for your first semester."

I almost laugh. I won't be here long enough to worry about the upcoming semester.

"We do things different here. You'll see." Reeve eyes me up and down. "If you need me, I'm just one floor below you, where I can promptly escape through the front doors—just in case my brother sets the place on fire. Also, if you're stuck in the building, I won't save you, so you've been warned. Oh, and if you bother me over stupid shit, I'll make your life an even bigger hell."

Nice pep talk. Very encouraging.

I shift my weight and prod a bit. "Aric," I say carefully, pulling my key card from my bag. "He seems angrier."

Reeve exhales like the question alone is exhausting, tilting his head as if considering what to say. "He's never angry, not in the way you're thinking." His fingers drum across the iPad. "Anger would be easier. It's loud. Predictable. But Aric? He's the kind of quiet that follows you, makes you paranoid, makes your skin crawl at times." He sighs. "It's like sleeping with one eye open next to a predator knowing that one wrong move"—he levels me with a stare—"will wake him."

I go completely still. I can't breathe.

He rushes on to add with a sloppy grin, "Anyway, it's kind of terrifying waiting for the quiet ones to snap. Am I right?"

I force a smile, then open room 209 and push my bags inside. "On that happy thought…"

He salutes me with his middle finger, then pulls up his iPad and clears his throat like he's about to get professional. "We at Endir acknowledge that you could have chosen any university program. We're delighted that you chose us and promise to exceed your expectations in—"

I take two steps back and grab the door, slowly shutting it in his face.

It closes with a soft click. "Wasn't done!"

"Yeah, you were!" I call back with a small smile. He might be annoying, but at least he's entertaining.

With a deep breath, I turn to take in my new home.

The room is furnished. Built-in cabinets, bookshelves, and desks span the right wall, windows straight ahead, beds to my left, and, judging by the fact there's two of everything, clearly this room is intended for more than one person. Not that I'll have to share; my father would've made sure of that. Fewer witnesses and whatnot. I wasn't expecting to be placed right next to my target, though.

Thanks, Dad.

But finding a six-foot-six Frost Giant on campus was never going to be the hard part.

Getting close enough to finish what I came here to do without losing myself in the process?

That's the part that might kill me.

Chapter Eight

ARIC

I had to leave. The air was soaked with her scent, which is weird to say even in my own head. Fuck, I really am losing it.

When I know the coast is clear, I go back to my room and down some of my meds, then stare at myself in the sink. My eyes are clear but lifeless. Looks about right.

I grip the sides of the sink and try to take some long, deep breaths.

Everything is going to be fine.

I just need to survive with *her* next door to me, moving around, breathing, existing, making noise, annoying the shit out of me.

I know the walls are thin.

Just like I know both of our beds are pressed against the same shared wall.

Inches.

Our bodies will be inches from each other, guarded by nothing other than some ancient stone wall that could crumble at any moment. God, I hope there's not an earthquake, not because I don't want to die under a pile of rubble but because I don't want my last moments to be spent lying next to her in that pile of rubble.

She smells sharp—cool air and wildflowers crushed underfoot.

Like rain just before it hits. Clean. Disruptive. Familiar in a way that puts me on edge.

A soft knock sounds at my door.

"Yeah," I rasp.

Reeve waltzes in. "So…this should be interesting."

I curse and toss my meds back into the drawer. "You think?"

He eyes the drawer, then me. "You feeling okay?"

I shrug. "As okay as ever."

So no, I do not feel okay. I swear if my therapist tells me one more time to journal my feelings when I have episodes or weird dreams, I'm going to explode.

I can tell by the way my brother's squinting at me, he's gonna say something stupid. "You look upset," he says finally.

"No shit, Reeve. Do I? Look upset?" I stomp over to the window and focus my gaze on the mountains past the lake. Frost forms between the panes of glass, distracting me. "Is it cold outside?"

"Huh?" Reeve plops onto my bed and leans back. "You do have a phone, you know. With a handy weather app. It's not any colder than normal. All the freshmen are currently out doing their normal weird pre-orientation shit, which means the dining hall shouldn't be super busy if you wanna grab some food to calm that temper of yours. I hear carbs work wonders."

"Yes, because fries always make me forget my anger. Good idea," I snap, then turn around. I take a deep breath and sit down in my desk chair, spinning to face my brother again. "Sorry."

"An apology?" Reeve's eyebrows shoot up. "I'm honored. And for the record, I'm annoyed she's here, too, all right? Let's just get through this semester without murder on our hands. People look up to us, you know? So keep your shit together as much as possible, which means avoid *her* as much as possible. And if you do run into her, well, try not to rip her head from her body." He hesitates. "Please?"

I scowl. "It's tempting. I mean, why the hell is she even here? At the college *our* family founded?"

Reeve drags a hand down his face and yawns. "I'm still trying to figure that part out. Point is, she's here. Her father's beyond powerful, and the last thing we need is a bad rep for Endir. It's the family legacy, right? We play nice for a few months, you graduate, we're free. Easy."

"Yeah," I mutter and run my hands through my hair. "I guess."

I flinch when something drops on the other side of the wall.

Rey. I clench my hands into fists, but I get up and move toward the sound.

Reeve looks from the wall to me, then back to the wall. "Are you sure you're okay?"

I'm never okay, but it's nice that he asked like the answer will be different, when we both know I haven't been okay in a long time.

A *very* long time.

I rub my hands down my face. "Yeah, sure, whatever. Let's just get out of here."

He goes to the door while I grab my phone from my nightstand.

I numbly follow Reeve out of the room, letting the door click shut behind me. My heart thumps against my chest faster than normal as I pass her door, and Reeve and I get on the elevator.

He hits the lobby button. "So, I hear goat yoga is really relaxing."

"Shut up, Reeve."

"What?" He holds up his hands. "Stop being so hostile. Goats are really cute! Or maybe a cat café. You can drink coffee, do your homework, have a nice little puss—"

"Do *not* finish that sentence," I grumble.

"It was a good opening." He sighs. "Anyway, point is, we just have to keep you distracted so you aren't fixated on her." He tries to catch my gaze, but I remain staring straight ahead. "Why *are* you fixated on her? I mean, I know we both hate her for good reason, but she's just a girl."

No. She isn't.

And I can't explain why I feel so strongly about that, other than when she was given the choice to run from his control, she stayed. I can't respect that. Plus, there's something deeper to her, something more sinister. My grandfather's done his homework, and so has Reeve. We know everything there is to know about her family and how she was raised. We know she's dangerous, yet nobody else seems to see it. Maybe that's what gets me. She's trouble, and yet she somehow seems to charm everyone she meets.

I'm so wrapped up in my own thoughts that it takes me getting to the lobby to realize that I forgot my wallet.

"Ugh." I shove Reeve out of the elevator. "I have to go grab my wallet. Wait for me."

"No worries." He salutes me and glances over at a group of female students. "I have ways to stay occupied."

He's such a sleaze; it should be written on his shirt as a warning to unsuspecting future partners. He says he loves love. I think he just loves the attention.

"Yeah, I bet." The elevator doors close.

I catch my reflection in the glass paneling—drawn features, jaw tight, something hollow behind the eyes. I almost don't recognize the man staring back at me.

I remember when I first arrived at Endir my freshman year. I was never what you would call an easygoing kind of guy like my brother, but I at least knew how to smile. Now I can't remember the last time my lips tilted up in anything even close to joy.

I look down and wait for my floor. I've lost my appetite entirely, my anxiety at her nearness making the blood in my veins turn to ice.

Back in my dorm room, I quickly send a text to Reeve to let him know I'll join him later and he should go on without me.

I sit on the edge of the bed, fists clenched against my knees.

Something's wrong.

Not in the building. Not out there.

In me.

I've felt it since the elevator. Since her.

I close my eyes, but the tension doesn't fade. It's not just in my muscles. It's under my skin.

And whatever it is—

It's waking up.

Chapter Nine

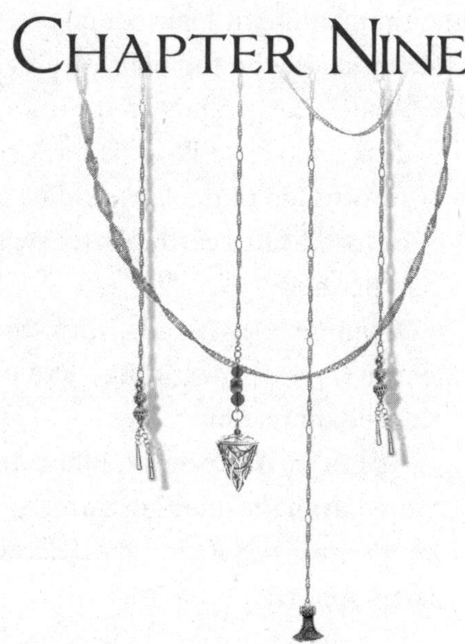

REY

The moment I'm alone in the room, I slide a hand into my jeans pocket. My fingers shake as I pull out Laufey's note.

It's crumpled and warm, and my heart races as I open the paper and spread it flat on my desk.

There are no words. No messages of love or encouragement, no mantra to persevere.

Just five runes.

ᚱ ᛞ ᚺ ᛟ ᚦ

Raido, Dagaz, Hagalaz, Othala, and Thurisaz.

Thurisaz was the rune I saw carved into the cobblestone not far from where Odinfather left me at the entrance of the university. The same one I tripped on and wanted to curse.

What does it all mean? There has to be some sort of connection to my mission. She wouldn't risk Odin's wrath to pass me this note for no reason.

The sound of Aric's door shutting has me jumping. I walk over to the wall and give it a soft knock. The echo I get in return nearly makes me jump. Great, so not soundproof. My mind suddenly fills with all the things I might hear coming from the other side of this wall, but I quickly shake the thoughts away.

When a tap sounds on the door, I freeze. Then I sweep the note off the desk and shove it in the back pocket of my jeans.

He wouldn't knock. Would he?

Before I can overthink it, I swing the door open. And it's not Aric standing there.

A tall girl—*very* tall—with thick, curly brown hair, the tips dyed electric blue, strides in like she owns the place, giant green basket balanced on one hip.

As I take in her outfit, I have to blink twice: flannel pajama shorts covered in chain-smoking cartoon cats, vintage Metallica tee that looks like it's survived actual battle, knee-high purple socks, and oversize shark slippers. It's…a lot.

Her dark brown eyes widen. "Please tell me you're not a morning person."

"I— What?"

She motions with her head in my general direction. "You know, the whole I-just-stepped-off-a-runway vibe you've got going on at what… only nine a.m.?"

I glance at my outfit, suddenly hyperaware of every detail. Black wool coat—structured, sharp. Underneath, a slouchy gray Dior sweater French-tucked into tailored jeans that somehow cost more than most people's rent. My Celine sunglasses hang from the collar of my sweater like punctuation, and the gold chain at my neck catches the morning light as I move. Chunky black boots, clean but worn in just enough to say effortless, complete the look.

"This is…just what I wear," I say, which sounds way more pretentious out loud than it did in my head.

"Cool. Cool-cool-cool." She nods, then taps her chin. "New life goal: introduce you to the concept of color. Maybe even glitter, if we're feeling brave."

She grins as she says it, and weirdly, it doesn't feel like an insult. Who *is* this person?

She sets the gift basket she's been holding on the second bed, full of snacks, energy drinks, and a pint of what I think is imported ice cream buried in dry ice.

"For you," she says.

"Um, thanks."

"I'm Ziva Morales. Suite 213 down the hall. Official greeter-slash-snack-whisperer for this floor. Unofficial gossip czar. You must be Rey."

I blink. "That obvious?"

She snorts and drops onto the edge of my bed like we've known each other forever. "Please. There was a memo. Mafia princess in 209. Possibly dangerous. Definitely hot."

My brows shoot into my hairline. "Excuse me?"

"Just kidding. But you're famous, babe. Whisper networks lit up the second your last name hit the housing list." She leans forward, her voice dropping conspiratorially. "Your dad's *that* Stjerne, right?"

I shrug a little, caught off guard. "We don't talk about it."

Ziva grins, unbothered. "Fair. Just don't stab me or anything. I'm very squishy under the boobs."

She grins again, warmer this time, and it strikes me just how unused I am to someone like her. People who barge in with snacks and boldness. Rowen never did things like this. Not because he wasn't friendly in his own way. But he was…quieter. The steady tide against the shore. Ziva is the opposite—fireworks in the sky and glitter in her wake.

"So," she says, popping open a bag of chips from the basket and munching on one, "you're next door to Aric Erikson, you know. Campus royalty. Sex on a mother-fucking stick." She says this last in a singsong voice, complete with matching head bob. "Also, sadly untouchable. Though if you're feeling frisky, go ahead and tap the younger brother. Everyone else has."

Her brown cheeks flush a little at her own joke. I arch a brow.

"Oh, obviously not me," she says, rolling her eyes like I just accused her of sacrilege. "Please. I have standards. And a calendar lined up with better options."

A startled laugh escapes me before I can stop it.

"Umm, thanks for the tip," I say. I don't bother to add I'd rather swim in a vat of sewage than "tap" Reeve Erikson. I think we're both on the same page with that one.

"Oh, I've got loads of useful tips about the social sitch on campus," she says and waggles her brows at me.

Without taking a breath, Ziva starts rattling off a laundry list of facts about the school hierarchy she's deemed important. Who's sleeping with whom, who's up for grabs, even who likes to share. It's a nonstop litany of names and sexual preferences, but I barely hear a word.

Somewhere in the middle of her spontaneous monologue, I got the idea that maybe she was being so friendly because she was just super susceptible to my Aethercall. So I consciously stop pulling and push a little. Not hard—just enough to test it.

But Ziva doesn't pause, doesn't blink, doesn't so much as mispronounce a name. She just keeps going like I haven't shoved an invisible wall between us. Like whatever I am doesn't matter.

It's shockingly refreshing.

Eventually, she waves a hand, as if to say *and that's all you need to know about Endir*, and stands, brushing imaginary lint off her cat shorts and plopping the bag of chips back into my basket. "Anyway, I've got a shift at the coffee cart in ten. If you want to scope out the local caffeine situation, I can show you the ropes later."

She reaches the door, then glances back. "Seriously, Rey—glad you're here. I've just decided, we're going to be the best of friends."

"Thanks?" I start like it's a question, but I don't know what else to say. No one's ever offered me friendship like it was no big deal. No conditions. No price. Just handed over like a hoodie.

She starts to turn back to the hallway but adds, "If you survive orientation, come find me later. I'll show you where the vending machines are that won't steal your soul."

"Thanks," I say again, and this time, I mean it.

"Don't thank me yet. Wait until you meet my ghost. She's super territorial."

And just like that, she's gone.

Chapter Ten

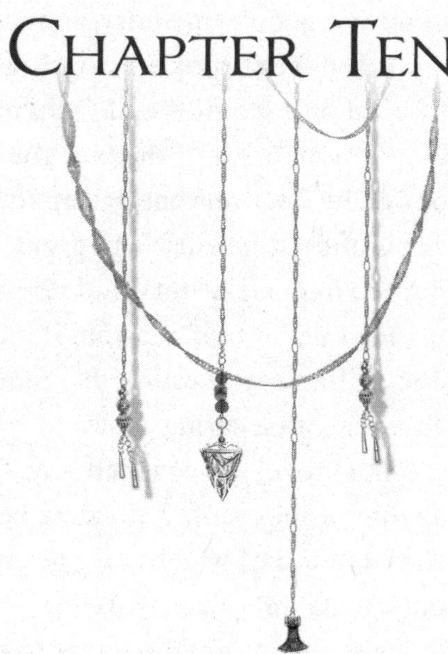

REY

I stare at the now-empty doorway, a little thrown.

Unsure what to do next, I pull the notebook from the blue bag my father gave me. When in doubt, choose war, I guess.

"It's just a notebook. It doesn't bite." I don't know why I'm talking to myself as I slowly open the first page.

It's a drawing of Mjölnir, Thor's hammer, the most powerful weapon in the world. I know almost nothing of the war between the Gods and the Giants, other than what Father has shared, and I have no illusions his version isn't heavily one-sided.

Long before "Norse" was a word, before men carved Gods into stone, Odin was not just a name. He was a force. And Mjölnir wasn't just a symbol stamped on rings and family crests; it was a sentence, a weapon of finality. It meant justice if you were on Odin's side and extinction if you weren't. The Giants—at least that's what stories called them—stole it, though not out of greed or chaos, like the myths say. They used it to destroy the Bifrost, and it changed everything. The Bifrost was a bridge linking our world to theirs, a shimmering, living connection between realms. Between Midgard, or Earth, and Asgard, the Gods' stronghold. The Bifrost was how Odin controlled the flow of power, people, memory, and magic.

But once it broke, everything fractured. Gods and Giants were trapped on each side, and Odin made sure that those trapped here no longer remembered the war that caused their separation. Using his power, he put everyone asleep to buy time. Their memories are locked away, and all because the great, benevolent Odinfather decided he wanted to erase history and rewrite it in blood and gold.

He's never told me what it meant for those trapped in Asgard. He doesn't like any question that may have an answer that exposes him as anything but a caring ruler.

Whenever I've asked my father about the Bifrost and why anyone would want it divided, he just says it was a mistake, a natural consequence of war, but it's always felt like he was leaving something out. The Giants already used Mjölnir to take down the Bifrost. Hiding it is just a giant middle finger to my father. He can't go home without it, and he can't restore his own powers, since they come from Asgard. The only people who can wield it need to have the blood of Odin or be worthy, and since Odin himself is evil personified now—that leaves, well, me. Jury's still out on whether or not I'm worthy, but at least I have the bloodline to steal it back—once I find it.

More importantly, why did the Giants hide an ancient weapon in this specific location, and why is Aric the only one who knows where? I think back on the runes I've been seeing scattered around campus. Are they working like wards? And if Mjölnir is protected here, meaning my father needed me to get in, are the runes making it impossible for it to call out to my blood? Something is suppressing it. Or someone.

I jump up from my bed and pace back and forth. Something important is right in front of me, I just know it. I have to walk through it. Step by step. This is what I've been trained to do.

The Giants don't want ultimate power returning to my father. Hiding the hammer means they were part of the war and at least retained their memories long enough to make those plans. They had to have done it after the destruction of the Bifrost. Because they're all still stuck here.

My heart skips in my chest, and my mind races, selecting and discarding reasons. The Eriksons' family legacy is this school. If it's protected by runes, that could mean it's also protected by a more ancient power.

When I first arrived at Endir, I could smell something ancient smoldering beneath the university, if my imagination wasn't running wild. Hell, even the mountains that surround the school feel mythical and unforgiving. Maybe they've hidden Mjölnir in a nearby cave or deep within the forest. Maybe getting close to Aric, gaining his trust, really is the key to discovering it.

I settle back on my bed and leaf through the journal again.

I turn to the page depicting Mjölnir and trace the drawing with my fingertip. Rowen told me stories of how the hammer had runes sketched all along the handle where Thor held it firm in his hand before thrusting it toward the sky.

Was Thurisaz one of them?

Lightning would illuminate the hammer as well as his eyes, turning them a terrifying silver before he'd let out the battle cry of the Berserkers. His warriors would rally around him as they emerged from the trees, wearing animals they'd sacrificed to the Gods. The Berserkers were so crazed, they would bite down on their own shields to prove they didn't need them in the first place.

But that was before everything shattered. Before the Gods fell. Before lives were lost and history was rewritten. Before everything humanity had once known was either erased or twisted into something unrecognizable.

The Gods and Giants—both betrayed and betraying—had become legends warped by time, half-truths, and propaganda.

What if the runes on the hammer match the ones on the note from Laufey? Is the note a map of how to find Mjölnir? Of course, that would be too easy, and yet, it would make the most sense. She might not be my birth mother, but she raised me, and the one thing I know down to my bones is that Laufey would die to protect me.

I take her note and slide it into the dossier, then turn another page on the many lives of Mjölnir. Apparently, before its theft, it was a simple-looking hammer, just metal and wood. But because Mjölnir is a living, breathing artifact, it continued to shift and change from battle to battle.

As Thor destroyed worlds and defeated his enemies, Mjölnir not only took on different shapes and sizes—it took on the knowledge and history of Asgard. Of every bloodline that had wielded it. Rowen told me once that the hammer was forged to answer to only one bloodline, Odin's, but if that's true, then how did a Giant use it to destroy the Bifrost? Half-truths and more half-truths.

I continue flipping through the notebook. The images quickly shift from ancient weapons and realms to my target.

Aric.

The pictures on this page make me pause. He's young, grass stains on his jeans. In one, he's playing football.

I don't know why I fixate on that, other than it's odd to think of him as a normal little boy. In another, he's holding up a fish in his hand. It's so small it probably has no meat on it, but he's proud.

His smile is wide. Bright. Anyone looking at that picture would think Aric was the happiest boy in the world. There's absolutely no trace of that boy in the man he is today.

In the next picture, he's standing with Reeve, who's wearing his high school graduation cap and gown. Aric's smile is less bright now, his posture tense. I compare the photo with those taken earlier. He doesn't even look like the same person.

What happened to change him?

His parents' deaths, no doubt. The thought makes my stomach sink.

I flip through the next few pages. They show his schedule, information about his hobbies, current favorite books and movies, and so on. All the usual intel. I'm sure Sigurd Erikson, being the mob boss he is, has a similar file on me—probably thicker. I pause a moment, my mind wondering what else Aric and his family might know about me.

Nope, don't need to go there.

Shaking my head, I keep reading. Aric suffers from insomnia. That makes two of us.

I skim a newspaper clipping of the time he was struck with lightning.

I remember this. Odin denies any involvement, though it's not like he'd tell me either way.

I flip the page. An allergy to kiwi?

Hmm. That, I didn't know.

I flip back to the pictures of Aric, of his dorm room, schematics of the house he shares with his grandfather. There's a picture of his SUV and another of the gym he works out at.

My chest tightens. The dossier is thick with endless information about Endir and Aric, and even Reeve has a few pages in here. No detail was too small to include. And yet, other than a crude drawing and a couple of scribbled notes, almost nothing about Mjölnir's potential location is included.

It's like my father wants me to struggle, then fail spectacularly.

Why would he not include more information about the object I'm meant to find? To steal? I understand it's not been seen in ages, but Odinfather is as old as time. Older than the hammer, in fact. So why wouldn't he have shared everything that might help me succeed?

I start frantically flipping through the notebook again, searching my father's notes. Page after page after page on the Erikson family.

But no sign of Mjölnir being used since the destruction of the Bifrost. Of course, Father already knew that. He prepared this dossier. He threatened everyone I love if I don't find the hammer.

There's a need to keep your secrets to yourself for the sake of power—but then there's intentionally keeping someone in the dark whose life depends on succeeding.

But Mjölnir *wasn't* lost. Was it? No one *misplaced* it. It wasn't a set of car keys. It was hidden on purpose by someone who could wield it. Someone whose bloodline called to the ancient weapon, was remembered by it. That's right. Mjölnir could remember…

My hands freeze on the page as the pieces click into place.

Aric does know exactly where it was hidden. *But he's completely forgotten.*

What's done can't be undone without Mjölnir. Father can't restore their memories. That's what Father's been hiding. That's why he needs me. I'm not really here just to steal Mjölnir.

I was chosen for this mission for a reason. There's more to it. Isn't there always, with Odin?

Bile rises in my throat. My father didn't send me because he believes I'm capable of anything. He sent me because, like most men who fear what they can't control, he'd rather a woman be the weapon than the one holding it.

That's what he saw in me two years ago, long before I ever saw it in myself: a soldier he can send into battle while keeping his hands clean. And this mission is no different.

I never let myself think about that day at the beach. But now, it comes back anyway—the wind, the salt, and the silence between us.

Aric and I weren't supposed to be alone.

The others had gone back to the house—sick of the sand, tired of the wind. But we stayed. Sitting too far apart to be anything and too close to pretend we weren't something.

I remember the way the waves crashed behind him. The sharp bite of salt in the air. The fact that he kept glancing at me like I was about to disappear.

"You don't have to be like him," I said.

I didn't say my father's name. I didn't have to.

Aric looked away for a long time. Then finally, softly, "Maybe I don't want to be anything else."

I think that's when I touched his hand. Or maybe he touched mine. It doesn't matter who moved first. What mattered was that it happened.

Just once. Just enough.

His hand was warm. Mine was shaking.

I don't remember what we said after that. I just remember the silence. The kind that feels heavy with things you're not ready to want.

We didn't kiss. We didn't even hug.

But something passed between us—something that scared us both enough to pretend it never happened.

And then the wind changed.

A gust tore across the shoreline, scattering shells and sand like something had exhaled from the depths. The air dropped ten degrees in a breath.

Behind us, the tide stopped. Froze. A sheet of frost crept out from where Aric sat, then across the wet sand—thin, precise, a vein of ice snaking toward the rocks.

Confusion, and maybe a hint of fear, shone in Aric's eyes as they briefly flashed white. He yanked his hand back like he'd been burned. Or broken. His hands shook after that. He stared at them, at the frost, like it was a death sentence.

"Go," he said. His voice wasn't cruel—but it was cold. Final.

I remember walking away, not turning back, not asking why the sea looked wrong or why my fingers felt numb.

I didn't know then what we'd triggered.

But I do know swift rejection of the betrothal followed, and while I expected my father to be angry, instead he was almost…pleased, like the whole thing had been a setup and they played right into his hands. He didn't care how embarrassed I was.

I think about Laufey's note.

About the frost Aric created from our held hands.

Getting close to him and finding Mjölnir.

He either knows and is hiding it from the world…or he's going to need a little help to remember.

I almost laugh. Well played, Father. If Aric knows what he is, then I was just sent to the wolves. He would die before telling my father a word.

So Odinfather is banking on my ability to crack him, to gain trust, to inspire loyalty—all the things I barely have within my own family, let alone with my enemy.

I sigh and try not to throw something. This isn't a quest; it's a hunt.

And hunters always forget one thing. Sooner or later, the hunted learn to hunt back.

Chapter Eleven

REY

For a moment, I want to call my father. Tell him where he can shove Mjölnir.

But I won't.

Nothing's changed. I always knew this mission would likely end with me dead. The only question was how. And now I know: most likely by a massive Giant pulling my arms from my body.

As long as Laufey walks away from Odin unscathed, I'll count that as a win.

Whether it's my father who breaks me or Aric makes no difference. Pain is inevitable.

But now, a deeper sense of purpose thrums in my chest. For once in his life, he really does need someone. He needs *me*.

Another sound from within Aric's room pulls me from the spiral, but it also gives me an idea. If I'm going to play this game, I might as well start now.

Let's see what happens when I walk straight into the storm.

I slam the notebook shut, shove my phone into my pocket along with my key card. Then I walk outside to knock on his door, maybe a bit too aggressively.

The door flies open, and Aric stares down at me. "What."

I smile up at him through gritted teeth. "I just thought I'd reintroduce myself, since we're dormmates now. I didn't make you muffins, but I do have—"

He starts to close the door. I put my foot in the jamb, examining his outfit through the slight opening left. He's wearing head-to-toe workout gear.

"Leg day?"

"Rey." My name comes off like a growl. He jerks me into his room.

Wow, that was easy. I turn around just in time for him to shove me up against the wall.

"Listen very closely," he whispers. This near, his profile is something from legends. His earth-dark eyes almost glow as he snarls at me.

I swallow hard, fighting the pull of his gaze. "I'm a good listener."

"I don't like you." He grins. His voice, however, is low, lethal. "I hate everything your family stands for. There will never be a day where I will want your *muffins* or anything else you can conjure up. I don't know why you're here, and it bothers me that I actually care." His breath is warm against my skin, but a chill still runs down my spine, his voice a slow, deliberate burn. "You were nothing to me then and are nothing to me now. And just in case you need some tough love, you're nothing to your father, too."

His words hit like a slap. But I don't flinch. Once, he and I had the beach—for a very brief moment, before we knew about the bad blood between our families. How easily things change.

He runs a hand down my cheek. "You're just a pawn in his empire, one dripping with the blood of the innocent. Innocents like my parents." He leans his head in and exhales against my ear. "We are *not* friends."

My entire body shivers, but not from the cold.

I heard of his parents dying years ago in a car wreck, and my fingers had itched to text him how sorry I was. But this anger blasting me, *blaming* me, was unfair. I lash out without thinking. "Calling your parents innocent is laughable, Aric. Yours were no better than mine. Ruthless. Cold. Power-hungry. Mine just happened to be better at it."

His eyes narrow, and the hairs on the back of my neck stand up. In a low voice, he says, "You don't know *anything* about my family."

"Maybe not. But I know you want to be just like *mine*," I whisper, reminding him of what we shared on the beach that day.

Like I pulled a cord from a socket, his fathomless mahogany eyes go lifeless.

He hesitates, his mouth right by my neck. "Just focus on surviving the semester and avoiding me at all costs." With that, he pulls back and opens his door, guides me through the doorway, then follows me out.

He's making a beeline for the elevator before I can even catch my breath.

"Good talk!" I yell after him, a bit stunned at how aggressive he is toward me and trying not to feel the loss of the guy I thought I knew.

"Goodbye, Rey," he barks at me as the elevator doors close between us.

If that asshat hates me now just for the blood in my veins—blood I never asked for—then maybe he deserves what's coming. Every bit of it.

Starting with a little invasion of privacy, since he's been so kind as to leave his room unguarded, followed by me attaching myself to him so painfully close, he's going to wish he were dead.

With a grin, I rush into my room and grab my lockpick, then jerk my door back open, coming face-to-face with Reeve as he's exiting the stairwell.

"Oh. Hello." I make a show of tucking my hair behind my ear as I quickly shove the pick into my back pocket.

He stares.

I stare.

His eyebrows go up. "I was just grabbing Aric. He was supposed to meet me at the dining hall but texted to catch him later. Were you headed somewhere or…?"

"Bathroom," I blurt. "It's an emergency!"

I'm better than this.

He nods in slow understanding. "All right then, well, happy…" I can tell he doesn't know what to say as his hands twist in front of him. "Times."

I wince. "Could have done better with that."

"I'm aware." He sighs. "Oh, and the lights have been going out on the floor, so in about two minutes we have a crew coming up to check things out. If you hear lots of loud noises, you aren't getting robbed. It's just maintenance."

Shit. "Oh. Good, thanks. I would have freaked."

"Somehow I doubt that, but okay." He crosses to Aric's door just as the elevator dings open.

Great. The maintenance crew is here already, meaning I can't just pick Aric's lock in broad daylight. Good thing there's always plan B.

Of course, I don't like plan B, but it's all I have.

I wait in the bathroom long enough for Reeve to realize Aric isn't here, then get back to my room and stare at my bag. It's not a big deal. Should be easy. I jump up and down to shrug off the stress, then crack my knuckles. He's out of his room. It's the perfect time to do a little recon. Figure out how he ticks.

"Fine. Let's do this," I say to myself and take a deep breath. Mist is swallowing the edges of campus when I glance out the window, and the gated entrance is empty. Good. No witnesses. Even if there were, my Aethercall would cover me.

My stomach growls, but I ignore it. I have more important things to feed.

I change fast: black leggings, tight top, phone in pocket, braid tucked under my hood, gloves on, a knife from Father's bag in a sheath at my waist. No dramatics. Just armor.

There are only two things I'm afraid of, heights and open water, but since Aric's room is right next door, all I have to do is climb out my own window, step along a ten-inch ledge two stories up, and then break into his room. All without falling to my death.

No problem.

CHAPTER TWELVE

REY

It's just a ledge. I'm very well trained in a lot of things. Jujitsu. Axe throwing. Even sleight of hand. But a tightrope walk, so not my thing. Something I'm reminded of as I lift the window and then the screen. The air carries the scent of the forest, full of pine and everything that should bring comfort. I focus on that as I climb out of the window and onto the narrow ledge.

Okay. Not so bad. I'm only two stories up. It's survivable if I fall. Maybe.

I slide my foot along the old cement and press my back against the wall, moving slowly, steadily. It's windy, but I can manage. What I'm struggling with is that I'm going to have to turn my body on this ledge when I get to Aric's window, then pull the screen off without making noise or falling to my death.

Would the dormitory door be easier?

Undoubtedly.

But now that I have a maintenance crew standing in the hallway, fixing lights of all things, I'm pretty sure that option is out, and who knows when Aric will be back. I don't have enough time to let any opportunity to gather intel slip through my fingers. Definitely not for a personal weakness like fear of heights.

Once I'm at his window, I manage to turn myself 180 degrees without more than a slightly panic-inducing teeter on the ledge. Then I pull the screen off and balance it on the ledge beside me before feeling around the edges for a way to lift the ancient latch and enter.

It takes a few minutes to use my blade to jimmy the latch, then another to inch the glass up from the outside. Every few seconds, I scan the grounds behind the dorm, where, aside from one couple cutting across the open yard toward the library, no one else is in sight.

Once I've raised the windowpane high enough, I slip inside, quick to turn around and reattach his screen.

His room is still dark, and I know he's not here. It's been mere minutes, and I'd have heard him return, plus he had workout clothes on and earbuds in his ears. He was clearly going to work out or for a run.

If he comes back early… Well, would he really expect anything better from my father's daughter?

There's a strong scent of cedar and fresh rain in his room. I try to stop myself but can't help but inhale the addicting aroma. It smells like a home I've never belonged to and will never know. That's an intrusive thought I prefer not to dwell on, but dammit, it doesn't stop me from taking another deep breath and savoring the smell.

Why is *that* what I fixate on? I shake it off. It's probably some obscenely expensive designer cologne, and I'm just another person falling for his pheromones.

I glance around the dark room, noting how everything is meticulously placed—his shelves lined with at least thirty books, his bed immaculately made.

I need to know his interests so they become my interests. Karate? Cool, I can join. Run club? I'd rather not, but I'll suffer to get this over with.

If I'm right, I'll need to wake him up.

Odinfather didn't admit as much outright, but I suspect that he no longer has the power to wake someone from stasis. That he needs me. That his powers are waning. How much, he'll never tell any of us, but it must be dire.

It's my job to pull Aric out of whatever stasis he's in, since his memory of Mjölnir's location would be on lockdown. And if I'm going to break that kind of God-tier stasis, I need to understand what keeps Aric standing in the first place.

What he clings to. What he hides. What he's willing to bleed for.

I haven't let myself plan much further than that.

Seduce? Marry? Kill?

I laugh at my own joke. I can't kill him. Marrying him is even funnier, and seduction? He'd hold a knife to my throat.

Good thing I brought my own.

I flash my phone light around the sparsely decorated room. He has a beanbag in the corner that looks like it's never been sat on. I plop down, put a piece of gum in my mouth, and assess his bookshelf.

He has a few books about architecture and behavioral science. Several history tomes. A whole shelf of classics. I refuse to respect him more just because I see Virginia Woolf.

I get up, walking over to the poster he has up on his wall. It's a picture of the sea. Fitting. I bet he wants to return and has no idea why.

"You were born of the sea and forests." I tap the colorful image with my finger and move on to his closet. "It's only natural to be drawn to them."

With a sigh, I run my gloved hand over his sweatshirts and pants, his loafers and hiking boots, then bring a T-shirt to my face and inhale.

Forest. Mist. Fire. Water.

Got it.

I may not have a ton of power, other than influencing people's emotions, but my sense of smell is amazing.

I tuck the shirt under my arm and keep looking around.

Would he be drawn to the hammer's hiding place the same way he's drawn to the sea?

I slowly walk toward his desk when footsteps sound, along with Aric's familiar voice.

"Yeah, I'll be right there. I just forgot my book and wallet again. You know, the whole purpose of me coming up here last time," he calls.

"Hurry up!" Reeve whines. "I'm starving."

Shit. Short run, apparently.

A shiver runs down my spine, and I don't even think. I just duck down, his shirt still clutched in my hand, and roll under his bed. Good thing he actually makes it. The comforter hangs just low enough to hide me.

I pat my waist to make sure my knife is handy. Just in case.

"You're always starving," Aric yells back. He's close.

I'll need to acclimate to his hypnotic voice. Damn, maybe that's his superpower. Except...do Giants even have any sort of powers, other than strength? The gaping chasm of what I know about Gods versus Giants has never seemed wider. Fuck you, Odin, for not preparing me better.

I race through my memory of Marvel movies, which were about half right, according to my father. What the hell can Giants do? Make shit cold? Or is it that they like to *live* in a cold place? I shake my head. If they scared Odinfather enough that he wiped their memories, they *definitely* had more going for them than excellent body heat and the ability to make a snowman.

My breath catches in the back of my throat when the door to his room opens, and the wind carries his scent through the open window I forgot about.

Shit. He'll know I was in here. First things first...I pray he doesn't realize I'm *still* in here.

Floorboards creak as he slowly makes his way toward the edge of the bed.

"Reeve, I swear, if this is another prank you put a freshman up to, I'm going to murder you." He sniffs the air. "I mean it. You know I haven't been able to sleep for two days; stop messing with my head. You got me. Can we please go eat now?"

The floor creaks with each step Aric takes across the room until he's leaning over to close the window.

He fishes something out of a dish by the door, muttering about dumb-shit brothers under his breath, then heads out again, pulling the door closed behind him.

My heart is lodged so far up my throat at the near miss, I just lie under his bed for a full five minutes. Not smelling his T-shirt. Just catching my breath.

When I'm sure he's not coming right back, I slide out from under the bed, pausing just long enough to smooth the comforter.

The next five minutes are spent moving through drawers—methodical, fast. I pretend not to notice the tight pull in my stomach after confirming what I already suspected: black boxer briefs. Of course.

My face is still warm when I open the drawer beneath his sink and three pill bottles rattle against one another. I lift each one, read the labels. Nothing I recognize.

I slip out my phone and snap a photo.

I tell myself it's for his own good. That maybe this will help free him.

But the justification lands hollow in my chest.

Ten minutes later, I've searched everywhere and, other than the mystery medication, know absolutely nothing useful.

My stomach grumbles, reminding me yet again I still haven't eaten.

I glance at the closed window but dismiss it. I never really planned to climb back out that way. Not when the dorm room door will lock behind me just fine.

After hustling back into my room and trading my black leggings for joggers, I head to the dining hall, taking my time to avoid any more unwanted run-ins.

It's crowded and noisy, and I'm bombarded with smells—cheap cologne, tikka masala, chocolate chip cookies, and all things greasy. I grab a tray and follow the line along the buffet, piling on fries, a sad-looking turkey sandwich, and a salad I don't plan to eat. Then I find a table tucked near the corner—out of reach, just how I like it.

The first fry is glorious. I'm halfway to forgetting the day thus far when Aric walks in, and I nearly choke. They should have already been here and left by now.

He's alone. Not with Reeve. And he's scanning the room.

Don't sit here…

Don't sit here…

I'm not ready.

The place is packed, but the two empty chairs beside me haven't been touched—thanks to my Aethercall. I've been pushing out waves of silent threat since I walked in, but only so I can plot. Apparently, it's working.

Usually, I like that.

But I can only assume the Eriksons are immune to my gift. Otherwise, all those years ago, Aric would have reacted to it in some way. He would have felt it, right? The way I couldn't hide the rejection or my heart dropping in my chest? And the way they've behaved today confirms it. Needling me. Approaching me, leaving too abruptly. Getting under my skin.

I glance around, debating whether to reverse the effect and pull someone into the open seat. But the students nearby are too busy filming themselves or scrolling mindlessly to notice an invitation.

I lower my gaze and keep eating—slow, mechanical, like that might somehow make me disappear.

A chair scrapes beside me.

Be anyone but him.

Seriously.

Anyone.

Chapter Thirteen

REY

"Rough morning?" he asks, not even pretending to hide his focus on the small nation of fries occupying most of my tray.

I glare at him. He just got done saying I needed to stay away from him and, while there are only a few empty seats, I figured he'd rather sit on the ground than across from me. So what's his deal? Does he suspect that I was in his room? Or is he playing at his own game now?

I dip a fry into my ketchup. "Just trying to get adjusted."

His eyes—sharp, dark, deliberate—drag over me, from my ballet flats to the edge of my hoodie. When they finally lift to land on mine, the weight of his gaze *scorches.*

And he hasn't even sat down yet.

No, he's choosing to tower over me like a complete jackass.

Everything Aric does is calculated, even the way he watches me. This is a ploy to exert dominance. "From the looks of it," he murmurs, his lips tipping up in a sexy smirk I itch to smack right off his face, "that might take some time."

I force my fingers to unclench and casually drop my fry onto the tray, despite the fact that my heart's ready to hammer out of my chest. It's almost cruel, how pretty he is.

I shrug, masking my nerves and increasingly rapid heartbeat. I blurt out the first thing I can think of from my perusal of his closet. "I like to hike. Makes me hungry."

"Hmm," he says, assessing me with a slight cock of his head. "Same. There are a lot of trails around here, but"—he sets his tray down next to mine as he takes the empty seat—"you don't seem like the hiking type."

"That's borderline insulting." I grab another fry and shove it into my mouth. "Though not as insulting as what you said earlier."

He shrugs. "If the hiking shoe fits…"

"So why are you here, Aric?" I ask, genuinely curious. "Didn't you just tell me to stay the hell away from you?"

He shrugs. "Know thy enemy."

"Ah," I say. "Okay, then. So how is your day going, enemy?" I lean in. "Eventful?"

His eyes narrow, and then he completely shuts down. "No. I've been reading."

Liar.

"What're you reading?" I prod.

"'The Epic of Gilgamesh.'"

I try to look unimpressed, but admittedly, that's not what I expected. Although a poem about immortality and doomed gods—an echo of their world—tracks as something he'd be drawn to. "Is that required reading? I haven't had a chance to look at my syllabus yet, with all the hiking I've been doing."

"Reading should never be required." He leans back, the fabric of his black T-shirt pulling tight across his chest. His voice drops, and yet again I'm reminded that the sound of it can be as hypnotic as a siren's call. "It should be for *pleasure*. Don't you think?"

His gaze flicks to mine, a slow, deliberate challenge.

I swallow. Hard. But I don't answer.

"The right book can consume you. Make you forget to eat, to sleep." A smirk tugs at his lips again. "Make you ache for just one more page even when you know you shouldn't." He leans in, close enough that my breath stutters. "It can be temptation itself."

I keep eating—not because I'm hungry, but because if I look at him any longer, I might do something reckless. The way he said that… It's not fair.

"Tell me, Rey," he murmurs, eyes dark and dangerous. "Have you ever been *ruined* by a story?"

My throat tightens, and I glance away—only to see Ziva waving at me from the trash cans behind him. She dumps her tray with a flourish, taps her chest, and points at me in the universal gesture for *need me to come over?*

I hope to every God in the Nine Realms she didn't hear Aric asking if I had ever been ruined.

Aric glances over his shoulder, his eyebrows shooting down. "Hey, Z," he says, voice flat and cool. Like he's already bored with whatever history they share.

"Hey, Douche," she answers, and I choke on a fry.

If Ziva hadn't already pronounced us best friends earlier, I'd have gotten on bended knee right then and begged to worship her for life.

Aric ignores both of us and picks up his burger, taking a huge bite.

"Catch you later, Rey." Ziva tosses me a wink before heading out of the dining hall.

"I see you make friends as well as I do," I say, breaking the silence.

"Apparently not," he says. "She likes *you*."

I shrug and snag the ketchup bottle from the caddy of condiments. "You're being nice. Why?"

"Don't get used to it." He grins, and this time it's pure malice. "I don't want to be anywhere near you. But at the same time, I find myself unable to stay away until I can figure out why you're really here. I know you don't give a shit about anything, least of all your education."

I force a polite smile. "Who says I don't give a shit?"

"I do." He makes a fist on the table. "You only learn what he tells you to. Everyone knows it. So what is it? What's the reason this place suddenly matters to the Stjernes?"

"You're paranoid."

"This school is my family's legacy. The only thing not tainted by *your* family." He looks down. "And I won't let you poison it."

A shiver runs along my spine, and I reach for another fry. "I can't tell if you're trying to intimidate me or seduce me."

"You're pretty," he says, standing. "But the prettiest toys always come with teeth."

"So I'm both a toy *and* pretty?" I bat my lashes at him. Jackass.

He raises his arms above his head like he's frustrated, giving me a view of his abs before he turns and walks away.

I refuse to be affected by muscle. That would be ridiculous and weak. Just because my mouth went completely dry, that's not my fault. It's the weather.

So he likes working out.

Maybe hiking.

Hates me but is drawn to me.

I push back my chair and stand. I guess I'm about to find out how well he plays with others.

Chapter Fourteen

ARIC

I feel rather than see Rey follow me through the rest of my day. Does she seriously have no pride? I spend hours in my room, failing to focus, sensing her mere inches away on the other side of the wall. When I leave, I hear her door open to follow me before I'm in the stairwell.

I lose her on my second run of the day, as dusk begins to settle like a blanket over the forest. Guess her little black shoes weren't enough to keep up with me. Into hiking, my ass.

But she's waiting outside the dorms when I return. *Shit.* She's not looking at me, though. She's shaking her head at the students walking toward the path that leads into the woods and down to the lake, through an ancient archway.

This ritual's ridiculous, yet people swear by it year after year.

I notice Reeve nearby, leaning against a giant redwood and watching all the freshmen light their candles and walk under the arch. Each time someone passes through and the candle doesn't go out, they all cheer.

Reeve raises a brow as I approach. "It's sad what people want to be true. There's no God up there looking down on them, choosing whose candle stays lit."

I shrug.

"I suppose it's good to let them have their fun," he muses. "Plus, most of them are probably hammered anyway."

"Most of who are hammered?" Rey. I'd know that voice anywhere. I clench my teeth.

Reeve sighs. "All this talk of God, and Satan's pet rears her ugly head." He tosses her a smile over his shoulder that softens his words. "Did you need something, princess?"

Rey pauses near us. I take a step back—not out of fear, but necessity.

She's been here less than a day, and already the tension in my body feels unfamiliar. Coiled too tightly, like I'm not entirely myself.

It's always been that way when she was near me, though. I can't help but notice how she walks into a space and people move without knowing why. They soften. Adjust. As if gravity itself has chosen a new center.

I've spent my entire life carving out room for myself within my grandfather's world. For her, the world seems to make that room on instinct.

I don't resent her for it, but I recognize it for what it is. She was made to draw people in. I was made to push through them.

If she ever turns that gravity toward me with intention, I don't know what I'll become in its pull. And I don't think she does, either.

Even if we both pretend like it didn't happen, I remember the real reason our families were at the beach that day two years ago. Both fathers called it a truce, but in reality, it was a transaction. Her father offered me unimaginable power—and *her* if I wanted. Our families would be bound by marriage, and a lifetime of bloodshed would cease.

Our parents had it all figured out. We would wed on her eighteenth birthday, *if* I had wanted to accept our betrothal that day.

And I did. That's the truth I've never said aloud.

I went to her on the beach to tell her I wouldn't accept the deal. That I wouldn't trade her future for mine. That she deserved better than to be used as leverage.

But sitting beside her, I faltered. I remember the salt air and the space between us, close enough to feel like there was something huge hanging there, something I wouldn't come back from.

And then she reached for my hand.

Her fingers brushed mine—warm and unsteady—and something in me tilted off center. Then she spoke.

"You don't have to be like him."

She didn't say Odin, but she didn't need to.

I've thought about that moment more than I should in the last two years. Lain awake and played it in my head over and over. At the time, I told myself she didn't know what she was saying. That she didn't understand what she was accusing me of.

The truth is worse. She wasn't wrong.

For one unbearable moment, I considered the deal. I imagined what it would be like to take the power her father offered—and take her with it.

I don't know what horrified me more: the offer itself or the part of me that was tempted.

But when she spoke those soft words, I felt exposed. Judged. As if she'd seen through whatever mask I was wearing and into the man I was becoming.

So I left before I could become him, and I didn't look back. At least not until my parents died less than a week later.

I remember how my chest felt after hearing the news—tight, raw, like something cracked from the inside out. I didn't sleep. I didn't speak. I just stared at the floor until my grandfather pulled the phone from my hand.

Everyone tried to convince me it was just an accident, that I wasn't to blame. But I knew it wasn't. *He* did this—because I rejected his daughter. And she woke something inside me that will never grow warm again.

Glancing over at the half smile lingering on her full lips, I can't help but wonder what my life would be like if I'd just said yes. At least my parents would be alive.

My fists tighten. My skin aches, like it's stretching to contain something it wasn't meant to hold.

A sound—small, brittle—escapes from my palm. I glance down to find a dusting of frost curling across my skin, delicate and shimmering in the light.

I wipe it away quickly, as if that will make it less real.

It's nothing.

Just her.

Just me.

Sure, *now* it wants out. Back then, I would have done anything to awaken a monster that could avenge my parents, but it was buried deep.

"Must be another cold snap," Reeve mutters, rubbing his arms as he looks up at the sky. "Didn't feel like this ten minutes ago."

Rey finally speaks again. "What are they doing under the archway?"

"Witchcraft," Reeve deadpans. "Or in this case, they've heard all of the ridiculous stories about the ancient archway that they believe is a gateway to the Gods. In fact, Endir was built around the archway to preserve it historically."

I roll my eyes, but ever the tour guide, Reeve keeps going.

"Lake Stevens having any sort of Viking influence that old is kind of wild." He points out the ancient runes inscribed above the arch.

"Norse, not Viking," Rey says.

Reeve's eyebrows shoot up. "Norse, not Viking what?"

Rey huffs. "Viking was a job, not a people. So, all Vikings were Norse, but not all Norse were Vikings."

She says it like it's something taught in grammar school, but I have to admit I've never thought of it that way before. And she's right. "Like how all sneakers are shoes, but not all shoes are sneakers."

Her eyes catch mine and twinkle, a slow smile lifting her high cheekbones even higher. Not that I notice. "Exactly."

I drag my gaze from Rey's and fix it on the arch. A short guy with a cloud of black hair sprints through, shielding the flickering of his candle with one hand, like speed alone will keep something ancient from snuffing out the flame. He reaches the other side, and his friends erupt in cheers, slapping him on the back. He lifts the candle overhead, his grin as bright as the fire he managed to protect.

A blond girl steps up next. One foot under the arch, then another. She inches forward like every step might collapse the ground beneath her.

Behind her, a taller girl with a long black braid jogs past, offering an encouraging smile over her shoulder as she clears the threshold in a single breath.

More freshmen follow—some cautious, some confident—raising their candles like trophies once they make it to the other side.

I keep my focus there, pretending to track who makes it through and who falters. It's easier than letting on that I'm hanging on every word of the conversation unfolding just a few feet to my left.

Reeve is giving Rey the full campus tour in lecture form—names, histories, rumors. I could probably recite it in my sleep. But hearing it from his mouth feels different with her standing beside him.

She listens like it matters. Like any of this—our legacy, our fractured past—is something she wants to understand.

Reeve gestures across campus toward the old stone path that disappears into the woods. "There's a temple out that way. You'll see it on the expanded tour..."

Rey leans in, curious. Enthralled.

Eventually, he brings the conversation back to the mystery of the arch, and she steps closer to the stone—one foot away, maybe less. She stays to the side, out of the path of the freshmen still rushing through, and lifts a hand toward the arch like she's reaching for something precious. Her hand glides across the runes, moving up and down with the indentations.

She turns to Reeve and gives him a smile I've never seen before. It's easy. Genuine. The kind of smile that warms people, that opens doors.

It pulls the air from my lungs. I don't know why it hits so hard—only that it does.

"It's one solid basalt arch," she says, wonder tucked into the curve of her voice.

Reeve moves to stand beside her without hesitation. Like he belongs there.

I stay where I am. Because I don't.

"Lots of ancient fishermen claimed it was here before they even settled the land, but who knows. Some say it's a gateway, others say it's a shrine to the Gods. Either way, it's tradition to pass through with a candle." He motions at the arch and tosses her a grin. "If the candle goes out, it means the Gods have forgotten you and misfortune will follow. If your candle stays lit, it means the Gods still remember and will favor you. It's why students cheer when they go through."

Rey laughs. "Ah, meaning the Gods remember them. Do they even realize who the Gods are?"

She freezes like she said something wrong and bites her lip.

I tilt my head, then catch myself. I do *not* need to hang on every single thing this woman says. As if to prove my point, I shove my hands in my pockets and grumble, "I'm headed to bed."

I don't wait for anyone to answer, just start walking off, and Reeve rushes to catch up to me. He grabs my arm, pulling me to a stop, a mischievous twinkle in his eyes, and says under his breath, "We should make her go through it and blow out her candle to scare her."

"Yes," I shake my head and mutter. "Because blowing out a candle will definitely scare the daughter of Satan. Not interested."

Reeve rolls his eyes. "Bro, you didn't see her expression."

I roll my eyes right back. "Why do I have to participate, then?"

"Supervise." He shrugs. "You're supervising."

"I'd rather not."

"Hey, Rey!" Reeve calls back to where he left her beside the arch. "Aric wants to see you try!"

Great. Killing him later.

He's wearing his most charming grin, which means she can't really say no. Not that he gives her any time to do so. He's already dragged me over and is leading us both to the back of the line of freshmen waiting to cross through.

Rey starts pulling away. "No, I'm good. I'm actually really tired."

"Afraid?" I scoff, the word sharper than I mean it to be. Something tightens between my shoulders at the sight of her hesitating. "It's just an old archway. I've done it a ton," I say. Total lie.

I've never gone under the damn arch. Not once.

There's something about it that puts me on edge. Not in some mystical, haunted way—just enough to keep my feet moving in the other direction.

I've already experienced enough weird shit in my life. I don't need to add "creepy magical college architecture" to the list.

"Of course, he'll go with you," Reeve volunteers, clapping me on the back. Yup, I'm going to murder him. My own brother. What's that called again? Fratricide?

By the time we reach the line of freshmen still waiting to go under, many have backed up, some actually silent in awe. Reeve and I have a reputation in school for rarely talking to lowerclassmen, never mind joining them in their ridiculous games. Feels like the whole group has been stunned into silence while Reeve grabs two of the plain black candles from the stack on the wooden stump and lights them, handing one to me and one to Rey. "All right, off you go!"

"I hate you," Rey says to him under her breath. "I told you I didn't want to do this."

"Feeling's mutual." Reeve winks, then shares a look with me. Right. I'm supposed to blow out her candle. Of all the elementary things, I swear.

"This is stupid," I say out loud, my breath fogging in front of my face as the temperature continues to drop outside. A chill runs down my spine as Rey and I stand in front of the basalt archway. "Let's get this shit over with. I'm tired."

"Same," Rey mutters next to me.

We both slowly walk under the archway as a mist crawls from the forest and down the pathway toward our feet. Once we're all the way under the arch and to the other side, I turn to blow out her candle and notice the flame's already gone.

Extinguished.

The Gods have forgotten her, then?

I slowly look down at mine.

It's covered in fucking ice. Completely covered, as if I've just dipped it into water and frozen it.

I drop the candle immediately and stomp on it, breaking both the candle and the ice wrapped around it. The last thing I need is Odin's daughter seeing it. "What'd I say? Dumb."

Rey does the same and rubs her hands against her pants. "Yeah, weird. Mine didn't even last. Guess I'm forgotten. Too bad."

If I didn't know better, I'd think she looks a little sad.

Reeve groans. "The stupid mist rolling in blew both of them out. You should go again."

I level him with a hard look. "If you're so obsessed, you go. I'm headed to bed. It's been a long day."

My hands shake the entire walk back to the dorm. It was just a stupid cold snap.

I repeat this in my head over and over again as I make my way to my room. I'm still muttering it as I change and get into bed. I'm still repeating it when I hear Rey's door open and close and when she finally rustles herself into bed. I turn toward the wall and stare at it. She can't get comfortable, either.

Annoyance hits long and hard when the sounds of her flipping over only to flip again drill directly into my brain. I'm half tempted to bang on the wall and tell her to lie still before I strap her to her bed. But then a flurry of visions of *actually* holding her down in that bed and pressing my mouth against hers fills my brain.

I jerk to a sitting position and smack my face. "No. Nope. None of that. No."

"Stop talking!" Rey yells from her side of the wall, banging with each word.

I bang right back. "I wasn't talking to you!"

"Then stop talking to yourself! Some people need sleep!"

I'm going to kill both her and Reeve at this point. "You stop yelling."

She pounds the wall again. "Sleep."

She says it like a command, and I find myself lying down in obedience, staring at the stupid wall. Again.

"Ass," I hear her say under her breath.

That's it. I raise my middle finger toward the wall.

One whole semester.

Only one of us is going to survive.

I gave her a chance to run years ago.

Now I'll feel zero guilt over a little blood spilled, because she was foolish enough to stay.

Chapter Fifteen

REY

"*M**ost of the Giants are sleeping, along with the Gods."*

"But why?" I ask.

My father's grin is menacing.

"Because they have no choice."

My alarm jolts me awake from my dream, and not for the first time, the familiar tune makes me want to hurl my phone across the room. Why I thought it would be a good idea to use Simon and Garfunkel as my wakeup call is beyond me. I mean, "The Sound of Silence"?

I *want* silence. I groan. I *need* more sleep. But by now, I'm committed to the irony, so changing it just feels wrong and messes with my entire headspace.

I was up late tossing and turning after that weird experience walking through the archway. My flame went completely out. The only good news is that everyone will just say it's a trick of the wind, while I know the truth.

That damn archway does actually have some sort of ancient power. I felt it. A subtle shimmer of energy, similar to what I feel when I'm around my dad. And yet my father never mentioned it. Maybe it's just another relic the Giants are trying to protect that's as dormant as they are. That would make the most sense. In theory. None of the runes on the arch matched the ones Laufey wrote out for me. I should have searched the area for more runes last night, and I make a mental note to do that every time I'm out and about on campus.

I'd been desperate to see what Aric's candle had done, but he'd already grumpily thrown it and ground it into the grass like some petulant child before I was able to see the effect of the arch.

Should I be surprised? No.

But the entire experience shook me a bit, making it impossible to sleep. It didn't help that the wall between our rooms seems to be made out of actual paper. I could hear every single sound coming through from the other side.

I shake my head, then pull a pillow over it. After tossing for what felt like forever, I heard his door open and close around midnight. Minutes later, when he returned, I could hear him pacing his room. Apparently, he wasn't kidding about the insomnia.

When I heard his footsteps heading toward his door a second time, I chose that moment to go out in the hall. Grabbing my toiletry bag as cover, I managed to run into him as he passed by my door. He smelled like water and moonlight.

"Midnight swim?" I asked, cursing myself for the crack in my voice.

"Please stop talking to me. It's late and I've had enough of you for the day." He sounded tired, irritated. He took in a deep breath like he was gasping for air. What was he up to now?

"Just curious." I sidestepped him, determined not to fall for… whatever this was he was playing.

But when he reached for the wall and then grabbed my arm, holding on in a death grip, even I couldn't pretend not to be concerned. "Are you okay?" I asked.

He opened his mouth like he wanted to confess something, then clenched his fists. "Dreams are nightmares. Nightmares are dreams. I just need it to stop, to finally stop…"

And then, like we hadn't just been in the middle of a conversation, he stalked away from me, slamming the bathroom door behind him.

Expected.

After all, he's a jackass. A jackass who is sleeping. *Sleeping*.

A sleeping Giant.

A sleeping deity.

Most are sleeping.

I've heard that phrase for my entire life. *Most.* But not all. Who, then, isn't sleeping? Another question I repeatedly asked my father, always getting the same answer.

"Humanity is awake," he'd say, as if that answered my question, as if this was the end of the discussion.

But of course it wasn't. I wanted to understand. "The Gods and Giants? Are any of them awake?" I'd ask, never sure if I wanted the answer to be yes or no.

His answer was always the same. "I am all you have in this Godsforsaken world."

I asked him this yesterday morning. And got the same answer. *I am all you have.*

He got me my first actual birthday cake yesterday. I'd been so excited that we were celebrating, that he and Laufey were finally acknowledging my birthday, that he allowed Laufey to publicly give me a cake rather than in secret, as she did throughout my childhood. I felt almost loved. We sang "Happy Birthday," I blew out the candles, and then he gave me a present.

I was so eager to unwrap it, hoping for something special. Maybe a necklace? Earrings? The bloodthirsty half of me would have even been happy with a throwing knife.

My smile was so big, it hurt my face. And then my father told me to close my eyes. I complied, of course, and heard the sound of wrapping paper being ruthlessly torn away.

"Hold out your hands," he whispered.

I did. The object was somewhat heavy. I opened my eyes, and the present slowly came into focus.

It was a chess piece.

The queen, to be exact.

The most important chess piece on the board. It can move horizontally, vertically, and it's often either given a pawn or the pawns on the board have the opportunity to rise up as a queen.

His message was clear. I had been a pawn, and now he was making me the queen. I was supposed to be thankful.

He grinned at me, whispering under his breath, "You'll do beautifully serving the family. Remember, only the Gods can be trusted." I saw Laufey flinch. How could she not, being a Giant herself? "It's time."

We left soon after that. I shake the memory loose and drag myself out of bed.

Orientation's at eleven, which is why I set my alarm for seven last night—like an idiot. Four more hours of sleep would've been the smart move, but if my father drilled anything into me, it's this: once you commit to a plan, you bleed for it.

So I don't second-guess. I just grab my bag.

Inside: snacks, water, journal, phone. The usual essentials, minus my knife, which I leave beneath my mattress.

If anyone stops me, I'm just a college girl exploring campus and stalking a very dangerous Giant in possession of a very dangerous hidden memory.

Totally. Normal.

I leave my room and hit the down button for the elevator.

The scent of the outdoors fills the air, and I can feel someone approaching from down the hall, but it's not Aric.

I don't have to look to know Reeve is wearing that same easy grin that never seems to leave his face. "Going hiking? Meditating?"

"Reeve," I say through clenched teeth. "You're up early and on the wrong floor."

"I like to bird-watch on the roof," he says dryly.

The elevator doors open. We both get in.

The silence is uncomfortable. "Why are you here, Rey? Really?"

"Education," I say smoothly. "Why else would I be here?"

"You're not welcome, and you know it. Aric believes your father had our parents killed, and I can't say I disagree."

Well, at least he came out and acknowledged the giant-ass elephant in the room. I'm surprised it took this long.

"I'm sorry for your loss," I say, and I mean it. "But from what I saw in the news, it was a tragic accident, your parents." I want to believe this is the truth, but part of me has always wondered if my father—and by relation, me—had any hand in their deaths.

"Bullshit," he snaps, and I flinch as his voice echoes off the walls of the elevator.

I probably deserved that. "I've just apologized even though it's not my fault. Maybe you're just prejudiced against me because of my name. If so, work on that. Your family isn't innocent, either." I barely tamp down the rage. He might not remember what the Giants did in destroying the Bifrost. But I've been told—and I've spent a lifetime suffering under Odin for it.

Thankfully, the elevator doors open, and I'm through them before he can even gather a breath.

I walk across the campus, headed toward the dining hall for breakfast, but at the last second, I veer left toward the forest path. I need to calm down. I don't resent Reeve for rehashing the past, but it doesn't accomplish anything, certainly not peace or healing.

Not to mention, no matter what, I'll still be found guilty because of who my father is, because of what he's capable of doing. What he's done.

I shake it off.

I know from the intel in the notebook that Aric normally does some meditation in the woods around this time. Fantastic. I walk farther past the tree line, carefully avoiding the arch, and down the trail.

The only time I've ever seen something unusual happen around Aric was that day at the beach with the sheen of frost. He'd walked away, his back to the ocean, so it's possible he didn't even notice. But what set it off?

One minute we'd been sharing a moment—and the next he'd been cruel and stormed away. Well, if showing your cruel side is what powered a god, no wonder my father was the most powerful of them all. He'd mastered that before I was out of diapers.

As I round a curve in the path, I see Aric stopped in a clearing. A few feet beyond him, the still water of a spring reflects the eerie gray light of the sky.

I dodge behind a tree and peer out around it just in time to see him shrug off his jacket, followed by his shirt. He tosses them onto an old wooden bench, and my breath catches.

He's facing me like he's putting on a show. Um, not what I expected.

He's not making eye contact, but his stare is so direct, I think he must have seen me duck behind this tree. Mouth dry, I keep watching. I can't tear my eyes away.

Maybe he didn't spot me and he's just an exhibitionist? I still can't see all of him because of the typical Washington early-morning mist, but when it finally clears, it's to see him slowly starting to unbutton his jeans. What the hell?

"Is this your first time?" he calls. Shit. He did freaking see me. But maybe he doesn't know it's me?

Wait, what did he just ask me? Embarrassment burns my cheeks.

"Reyyyy?" He says my name like a taunt, stretching it out way longer than necessary. "I mean, if you want to join me in skinny-dipping, I won't complain. But I can't promise I won't drown you."

Caught.

Chapter Sixteen

REY

I'm seriously better than this.

Is that going to be my new mantra? I'm better than this? Shit.

I stomp out from behind the tree and do the only thing I can think to do to get him as off-balance as he's gotten me. I start stripping right in front of him, starting with my jacket. Two can play this game, and considering I literally have everything to lose, I'm all in.

"Thank you so much for the invitation," I say, toeing off my shoes. "I've been waiting years to get naked with you."

Aric looms over me, eyes burning with unreadable emotion. Is it rage…or something worse? "Why are you here?"

I clench my fist around the hem of my T-shirt and yank it over my head, willing my pulse to chill the hell out. He's the enemy. He's furious. And he's half naked.

Get it together, Rey!

"Your brother just asked me the same question. Education," I say sweetly, as if this isn't the worst idea I've had in at least a week.

I unhook my bra, toss it onto the bench, and shove out of my pants in one clean motion. Panties stay on. Can't give the people everything they want.

Our gazes collide, then drop as one. Boxer briefs, like I saw in his room. My skin feels tight and my mouth waters as I step a bit closer. The air between us is charged, heavy with unsaid things, confessions, discussions about our past, all of it.

"You were right," I tell him. "It's my first time." I nod toward the spring behind him. "So go ahead—teach me."

His face goes deathly pale, then seconds later he's flushing fire-alarm red.

"It's more of a learn-as-you-go kind of thing," he says finally, his voice rough as it skips across the suddenly frigid air hitting me in the face with such intensity that I suck in a breath. "I'm getting in."

He backs up into the spring, his mahogany eyes dark and unblinking, which would be unnerving enough, but add to it that he never once breaks eye contact, causing heat to unfurl low in my stomach… Is he trying to intimidate me?

Well, I'm here. I'm naked. Does he really think I'll fold that easily?

Then it hits me. He's not trying to intimidate me.

He's *daring* me.

His nostrils flare again, his jaw tightens, and then he swallows like he's doing it to keep from saying something. I chalk it up to his hatred and absolute doubt that I'm here for charitable reasons.

My pulse is frantic, my breaths too shallow as I watch him disappear into the mist rising from the spring. The early-morning quiet is broken only by the sound of water rippling as he slips in. No pressure, no panic. I can do this.

I follow, stepping carefully over the rocky path until I reach the edge of the small spring. I'm not a fan of water. Ever since I was a kid, I've had nightmares about drowning. Probably a result of Odin tossing me into the mansion's deep end as a child. His form of parenting was literally sink or swim. But this pool doesn't trigger the lurching feeling of dread in my stomach—the water's clear, and I can see the stone lining the walls and edges. The air is cool against my bare skin, but the moment I sink into the water, warmth overwhelms me.

What the hell am I doing?

"Reckless" doesn't even cover it—I must be losing my mind…

knowing what he could be capable of.

I need to get close, but this is too close, too soon.

I've only been here a day, and I'm already skinny-dipping with the enemy.

Now that I'm close enough to see him again, I notice Aric's eyes are closed, his expression unreadable. I'm almost naked. He's almost naked. And completely unbothered. I don't know if I should be offended or thankful that he hasn't said anything.

The charged silence stretching between us is heavy with an unspoken challenge.

I open my mouth, but before I can speak, his voice cuts through the stillness.

"Shhhh." His tone is low, warning. "This is a quiet place. Make noise, and you might get eaten."

I roll my eyes and flick water at him while dying a bit internally at the possible double meaning.

His reaction is instant. His eyes snap open, dark and intense, and then suddenly, I'm shoved against the muddy wall of the spring, my back pressing into the slick surface.

"Do that again." His voice is a dare. A threat. He tilts his head to the side. "I liked it."

His eyes flicker to my mouth.

I try not to react, but it's impossible with Aric. I want to ask him questions, dig deep, for my own personal reasons but also because it's the only way he'll let me in. "You hate being challenged."

"No, I never back away from a challenge. I hate losing," he says quickly, and his eyes soften a bit. "And although I might be able to forgive you, fair warning, I'll never forgive your father."

"It's unforgivable. All of it." And it's true. What my father did, what happened during a war Aric can't remember his bloodline having any hand in…it's all unforgivable.

He sighs. "It is, and yet, all I keep thinking is 'damn, the lips of my enemy look so soft, I should indulge for just one second and take a bite.'"

It's part of my plan, but his words shouldn't make my blood rush. I suck in my bottom lip and imagine it's him. "What's stopping you?"

His eyes dart from my mouth back up to my eyes. "Loyalty." He tilts his head. "What's stopping you?"

"Self-control."

He leans in and grazes my ear with his lips. "Surprised you have any left after living with Odin."

I freeze. Even knowing he's sleeping, it's shocking to hear him refer to my father as Odin, not realizing the power of the name.

"Is this how it's going to be the entire semester?" I ask him, breathless.

He pulls back. "Probably."

"You mad about it?"

"Again, I like a challenge. Plus, I think you're in over your head with Endir and especially with my family. I know you're here for a reason. You want to get close to us and find out all our secrets? Be my guest, but the closer you get to me, the closer I get to you. Better tread carefully."

"Mm, okay." I nod. "I'll take your advice to heart."

I bite my lip again, heat pooling in my belly as he watches. Heart hammering, I throw caution to the wind and flick another drop of water toward his face. "Oops," I murmur. "It slipped."

A slow, wicked grin curves his lips. His hand disappears beneath the water, brushing against my thigh. I freeze again, my pulse racing as his fingers trail upward—slow, deliberate—gliding along the curve of my waist, up my ribs, until his palm is at my throat.

And then his lips are on my neck. Warm and decisive.

Not tentative, not testing. Just there, like he's always known he'd end up exactly in this spot.

A breath catches in my throat. My hands hover, useless, unsure if I should shove him away or pull him closer.

He moves higher, slow and infuriatingly confident, dragging his mouth up to my jawline.

And when he bites—just enough pressure to make me gasp—I hate how much I want him to do it again.

He murmurs against my cheek, "I told you, I never back away from a challenge. You smell good, by the way. Too bad…"

Something cold and wet smears across my cheek. Is that...*mud*?

He releases me and shakes the excess from his fingers, his smirk dark and satisfied.

"Sorry," he murmurs, voice rich with amusement. "It slipped."

I wipe the mud from my face and flick it back at him, a genuine grin on my lips. "No apology needed. I like a good mud mask."

"Oh, I wasn't being helpful; it just pains me to see your face."

I wrap my body around him and shove him down into the water. He goes easily, and when he pops back up, his expression is all amusement. He may be asleep, but he's not dead inside after all. He can feel.

Better yet?

He *wants* to.

"Oops." I shrug. "I slipped."

He pushes me up against the wall of the spring again and grins. "You're a real handful. Too bad you won't last long. You might have been entertaining."

I shrug again. "Who knows what the future holds."

Aric presses his hands on either side of my head against the spring wall, caging me in, then lightly shoves back. The distance quickly grows between us. "Who knows indeed."

Chapter Seventeen

ARIC

I grab my clothes from where I left them on the bench and head back up the trail, stopping partway to put on my pants so I'm not walking half naked back to the dorms. My whole body is buzzing from that interaction with Rey. I shouldn't have let her get under my skin, but damn if there isn't something about her…

I use my shirt to wipe down my body as I walk until I find myself right next to the archway again.

"Stupid legends," I say, shoving my arms into the damp shirt, and walk right underneath the arch. Immediately, a chill runs down my spine. I shake it off and keep walking, but something feels funny beneath my feet. Frowning, I look down and lift up my foot. Perfect icy footprints press into the grass.

Mine.

I slowly swallow and look over my shoulder, then notice a path from the archway to the actual trail. Within seconds, the footprints are gone. Shit. Maybe they really do need to increase the dosage of my meds this time. It's been years since they've adjusted them.

I don't blame Reeve for being worried that I might be losing control. I haven't been the same since I heard she was coming to campus.

I almost kissed Rey back there in the hot spring. It was like something came over me, something familiar. Even though I could see the steam coming up off the heated water, all I felt was cold inside. Freezing, yet burning as well. Burning for Rey.

I keep stomping toward the dorms and try to ignore the way my heart feels like it's beating out of my chest when I think of Rey's mouth, the way she felt in my arms.

Everything about her is wrong.

She's from a line of murderers, and nothing can change that. I need to seriously refocus and not overthink why my body is betraying me by responding to her the way it does. It's not rocket science why, though I'd die before admitting that to her.

She's so beautiful that it's hard to look away.

She's snarky and clever and just a little bit vulnerable.

Even her voice is hypnotic—it warms me from the inside out, only to turn into such a searing burn that my brain tells me just one touch would be worth it—even if she did shove a knife through my chest after the fact. She's a black widow, and I refuse to be caught in her web…

But wouldn't it be nice to have just one taste?

I quickly get on the elevator, needing the safety of my room before I shatter. It takes maybe thirty seconds to reach my floor, but even that is way too long. Lights flicker overhead like they have been for the past few days as I make my way down the hall. A sudden wave of nausea washes over me.

I quickly stumble into my room, grab the water bottle next to the sink, and pound it while the ceiling starts to spin. My vision doubles, triples. I finish the water and brace myself against the sink, looking up into the mirror.

Blood drips from my face. I yell and throw the water bottle against the mirror at my own reflection. "Stop, no!"

The lights flicker off, and when they turn back on, my reflection's back to normal. My dizziness is gone, too, and the room seems to have stopped spinning. But still, my throat burns with a fiery ache.

More.

I need more water.

I fill up the water bottle three more times and take some deep breaths, then grab my meds and take them.

My phone rings. Grandfather, or Sigurd, as I always reference him when I'm back on campus. Shit.

I debate not answering. But he'll only keep calling, so I swipe the phone and his face pops up on the screen. He's on campus, in his office. I can tell by the artifacts displayed behind him—rune-cast steel Asgardian chains; a gleaming bronze replica of Gjallarhorn, the cursed horn believed to summon Ragnarök itself; a fragment of volcanic basalt carved into runes rumored to be from the shattered stones of Jötunheim; and a small, iron-bound chest in the corner, its lock shaped like a serpent's eye. Honestly, anyone hopping onto a Zoom call with the guy isn't going to feel all that encouraged about their future—his office is littered with reminders of death, destruction, ruin, and what will happen if you cross him. Just like the runes, he surrounds himself with powerful artifacts on purpose.

"Yes, sir?"

"Control is vital, Aric. Do you need to be reminded of this?"

How does he know mine is slipping? Did he see the trail of ice I left coming back from the hot spring? I don't want to admit that it's getting harder, but… "It's probably better if I move back to the house. I can commute in for classes—"

"No."

The word hangs in the air. No explanation. Just his decree.

I don't bother arguing.

"You're awakening, Aric."

No shit. "Does Reeve know? Is he like me?"

"He's still sleeping."

I imagine my brother wielding my powers. "Probably for the best."

"You think?" Sigurd barks a laugh. It's a rare display of real emotion from him. One that has me smiling, because yeah, totally agree about Reeve.

All I can picture is a shit-ton of naked snowmen or forced frigid temperatures and a call to use body heat to survive. Yeah. With great power comes great responsibility, something Reeve lacks in spades.

"I have questions—"

"And you have an enemy to manipulate."

Rey.

"Why is she here?" Before I can voice all my questions, Sigurd is waving at someone else.

"Professor Higgins! Yes, do come in." And with nothing more than that, Sigurd ends the call.

Right. First week of school. My grandfather is the president of the university. But would it really kill the old man to carve out a few actual minutes to communicate with me?

I angrily toss the phone onto my bed and grab my shower caddy. When I walk out of the room, it's to see Rey just getting back. As she brushes past me, I can tell she still smells like a fresh spring day. It's like she wasn't just covered in mud minutes ago.

Lights continue to flicker overhead. It's not helping with my bad mood.

"Are they going to do that all semester?" she asks like she wants to spark up a conversation with me, despite all outward warnings that I'm ready to explode.

I roll my eyes and pass her, giving her a wide berth. "Maybe we're cursed because you're on this wing now."

"Very funny," she says, her gaze focused on the key card she waves in front of her locked door.

"Wasn't joking."

The lock dings, and she turns. "Hey, Aric—"

"Nope." I ignore her and go into the bathroom, shutting her out of my life and my thoughts as much as possible.

The moment the door closes behind me, I can finally exhale.

I cross the room in three strides and turn the shower on—hot, as hot as it goes—then brace both hands on the sink while steam curls up the mirror like fingers trying to blur me out of the picture.

I strip. Step in.

The heat hits like a punch, and I welcome it.

The minutes tick by as I stand there too long, water pounding over my head, down my back, trying to scald the memory of her from my skin. It doesn't work. The heat just makes her feel closer.

Her voice still echoes in my ears. That look she gave me—half challenge, half invitation—like she was daring me to lose control.

And I almost did.

I tip my head forward, press my forehead to the tile.

This can't keep happening.

Since my parents died, I've kept everything contained—my grief, my anger, the expectations from my grandfather to take over what's left of the family's legacy. I didn't ask for this weight. But I carry it all the same, because someone has to. Someone has to wear the crown before it's taken from us.

Just thinking of Odin and what he did to my parents makes my muscles lock tight, fists clenching on instinct. Fuck me. I came in here to calm down, not ratchet my rage higher.

I close my eyes and take a deep breath, steam filling my lungs as I drag the heat in and hold it there. Inhale, count to three. Exhale, count to three. I repeat the exercise my therapist taught me, and my pulse slows, shoulders ease, a semblance of control seeping back into my bones.

Control. Such a simple word. And the only thing keeping me from breaking.

Yet when Rey's in the room, I have none.

She tears the ground out from under me without trying. Looks at me like I'm a puzzle she already solved and resents the answer.

And I hate her for that. Almost as much as I hate the part of me that wants her anyway.

The water turns cold, but I stay under it. Let the sting anchor me as I think through what to do about this woman. It's obvious she's not going to give up. Maybe even can't. But that doesn't mean I can't seize control of the situation. Use it to my advantage.

When I finally step out, I've made my decision. I move slowly, deliberately. Let the plan settle against my chest like a familiar blanket.

I grab my towel, sling it around my waist. Breathe.

Dragging my fist across the fogged surface, I create a clear slash across the mirror. The reflection that stares back at me? Good. I look like a man who has it together.

And all because of one simple plan.

She wants to get close? I'll let her. I'll play along, give her what she *thinks* she wants—access, proximity, influence.

And in return, I'll get what I need: the truth. About why she's here, what her father wants, and how to stop it.

Then maybe—if I'm smart—how to burn this obsession out of my system before it takes the last piece of me that still feels human.

Chapter Eighteen

REY

Aric slammed the door in my face before I could even finish the question.

Cool. That went well.

I stand there a second longer than I should, my hand half raised, as if I might knock on the bathroom door and try again.

"You know," a voice says from behind me, "some people would take that as a sign."

I spin around to find Ziva leaning against her doorframe, a toothbrush hanging out the side of her mouth like a lollipop. Her hair is a wild halo of electric-blue-tipped curls, her cat-print pajama shorts still riding low on her hips beneath her Endir hoodie. She looks equal parts chaotic and smug.

"He's not a morning person," I mutter.

"Neither am I," she says, yanking the toothbrush from her mouth and pointing it at Aric's door. "But at least I don't weaponize it."

I can't help it—I snort.

Ziva grins, then drops the brush into a mug in her left hand. "Let me guess. You tried to say something human, and he responded with a death glare and a shut door?"

"Basically."

She folds her arms. "Don't take it personally. He's like that with everyone. Especially people he thinks might actually matter."

I raise an eyebrow. "Sounds like you speak from experience."

Ziva's expression shifts—just a fraction—but it's enough to pull me up short.

"Let's just say Aric and I go way back. Used to be best friends when we were kids. Grade school stuff—he'd share his pudding cups, I'd let him cheat off my math homework. Totally platonic, tragically adorable."

I blink. "So…what happened?"

Her mouth quirks, but there's no humor in it. "His grandfather happened. One day, I just wasn't welcome anymore. No explanation. No warning. Just a very polite reminder from a very old man that some names don't mix."

My chest tightens. "Because you're—?"

Ziva gasps, hand to chest. "Mexican American?"

I wince. "I didn't mean—"

She waves me off, laughing. "Relax, Snow White. No, apparently, I'm dangerous because I have opinions. Loud ones. Also, I once threatened to set a kid's pants on fire for calling me spicy."

"Did you actually?"

Ziva lifts a finger. "Allegedly."

I chuckle. I can't help it. There's something disarming about her, like she's already decided I'm not a threat, not competition, just… someone to root for. She doesn't know how rare that is.

"I'm not into Aric," I say before I can overthink it. "Whatever you saw in the hall—he slammed the door in my face five seconds later."

Ziva raises an eyebrow like she's heard that one before. "Not saying I care, but if I did? I'd tell you to be careful. That kind of power doesn't come free."

I nod slowly. "Good thing I'm not looking for handouts. Just answers."

She studies me another beat, then gives a sharp nod. "Cool. Then I'm going back to bed for fifteen minutes and pretending the world doesn't exist." She points her toothbrush at me again. "You need me, scream. Or just send psychic vibes. I respond to those, too."

I wait until her door closes behind her before I retreat into my own room.

Plopping on the edge of my bed, I sigh long and low. I know he's the enemy, but for one minute Aric almost felt like my friend as we flung mud at each other in the spring. Of course, he also threatened my life *and* dragged his teeth along my neck—but I tell myself he didn't really mean any of that.

Is that how starved I am for attention?

Probably. I swear, at this rate I'll never grow out of the need to be seen or heard.

Just as quickly as our little playtime started, it was over. But he can't get away from me that easily. I say this even though he just slammed the door in my face. I'm playing the long game. It's fine.

Jumping up, I walk over and sit at my desk, pulling out the notebook.

My fingers trace the scrap of paper from Laufey.

This—all of this—is for Laufey.

I can't get distracted. Can't fail. She is the one bit of leverage my father has over me, and he'll use it. Use *her.* Mercilessly.

Is she safe? I wonder. Sad? She's always been sad, even in my earliest memories. Though she'd smile as she braided my hair, and she'd look so peaceful when she'd sing me to sleep and tell me stories when I was scared.

Stories of a kingdom far far away, except this one was real. I was the princess. But the king was evil and there was no savior but myself. The people only had me to rely on, and in order to defeat the evil I had to learn how to be patient. Her stories all had a reason for them, a hidden meaning. Just like her actions, Laufey chose her words wisely and with purpose. Nothing was by accident, everything by design, and now she's dying—or will die if I don't find Mjölnir in time.

We don't speak of Frigga. We don't speak of how life was back in Asgard. Just like we don't speak of why she would marry him here, other than he saved the life of someone she loved for her healing power. She's been more employee than wife ever since.

"I'll find a way to free you," I whisper.

I study the rune-laden note. I've seen one of these already at Endir. I know what the others mean, so if I come across any of them on campus… Maybe they won't lead me to Mjölnir, but maybe they create a sort of ward or shield for me?

I pore over the notes, looking for any reference, and stop on the picture of Mjölnir again.

I read the bullet points: "Holds the history of Asgard and all the wars. Holds the power to both build and destroy worlds. Can only be wielded by those it deems worthy. Created for Thor by the dwarves Brokk and Eitri—Mjölnir helps control Thor's power. Has a personality like any other artifact; it can feel, speak, engage. Original owner: Thor."

I shut the notebook.

Mjölnir can *communicate*.

I wonder if it's communicated with Aric at any point? Maybe through dreams or visions? Was Mjölnir speaking to him through the nightmares he mentioned last night? How did I miss this earlier?

Curiosity has me sending a text to my father, even though he's the last person I want to talk to.

Me: *Did Mjölnir ever talk to Thor*

I wait.

Finally, the dots pop up on the screen.

Odinfather: *Thor is dead. We don't speak of the dead.*

Me: *We're talking about a hammer. Did it though*

Odinfather: *They were inseparable before the war. Like family.*

Me: *And during the war?*

Odinfather: *You know the history. Thor died, Mjölnir was taken.*

Me: *So it mourns for him then?*

Odinfather: *As do I. Daily.*

I swallow the lump in my throat.

Me: *May Thor's storm rage on in the sky, eternal and unbroken, in the Hall of Bilskírnir, the largest hall of the Gods.*

Odinfather: *May he find his peace amongst the storms he created.*

I set the phone down and stare at the words. I never met my half brother. But something about the silence beneath Odin's answers tells me he loved Thor—in his own twisted way. And if Mjölnir was forged to reflect its wielder, then what is it now without him?

Grief and power wrapped in a relic that doesn't forget?

If the hammer is mourning, then I understand it better than I thought.

And I know one thing for sure:

Mjölnir belongs with the Gods. It belongs with my family.

And I'm going to be the one to bring it home.

I glance at my phone. Fifteen minutes before I need to head downstairs for orientation—just enough time to tug on some fresh clothes and pull my hair back. I fix my face in the mirror. Lip gloss. Powder. High ponytail. I look like a girl who slept well and has zero blood on her hands.

I grab my orientation packet, sling the rucksack over one shoulder. The notebook and blade stay tucked under my mattress—until I need them.

Aric might think he has the upper hand, but he overplayed today. He wants me. And I can use that.

Like I told Ziva…I need some answers.

Chapter Nineteen

ARIC

Sometimes I hate Sigurd. He knows I don't do crowds, don't do people, and yet he's insisted that his grandsons—both of them—will be the draw that gets students to sign up for the sunset campus tour. So here we are.

I'll admit, Reeve can pitch Endir like nobody else, making it out to be some Ivy League utopia. It's almost impressive—if you ignore the fact that he's never once attended class on time.

Besides, pleasing our grandfather by agreeing to these tours comes easy to him. Everything comes easy to Reeve. He's the golden child. Always sunny, always popular.

Yet despite his many admirers, the one who loves Reeve best has always been *Reeve*. I swear, the sound of his own voice could probably give him an orgasm at this point. He's a great brother, loyal, trusting, but the narcissism is strong in that one, and he isn't even apologetic about it.

I'm waiting outside our dorm for him to grab the rest of his school spirit rah-rah tour shit when he rolls out the front doors with a giant green flag in his hands.

"No." I point at it. "You are not holding a flag like we're in some parade. Put it back."

He grins and flips it over. “It has my face on it.”

“For fuck’s sake, can you give it a rest? Just once?”

He tilts his head. “No, I don’t think I can. Plus, it’s comic relief for what’s going to be the most boring two hours of these new students’ lives. I was seriously tempted to make brownies laced with weed just to help them through it, then realized that, even though it’s legal in Washington, I’d still be drugging people without their knowledge.” He seems genuinely sad about it.

“Wow, how astute of you.”

“I do have boundaries,” he says, but even he can’t keep a straight face while saying it.

“No you don’t.” I pinch the bridge of my nose, already feeling a headache coming on.

He shoots me a sloppy grin, then puts his stupid Gucci hat on his head and starts walking away. I follow him to the tour meeting location, and when I get there, I choose a spot next to the Endir University welcome sign, conveniently placed a few feet away from where about forty students have already begun to gather.

Everyone’s chatting and laughing like it’s going to be the best tour of their lives. I know they’re just running off the whole freshman first-week-of-school thing, but I wonder what it would really be like to look forward to something like that, with pure, unadulterated joy.

I know part of what keeps me from feeling that way is the medicine I’m on. It makes me feel numb. It used to work better before Rey showed up at Endir. No question, I prefer numbness to the out-of-control feelings I have around her, the constant threat that at any moment, I’m going to snap.

And just like conjuring up Beelzebub, she joins the crowd, moving through it until she’s right in front of me with a big, knowing grin. She’s in baggy jeans and tennis shoes, a crop top black sweatshirt, and has her hair pulled back into a high ponytail.

She’s effortlessly pretty.

Annoyingly so.

I don’t trust pretty things. There’s always something lurking beneath the surface, or, in Rey’s case, a hell of a lot of somethings, just waiting to pop out and slit your throat.

She smiles at me.

I ignore her and join Reeve.

"Welcome." Reeve holds his flag high. "Make sure to follow the green flag, aka me, at all times." A few girls around us giggle. Of course they do. "And know that my brother and I are so honored to be giving you a tour of the university. Most of you have seen the dorms and dining hall already, so we'll be taking you through the science building, business building, arts, and music." He pauses, and I know it's for dramatic effect. "Then, to end the tour, we'll make a stop at the Hall of Ormir!"

Everyone starts talking at once. The Hall of Ormir is legendary. Theories abound about the temple. It's been called the product of an eccentric billionaire. A meeting house for a pagan cult. Others believe it really is of Norse origin. Ghost-hunting shows consider it one of the most haunted places in the Northwest.

It's not. Haunted, that is, though some scary shit has been rumored to go down there.

The whispers people hear in that hall are nothing more than the wind moving between the ancient building and the water that surrounds it, but people still believe.

Because people are stupid.

Reeve holds his flag high and waves it. "Shhh. We'll go over the rules once we're there. Let's start with the boring stuff first." He turns and starts walking. I follow and suddenly feel Rey at my side.

I smell her, too.

"What?" I don't turn. "What do you want?"

"Nothing," she says quickly. "I'm just walking. Is that okay?"

I grunt.

She keeps pace with me—which I have to admit is impressive, since my legs are at least six inches longer—but at least she's not talking to me or touching me.

After we visit the science building and move on to arts, I'm a bit perplexed about why she hasn't tried to charm me at all.

An hour later, we're at the last building—business. Reeve is spouting off about Sigurd and other donors whose contributions landed their names on each wing. I turn to finally say something to Rey, only to realize she's wandered off. I scan the crowds and finally spot her next to Reeve. Figures.

I feel my frown deepen. Why the hell do I even care?

Reeve starts laughing at something Rey says, and irritation burns through my veins. He knows she's the enemy. He shouldn't be laughing with her even if she were the funniest person on the planet.

I cough into my hand to get his attention.

Reeve doesn't look up.

"Reeve," I finally snap.

His eyes lock on mine. He knows exactly what he's doing. "Yeah?"

"We should go to the Hall of Ormir before it gets too late."

It's a valid excuse. People aren't allowed to pass through the gates after dark; too many students have either drowned or gone missing over the years. Some think the drowning has to do with the way the current runs in the spring-fed pool that the hall was built over, while others say people drown because they stay too long in the water, thinking it's going to give them special powers. Nobody really knows anything except it's not smart to be here at night. And it's never safe to swim.

"The university is liable for everyone we take past those gates," I remind Reeve.

He nods. "True. True." To the freshmen, he says, "All right, Endir fam, let's get moving!"

Rey leaves his side and returns to the group. She doesn't bother to find her spot next to me again as Reeve holds up his flag and starts walking us toward the Hall of Ormir in all its daunting glory.

A chill runs down my spine, growing stronger the closer we get.

As we pass through the gates, a cool breeze suddenly picks up, swirling around the group before everything goes quiet and still. I can't explain it, but my heart is suddenly racing.

A kid shouts, "It's the ghost!"

Rey's suddenly next to me, whispering under her breath. "Or some angry Gods."

I roll my eyes and feign ignorance. "Don't tell me you believe any of that shit."

She hugs herself against the chill coming off the forest and keeps walking. The closer we get to the ancient temple, the colder the air becomes until I can see my breath in front of my face. I need to calm the hell down, but I can't.

My fingertips tingle. Chills move through my veins. Frost covers my hands.

Again.

In a blink, I'm back on a windswept beach, waves crashing against the shore, salty spray on my face and the daughter of my enemy sitting close enough to kiss.

Something changed in me that day.

A dam breaking, a door unlocking. I don't have the words to describe the way a part of me chipped away.

All I know is that Rey is the common thread. Her presence is a flame to the cold I can't escape. Every contact widens the rift, making more and more of the monster inside me want to break free.

I shove my hands in my pockets. My heart starts to race, a clammy sweat breaking out along my forehead. Damn it, it's happening.

When I sneak a glance at Rey to see if she's noticed, I realize her breath is doing the same thing, so it must actually be cold outside. I hate the sigh of relief it brings—knowing her air also carries frost but from the actual temperature, not me.

A small voice in my head whispers…*for now*.

I shove it from my consciousness.

It's getting harder and harder to hide, to explain away—and one day, I know, it will be impossible.

"We should stay with the other students." She nods jerkily, and we catch up to the rest of the group.

"All right." Reeve stops at the massive stone entrance.

The iron door itself is at least twelve feet tall. The rest of the building is constructed like an ancient temple with icons and runes etched into the stone. "You'll have around thirty minutes inside. Please don't go into the pool at the bottom of the stairs. Trust me when I say you won't come back. It's roped off for a reason, so don't be a dick, all right?"

Everyone mumbles their agreement and starts to go into the building. Phones out, cameras clicking or live streaming.

"That's a massive beast if I've ever seen one," Rey whispers next to me.

"Well you do live with Odin, so." I glance up, following her gaze to the massive structure. Built from ancient black stone, it rises at least three stories high, the forest seeming to fold around it—trees growing against its sides like it belongs to them. At its peak, nine twisted iron spires form a serpentlike deity reaching skyward, mouth open in a silent scream, eyes hollow.

The steep roof is shingled in black slate. Another serpent coils over the oak door, iron-banded and scarred with faded runes etched deep into the stone.

The whole place feels alive. And ready to eat someone.

My father used to bring me here when I was a kid. I'd cry until he gave up trying to explain the carvings, the runes, the stories in the stone. Funny—I haven't thought about that in years, probably because I usually avoid the area like the plague.

Rey studies the front of the building, her gaze tracing the runes as if she's trying to memorize every detail.

"After you?" she asks.

I realize I've been staring. Not at the temple. At her.

"Yeah." I touch the door and immediately yank my hand back.

I'm sure it must have burned me, but when I look at my palm, it's totally fine.

"Everything okay?" She frowns.

"Worry about yourself." I shove past her, shouldering the door open without touching it again, and keep walking into the large sanctuary. The air is damp from the open lagoons near the very back and the constant water that runs into the pool beneath the temple. The smell of incense is still eerily strong, like it became a part of the building and refused to leave. The high beams arch like ribs from a corpse, their surfaces carved with bodiless faces, each of them looking like they are people crying out in pain.

Rey moves closer to me. "This is creepy as shit."

I almost laugh.

Nope. Don't let her break your defenses. "History usually is."

Reeve is guiding the freshmen around the hall, snapping selfies with the group in between his show-and-tell. True to form, his stories are heavily embellished.

Rey hangs back by me. Her eyes narrow as she walks toward the nearest wall and reaches for it, then jerks her hand back. "Why are there burn marks?"

I want to be an ass and walk away, but I answer her instead, like a glutton for punishment. "They say the priests made sacrifices to the Gods here, offerings to welcome them back. But I don't buy it. Those weren't gifts; they were penance. Humanity bleeding itself dry to make up for all its mistakes."

"That's…dark." She licks her lips and stares back at me, expression blank. "Which Gods?"

"Does it matter?" I snap.

"Maybe."

"Norse, I'd imagine." I shrug. "It's a Norse temple, after all, despite no one being able to date it."

"Really?" she asks skeptically. "An ancient Norse structure on the West Coast of Washington state."

"History doesn't always get it right." I shrug. "Leif Erikson journeyed to the Americas long before Columbus ever did."

"Wrong coast. But…fair."

"You can tell by the carved runes around the temple door. Nine runes for the Nine Realms."

"It's said the Bifrost connected our world to others long before recorded time. You know, if you believe in that sort of thing." Her eyes look almost expectant.

"Sure, why not. There you go. Mystery explained. Any more questions, or can I walk in the opposite direction of wherever you're heading?"

Her smile seems forced when she looks up at me. I guess that makes two of us, though she hides it better. "You shouldn't have left an opening."

"Rookie mistake," I grumble.

She smirks, then points at the rear of the hall. "What's that?"

I keep my annoyed sigh in. "A very creepy obsidian mirror that tilts down to reflect the water."

Rey moves toward the pool, and I follow. So much for walking away.

"That pool's pitch-black." She shudders. "I bet it's super deep."

"You don't like water?"

"Not especially." She inches farther away from the pool's edge. "Why reflect the water with the mirror?"

"Why so many questions?" I counter with annoyance. "Reeve may know more about it. He's into all of this shit, but I think it has something to do with trapped Gods in the water or something like that. They'd sacrifice humans as an offering and then put the mirror on the water and wait to see the reflection of the Gods coming to the surface to collect their souls as they were released from their imprisonment." I glance over to see her staring at me like I have three heads. "Since you can't look a God right in the eye."

"Um, why can't you look a God in the eye?"

"Because humans aren't worthy." I roll my hand. "You have to use the mirror to see. Kind of like Medusa—wrong mythology but similar concept."

Why I feel compelled to help her out with this explanation, I have no idea. It's like I can't control the words spilling out of me any more than I can control breathing. Plus, I can't tell if she's asking because she really doesn't know or if she's baiting me.

"Ah. 'Kay." Rey nods and peers into the mirror, observing the murky lake water. "I see nothing but darkness."

"It's all a myth," I say quickly as a twinging zap of cold starts building in my chest. Epic timing. "We should go. You don't want to be here at night. It's even creepier. Then again, if that scares you away, take your time."

Rey rolls her eyes. "I don't scare easily. I think I've seen the worst."

"Well, your father *is* a notorious murderer. I'm sure he gets extremely creative when he dismembers people."

The cold continues to build. Where is it coming from?

She looks back at the mirror, her gaze narrowing. "There's something etched on top of the obsidian," she mumbles, leaning in closer.

A sharp whistle has us both jumping.

Reeve.

Shit For Brains blows again, then waves that ridiculous flag, and the other students follow him out of the hall like a herd of lemmings.

"We should go, too," I tell her.

"In a sec. I think I recognize this rune." She goes up on her toes.

My added height makes it easier to see.

"Raido," we say at the same time.

The front door slams shut, causing a gust of wind to swirl through the room. Rey turns away, but it's too late—the mirror suddenly flips, the huge stone slab slamming into the back of her head, and slices me when I try to stop it from hitting her again. Its edges are sharp and jagged. She falls to the ground.

"Shit!" I catch her, kneel next to her. I reached her before her head hit stone, but blood's trickling down her neck. "Are you okay?"

She sits up and gingerly touches the back of her head. "Ouch, yeah, that was weir—" Her eyes go unfocused.

"Rey? Rey?" Panic spikes.

I grab her face, but the minute my skin brushes hers, the air shifts. The once-still pool ripples violently, waves splashing against the stone edges like something in its inky depths just woke up. Cold biting through me, I try to pull back, but my hands won't move; they're frozen against her skin.

My back ignites like it's on fire while my body shudders.

We have to get out of here.

Chapter Twenty

ARIC

Frost covers Rey's face where I touch it. I jerk back, causing her to fall against the ground a second time.

Damn it. I reach for her again.

She's still disoriented and mumbling something about the water, but I manage to walk us out of the building and slam the door behind us. I don't know why, but I turn and look up, my gaze drawn to the phrase etched above the door in ancient Norse.

Where water remembers and blood mourns.

I'm shaking by the time we get back on the path to Endir. She's still silent, but at least she seems okay—though I use that term loosely. Her eyes are glazed, but I don't think she fell hard enough on her head to be concussed. The wound would be the mirror's fault, but the concussion would totally be on me for not catching her that second time. My back still burns below my neck, right on my spine. Shit, what did I do? I keep my eyes trained on her.

Reeve gives me a raised eyebrow when we get closer to the group, but I ignore him and angle Rey away. "We're heading back to the dorms."

When we get there, I tap my card against the door, hands still shaking. We walk in silence to the elevator. I hit our floor and stand on the opposite side of her. We aren't touching anymore, but she's close enough that I can feel her breathe.

"You should really have the school nurse check you out tonight after you clean up that injury. I doubt it's a concussion, but you never know." The air feels too thin, the elevator too tight for both of us. I want to ask if she's okay, but I shouldn't care. It's Rey.

She can deal with whatever nightmare she saw while I go into my room and try to prevent myself from completely losing it.

"Yeah, that fall shocked me a bit." She nods. "But I feel fine now. I'll be ready for classes after some sleep." Rey touches the back of her head. "No more blood, so that's both nice and alarming. At first, I thought I had this huge head wound."

I think about what happened when I touched her face. Maybe I was mistaken? Maybe she heals fast?

But the frost, the burning sensation… I ignore it. It's in my head. It has to be.

"Any nausea? Headache?" I ask. I can't just let her go to sleep if she's concussed.

"None at all," she says with a small smile. "Just a bit of blood."

"Let me see?" I walk over and lift her hair, needing the distraction from my own paranoia, even if it is my parents' killer giving it to me.

She's right; there's fresh blood.

But where there should be a cut from the sharp edge of the mirror…

There's nothing. Only smooth, soft skin.

My own hand is already healing—not surprising—and she's too out of it to notice that I'm healing fast.

I drop her hair and step away. "Yeah, you just need to wash the blood off. The cut must be in your hairline or something," I lie. I have no answers for her, for *myself* about why that would happen. Best we forget it.

She nods. "I will. Don't worry about me. I'm no stranger to getting injured."

What the hell does that mean?

She seems perfectly calm walking into her room and closing her door in my face—while I'm having an internal breakdown in the hallway.

My hands turned to giant mittens of frost and froze on her face, and now she has no wound at all—and neither does my hand. Thank God she didn't see my reaction, but why now? Why her?

I pace my room, then stare at myself in the mirror. "You're not losing control. It's her, the stress, the circumstances—it's not you."

And yet, even as I say it, I know something's wrong.

I flex my back in an attempt to alleviate the pain still dogging me. Did something hit me, too? I peel off my shirt, toss it to the ground, and turn around.

Clear as day, an angry black rune stares back at me, starting just below my neck.

Raido in its simplest of forms.

A warning.

Normally of the journey ahead, but this one may as well be fucking waving back at me.

ᚱ

Well. Shit.

And I thought controlling the frost and my emotions was my biggest problem.

Chapter Twenty-One

REY

It's the first day of college.

And I'm already late.

Crap.

That weird run-in with a mirror still has me a bit shaken as I scramble to get my stuff together for my first class.

I've looked a dozen times since last night, but I still can't find the actual wound. Lying in that creepy-ass temple, for a few seconds there, I could have sworn Aric's dark eyes burned bright when he was staring at me, asking if I was okay. He held my head briefly, and a cooling sensation washed over me so fast, I forgot all about the pain. It was strange, to say the least, and then suddenly we were out of the building and walking back like nothing had happened. The only other time I've ever felt that cooling sensation is when Laufey would heal me—but if anything, Aric would be the first to leave me to die, so there's no way.

Maybe he's sleeping but his powers aren't?

Maybe the chill I felt was because of the very eerie atmosphere of the temple or the fact that I one hundred percent believe human sacrifices took place in that pool. How foolish, killing people to summon the Gods when the Gods have been here all along, just unaware of their own presence.

Imprisoned. Alone. Forgotten.

I can almost, *almost* understand the bitterness that overflows from my father.

The only real question I have is, what Gods were they trying to summon? The Giants? Us? I wonder if my father knows—not that he'd tell me, since it has nothing to do with Mjölnir.

Could that temple tie to Mjölnir? I feel like he would have said something if it did, but then again, he only ever speaks to me in half-truths.

I chew my lower lip as I riffle through my purse, looking for my key card. None of the runes outside the temple matched Laufey's note. But the one on the mirror did. Raido's a powerful rune, one associated with journeys and pilgrimages. So, not surprising to find it in a place of worship.

The campus, from what I've seen so far, is littered with runes, from the pathways to the buildings themselves. Sigurd Erikson has clearly set up wards of protection. To keep people out? Or to keep people *in*?

Hell, maybe they're inactive. I stepped on Thurisaz when I first got to Endir, and the rock just stared up at me mockingly, no magic, nothing. If there's any connection between the note from Laufey and the runes, it's something I'll have to investigate later. First things first. I need to focus on the new task at hand as my fingers close around my key card.

Finding my syllabus.

I quickly grab the printed schedule off my desk and shove it into my bag, snag my phone and tuck it into my jeans pocket, then pull open my door. Reeve is already standing on the other side, hand up and ready to knock.

"I was coming to make sure you survived the night after going through the Hall of Ormir," he says, giving me an eyebrow waggle for good measure. Why are all the good-looking ones complete psychopaths?

"It was touch and go there for a few minutes." I shrug and click my door shut behind me. "But I made it."

"Damn." Reeve makes a face.

I flip him off in response.

I can't hear Aric in his room. Did he already leave? Am I that late? Reeve said yesterday that every student would be attending a brief opening ceremony today before our first classes.

I have the sudden urge to check on him. He seemed pretty shaken last night, too. Except...why am I worrying about my enemy? Why did it matter? "Um—" I point at Reeve. "You should just go without me. I have to use the restroom."

He frowns. "Are you sure? I can wait."

"Yup! Save me a seat."

"In hell? Absolutely. Front row."

I roll my eyes at him as the elevator doors open, then shove him inside. "You're a nuisance, Reeve."

He grins. "You have no idea."

The minute the elevator closes again, I bolt over to Aric's door and press my ear up against it. I don't hear anything.

I lean in harder, until suddenly the door yanks open. I tumble forward and crash into him. "Sorry, I was just—" *Just what, Rey?* There's no answer that can hide the cringe at being caught eavesdropping.

His chest is solid and warm. I try to pull away, but he drives me backward, pinning me against the wall. Nostrils flaring, he leans in, his mouth brushing close to my skin like he's seconds away from breathing me in. "What do you think you're doing?"

Worrying about you? Stalking? A little of both? "I was getting ready to go to the opening ceremony. Reeve already left, and I figured I'd knock just in case you were sleeping and missed your alarm."

Because I care? Damn it, like he's really going to buy that.

His lips curl into a cruel smile. "Yes, because we're close enough that you'd be looking out for me." His eyes search mine in a cold, unfeeling manner. At least he's made it painfully known where we stand.

"Like you were looking out for me last night?" I counter.

"That was different," he growls. "You had a goddamn head wound."

I cross my arms with a huff. "Well, I feel fine now." I tilt my head. "And why *can't* I look out for you? We're all in this semester together. Plus, it's not like we're strangers. We've known each other a long time, and we've already skinny-dipped together, so that basically bonds us for life." I just had to bring it up, didn't I? Like my brain needs a solid excuse to remember what his naked skin looked like. My cheeks flush hot.

"That was a mistake." His words are low and menacing.

"Huge mistake," I agree, but my voice is barely a whisper.

"You should go. You don't want to be late."

I blink up at him. "You're too tall to climb over, and you're crowding me against the wall. I'll leave once you back off."

"This isn't crowding." He presses closer. "This is." His body is hard and hot against mine. He's so close I can feel his heartbeat like it's my own.

My breath catches in my chest. I'm supposed to be the one hunting him, not the other way around.

For a few seconds, I falter, panicking at my own weakness—because while he's supposed to be this unfeeling zombie, I have to admit I like the way he feels this close to me. I think back to last night, to his hands on my face.

I tentatively run my finger down his chest.

He grabs my hand but doesn't release it.

No, he grips it. Hard. Like he's memorizing the way my fingers fit in his palm.

I'm suddenly thrust into a fever dream. We're against a wall of ice I've never seen before, and then, just as quickly, we're back in his dorm room. His mouth runs down my neck, taking small bites while he rips at my clothes. I tug off his shirt, his eyes burning bright mahogany, lips parting as he lets out a groan that shakes the walls around us.

Next thing I know, he's picked me up by my waist and set me across his hips. He's walking me toward…

With a gasp, I come back to myself, still pressed against the wall, dizzy from whatever the hell kind of vision that was. I jerk my hand away from his. "I have to go."

Chapter Twenty-Two

REY

I get off the elevator and stumble across campus toward the Assembly Hall, trying to figure out what the hell just happened.

Kissing. Moving toward his bed. And…ice? The vision made no sense. For starters, I don't get visions. Yes, it's a power, but it's not part of my skill set. I'm strong, I'm resilient, and I can glamour people with my Aethercall, making them feel things.

But trippy mental projections? Not on my résumé.

Maybe they were part of Aric's power? Which then begs the question: What sort of other gifts are lurking beneath his surface, just waiting to burst free once he's awake and able to access them?

My stomach twists. If that was a glimpse of his power, no wonder the Gods fear the Giants. He hijacked my mind so completely, I wouldn't have known it was fake even with a gun to my head.

I felt his lips, the way they glided icy cool over mine while his hot tongue invaded.

I felt the heat of his mouth, the scrape of his teeth down my neck.

That, at least, was real.

I shiver and cross my arms, walking faster until I nearly run into someone. "Sorry!"

It's Reeve. He's holding a paper cup and shaking his head like I'm a disappointment. "Almost sent out a search party." He pitches his voice low as two other students walk past us. "And I got you a tea. I skipped on coffee, since I didn't want you to shit your pants again."

I glare. "I didn't shit my pants, you ass."

I reach for the cup, too exhausted to argue. But before I can touch it, another hand intercepts—Ziva's.

She steps between us like a curtain dropping mid-scene, her fingers curling gently but firmly around my wrist as she steers it away from the offering.

"Don't take anything from this one," she says, not looking at me. Her voice is calm, but there's steel under it. "He smiles while he cuts."

Reeve opens his mouth. Closes it. Blinks. Tries again.

But nothing comes out.

No teasing. No careless smile. Just the guy who never shuts up blinking like his soul depends on finding the exact right word to say next. And failing.

My eyebrows shoot up. "Holy hell," I whisper. "You broke an Erikson."

I turn to share the joke with Ziva, but what I see on her face freezes the words in my throat. Not triumph. Not sass.

Hurt. Quiet and buried but unmistakable.

And I know that look. I've worn that look. I've carried it.

I shift slightly, hand sliding into my rucksack to reach for the knife… that is tucked beneath my bed. Right. Blades not welcome on a college campus.

It's just…instinct that I always have it with me.

My hand comes back empty. No knife.

Ziva slips her arm through mine, eyes still forward. "Come on," she says softly. "He's not worth the bruise."

She doesn't know what I almost did. But she pulls me away like she does, and I'm thankful for it. For now.

We move through rows of white folding chairs toward the stage, where an old man in full school regalia is fiddling with a microphone.

"Sigurd," I mutter.

Ziva makes a face. "Why do all evil men dress like they've been shopping drunk on Etsy?"

I half laugh, half wince as feedback screams across the auditorium.

Sigurd taps the mic again, causing more feedback. He looks to be in his mid-sixties, dressed head to toe in the school colors of crimson and gold. How…cliché. And yet, he almost looks cheerful. I've been told my entire life that the only person more dangerous than Aric and Reeve is Sigurd, and yet he just seems like some eccentric old grandpa with too much money and time on his hands.

Sigurd's dark brown eyes lock on mine with keen interest. His stare isn't threatening. It's more of a knowing gaze, which still has me wanting to sink down into my chair. I don't like the intensity of it.

I make a mental note: his smoke screens are the school, his clothes, the mild way he carries himself. But the way others perceive him matters—approachable to some, untouchable to others.

Deadly to me.

Aric joins him on the dais, and Sigurd turns to shake his hand, then gestures for his grandson to take a seat in one of two empty chairs to the side of the podium.

Aric nods and, somehow, manages to fold his six-foot-six frame gracefully into the rickety chair, kicking his legs out and crossing his ankles. Crossing his arms next, he leans back, and our gazes collide.

My heart rate picks up, my breath catching in the back of my throat as neither of us looks away. Images flicker in my mind. Tongues. Lips. Bodies sliding against each other with hunger.

Heat stains my cheeks, the moment stretching between us, but I can't look away. I'm drowning in his mahogany gaze and the memories of a moment we never should have shared. The corner of his mouth kicks up like he knows it, too, and something about it shatters the hold he has over me.

I shake my head, drag a heavy breath into my lungs, and stare at my knees like they're the most important thing in the world.

"You okay?" Ziva asks, leaning over.

I don't even bother to deny what she must have seen. "Getting there."

"Just don't fall for him," Ziva says, her voice low and steady. "Or do, just don't mistake obsession for intimacy. That's how they win."

The words land like an anchor in my chest—sinking, dragging. It's almost like she's talking from experience. I mentally file the observation away.

Up onstage, Sigurd is still talking, but I can't hear a word of it.

Ziva's gaze is fixed ahead, calm and unbothered. But I'm rattled.

Don't mistake obsession for intimacy.

I grip the edge of my chair, heart tripping over itself. Because I think that's exactly what I'm doing. And the worst part? I don't want to stop.

He doesn't just pull at me. He's pulling me under bit by bit.

And the more I fight it, the more I realize—I was never meant to swim free.

Chapter Twenty-Three

REY

After an hour of hearing former Endir graduates and prestigious—their word, not mine—alumni make speeches, Sigurd's at the mic again.

He's beaming like a game-show host as he introduces the faculty like they're the starting lineup of an NFL team. When will this end?

I clap when everyone else claps.

I'm here. I'm totally normal. Not a killer. Not from a notorious crime family. I'm participating. Go Endir!

As if sensing my inner sarcasm, Sigurd pauses. Hand to his brow, he gazes out across the Assembly Hall. "Ladies and gentlemen, you're a part of Endir now. This school is your legacy! Your fellow students and alumni will become your friends, your family."

Where is he going with this, and why does it feel all sorts of wrong?

Cue the psychopathic villain chuckle in three, two, one.

He laughs.

Bingo.

I'd take pride in my prediction, but it's just too easy.

"Don't be shy," Sigurd says. "You're all so spread out. That's not the way to make lifelong friendships."

Is he serious right now?

"Come on," he cajoles. "Everyone to the front. No sleeping in the back. Fill in the gaps, introduce yourself to your fellow classmates. Celebrate your differences, your commonalities. Form alliances!"

Alliances, hmm? What an interesting word to use.

Ziva laughs a bit too loud, too forced. But she stands, so I do, too.

I follow her out of the row and toward the front, not because I want to but because disobeying Sigurd's directions would draw too much attention, and again, I just want orientation to be done.

I file in behind her, and we settle into our new seats, maybe ten rows from the stage.

The students in front of and behind us lean in expectantly. Time to make friends. Wow. This is really happening.

"I'll start!" Ziva smiles brightly. "I'm Ziva." She rattles off a list of hobbies that sounds like a dating profile. Something about hot yoga, candle making, and, "I love long walks on the beach."

Girl, please.

Her lips twitch. Okay, so she knows she's being ridiculous. Our other classmates nod and clap like she just recited Shakespeare.

"Hi, Ziva," the surrounding students chant.

One little push of my Aethercall and they'd all be too dazed to notice me. But no. I'm on my best behavior.

The dark-haired girl in the row in front of us turns around fully and raises her hand. "I'm Gaby Smith from Tacoma. Business major. I bake, but not cookies, too basic. Cupcakes only. I'm going to open a shop on the pier and marry a fisherman." She shrugs at our blank stares. "So we can live off the land. Sustainably."

Cute. Self-sufficiency via cupcakes and salmon. Why does she sound so damn cheerful about it?

By handshake number two, she yanks another student into her orbit. "I'm a hugger!"

Please don't touch me. Please don't touch—

She reaches for me, then jerks her hand back, shaking it. "Whoa! Shock. Your aura's spicy!"

I force a laugh. "Static. Happens."

All eyes fall to me. Oh shit, it's my turn.

"Hey, everyone. I'm Rey." I deliberately leave off my last name, then gently push my Aethercall. Not enough to alienate, just enough to distract. "Undecided on my major. But looking forward to discovering the path I'm meant to take. Life's a journey, you know."

"Word." Ziva coughs to my right.

I shoot her a smirk. Yeah, she barely knows me and already can tell I'm full of shit. Well, at least that's one person in my corner.

I sit back down to the chorus of "Hi, Rey!"

Next we meet Jameson Jacobs. A nice if not overly bookish guy, with floppy bangs and enviably perfect skin, who seems to have the unfortunate luck of being named after a porn star. Not information I would've known. Yet he led with that.

Jillian Merritt from Arizona's a psych major. And on the basketball team.

Hector Salas from California, premed.

Engineering. Finance. English lit. Biochem.

A dozen total strangers offer insights into their goals and personalities.

It hits me like lightning: I'm jealous. And not just a little. So jealous it burns behind my eyes.

What would it be like to bake cupcakes and make study dates? To rush a sorority? To plan for a future, a real one, that didn't involve blood and death and violence?

I glance up—and freeze.

Aric.

He's watching me from across the room.

My heart thumps wildly against my chest like it's begging to be noticed—heard. Adrenaline surges through my system. He's my target. My enemy. The first and only person to ever really see me.

That's what made his rejection of me all those years ago cut so much deeper.

Just when I think I'll have to look away, he does first. Like I'm not worth staring at.

Students continue chattering around me, but I can't get the gnawing in my stomach to go away. I didn't expect being smack-dab in the middle of a normal college campus to affect me so much.

The way these humans coexist with no clue of the war that shaped the world.

The way they can hope and dream. And I never will.

I've been trapped and isolated with my father for years, but I've never felt lonelier than I do in this moment.

Feelings have no place here, I remind myself. So I bury them. I bury them deep.

The round-robin continues until we land on Eira Helian. She arches a brow at me. "We already know each other, Rey," she tells me.

We do?

"My father works at Odin Enterprises."

My father's company, of course, but a fact I would've preferred not to be widely known. Ziva leans closer to me. But I easily deflect. "I'm not involved much in my father's business."

Lie.

"But it's really nice to meet you." I give my Aethercall a stronger push, and the students around me shift their attention away. "Tell us more about yourself, Eira."

She takes a long, steadying breath. Though not to steady her nerves or prepare her thoughts, I discover—she's drawing air so she can launch into what might be one of the longest speeches known to humanity. Okay, that's hyperbole. But you know the type. Addicted to the sound of their own voice. Desperate for constant attention.

"Well, my day started off like complete shit, for one. We were out of bananas…"

Just once, I'd like to be wrong about these kinds of things.

She rolls her eyes. "Naturally, I fired the housekeeper. Not just because of the bananas; I'm not a total monster. She knew it was my move-in day and forgot the grocery list again. She texts her family nonstop! She has one job."

"The audacity," I whisper under my breath. I mean, to text family, the horror.

"Right?" she yells. "Thank you!"

Doesn't understand sarcasm. Got it.

"Anyway." She takes what I'm assuming is a soothing breath. "The moving crew dropped two of my favorite succulents, shattering them into pieces—I've had them at least six months."

Dear God, give this woman a medal.

"Then I came here… Nobody seems to understand how important this is to me, my parents included, and my room is all wrong, not even close to how big it looked in the brochure, and I'm pretty sure the girl next door hissed at me."

She leaves so many openings, it's hard not to respond. I bite my tongue and nod, then, along with everyone else, say, "Hi, Eira."

Another rough exhale escapes her bright red lips. "Hi, whatever, oh, my food's almost here." She starts tapping away on her phone like Bananagate never happened and the world is right again.

"You can't make this shit up," I whisper to Ziva.

"Preach."

By the time Sigurd calls the assembly back to order, my right eye is starting to tick. The students quiet around me as he resumes talking, and I completely tune out. The relative silence after all that socializing is bliss.

Ziva hands me a sleeve of Oreos. "I think I love you," I say.

"I hear that often."

I tear into the cookies and barely keep my moan at bay.

I've finally started to relax when my phone buzzes in my pocket. Mid-chew, I use a free hand to grab it and stare at the screen.

Odinfather: *Ticktock.*

Sonofabitch.

My palms start to sweat. The Oreo goes completely tasteless in my mouth when another text follows.

It's a simple picture of a chessboard.

While the Cosa Nostra hands out patron saints when you've had your first kill, Odin gives you a chessboard.

From that point on, you play his game.

I pinch to zoom.

It's missing the queen.

He didn't send me a picture of any board.

He sent me a picture of *his.*

His way of saying the game has started—and he's willing to sacrifice me to win.

Chapter Twenty-Four

REY

I check the time on my phone. My ass hurts from sitting for the last ninety minutes, and I'm a nervous wreck.

How did it all seem so much easier only twenty-four hours ago? Wake a sleeping Giant. Threaten him or whoever necessary to get him to lead you to Mjölnir, steal it back, get away clean. Done. Oh yeah, and do it all in seven freaking days.

I silently groan. As plans go, that might be one of the worst ever.

First of all, the blueprint of the "wake a sleeping Giant" plan could be anything from feeding him kiwis to setting him on fire. I vote fire.

Secondly, stealing a mythical weapon that is apparently sentient is just…ridiculous. What if it zaps me unconscious when I touch the handle? Then again, according to my father, it responds to our bloodline so I should—*should* being the key word—have nothing to worry about.

Because, of course, I can trust everything my father says.

And finally, and most importantly in my opinion, what on the Gods' green earth did I think would happen if I managed to actually steal the hammer and secret it away from the Eriksons? I'd be the first person they'd assume stole it, and they would come for me. There would be nowhere Laufey and I could hide from their wrath. I'd have finally freed us from one bloodthirsty man only to get us killed by another. Super.

In summary: shit discovery plan, shittier theft plan, and a retirement plan worthy of a Darwin Award.

I squirm in my chair and mentally chuck the entire plan. I need a new one.

I start to stand, ready to sneak out a side door, eager to use my time plotting Sigurd's demise rather than listening to him wax poetic about honor and education.

"And that's why I'd like to ask my grandson to say a few words," Sigurd finishes, and I stiffen. My gaze lands on Aric's narrowed eyes. It's not obvious, but I can tell he had no idea he was going to be asked to speak.

I settle back into my seat, a genuine smile spreading across my face.

"This should be entertaining," Ziva murmurs.

I'll give him credit, he gets to his feet and approaches the podium with minimal prodding. "Fine. Welcome to Endir."

The crowd goes absolutely wild. Cheering, catcalls, the occasional "Dude" shouted like he's their idol.

I glance at Ziva, but she just rolls her eyes and mutters, "Fucking Eriksons."

Aric lets out a heavy sigh and, no joke, says literally ten sentences. It's almost like bullet points. Family legacy. Endir pride. Job placements. Test scores going into masters' programs. Let's have a great year.

He looks like pure violence and sounds like he wants to be anywhere but here. And then I notice his grandfather standing to the side of the stage.

Sigurd's arms are crossed, and he's looking at Aric, his smile frozen. Interesting. Not what I'd expect from a "doting" grandfather.

Strange. As strange as the fact that Aric is his own celebrity here.

I narrow my eyes.

It's obvious that he hates the attention.

Suddenly, it occurs to me.

Aric's a puppet on a polished stage. Just like me.

Don't feel sorry for Aric just because he's as trapped as you are,

I remind myself as Aric finishes what might have been the shortest, angriest speech ever delivered. I'm grateful for the renewed chatter around me breaking me out of my swirling thoughts. I need to focus.

Remember where I am.

And why I'm here.

And figure out that damn plan B.

"Sorry I'm late. What'd I miss?"

I whip my head around at the familiar voice, feel my jaw drop open as I take in the sight of the absolute last person I ever expected to see here. "R-Rowen?"

A genuine smile I don't even try to hide overtakes my face. Rowen. Is here. Smiling at me.

The one person who might actually have a plan that isn't total shit. Gods help me, I'm beyond glad he's here.

I just wish I knew why.

CHAPTER TWENTY-FIVE

ARIC

The crowd's finally starting to break up when movement to my left catches my eye. Normally, I wouldn't give it much thought—but the guy's tall.

Really tall.

He's talking to Rey—and her face is lit up like a star that just found its place in the sky. Odd for her, and completely irrational for me to notice.

Sure, I lost myself for a few minutes back there in my room, my body reacting to her proximity in ways I still can't explain. But there's nothing like standing in front of a few hundred of your closest acquaintances to throw some cold water on a guy's libido.

Not to mention watching her flirt with another guy.

I grit my jaw and angle around a row of chairs to get a better look at whoever has her so animated, then immediately recognize the driver who dropped her off on her first day. The same guy who stood too close when they said goodbye.

He looks about my age, but there's no way he's a student. The all-black three-piece suit says security detail, and the earpiece he's wearing like some budget mall cop just confirms it. Rey keeps talking, but his eyes are scanning the crowd.

I keep walking. It's not my business. Not my problem.

But when she tucks a piece of hair behind her ear and looks at him like she's glad he's here, I change course.

I don't need a reason. I just do.

I get close enough to see his eyes flick toward me. He doesn't flinch. Doesn't stop smiling. Doesn't take his eyes off her for more than a flash.

"Hey, Aric." A short brunette grabs my arm as I pass. "Great speech."

I glance at her, half checking her pupils. Has to be high. That was objectively the worst speech ever delivered in the history of orientation addresses. Reeve was the one meant to dazzle the crowd, but he pulled a vanishing act. So when Sigurd tapped me to fill in, I had nothing. No notes. No plan. Just a vague memory of Endir's graduation rates and a bad attitude.

"Thanks, Becks," I mutter, already moving.

"I was thinking—" she starts.

"Wonderful. Let's circle back to that later," I say, brushing past her.

Yeah, it's a dick move. But I've got bigger problems. I've lost sight of Rey's driver.

I weave in and out of clusters of students, their voices rising in bursts—griping about professors, trading rumors about class assignments. It's the usual first-day-of-school buzz, and I envy how easy it sounds. Like none of them have anything to protect. Nothing to lose, while I'm over here hunting the driver of the girl I loathe, dealing with daily breakdowns, and wondering why ice keeps appearing randomly in her presence when I've always been able to control it. But sure, yeah, that Human Anatomy class is gonna be rough.

A few minutes later, I catch a glimpse of him again—this time in the far corner of the room. He's peeled away from the crowd, standing near the exit, hands in his pockets, pretending not to be watching anyone in particular.

But I know better.

I shift directions and head straight for him. There's a tension in my shoulders I can't shake, and the sooner I figure out what this guy wants, the sooner I can get back to my day.

He's already seen me coming. Doesn't flinch. Just shifts his weight slightly, like he was expecting this.

Good. Let's get on with it.

I walk up to him, arms crossed. "You new?"

Of all the things I could have said, that's what comes out?

His jaw twitches like he's debating whether to answer. "Something like that."

The guy's got a slight accent—can't place it—but what really stands out is his size. Not just tall. Broad. Built like a security detail for someone important. Muscles fight for their life beneath his black suit, and I can't tell if he wants people to know he works out or if he just doesn't care that his suit is tight and has better things to worry about.

I'd thought he was just a driver, maybe two-bit security. "Bodyguard?" I fish.

He doesn't answer right away. Just keeps his eyes on Rey, who's moved to talk to someone else now. Finally, he says, "Not for her."

"Kind of creepy that you're watching her so intently then, right?"

That gets his attention. He turns slowly. Cold, unbothered blue eyes meet mine. "Who says I'm watching her?"

"I do."

A pause. Then a shrug. "I guess not everything is as it seems."

My knuckles tense. I ignore the cold prickling my fingertips. "You're wasting your time."

His blue gaze slides to mine finally. "That depends. On how much time you've got left."

There's no malice in it. Just certainty. Like he's already read the ending and I'm too stupid to skip ahead.

"You Erikson?" he asks, like it's a dirty word. God, how I want to punch the smirk right off his face.

"Aric."

His mouth twitches again. "Right. The heir."

I bristle. Not at the title. At how easy it comes from his mouth. Like I'm just another one of Sigurd's artifacts.

"Whatever you think you're doing here—" I start.

He cuts me off with a tilt of his head. “Relax. I’m just observing. For now.”

I don’t like the implication. I like even less that Rey trusted him enough to smile at him like that. What the hell is wrong with me? Who cares who she smiles at?

My fingers curl. That chill races down my arms, and I flex against it hard, shoving my hands into my pockets.

“Enjoy the show,” I finally mutter, turning to go. I should leave it there. Should walk away.

But I glance back once, just for a second.

He’s still watching Rey. Not leering. Not assessing.

Guarding.

And that’s worse.

Because whatever game I thought I was playing with her, I’m not the only one playing anymore.

And though I don’t lose…

Something tells me he doesn’t, either.

CHAPTER TWENTY-SIX

REY

"So what's next?" I ask, watching Aric's back as he walks away. We've moved to a corner of the room. Most of the freshmen are raiding snack tables or wandering off to mingle with one another or to chat with their advisers. But a few of the others from our getting-to-know-you group are lingering next to Rowen and me, clearly unsure what to do next.

The hall echoes with a low hum of too many conversations, and I could curse my overly sensitive nose. I'm picking up stress sweat and cheap perfumes, an assortment of body lotions, soap, and coffee. It's distracting.

Eira sighs and checks her watch. "Please tell me this is actually over and we won't be forced back into some team-building exercise, because I say no."

Rowen clears his throat next to her, as if to say, *you don't really have a choice*. Seriously, why is he here? And why hasn't he said something? His silence is worse than the lingering stares he keeps shooting in my direction, like I should be able to somehow read his mind or something.

Eira glances over her shoulder before he can open his mouth. "You've been working for like an hour. Shut it."

He holds up his hands. Normally I would laugh, because I'm the one who bosses Rowen around, but instead, I'm just extremely confused.

"Working?" Ziva asks. "Working in what manner?"

"Yes," I add. "Working for *who*?"

Eira waves her phone like it's obvious.

Ziva and I share a look. No, no it isn't.

"I'm a makeup influencer," she says, as if that explains everything, and honestly? It explains a bit.

"You don't say," Ziva deadpans. "So he's your personal protection from someone trying to steal your eyelash curler?"

Eira shrugs. "A threat can come from anywhere."

All right, that's actually a valid statement.

"Besides," Eira continues, "my dad's high up at Odin Enterprises. It would be a publicity nightmare if something were to happen to me. I mean, can you imagine?"

Oh, I am. Imagining.

She realizes I'm the boss's daughter and *I* don't have a bodyguard, right?

But this is an ingenious way to get Rowen on campus without looking suspicious. Although I wonder why Father didn't just send him as my bodyguard. Or have him enroll as a transfer student or something.

More than that, a few days ago, Rowen wasn't permitted to help me at all.

What changed?

I jolt when Aric returns, sidling up next to me. "Friend of yours?"

"Wow." I slow clap in an attempt to recover from my own dark thoughts. "You know what friends are? Color me impressed."

Reeve comes up behind his brother, putting an affectionate arm around his shoulders. "He can spell 'cat,' too. It's wild. I'm still dumbfounded."

Aric shoves him lightly, and Reeve pretends to clutch his arm in pain.

I lift my chin. "Nice speech, by the way."

He grimaces.

Sigurd clears his throat into the microphone, causing feedback to fill the air, and several hundred students collectively groan.

"Not again," Aric mumbles.

"Sorry. Sorry 'bout that." Sigurd smiles like, *little ol' me doesn't know how to work a mic*. "This concludes our ceremony. Thank you for attending today's assembly! Remember to download the Endir app, and new students and transfers can collect your final enrollment packets at table three." He points to the left corner of the room. "Lastly, don't forget to sign up for this week's activities!"

"There's more?" I choke.

"So much more." Reeve's smile is creepy big.

Sigurd speaks with a flourish. "Throughout the week, we'll be having an ice cream social—"

"Which we will not be attending," Reeve says under his breath.

"Followed by fireworks over the lake."

"Also not attending, because the fireworks at our end-of-the-week house party are better," Reeve adds.

"And our annual capture-the-flag-slash-Nerf-battle."

Reeve's hand shoots up. "That I *will* be going to."

"And finally, as has long been an Endir tradition, we will welcome our esteemed alumni, parents, students, and faculty to participate in the Wild Hunt for good luck! Feast and games provided, of course. If you make it through the treacherous trails, that is."

Everyone laughs.

Reeve smiles. "That I *will* be planning."

"There are also several department-led mixers so you're able to get to know other students within your major. Good luck." Sigurd finally gets off the microphone and hands it to one of the staff.

Reeve breathes a sigh of relief. "Hide that microphone. Put it in your pants if you have to. Do not hand it back."

And just like that, my first and final week at Endir is officially underway.

Gods be with us.

Chapter Twenty-Seven

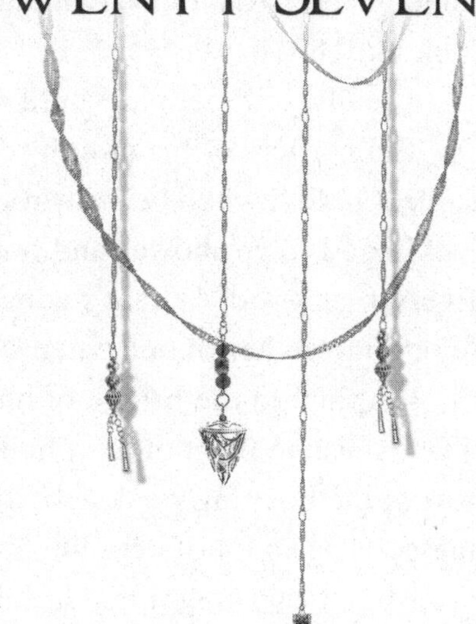

REY

I quickly download the Endir campus interactive app on my phone, then follow the herd to the activity tables. I make a show of studying the sign-up sheets without actually signing up for anything, then grab my final enrollment packet and beeline out the door.

I've got two hours before my first class.

I jog back to my room, ready to plan or plot, or possibly take a quick power nap before classes, but when I jerk open my door, something goes whizzing by my face.

I snatch it out of the air and slam the door shut behind me to assess my attacker.

"A rock, Rowen? Really?" Only when I look, it's not a rock. It's a marble chess piece. The one missing from the photo Father texted me earlier.

The queen.

I set it down on the nightstand.

"A gift from your father," he says.

But we both know it's not a present. It's a warning.

"You didn't have to throw it at me."

"I knew you'd catch it," he says, as if that makes up for it. He stands from my bed and looks me over, so I do the same. His blond hair is pulled back into a tight man bun, and he's still in his black suit. "You look like shit, by the way."

"I really wish people would stop stating the obvious."

The corners of his mouth reveal his dimples. I've missed his easy smile. I hate it when he's always on guard.

"I need to go shower and possibly fit in a nap before my first class. Everything good? Where's your little texting shadow? Does she even look up from her phone when she speaks?"

He pinches the bridge of his nose. "Where else? She's putting on a face mask in front of her phone. You know, to prep for class and the rest of the opening week activities, all while delivering content to the masses. I see a lot of peopling in my future."

I burst out laughing. God, it feels good to relax, even just a bit. "Your absolute favorite thing to do. Lucky you."

"I don't think she understands that I'm not a paid friend but a bodyguard because her father's a paranoid board member who thinks someone's out to get him." He rolls his eyes, but then his face goes grave. "Odin's mostly placating him, but there have been more threats lately, so…"

I yawn. "Who did my father piss off this time?"

"I didn't ask. Don't want to know." His gaze darts between the door and me. I don't like the look he's sending my way or how he takes a breath like he's preparing to drop some seriously bad news. "Odin had another rage-fueled episode today. They're getting worse, Rey."

"What happened?"

"Hell if I know. Something set him off. He broke four chessboards. Four people dead without batting an eye."

"Gods."

He shrugs. "Most of his inner circle, they aren't saints by any stretch. But within the corporation, there are hundreds of employees. Inevitably, innocent people are going to get hurt. Not only is it bad for business, but it brings unwanted attention at a very critical time."

My thoughts drift to the other students. They have families, friends. I just met Eira, and even though she isn't one of my favorite people,

I wouldn't want harm to come to her or to her dad. And then there's Ziva. She's already had my back more than once. Can I really live with putting her in danger?

"The more his power wanes, the more he loses his grip on reality."

I've always suspected it was getting worse, but to hear Rowen state it so bluntly...

Odin's life force is tied to Asgard. Being cut off from the source for so long, of course he's growing weaker and lashing out at people. Power is just like time—eventually, it runs out.

"How is Laufey?" I prod. I haven't texted her, knowing that my father will be monitoring her phone, and the last thing I want is to get her into trouble.

Rowen lets out a sigh. "You know how she is. She loves baking and her garden. She's been outside a lot more recently. I think it's to get some breathing room from Odin, but he always checks in on her."

"Checks in on his prisoner, you mean?" I let out a snort. "It's good that he's not hurting her—"

"He will, though. Soon. If her illness doesn't take her first. Odin doesn't make empty threats." He sighs. "He does care for her...in his own way."

But that's the whole of it really. What little emotion my father *is* capable of will not sway him.

"Don't defend him, Rowen. It only makes me want to punch you, and I actually like you. Can we be done with this conversation? I'm doing the best I can, but it's been *two days*. I can't really skip around campus asking questions, and getting close to the Erikson heir hasn't exactly been a thrill."

Aric's hostile.

Angry.

A dangerous bottle of uncontrollable emotion that could break at any time.

"Do you feel anything..." My voice trails off. "Different at Endir, I mean. I know you've always had your secrets, but do you feel weaker here? More unbalanced? From Sigurd's power? The ridiculous amount of runes?"

Rowen looks down at the ground and tenses. "You've seen my scars. Since I set foot on campus, they burn as if they're brand-new cuts, Rey. How's that for different?" He squeezes his eyes shut. "Sorry, you didn't deserve that."

I stare at his right arm. It looks like someone raked their nails down his skin, trails leading up to his fingertips scarred so severely, he almost looks like a burn victim. "The Eriksons, their entire bloodline, will pay for what they did to you."

He doesn't flinch, but I see the rage in his eyes, rage from a lost war, lost family—lost everything. "It's deeper than that, and you know it. You need to work faster. Aric isn't an idiot, and neither is his grandfather. Odin and Sigurd were at war for millennia. Being trapped here may have kindled some temporary ceasefire, but that's all it is. There will never be peace."

His words leave me feeling hollow.

"They've let you into their world for now, and they might be content to toy with you and play nice for a little while. But don't make the mistake of thinking the Giants are weak. Tread carefully and move fast."

Helpful.

"You're Odin's daughter. Mjölnir should be drawn to you."

I know all of these things, but hearing them repeated out loud makes my task feel so much more daunting. I toss my phone on the bed and pull my hair back into a low bun. "Odin says you have a claim to the same bloodline through your family, though diluted. So why won't it react to you, too?" I finish my hair and cross my arms. "It would be a lot easier to tag team this, you know."

He licks his lips. Something he does when he's buying time to think about his answer—because he never just reacts. Always assesses first. "I wish it did. But what little trace of Odin is left in my blood isn't enough to wield the most powerful weapon in the world. The accident ruined me—I bled out so much that sometimes I wonder if the part that mattered is still even there." His face darkens. "Can we not talk about this right now?"

"Sorry, it's just that you've never told me, and maybe it could be helpful to talk about it."

"It won't be." He shakes his head. "I've already lived through enough trauma for a lifetime, Rey."

"I didn't mean to dredge up—"

"Forget it," he says quickly, walking over to the window, body tense.

I know he's scarred, inside and out. Though it shouldn't, it makes me think of Aric. Losing his parents. Being struck by lightning in that freak accident.

"How many volts are in an average bolt of lightning?" I ask Rowen.

He whips around, nostrils flaring like the question pisses him off. He quickly recovers and rubs his eyes. "Sorry, I'm tired and not used to you asking questions that have nothing to do with revenge, fighting, death, or fries. Plus, I'm exhausted over Odin's Mjölnir obsession. I get why we need it, but it's not…his."

"I mean, technically it's his. My father's the one who had the hammer crafted."

Rowen's still rubbing his eyes, but his back stiffens, his hands balling into fists. Concerned, I reach for him. "Hey, are you feeling okay?"

In an instant, he has me pushed up against the wall, his hand at my neck while my feet dangle in the air. I tug at his hand, panicking, needing air. What is going on? He's never once tried to hurt me.

"Rowen," I choke. "Rowen!"

His eyes are fathomless, like dark holes, before he leans in and runs his nose up and down my neck. His voice is raspy. "It isn't Erikson's or Odin's! It was gifted to the most powerful God in the realm, and I'm fucking tired of people ignoring his sacrifice!"

"Put." I kick at his legs. "Me." I kick harder. "Down."

If I don't get through to him soon, I'm going to pass out.

I'm going to die.

Chapter Twenty-Eight

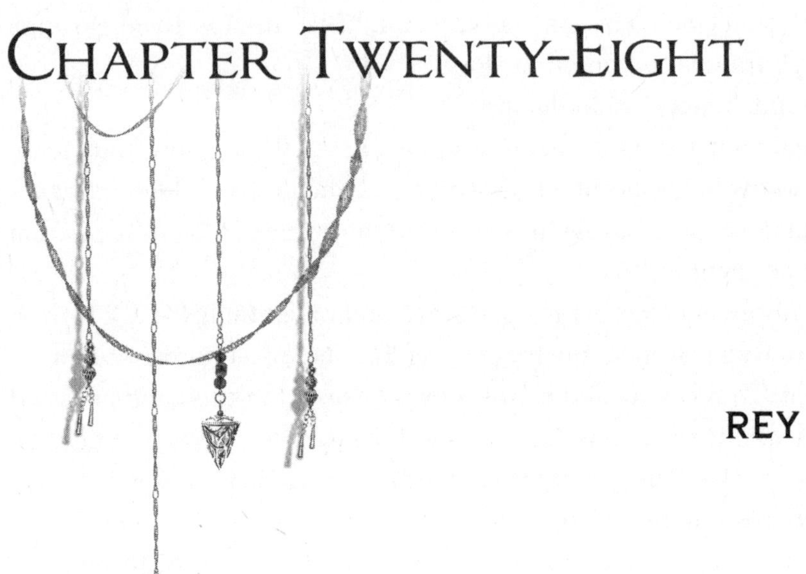

REY

I go from stunned to helpless to really fucking angry in a snap. I'm basically his family. He's never lost his temper with me, not once. I know, deep in my soul, Rowen would never harm me.

I don't want to hurt him, either, but I have no choice. I shove a hand right into his chest, sending him sailing backward against the empty second bed. It splits in half on impact.

And sure, I'm strong, but I'm not *that* strong. I stare down at my shaking hand.

I only used one hand. And sent a six-foot bodyguard slamming into a bed? That's not normal.

Could it be my blood responding to being here?

Despite the weirdness of it all, I actually feel good about it. Good that something's happening at being this close to Mjölnir.

Rowen groans. "Fuck, are you trying to kill me?"

"You had me in a chokehold, you asshat!" Heart racing, I offer him a hand and pull him to his feet.

His eyes narrow before he takes it. "What are you talking about? You just said you had a question about lightning and were droning on about Odin." He gets up and dusts off his clothes. "By the way, it can be up to a billion volts."

A billion.

Volts.

Would Aric survive that?

Unscathed? I mean, I can testify to that after our time in the hot spring. There wasn't a mark on him. Just dense muscle and bronzed skin.

But more importantly…

"What's going on with you?" I eye him warily. "You just lost your shit, and you've never so much as yelled at me. Did something happen?"

"Oh God." His face softens. "I am so sorry. I just— Maybe it's affecting me, too. Being here so long, being away from our homeland, surrounded by God knows who."

My ears perk up. This is the most he's ever told me. "So you weren't born in Washington, then?"

He bites down on his lower lip. A knock loud enough to take down the freaking door interrupts us.

Bang.

Bang.

Bang. "What the hell are you doing in there? Remodeling?"

It's Aric.

He bangs on the door again.

"Don't make me break down this fucking door!"

Is everyone taking rage vitamins today?

I quickly glance at Rowen. "Sorry." I kick him toward the bed so Aric doesn't see him and suspect me of anything. "Yes?" I ask as I open the door a sliver.

Aric's dark eyes are wide, and I could swear he looks panicked as he glances over my head, then around to the destruction behind me. The broken bed.

"I fell."

His eyebrows shoot up. "From crawling across the ceiling? You do know it's illegal to damage school property."

"Yeah." I cross my arms. "Don't really see a little badge on you that says campus security. And it was an accident, all right? I really did fall."

"The spare bed in your room is literally split in half."

"I weigh more than I look."

"It looks like you kicked it." He starts to walk in.

"Nope." I shove the door against him. "I'll pay for the damages. Worry about yourself." Damn it all, I need to get close to him, and this would be the perfect opportunity if Rowen wasn't hiding behind the door by my bed. Can't have my lie exposed now.

"I heard talking," Aric adds.

"I was on the phone," I hiss. "Can you go now?"

His eyes narrow. And then with one big shove, the door flies back and nearly off its hinges, and Rowen is fully in view, looking a bit worse for wear, hair tousled from being kicked into the bed, shirt torn. Great. Perfect.

Aric swears, and whatever it is I thought I saw in his eyes moments ago is gone. Now they are pure ice.

"Wow, wondered why you sprinted back to your room, and it suddenly all makes sense. You're the black widow that kills after mating." He's talking about me, but his eyes are pinned on Rowen. "Not worth it, person I just met. There are better ways to go than in Rey Stjerne's bed."

Rowen smirks, playing his part perfectly. He saunters over to stand beside me. Oh no, what's he doing? This man is like a brother to me. "I highly doubt it."

I'm killing him.

Aric glances at the broken bed and points. "I'm assuming that's where you ended?"

"Or started," Rowan says in a cocky voice. "Some of us last longer than others."

"Some of us could have lived a lifetime without knowing any of those details." Aric shakes his head and leaves my doorway.

I watch him walk back to his room, and once he's inside, I shut my own door and shake my head at Rowen. "Could you have thought of anything less weird, Rowen? Seriously."

He rolls his eyes. "You told him you fell from the ceiling like you were Spider-Man."

"I panicked, all right? Also, fix your clothes. You may be adopted into our psychotic family, but we both know Odin would behead you with more precision than a guillotine if he saw you in my bed."

Rowen fixes his hair and tucks in his shirt. "Don't worry. You're not worth the risk, even if you are pretty."

What's with him? He isn't acting normal. Even his eyes have taken on a darker hue. Is it me? Or the weird heaviness of this campus? Maybe the overflow of runes causes people to lose their shit. Would it surprise me if Sigurd did something like that in order to somehow control his students? Not at all.

"Stop messing around. Seriously." He would never hurt me—at least I thought not, but now I'm wondering how fast I can reach my knife.

Note to self, beneath the bed is too far away.

"I'm doing my job just fine." He says this like nothing happened, like he didn't just lose it a bit ago. "You're the one who's disappointing Odin." Story of my life. "Maybe try a different tactic?" I want to smack the raised eyebrows right off his face.

"I'm not seducing Aric with my body, you ass."

"You don't seduce men like Aric with your body—you seduce them with your bad attitude and make them curious why you aren't falling all over yourself for them like everyone else is." He shrugs and walks toward the door. "Plus, who's got more of a shit attitude than you?"

He leaves me alone with all my confusion, which is the last place I want to be. Being alone means spiraling, remembering Aric's expression when he opened the door. When he saw Rowen and the bed and *me*.

I know what Aric assumed. Not that I care what he thinks of me. I inwardly cringe. Yeah, that's a total lie.

I hate that I care, just a tiny bit, and that an even darker side of me was happy at first. Because when Aric first beat down my door, I think it was because he was worried.

About me.

We didn't always hate each other.

I touch the handle to my door and stumble forward a bit.

I imagine his lips trailing down to my jaw, his mouth brushing the edge of my throat. Each featherlight kiss would feel like a wave of frost blowing across my skin. Goose bumps rising. I would suck in a breath when his lips linger at the hollow of my neck. He would hesitate, then blow cool air right across my pulse.

It would pick up immediately.

I'd dig my fingers into his shoulders in an attempt to anchor myself. Needing more. Needing everything.

My senses would blur around me as thunder pounded in the distance, in perfect cadence with my erratic heartbeat. A storm might brew outside, but with each kiss he'd start another one between us. I want to surrender, to give in to the ice. To let go. So I'd wrap my arms around his neck, our eyes locking.

He would smile against my lips. "I like your warmth."

I would shiver as I sank down on him—

Whoa there. Nope.

I smack myself in the head and realize that my door's still partially open.

Ziva's standing there, cup of coffee halfway to her mouth. "You good?"

"Yup!" I say too quickly. "Just…forgot what I was doing and, uh, catch you after class." I shove the door closed and lean against it.

I really wish someone was on my team—anyone—and now even Rowen's snapping, forgetting himself, getting violent, speaking for my father, watching me. Can't they see I'm trying? Plus, it's been two days! I can't create a miracle in two days.

I collapse onto the bed and reach beneath it to pull out the note from Laufey.

ᚱ ᛞ ᚺ ᛟ ᚦ

Raido, Dagaz, Hagalaz, Othala, and Thurisaz.

I read the runes over and over again, then pause.

Raido. The rune from the Hall of Ormir.

Frowning, I dig through the black orientation packet Reeve gave me, pull out the brochure of the campus, then circle the rune at Raido. Does Endir have a map of the runes? A guide? Google has a guide for everything—there's probably a Reddit thread, too. Maybe even a useful one, if I'm being optimistic.

Did Laufey mean for me to be hunting something, or did she just give me some sort of ancient blessing because she's a Giant and they know their runes? At this rate, I wouldn't be surprised if it was a freaking warning about which to stay away from.

Laufey wouldn't risk her life to hand me runes for nothing; they're too powerful for that, the meaning too important. Everything she does has purpose. I can't forget this. She's patient. Brilliant. I have to figure it out.

I'll need to pay more attention to them when I walk around campus. Maybe in trying to understand what she was hoping to communicate, I'll find Mjölnir faster.

I glance out the window and see Aric. He's walking toward the forest and seems angry. Because he walked in on Rowen and me?

He kicks at the ground and suddenly stops as ice builds beneath his feet. He stares down, seemingly confused, then keeps walking. Interesting. He's unknowingly creating ice when his emotions are high.

More interesting—he may not be awake, but something inside is.

Maybe it's time I help him let it out.

Chapter Twenty-Nine

ARIC

I jog out of the building, unable to see straight. I don't remember slamming the door behind me, but apparently I did, because someone yells at me to watch it. This is why Reeve keeps warning me away from her. It's like I can't control shit around this woman—my temper, my need to talk to her even when I know it just makes things worse.

Shit, does she have to be everywhere?

I stop and look down. Icy footprints stare up at me.

I kick at them and rein in my breathing, then stomp down the trail leading toward the lake. My senses are attuned to anyone else who might be nearby, but it's quiet. First day of classes and all that.

I feel like I'm losing control, but the last thing I can do is go to Sigurd and admit it. The drugs are no longer suppressing my heightened emotions now that Rey's on campus, and he fucking allowed her to just waltz right in. Is this punishment for two years ago?

These last few days, it's been one trigger after another.

It's her. Rey is fucking with something inside me, and I need it to stop.

Now.

I reach down and grab a log as big as my thigh that's fallen across the path. But as I crank my arm to whip it into the forest, I see I've actually made a half-inch dent in the bark where my fingers dug in.

Stunned, I drop it to the ground. I stare at my fingertips. I don't have any scratches or other signs that I've just pressed my fingers through wood.

Well, that's new.

"You're from a long line of Giants," I was once told, "but don't worry, the medications should help you. Just try to control it—you're the first who's been born away."

"Away?" I asked.

"From Jötunheim."

Home.

I could taste it, smell it, wanted to experience it. "When can we go back, Sigurd?"

His eyes went pitch-black. "Never. The Gods burned it to the ground. You can't return to ash."

"Did you make them pay?" I asked.

"No. But one day, I will." He smiled and patted my head. "Until then, just enjoy the fresh snow around us, focus on the cold, and all will be okay."

My stomach clenches again.

I'm bending over to examine the branch when something dark and sinister swirls inside my chest. The pressure builds, and it feels like whatever it is, it's trying to break free. I want to scream into the void, rail against whatever the hell this is, but instead I do something I've never done before. Something Sigurd's warned me about. The one thing I've been told never to do because this world is made for men, not for the likes of Gods and monsters. Not for the likes of me.

I give in to the darkness and free-fall into the all-consuming cold around me.

And for the first time in a long time, I feel freedom.

My back starts to heat up, my jaw aching from clenching my teeth. Slowly, my lips part, and when I open my eyes, every exhale shows my breath turning to frost in front of me.

I think about Rey and Rowen.

Unreleased fury builds like a storm inside my chest until I let out a scream and crash my hands against a tree. A crack sounds as the tree splits in half and slams to the ground.

Frost lingers around the crack in the bark, along with a sheen of ice, and my fingertips are numb with the feeling of rightness.

I take a minute to relish in it, to breathe in the cold, crisp air.

What am I capable of? I'm not sure. I don't think anyone is.

I shake my head.

What hasn't Sigurd told me about being a Giant and everything it entails? Especially being that I was born here. Whenever I bring up my parents and my past, all I get are warnings, a lecture, or my favorite, silence. He wants me to be patient, but it feels like time is running out and I can't figure out why.

And what does it have to do with her?

My stomach aches again.

A maelstrom churns beneath the surface. I can feel it: cold, ancient, bloodthirsty.

Hungry.

I stare at the broken tree and feel myself starting to smile. It should be terrifying to want to destroy, so why does it feel so good?

My phone buzzes in my pocket.

It's probably Reeve.

I pull it out and stare at the screen.

Reeve: *where are you? i'm about to leave the dorms for class. the games are tonight and we have to win this year or i'm disowning you*

I almost tell him what happened with Rey, but already I feel the darkness leaving, along with my twisted thoughts. I can control this, whatever this is. I have to for now. I have no choice.

Me: *Be right there.*

CHAPTER THIRTY

REY

I'm still reeling from a stupid nightmare.

In it, I was drowning, of course, as a whirlpool dragged me into the inky-cold depths of the sea. My father, Rowen, Aric, Reeve, and even Laufey were standing on the shoreline, watching.

The downward spiral. The crushing weight of the water—clearly, a metaphor for my responsibilities. It's like my brain threw the worst of my stress onto a giant TV screen and forced me to watch.

I drag myself toward the mirror over my dorm sink. My reflection looks like hell, but there's no time to feel sorry for myself. Ponytail, black spandex shorts, oversize black hoodie that nearly swallows them whole, and tennis shoes. Good enough. It's not my usual designer uniform, but it helps me blend in. And tennis shoes beat heels if I end up chasing—or being chased. Yay college and possible death traps.

I'm already sweating by the time I pass through the lobby. I make a face when I shove open the front door of the dorm. One day at a time. One asshole at a time, too: also known as one Erikson at a time. I'll be fine.

I pull out my phone to look at the campus map and start walking.

Everything from the ginormous trees to the heavy air is so damn thick up here, it feels like I'm wading through soup. And whose brilliant idea was it to design the different buildings so far apart from each other? Must it be an actual nature walk to get from point A to point B?

Gods, forget my earlier resentment of Bellevue. I miss the city. My attitude doesn't get better as the Everett humidity assaults me like it has a personal vendetta against me or my kind.

Maybe the campus is cursed. Maybe it senses my blood and is already out to get me. I notice a few runes on the ground, spaced out like a sick version of hopscotch, and I sidestep them. Paranoid much? Yes. Absolutely.

Runes are used much like wards or a talisman. By themselves, they are powerful, but together, you've got yourself some serious waves of protection and a giant-ass warning sign for all to feel. I mean, most people won't know what it is or why they feel like it's hard to breathe, but ancient power is like that. It chokes you slowly.

By the time I stumble into the clearing beside the arts building, I'm fuming. And then I gasp—because it's gorgeous.

An outdoor classroom is tucked among the trees, ringed with cement benches, sunlight scattering through the branches above. And right next to the classroom are the blessed double doors to the arts building. Advanced Ancient History. Can't wait. I click through my schedule again on my phone. Room nine, Dr. Tyrson. I scowl at my phone screen, then try to take a deep breath. It's fine. It's just a job, a mission. I'll have Laufey free from Odin's clutches in no time and bouncing away from campus with Mjölnir in my hands, flipping off the Eriksons the entire way.

And if I learn some cool facts along the way, more power to me.

My vision suddenly blurs as the feeling of Aric's hot mouth on mine takes over—seriously, why at the most inconvenient times? Nope. I'm burying that vision, it didn't happen, will never happen, and it's just a distraction. Can runes bring on visions?

I wouldn't put it past Sigurd. If he can steal the most powerful weapon in the world, I'm sure visions are mere child's play. It's not like he isn't powerful in his own right.

I need to remember that. Right now, it's an even playing field, but

I aim to change the odds to our favor.

The smell of cleaning solution fills my nose the minute I walk through the doors. I make my way through crowds of eager students, and it's so normal that it's almost unreal to me. Everyone' s just existing, talking about their majors, about rushing, sports, life. They have no idea, and the more I listen, the more bitter I feel.

Lives are on the line.

And these clueless kids are on dating apps.

People will die, and someone's pissed that their TikTok didn't go viral.

I roll my eyes and sweep past a group of guys, a few of them looking in my direction like they're waiting for me to smile. I ignore the usual stares, push my Aethercall, and keep walking. I don't have time for boys. I already have to tolerate Reeve. And Aric.

I finally make it into room nine and stare.

How typical—Aric's sitting in the back, Reeve right next to him, engaging with a gaggle of women while tapping his pen on his thigh. Of course they're hanging on every word he says. I narrow my eyes and peer past him to Aric.

Aric looks like he'd rather be anywhere else. If I didn't know better, I'd think he wasn't even breathing—or maybe he's just as irritated by the chatter as I am. He radiates intensity, from his steady breaths to the way his pen spins between his fingers over and over again. Then his eyes catch mine. He holds the stare for a beat before a smirk tugs at his lips—the same lips I can't stop imagining.

There's no softness in his gaze. Murder? He wears it like a second skin.

I move to the long desk in front of them and start putting down my things. I start with my black Stanley, then pull out a pen, my notebook, my syllabus, and my planner. See? I can be normal, too. I feel a weird sense of accomplishment when I grab my textbook, my fingers lingering over the front page. Ancient History.

A subject I know more about than I should.

"Hey." A guy sidles up to me—low voice, bright blond hair, a pencil tucked behind his ear like a weapon he's not afraid to use. Endir sweatshirt, arms crossed, staring me down like I owe him my number followed by an aggressive text followed by a heart emoji.

"Hey." I look back at my textbook.

"Aren't you a freshman?"

I clench my teeth. "Yup."

"This is an advanced-level class," he points out. "You must be beautiful *and* brilliant."

"Yeah, okay." He's either trying to flirt or just doesn't know how to talk to girls. I stand. "Listen—" I pause, waiting for his name. I have manners; they're just buried under my zero tolerance for bullshit and guys who think the world owes them something.

"Zane," he says proudly.

"Great, Zane, I'm going to save you the trouble. I'm one nervous breakdown away from turning into a serial killer, and my dad knows how to bury bodies very well. I wouldn't touch me with a ten-foot pole."

"So true," Reeve says under his breath from behind me. Okay, I may have been hoping for someone on my team, but this was not what I meant. Thanks, universe.

I keep talking. "I know I look fun, but I'm not some shiny trophy you pull out and polish when it suits you. I'm more the type who waits under your bed with a knife—"

"Or the closet," Reeve says behind me helpfully. "Or the living room with the candlestick, the kitchen with the rope—honestly, dude, it doesn't matter what objects she has, the end is always death. I'd run, don't walk."

Zane slowly backs away from me and whispers "bitch" under his breath.

"Nice to meet you!" I say cheerfully and take my seat again.

"Your first class and you already made someone cry. I had my bets on a professor, not a transfer for the football team," Reeve grumbles. "Do you even know how to smile or talk in any way that isn't dripping with sarcasm?"

"Sarcasm is supposed to be a semi-intelligent deterrent from idiots, and yet it never repels you. I can never figure out why."

Reeve elbows Aric. "We're drawn to danger."

Aric snorts out a laugh. Okay, so he does still have a pulse. "I must admit, I'm curious about one thing."

"Ah, he speaks." I cross my arms. Finally. "Yes?"

"You were homeschooled the last two years, and even with AP classes, you still wouldn't have the credits or prerequisites for Dr. Tyrson's course. I call bullshit. It kinda feels like stalking at this point. Hate to break it to you, but the answer was no two years ago, and it's still no now."

Indignation scorches my throat. "Check your info again. I aced all my AP exams to be here. Sadly for you, that means you're stuck with me all semester. May your eyes bleed from the torment."

"I'm sitting behind you. Trust me, they already are." His dark eyes flash white briefly before turning back to normal, and suddenly I'm very aware that I have my back to a dangerous enemy, one who has no clue how powerful he really is and who I really shouldn't piss off right now. I calmly reach for a pen so I have something I can use as a weapon and wait.

A loud voice breaks the tension in the room. "If you haven't already, open the app you were instructed to download along with your packets, locate your partner, and please sit next to them. Hurry up now; we don't have all day."

Dread washes over me.

This is a good thing, and yet…

I count the heavy steps moving in my direction.

I almost wince when the notebook drops, followed by the bag, then a pen that slowly rolls until it hits my hand. I look up into bright mahogany and extremely angry eyes. "Move over."

Chapter Thirty-One

REY

"Grab your partners and get comfortable." Dr. Tyrson's voice booms across the room, low and commanding. He isn't loud, but it doesn't feel like he needs to be. I imagine every word that comes out of that man's mouth is deliberate and carries weight. I hadn't even heard him walk in.

He stands at the center of the room, tall with broad shoulders and deep brown skin. His close-cropped black hair has silver at the temples, and a neatly trimmed beard sharpens his already strong jawline. He's wearing a simple black Endir sweatshirt that makes him look approachable—almost. Maybe that's a theme here with the professors, what with Sigurd's garish gold outfit setting the tone.

I steal a glance at Aric and freeze.

There's not even a dip in the temperature. But the vision hits me like an avalanche all the same.

My hand's on his neck, his on mine. His eyes move from my mouth, lower, lower. We lean in, breaths heavy, puffs of frost appearing before our mouths, mingling, tempting. His full lips whisper my name as his hand comes up to my throat—

"You done?" Aric asks. His smile is slow and deliberate. "Don't misunderstand, I was just measuring how much rope I'd need later. I like to be prepared."

He's in my head. My *visions.*

Now that's a complication I wasn't prepared for.

The classroom hums with noise—backpacks unzipping, laptops clicking open, whispered gossip carrying over the scrape of chair legs. The air smells faintly of coffee and old books as I lean forward on my desk, tilting my head toward Aric. "Wow, and you already know my number one fantasy about being tied up. You really are a good partner."

I can do this. Charm him.

I lick my lips, let my gaze linger too long, and pull—just a little. The Aethercall slides from me, warm and soft, wrapping through the air like the faintest brush of a hand. Not much, just enough to test him. To see if he responds.

He's gripping his pen so tightly I think it might snap, but slowly—painfully—his fingers unclench. His jaw eases. His shoulders drop. It's like I just cut invisible strings that had been choking him.

He lets out a low groan, barely audible over the noise, but Reeve hears it. A sneaker jabs the back of Aric's chair. "You good?"

"Fine." Aric's voice is iron through clenched teeth. His gaze cuts to mine, sharp enough to pin me to my seat. "Stop it."

I widen my eyes, feigning innocence. "Stop what? I'm not even talking to you."

The thing about the Aethercall is that it's tricky—it can feel like a hug, like warmth spreading across your chest, like someone smoothing your hair and telling you everything's going to be okay.

But I'm not touching him. Not even close. He feels it. He's aware of it. But it's not compelling him. He's just…calm. And it takes him a second to realize that.

The irony stings: I can make other people feel safe, calm, wanted—but I've never had a clue what that would feel like for myself.

"All right." Dr. Tyrson's voice cuts through the classroom hum. "Open your syllabus. I know, I know—now the real work begins.

If you haven't already figured it out, you're in Advanced Ancient History."

Zane—of course it's Zane—lets out a cheer. Reeve immediately starts kicking the back of my seat like an overgrown toddler. I'm surrounded by children.

"You and your partner will have several group projects throughout the semester. And to kick things off—"

Oh no. Bad news incoming. I can sense it.

"—you'll each be assigned a local landmark to visit. I expect your paper by the end of the week, just in time for all of you to turn it in before I lose half of you to parties and the chaos of rush."

The room erupts with groans, scattered cheers. I glance down at the syllabus, my stomach sinking. Our names are right there, paired together, next to our assigned site: the Ice Caves.

Perfect. Just perfect.

Not only are we not given much time, but the thought of being trapped in a car with Aric Erikson is its own kind of torture. And I know why this pairing happened—why my father engineered it. He doesn't just want a paper turned in. He wants me close to Aric.

Forced proximity. Forced awakening.

He knows I can handle myself. But does he have any idea what being near Aric does to me? Not just emotionally after his rejection years ago but to my Aethercall, my control, my sanity? Does he know how dangerous this is?

He doesn't care. Throwing me to the wolves is exactly the point.

Ice Caves. Where Frost Giants are strongest.

What could possibly go wrong?

"Great." Aric drops his phone onto the desk with a thud and raises his hand like he's already done with this circus. Dr. Tyrson doesn't even look in his direction. Aric lets it fall, then slowly cranes his neck toward me.

"I actually want to make it through senior year," he mutters, "so if you could just nod your head, not cause trouble, and at least contribute, that'd be great."

His hand grazes mine. It's an accident, but it doesn't feel like one. It feels like a spark detonating under my skin. He flinches back. I ball my hand into a fist, trying not to show the fear—or the thrill—curling in my gut.

"When do you want to get this done?" I ask flatly, flipping open my planner like none of this is fazing me. "I've got Intro to Business Tuesdays and Thursdays, bio lab after that."

He doesn't even hesitate. He grabs my phone and flips it in his hand to face me, and it unlocks. His thumbs fly across the screen, and then he slides it back to me with his number saved.

"Normally people have to work a lot harder for that."

I look down at the screen and type in his name. Giant Asshole.

"You'll never see me beg, Erikson."

He wraps the leg of my chair with his foot and drags me close. "Too bad, since being on your knees seems where you're most comfortable… after what I walked in on today."

I freeze, heat rushing to my face.

Reeve clears his throat from behind us. "Um…what exactly did you walk in on?"

Aric ignores him. Ignores me, too, facing forward like nothing happened. I stare down at my phone, force myself to breathe, and try not to let his icy composure cut deeper than it already does.

The rest of class drones on in meaningless buzz. By the time I gather my things, both Aric and Reeve are already out the door.

Dr. Tyrson's deep in conversation with Sigurd.

Where the hell did he come from? And just how long has he been standing there?

He leans against the frame, patient, watchful, ancient.

I don't like him any more than he likes me. But I know exactly who he is. What he is. The whispers about Sigurd are as dark as the ones about my father. Older. Colder. Not royalty, but the closest thing to it. My father once said it's been centuries since his kind were forced to bow.

Every culture has an origin story. Every myth, a beginning.

And I'm standing in front of it.

When Dr. Tyrson looks down at his phone, then takes a call and walks away from us, I don't think. I just move. I press two fingers to my lips, extend my thumb to my throat. The old gesture. Once, it meant loyalty—that you would silence your own mouth and slit your own throat before betraying the Gods.

Now it's a mockery.

Sigurd's eyes narrow at me, glinting sharp, unreadable, as I leave the room.

CHAPTER THIRTY-TWO

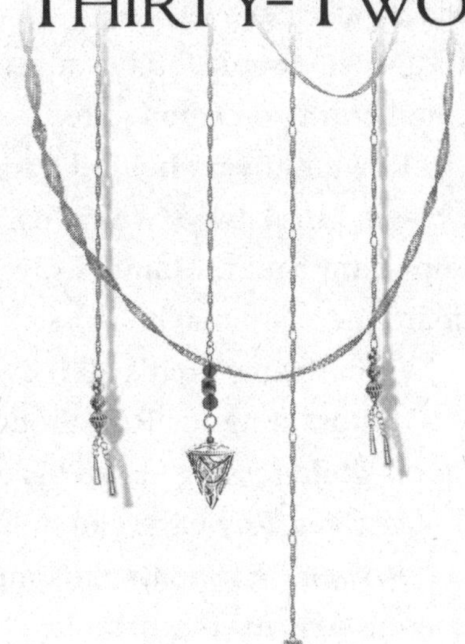

ARIC

Food tastes dull in my mouth. It's been exactly two hours since my class with Rey, and I still feel her in the air—what's worse is that the minute she was gone, I expected to calm down, but instead I almost feel *more* on edge.

A headache pounds between my temples as I shove the plate of food away and reach for my can of Coke.

Reeve drops down next to me. "You're not thinking of actually trying to tame it, are you?"

"Who?"

"Satan."

"Never." I scowl. "It's bad enough I have to be her partner."

Ziva chooses that moment to pop down at the same table and spread her two trays around. How many fries can a person grab? "Eriksons, I'd say it's a pleasure, but I'm only here because every other seat was taken and people are petrified of you two."

Another tray clatters onto the table. Eira.

She slides her food a few inches away from her body, her blond hair braided back in a crown that gleams under the fluorescent lights. Where most of the students look like they just tumbled out of bed, she's got on glittery eyeshadow and bright red lipstick. She smiles widely at Reeve.

"Most people," Ziva mutters between bites of fries, like she's commenting on a bad joke.

Rowen hovers behind Eira, scanning the room with those sharp eyes of his. Always watching, never missing a thing. Why is she so important again? Rumors say she's got an important father, maybe a board member, maybe worse.

Odin flexing, that's all it ever is.

It must sting for Rey, though. To see Odin protect someone else's blood while tossing her to his enemies.

And yet, Rey? She can hold her own.

"Rowen." Eira pats the empty chair beside her. "Sit down. You're making Aric uncomfortable."

I'm not uncomfortable. What I am is curious.

"So you work for Odin?" I ask, leaning back. "What, like a rent-a-bodyguard gig?"

Rowen doesn't even flinch. "My family's been in his service for years. It's only natural."

"Uh-huh." I shrug. "So you never went to college?"

That earns me the barest flicker of amusement. "Honestly, with the jobs I've had and the people I've been hired to protect, it feels like I've already lived a million lives. The last thing I want is to rot in Organic Chemistry."

Eira finally looks up from her phone. "So I heard you guys are hosting a party this weekend?"

Reeve lifts a hand. "Invite-only. House isn't big enough for everyone."

She gives him a slow once-over. "So what do I need to do to get in?"

His nose wrinkles. "Um, not what you're thinking."

Ziva snorts. "To be fair, it is you, so why *wouldn't* she think that?"

The tension between them is suffocating, bitter and sharp even though they're laughing it off. I nearly scoot my chair back from the burning resentment for each other they drag in with them.

"I forgot you were even sitting here," Reeve fires back.

Ziva's smile cuts. "I'm used to it. You forgetting your phone, your keys, the fact that you had a girlfriend."

I groan into my hands. "Can you two not bring your drama here?"

"Whatever." Reeve stands just as my phone buzzes. "You can all come, just don't ruin the vibe."

I glance down. Unknown number.

Unknown: *Done with my classes. Want to get our assignment over with or did you have another day in mind*

Rey. Of course it's Rey.

And of course, she chooses that exact moment to walk into the dining hall.

Ziva waves her over. I flip my phone face up, leaving her on read, but when her eyes drop to the screen, then snap to me, her glare cuts deep.

And suddenly, I can breathe. Or it feels like I can.

"Just texted you," she says flatly.

"Yup." I smile back, cool as I can manage.

"Hey, Eira." Rey's voice is deceptively casual. "Can I borrow Rowen really quick?"

The flare of jealousy hits so fast, I almost choke on it. No—not jealousy. Just anger. Irritation. Annoyance.

Eira shrugs like she couldn't care less, and Rowen walks over to her, throwing a casual arm around her shoulder.

My hand curls around my Coke can until the aluminum creaks. Frost blooms across the surface in thick veins, ice racing up my fingers until the whole can is frozen solid.

Eira gasps. "Wow. That must be really cold. I'm gonna grab one." She scurries off.

But I can't move. Can't breathe. All I see is Rowen and Rey walking out together.

Something's going on.

And the rune on my back—it burns. It's alive. I can feel it clawing under my skin, demanding to be noticed.

I keep telling myself it's nothing. A trick. Some accidental magic Rey stirred up in the Hall of Ormir.

It started there. But it needs to end now. A small voice reminds me it started years ago, but it wasn't like this then. Back then, I could still control things, but now? Now things are…changing. I shift uncomfortably.

Tonight, I'm done pretending. Tonight, I'm asking Sigurd why the hell I've got a living, breathing rune carved into me like a brand.

And how the fuck I get rid of it.

Chapter Thirty-Three

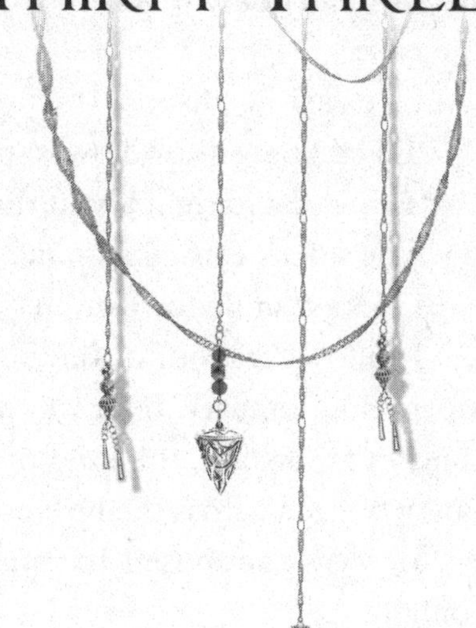

REY

"What's up?" Rowen crosses his arms and leans in. "You're not really squashing down the whole *I was in your room and we broke a bed* rumor right now."

My eyebrows shoot up as I self-consciously look around the dining hall. People are staring. Great. Perfect. "There's a rumor about us?"

He nods. "Though in the rumored version, you were naked."

I slap a hand over his mouth, then drop it. "That's ridiculous."

"Welcome to college." He almost seems sad when he says it. "You're young and pretty, and I'm not a troll, so people put two and two together. And I mean, the bed *was* broken. It doesn't matter, anyway. Better than them talking about you and Aric."

Fair point.

I hold up my phone. "Keep yours on you. I kind of told Aric we could do our assignment now. Field trip to the Ice Caves."

"Brilliant idea, Rey."

"Appreciate the sarcasm."

I know Rowen's right, but it's all I have, and as much as I would love to enjoy the delusion that this is normal, that I'm just attending classes, starting my own rumors, and headed toward a sex tape scandal all before streaking through the quad—that's not the case.

Lives are at stake.

"I'll be fine. I know how to handle myself."

"Hope you're right about that. Because here he comes."

Aric's dark eyes meet mine, and without a word, he nods.

I force a smile for Rowen. "That's my cue."

I follow Aric out of the building, toward the parking lot just as storm clouds muscle their way across the sky, thick and heavy. The day dims in an instant, the kind of wrong darkness that feels like a bad omen written across the heavens.

It wasn't supposed to rain today. Definitely not thunderstorm tonight.

I shiver and keep my eyes locked straight ahead, but my gaze still catches on Aric's fists—white-knuckled, clutched tight at his sides like he's one second from putting them through a wall.

Lightning suddenly charges across the clouds, jagged and sharp.

He stops short, spins on me, voice breaking, raw. "Do you have any idea what you're doing to me? What being near you feels like? You think this is some kind of game?"

I reel back, breath catching as a cool wind whooshes across my cheek. His chest heaves once, twice, and then he drags a hand over his face like he's trying to shove the words back inside.

"Forget it," he mutters, voice lower now but no calmer. "I know we have to ride in the same car. But if you could just...stay away from me. Unless it's absolutely necessary. That'd be great."

The storm deepens overhead, growling.

By the time we're settled in his black Defender, he's gripping the steering wheel so hard, the leather groans. His jaw is locked, eyes fixed forward like he's holding on by a thread. He keeps blinking, shaking his head, like he's losing focus.

My pulse spikes.

And for the first time, I wonder if I'm trapped in this car with him—or if he's trapped in here with me.

I haven't had a chance to fully look at the map, so I haven't mathed how far we're actually going. I assume I have a few hours for a partner breakthrough.

Aric apparently doesn't trust me to navigate. He takes his phone out of his pocket and pulls up a navigation app, then types an address and waits for it to sync on the car's console. I try not to let my irritation show.

Playing the long game is going to be the death of me.

"The Ice Caves are old," Aric starts. His voice is low, clipped, but steady enough to sound like a lecture. "Thousands of years old, some of the oldest glacial formations in the Northwest. People have used them as shelters, burial sites, even meeting grounds. That's why Dr. Tyrson assigned them. We're supposed to take notes about the structures themselves, how they've lasted this long—"

I cut him off with a sharp laugh. "I, too, have a syllabus, professor. And guess what? I can read. You don't have to tell me what to do—we're partners, remember?"

His jaw ticks. "I just don't trust you. And one of us actually cares about grades. Graduating. Escaping."

The word hits harder than it should.

I keep my eyes fixed on the storm-tossed road ahead. "What makes you think I don't want to escape, too?"

Silence fills the car, heavy and suffocating.

Finally he mutters, "You had the chance to run. You didn't."

I let out a shaky breath, trying for a heart-to-heart I'm not sure I have the courage for. "You're right. I had a chance once. A moment of hope. A cruel, fleeting moment in my life where what my father planned for me seemed almost like an escape. I dared to hope..." My throat tightens. "I saw it like a crack in the void, a slit of light I thought I could slip through."

He doesn't respond.

So I keep talking, words scraping raw on the way out. "But I forgot about the chains. The ones still wrapped around my legs. My mind might be free, my heart, too, but my ability to run? Frozen."

He doesn't say anything, but I swear I hear it anyway—the

faintest whisper of wind in the car, carrying words he'll never admit aloud.

Just like me.

I glance at my phone, desperate for distraction. Three missed calls from my father. Three unread texts. My pulse spikes.

Shit.

"So…the four big Ice Caves, right?" I ask, forcing my voice steady.

"Yup," Aric answers without looking at me. "We're going to the ice."

A shiver runs down my spine. I plaster on a smile I don't feel. "All right. To the ice."

My phone dings again. I take a deep breath and finally gain the courage to check my text messages.

Odinfather: *In class? Updates?*

He rarely says please, so I'm not sure why I'm expecting one now.

Odinfather: *I'm sure you've already made contact with Rowen. I sent him in so you're reminded of what you will lose if you don't succeed. The ice is very thin, daughter.*

A choking sensation wraps itself around my neck. Dammit. This is one time I did not want to be right.

Odinfather: *Rowen just told me you're off campus. I didn't send you there to play their games. You aren't one of them. You never will be. You have a job to do. Do not disappoint me.*

Rowen told him I'm off campus? It's a school assignment! Whose side is he on? But I guess he had to tell his boss. And Rowen would describe without any detail, so it's not totally his fault.

My phone goes off again.

Odinfather.

A picture of Laufey.

My stomach clenches. She doesn't look hurt, but that doesn't mean she isn't.

I don't need the reminder that she's waiting, that the clock is ticking. That her life hangs in the balance. I've seen Father kill. He's heartless. Laufey risked the very real and unhinged wrath of Odin to give me that note. It has to be significant. I refuse to believe otherwise.

I read off the runes again in my head.

Raido. It was there, in the Hall of Ormir. It means journey.

Is this going to be my journey, then?

I turn my gaze to a very still and focused Aric. I'm used to disappointment, I bathe in fear of my father, but the last thing I need is to develop a weakness for my enemy and wish for the one thing I've never truly had.

A friend.

Chapter Thirty-Four

REY

An hour of slow torture—no music, just the sound of the engine and my own breathing—and we finally pull into the gravel parking lot at the trailhead.

"Whoa." The word slips out before I can stop it.

I've seen plenty of strange things, but nothing like this.

It feels less like Washington and more like we've been dropped into the middle of Norway or Switzerland. Snowcapped ridges loom above us, their shadows stretching long and cold across the lot. Jagged boulders jut out at impossible angles, the kind that make you wonder how long they've been here and what they've witnessed.

There's a chill in the air, heavier than mountain weather—an eerie weight that makes my skin prickle, like maybe we shouldn't be trespassing at all. Like maybe we should get back in the car. Now.

The wind picks up as the storm brews overhead.

Aric slams his door, gaze cutting toward the trailhead sign half buried in snow. I'm very glad I changed into jeans before heading to the dining hall. Spandex shorts would *not* be it for this hike. "This path was used as a burial route," he mutters. "Old tribes brought their dead up here, left offerings at the caves. Some of the bones are still sealed in the ice."

My stomach flips. "Great. Haunted caves. Perfect study spot with my new partner."

He ignores me.

We start down the trail, the gravel crunching underfoot. With each step, the trees close in, the air sharper, colder. It feels like we've stepped out of one world and into another entirely. I wonder if this place, like Endir, has its own stories to tell and dark secrets from the past that nobody wants discovered.

Excitement suddenly bubbles up within me, only to be quickly tamped down. I'm not here for actual school. But how nice would it be if I were?

It's a full mile hike to the first cave—which I wish I'd known. Every three steps I take is just one giant stride for Aric, so I'm winded by the time we reach the mouth of the first cave. Its massive entrance is encompassed in white ice compounded from years of snow melting and freezing over and over again.

The inside is brighter than I imagined, but the ceiling starts to get lower the farther you walk. Aric disappears into the cave without calling back to see if I'm okay or even waiting for me. I have to step carefully as I follow him, thanks to rocks and ice chunks littering the ground.

A stream trickles to the left, the sound of dripping water not helping my nerves. It's clearly melting, the dome of ice over our heads.

"Hey, Aric?" I call into the eerie blue darkness. "I thought you said we'd explore around the entrance first. See if things are safe, then take some notes and pictures?" He keeps walking ahead of me; I can only tell because I can hear his feet crunch against the ground. The ceiling of ice gets lower the deeper I go into the cave, making me feel progressively more claustrophobic and panicked.

I hate the cold. I hate ice. This was a bad idea, miscalculated to the extreme.

There are better ways to keep your enemy close, right? If there is an avalanche or cave-in, we'll be dead.

I'm so distracted by the fact that I have to duck that I nearly run into Aric's back.

The cave opens to a cavern. The world around us is blanketed in blue and white.

His jaw unclenches. "It's breathtaking." His voice sounds awed, deep. Almost vibrating. The icy world around him feels like home—that much is clear. To me, it's cold, but to him, it's everything his sleeping half is missing. And I know more than anyone, the best feeling in the world is knowing who you are, and a lot of that comes with knowing where you're from.

"Aric." I grab his arm and discover that he's shaking. "Things don't look stable."

I send my Aethercall toward him, testing whether he really is immune. He shudders. Is he fighting it off?

If he awakens in here, there's no way I could fight him off safely, and if he suddenly realizes he can find Mjölnir and use it? I'm as good as dead. Would it answer to him without me? Or would he just cheerfully bleed me dry and see if that worked?

I take a deep breath and look down at his right hand. It's still trembling. He reaches up and runs it through his inky hair.

He shakes his head and blinks like he's trying to refocus. "Yeah, this feels wrong. We should go."

Thank the Gods. "We finally agree on something." I turn too quickly and slip on the ice, but Aric immediately grabs me by the shoulders. We share a sigh of relief right before we hear a thunderous crack reverberate through the cavern.

"Stay. Still," he whispers, and his hot breath against my neck sends a bolt of electricity straight down my spine.

He doesn't have to tell me twice. The cave groans with more loud cracks. He pulls me closer against him and wraps his arms around me. I can feel the power, the heat pulsing through him.

Another loud crack rips toward the mouth of the cave as snow and ice start to crash from the ceiling above us.

"Run!" he yells.

I do as he says, dodging shards of ice as more of the ceiling collapses above us. We're going to die here. I'm going to die in the Ice Caves with a Frost Giant. There's irony in there somewhere.

Maybe if I make it out alive, I'll laugh at how ridiculous the thought is, but I'm currently trying to dodge falling daggers of ice. One narrowly misses my foot. The cave is collapsing at an alarming rate, and I can't run any faster.

Another large piece of ice falls to my right, but I can see the mouth of the cave up ahead.

We're going to make it.

Aric is turning around to ensure I'm right behind him when a sudden jagged shard falls right between us. He grabs my hand and jerks me toward him just as the ground starts to slide beneath our feet.

Another shard of ice comes at us, and this time it hits me square between the eyes. Pain lances out everywhere, and the last thing I think before I lose consciousness is…

We're not going to make it.

Chapter Thirty-Five

ARIC

I cough and shove a pile of ice away from my face. My eyes burn as I stare straight ahead. Rey's in my arms, unconscious. The cave collapsed around us, but in front of me is pure light. I reach out to touch it, but a wave of nausea hits me and I feel my eyes roll to the back of my head.

"You're not worthy!" the man standing in front of me shouts. "You'll destroy the world and bring about Ragnarök! It was never yours!"

I'm holding a hammer straight above my head as lightning streaks through the sky and splits into the hammer—and into me.

"Do you really think you deserve to live?" I growl as a second man appears. "After everyone you've killed? Either of you?"

"We are Gods!" The sound rains down on my ears like thunder, like truth, but I reject it, I reject them *as Mjölnir groans in my icy hands.*

"You are weak!" I roar, sending the lightning directly at the Gods.

"You'll end us all!" The man with a broken hammer etched into his golden armor and a helmet sliced half off his head takes a step closer. His eyes are blazing white as he points at me and collapses to the ground, silver blood spewing from his mouth.

I turn to a woman standing next to me, bloodied, bruised—it's Rey.

What the hell is she doing here?

She reaches for me only to pitch forward, eyes open wide, like she's just been hit by something. It's too dark to see. Dammit, why can't I see?

A knife sticks out of her stomach. "Aric!"

"With the perfect sacrifice," a rough voice whispers, "Ragnarök…has already begun."

My body buzzes with an electrified rush, and I can feel the power gathering in the hammer. The sky lights up with another flash of lightning, and suddenly I can see we're on a battlefield. It's bloody, everyone is fighting—we're losing the war even with the hammer on our side.

We can't lose.

We can't.

We need it, the hammer needs it.

Frost. It needs frost.

What?

It's a hushed whisper, but from where? The wind? The hammer?

"Do it now!" someone shouts.

Do what?

What am I supposed to be doing?

"No!" the man with the hammer on his armor shouts. "Don't do it, you fucking abomination!"

I stare him down while another voice whispers behind me. "You know exactly who you are."

I let out a roar and jolt awake.

I'm alive. I'm in the cave.

And my entire back burns as if the fires of hell are licking at it. My skin has a pulse, my blood rushes, and even though I see Rey next to me, all I hear in my head for a few brief seconds is…

"Frost."

Chapter Thirty-Six

REY

I'm covered in ice and snow. The only warmth I feel is coming from Aric's chest and the blood that's actively running down my temple. Is it mine? But oddly, I feel no pain. Could it be his?

I lift my hand and wipe it away.

"Aric?" I scramble off him and look up. He's in a weird daze. The collapse of the melted ice didn't just take us out—it took out part of the floor of the cave. Thankfully, it looks like we only fell a few feet, so we should be able to get out.

Aric sits up and touches his right shoulder blade. When he brings his hand back around to look at it, I can see it's covered with specks of red blood and spots of silver.

Does he see it? The silvery blood of a Giant? I'm Odin's child, and I've bled many times before, but I don't have that in my veins.

He quickly shoves his hand into the muddy ice water next to us and stands. Ah, so he's seen the silver before, has probably learned to hide it before people ask questions. If he's ever asked those same questions, I wonder what sort of answers Sigurd's had for him.

"Are you okay?" he asks, and I'm surprised by how steady his voice sounds, like we didn't almost just plummet to our deaths.

I nod and slowly get to my feet. "I've survived worse. Thanks for that, by the way."

"I'm not your father, Rey. I don't just stand by and watch people die—even if they deserve it." He shoves past me and heaves himself up like it's nothing, then offers me his hand.

I see something shining out of the corner of my eye.

"Wait." I kneel down on top of the pile of ice that fell through with us. "I see something."

Aric lets out a groan. "Another rune?" It's a simple rock slab with Dalgaz carved into it.

"A rune. Here?"

Aric shrugs. "This region is littered with old runes. Every time someone discovers one, they'll bring it to the campus for identification. The Anthropology Department has a whole collection."

"And what about the runes sprinkled all over campus?"

He smirks. "You noticed those, huh."

"Kind of hard to miss."

"Sigurd warded the whole university. He's superstitious. Says they're for protection."

"Funny, who would he need protection from when *he's* the villain?" I do laugh then. "Life is weird."

He sets the runestone down by his feet, then heaves me up. I fall against his massive chest, but he shoves me away, then grabs for me as if remembering I just almost died. "Sorry, instinct."

Yeah, I bet it is.

"No worries. I know you don't like people touching you."

"I'm only allergic to you. Everyone and everything else are fair game." He starts walking. The gash on the back of his shoulder already looks better.

We walk in bitterly cold silence back to the car. We're almost there when it starts to pour, hail and rain cascading from the skies as if nature's angry we disturbed its peace.

Turnabout's fair play, Mother Nature. You almost just killed me.

My teeth start to chatter as I get into Aric's car. Between falling in the cave and the downpour, I probably have mascara streaming down my cheeks, stringy wet hair, and clothes plastered to my body in the most unflattering way.

Not that I want to look flattering to him.

At all.

Aric peels off his wet and bloody shirt, then grabs a duffel from the back seat.

"Here." A towel gets tossed so hard my way, it smacks me in the head.

I grit my teeth. "Thanks."

Do not look at his chest. Do not look at his abs.

But holy shit, since when did this guy get tattoos? I definitely didn't see any in the spring yesterday. I can't get a read on the one along his side. It seems like it's faded or something. But the one on his back?

That one is most definitely a rune.

Raido.

What the hell?

He quickly drags a fresh black T-shirt over his head and stares me down. I feign ignorance, but my mind is racing. Surely, even though he's sleeping, he knows how powerful runes are. Did Sigurd do it to him? It looked like two. My brain nearly explodes with possibilities.

Dressed again, Aric digs through his black duffel and pulls out two prescription bottles.

They're the same ones from his room.

"What are those?" I ask, going for innocent.

"These"—Aric twists open a bottle of water—"are none of your business." He tosses back one from each container, then puts the bag in the back seat. "We'll wait out the storm here."

"Because you want to extend our time together or because you're too afraid to drive in the rain?" I ask. He's not the only one who can do deadpan.

He leans over the steering wheel. "Three, two, one." Immediately, the downpour increases, to the point that I can't see anything through the windows. "I know my storms."

Of course he knows storms.

Frost Giant.

"Neat trick," I murmur. "How long do you think we'll be stuck here?"

"An hour, give or take. Storms like this don't go that long, but people end up sliding off the roads up here. They forget that just because it isn't icy doesn't mean it isn't dangerous. It's nature, after all." He suddenly leans his seat back, crosses his arms, and closes his eyes. "I'm going to nap."

"Did you just take sleeping pills?" I ask. How the hell long am I going to be stuck in here with him?

"Sleeping pills don't help what I have. You'll need to trust me on that one."

"And what do you have?" I dig.

"Dreams," he whispers. "Worse than you can even imagine."

Chapter Thirty-Seven

REY

Aric's breathing evens.

I examine my fingernails like I'm making small talk and really couldn't care less. "What sort of dreams?"

"Didn't ask you to be my therapist." His eyes are still closed. "What makes you think I would ever tell you anything? Your father deals in secrets. You're his daughter, even if you're as powerless against him as anyone else."

I bristle. "I was just asking a question. You don't have to insult me." Or remind me of my place. I instantly think about the chessboard.

"It wasn't a question. You forget who I am. My family is just as powerful as yours, Rey, just as dangerous in our own way. You, of all people, know how I was raised."

"You talk a big game, but I highly doubt your upbringing was worse than mine."

One eye opens. "My parents are gone. Dead. They'll never see me graduate. Never celebrate a birthday or holiday or ask me how my day was again." He stops, takes a small breath. "My mom was kind, Rey. Really sweet. She'd make me give her a hug each time I left the house. I can barely fucking remember what that feels like now."

I jerk back. "The panic I would feel if my father actually attempted to hug me—he's more likely to hold a knife to me."

"I don't remember my parents' hugs anymore," Aric says. "All I remember are my grandfather's tears."

We're both quiet for a while. Lost to our thoughts and grief.

"I mean, at the very least, I bet your stepmother showed you some sort of affection," he finally says. It feels like an opening, like a fleeting moment I can use to connect with him. Gods know I need one.

I glance sharply at Aric. "Not so much hugs," I admit. "But she always had stories for me—some might argue that's better than physical affection because they lasted longer. Tales of Jötunheim, stories steeped in war and betrayal, unspeakable loss and timeless love."

My chest tightens. Laufey doesn't deserve Odin's wrath.

Aric studies me, his expression unreadable. "So, stories?"

"Yeah," I say with a shaky laugh, brushing at my damp cheeks. "I always had a favorite."

His lips twitch into a scowl. "Naturally, it's about betrayal. Murder. Evil."

"Of course." I shoot him a pointed look. "No. It's about true love. 'The Nightfrost Ring.'"

His head jerks up, brown eyes locked in on me.

I continue before he can interrupt. "How Thor fell so madly in love with the Giant Alvaldi that to prove his devotion, he had the dwarves—the master smiths of Svartálfheim—forge a tether to Mjölnir. A ring that tempered his power. He wanted an equal by his side, someone not from Asgard, someone his father didn't choose for him. He wanted true love."

Aric exhales like I just punched him in the ribs. "You finished?"

I frown. "Whatever. You're the one who asked."

He drags a hand over his face and mutters under his breath, "What did I do to deserve this?" Then louder, with a bitter edge: "That's complete bullshit, and you know it, right? I mean, the story of Nightfrost is legendary, sure, but Thor betrayed her. That's the part they sugarcoat. The ring's been lost ever since. Some say Alvaldi's heartbreak was so deep, she cursed the Gods and hid it. Others say she died still holding it in the woods of Jötunheim, whispering for Thor to rescue her. Who knows?" His eyes go dark as frost gathers along his knuckles. "End of the day, it's still betrayal. Tale as old as time. You trust someone, and they slap you in the face."

"Wow. Okay," I say, genuinely taken aback. I've always truly loved that story, always considered it as pure as pure could be.

His voice softens. "If you love that story…then you know it's for the best."

I glance up to find his mouth only inches from mine. "What's for the best?"

"Staying away from me, from my family, before you end up just like that woman in the story. Dead."

Chapter Thirty-Eight

ARIC

The drive back is uneventful, the silence between us tense as hell. My death threat could have been delivered better, sure, and I think she could tell I was losing patience with all the questions when I cranked up the music to tune her out. But how was I supposed to tell her I was in the middle of a breakdown?

I need space, and Rey sees everything.

From the car, I watch her walk back to the dorm, and every feeling I shouldn't have knots in my chest anyway. One minute, I'm pissed. The next minute, I'm panicking that she saw too much—like the silver flecks in my blood that rise like mercury. Or the way that being near her flips a switch I can't control. Rage or kiss, kill or keep—every instinct at war, and I'm losing ground fast. I slam my hands against the steering wheel and drive toward the lake, then park and get out of the car, leaning against it.

I take a deep breath. I need to find the silence or some other shit, because I sure as hell am not journaling about this right now.

I look up to the sky as I feel power surge to my fingertips. I stare down at my hands and focus on bringing the cold to the surface. Instantly, my fingertips are covered in frost. I wave my hand over the ground, more frost following in intricate little patterns. I wait for the calm when the sound of thunder rumbles in the distance. Like static electricity has charged the air, I can feel the weather's vibrations on my skin.

No, the vibration comes from me, driving the storm.

I flick my right hand toward the sky, then pull it down as a flash of lightning hits a tree right in front of me. I stumble back, and then the calm comes—not before the storm but during.

I let the power rise and surge and break free.

Maybe by embracing whatever power I have inside, I'll be able to end this once and for all. And bring Odin's head to Sigurd on a silver fucking platter.

I take my time coming back from the lake and approaching the admin building. Sigurd has an office at the very top with a wraparound balcony he often paces during the day—more often at night. He says he watches the stars, but he's never looking up. Sigurd is always looking across—at the archway and the numerous runes scattered around campus.

Once, I asked if he even knew how many he had. He just laughed, said he tended them like a farmer tends his garden, that I should be grateful for the wards of protection. Nothing Sigurd does is accidental. He's obsessed with the basalt of the arch, with this place—Endir is sacred to him.

It's hard to blend in on campus, so I do my best to nod and smile as people wave. I can't help but wonder, though: What if one day raising my hand to wave turns into something more sinister? I jerk open the glass door to the building, and it creaks in my hand like I've nearly taken it off its hinges.

Some faculty are lingering in front of the elevators. Nope. Not looking to make polite conversation in a confined space. So I bypass the lobby and slip into the stairwell.

I jog up the stairs, taking them two at a time until I reach the third-floor offices. His is at the end of the hall, and the large black door's already cracked open. I grimace as I walk down the hall of antlers, the eyes of his kills staring blankly back at me. Not one for hunting, I'll never understand why that's his specific hobby or why he feels the need to decorate with everything he's killed.

But maybe it's as simple as that.

He's a killer.

The brightly colored clothing and the Santa smile. All that good-natured bullshit is a thin veneer, a disguise to hide the cold-blooded ruler beneath.

I wave the rune in the air and place it on the desk just as he gets off the phone. He's changed into a black suit, his hair combed back, beard trimmed. To the world, he's eccentric and generous, but in this office, his true power beats like the war cry of a drum.

"You went to the Ice Caves with the Stjerne girl. I'm assuming things went well, though the assignment didn't ask for you to steal an artifact from the site. Which one of you struggles with simple directions?"

Both, actually. "It fell." I cross my arms. "After the ice caved in on us."

He stills. "She survived?" I can't tell if he's pleased or disappointed.

I scoff. "Do you think I'd be this calm if she was in my car bleeding to death?"

Sigurd shrugs. "If she were, I'd just assume you were being smart in bringing her body back to me instead of her father."

"Wow, with that mindset, I can't imagine why you ever wanted to force me to put a ring on it."

He stares down at the rune, then back up at me, his gaze sharp. "You know, this might be good for you. Having her here, sparking an old flame and all that." He leans forward, folding his hands. "If anything, think of it as an opportunity to get back into my good graces. You proved you couldn't be trusted then—I wonder if you can now? Blood over…pity, was it? For her? Your enemy. We have no room for that as Eriksons, not for the family responsible for your parents' deaths, Aric."

His words are tormenting and taunting all at once. Nothing is ever simple with him.

Nothing is ever simple with her.

I hadn't counted on how much Rey would affect me. Then or now.

Two years ago, she was terrified and hopeful, the way she looked at me making me feel ten feet tall. Her father was obviously willing to sacrifice her, the same way I already knew I was screwed with my own family. Always hoping my parents would help me find a way out and protect me like they swore they would.

She would have forever been a pawn, first to him, then to me.

I was almost thankful for that night when the water froze—for one second, I hoped for something greater—and then my parents died and all of my hope died right along with them.

I bottled up whatever she'd released and swore to never hope again.

It was safer that way—*we* were safer.

Another lie, because safety is nothing but an illusion in this world.

Now look at us.

Right back to where we started. Thrust together by two manipulative old men, though that's the crux of it, isn't it? They aren't men. They're Gods and Giants stranded in a world of mortals, imprisoned and angry, their power waning.

Desperate times. Desperate measures.

I step closer to his desk. "Nothing happens on this campus, in this state, without you having some hand in it."

Sigurd smiles.

"Letting Odin or one of his minions force their way into Endir and drop his daughter here, and in all of my classes, no less."

He doesn't reply. I loathe his arrogant silence.

I wait him out. It's obvious Sigurd has a plan. Rey wouldn't have been admitted otherwise. My grandfather designed her schedule—or at the very least he's turning a blind eye. What's his angle?

He drums his fingertips along the desk, once, twice, each time louder and more powerful than before, until tiny marks from his nails dent the wood.

"Would peace between the families be so bad?" he asks.

What a fucking lie. He never does anything that doesn't benefit him, and Odin is the same. Peace? They aren't after peace; they're after power.

"An alliance of sorts? Think about it. I know I have. I'm getting old, Aric, and it's time to pass the torch. You've been alone for so long, so why not take what's been freely given to you?"

"I don't need her. *We* don't need her. And word of warning, I might actually end up killing her before the end of the semester." Would that satisfy him?

He grins like I amuse him. "If killing came so easy to you, you would not have been the one chosen."

Chosen? What is he talking about?

"Play nice in the sandbox, don't forget to share your toys, and remember that we always keep our enemies close—so when the time is right to turn on them, we don't have to chase."

I get whiplash talking to him. "She's living next door, so chasing won't be a problem."

His smile widens. Yeah. He planned that. "Let's start thinking about next steps, shall we?"

"Next steps?"

"Graduation, your parents' legacy, mine, your future, what *you* are." He holds out his hand.

"Am I supposed to shake it or…?"

"Your vow that you'll do everything in your power not to let me down—or let your parents down."

I shake his hand. It's cold as ice, just like his demeanor. Deep down, I know he cares. He's just obsessed with his hatred for the Stjernes and the need for revenge for my parents' deaths. I get it.

I tuck my hands deep into my pockets as I feel the tickle of ice forming along my fingertips.

His eyes zero in on my hands anyway. "A bit cold?"

Is he seriously in my head? "No, sir."

"You're dismissed."

He turns his back to me. So much for asking about the rune burned into my skin. When Sigurd dismisses you, you're dismissed.

I leave wondering two things.

Can he read minds?

And why is he encouraging me to spend time with the one girl who has the power to destroy everything?

Chapter Thirty-Nine

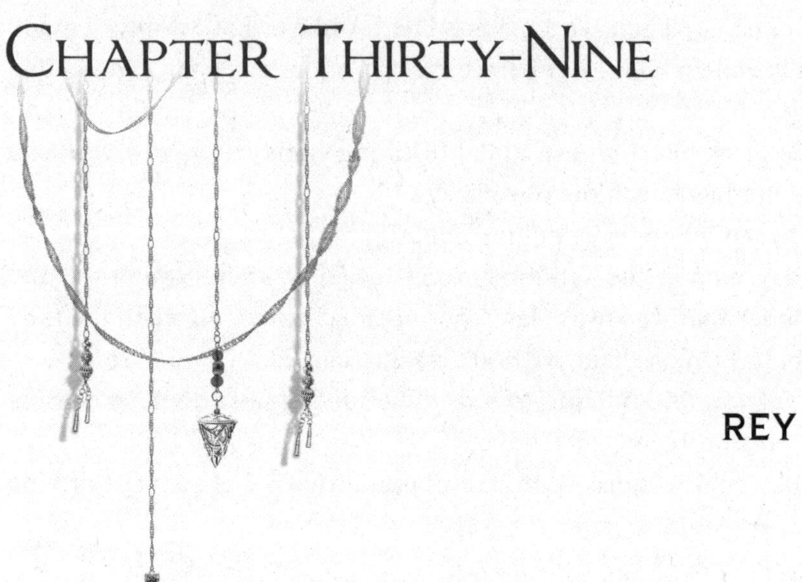

REY

"Hold the elevator!" Reeve calls the second I step inside.

No. I don't think I will.

But Reeve slips through the doors before they close and gives me a once-over that has me crossing my arms. "Judging by that resting bitch face, and the mud stains and wet clothes, I'm guessing the Ice Caves weren't all laughter and doodling Aric's name on your report?"

I try not to think of all the ways I can impale him with my pen. "I mean, we almost died in the name of ancient history, but we did just fine." I leave out the questionable rune we discovered and the rest of the strange things that have happened because, first off, it's none of his business and I'd rather drown than ask for his opinion. But more than that, because he's an Erikson. He'd be the last to throw me a life raft.

Reeve slams the emergency stop button on the elevator, making it jolt. It doesn't trigger my fear of heights, but plunging to my death is still not how I want to go out. I brace myself against the wall.

"I'm going to level with you," he says, and for once, he sounds serious.

"Could you not have leveled with me anywhere else?" I ask.

Literally anywhere else. Okay, so maybe I am afraid. I hate heights. Even small ones.

"If we plummet, the worst that would happen would be falling on your ass. Gravity might just make some of the mud and dirt fall out of your hair." He grins. So much for serious.

I flip him off. "Okay, do your leveling so I can get out of this death trap."

"You have no idea how desperately I want to jump in the air right now." He shoots me an evil smile.

"It'd be the last thing you do."

He chooses to lean against the wall instead and suddenly sobers. "You can't push Aric. He's seen multiple therapists, but he can't get past— " He sighs and leans in. "Shit, you take this to your grave, all right?"

"We're still dangling in the air here. Talk faster, Reeve."

"You remember after our parents died and after he rejected you and all that shit." Good reminder. Fantastic. "He was in his room sulking like Aric does, and it exploded. I'm not talking like, *oh look, a small gas leak, that's unfortunate*. He blew out the windows, the doors, melted his chair. The firefighters said it was a freak lightning strike."

I know he was struck by lightning. Everyone in the area does. It was a huge story when it happened. Not Aric's involvement, but about Sigurd's mansion catching fire.

Reeve shakes his head, and his light brown hair falls across his sculpted face and high cheekbones. "I ran in expecting flames, but everything was just ash. Everything but him. He was completely fine. Sort of."

"What do you mean, sort of?"

"He was angry, confused, and one thing I'll never forget."

"What?"

"His eyes," Reeve rasps. "They fucking glowed white."

I step closer to Reeve, feign a worried tone. "That sounds horrific. He must have been so scared." *Tell me more.*

Reeve pauses. "Actually, I think he thought it was pretty fucking cool, not that he ever used those words." Reeve hits the button, giving the elevator a jolt. My stomach jolts with it. "He said the lightning went straight through him."

"Do you believe him?"

He smirks over at me. "Don't forget, I, too, am in therapy."

When the doors open, I follow him out of the elevator. "But did he—"

"Ask him yourself." He shrugs. "That is, if you can get on his good side, which I guarantee you can't. He doesn't like people, mainly because his entire life people have either let him down or told him he was crazy… Well, that part's sort of on him. There was a while where he kept going on about visions. Freaky monsters, lots of dead bodies, a black-and-gold bridge. Didn't really help his case."

My body breaks out in an immediate cold sweat. "A bridge?"

He ignores me. "And that was before the attacks over the last year. Sigurd hasn't let him leave this area since last fall, did you know that? For his own protection?"

We stop at my door. "I didn't," I admit.

"Kidnapping attempts," Reeve drawls. He leans against the wall beside my door. "Know anything about those, daughter of Odin?"

No. But suddenly it makes sense—we learned about Mjölnir's location a year ago. Of course my father has been trying to get his hands on Aric ever since. And of course Sigurd wouldn't let his grandson off campus, outside his protection. I wonder if he's been adding runes for exactly that purpose—keeping my father away.

And that's why Odin sent me.

"So maybe don't push him so much," Reeve is saying. "He's fit to blow. This isn't one of those stories where you jump in to save the sinking ship. I love my brother, don't get me wrong, but he's not someone you can save. He's someone you run from. And whatever twisted little game your degenerate daddy is playing at…you won't win. Consider this my last warning."

"Wow," I say slowly. "You really care about him."

Reeve's eyebrows furrow. "Of course I do, Stjerne. Now go on. Maybe get into some warm clothes. And don't forget, tonight's the Nerf battle. It's one of the only fun things we do around here."

"Yeah." I nod slowly, considering it. "I'll see you in an hour or so."

"Make good choices." Reeve winks.

I quickly make it into my room and shut the door behind me.

Would truly ignoring Aric, giving him space, be a good choice?

And could I even walk away now if I wanted to?

Chapter Forty

REY

"Wow." Ziva eyes her rapid-strike Nerf gun appreciatively, then holds it up and attaches more ammo to her body.

Aric and Reeve are the team captains for the Berserkers. Shocker. Ziva and I volunteered for team Viking, while Eira's over collecting butterflies. Okay, not really, but I've seen her skip at least twice with her Nerf gun in the air, and she keeps aiming at Reeve. I can't tell if he thinks it's a threat or that she's suddenly set her sights on him.

Rowen's off on the side of the field monitoring, probably taking pictures to show my father I am in fact yet again "playing" when I should be hunting.

But I am—hunting, that is.

With all the chaos going on around us, it's not going to be hard to slip away during the game and do some investigating. First stop, Sigurd's office.

Why there? Because Mr. Collector of Creepy Rune Gardens may just have more of the ones I'm looking for.

If Sigurd is anything like my father, then he'd want to keep his treasures close.

Aric and Reeve walk over to position themselves across the line in the middle of the field. I point my gun at Aric's stomach and fire two shots. Gods, that felt good. "Sorry, I was just making sure it worked."

He narrows his eyes. Reeve steps in front of him. "Save the rage for the field, man, save it for the field."

Apparently, they run this tournament-style, with teams assigned to battle it out before progressing to the next tier. I can see a scoreboard and an array of sweaty students lingering along the sidelines. I wasn't expecting to go head-to-head with Aric's team in the first round, but win or lose, he'll be distracted.

Sigurd walks down the line between the two teams wearing a black track suit, paired once again with his Endir hat. "All right, the whole point is to capture the other team's flag in their territory. The Viking flag is in the dining hall, and the Berserker flag will be at the fountain."

That's on the same side of campus as the admin building. Not too close, but nearby.

"Safety first!" Sigurd warns. "And good sportsmanship. If you're hit with a Nerf dart, remove yourself from the game."

"An honor system among college students during a Nerf war," Ziva muses.

Yeah, it's gonna be a freaking free-for-all.

"You have ten minutes to come up with a plan of action," Sigurd tells us. "And yet again, welcome to— "

"Endir University," we all say in an array of bored tones.

He's already got us trained. Maybe that's his plan? Get the hammer, control the world, and fill it full of mindless drones.

"Lovely, lovely." Sigurd claps along as more cheers erupt around us.

I tilt my head and stare at the oblivious look on his face. "Can we shoot him?" I whisper.

Ziva lets out a long exhale. "Yeah, methinks he's perpetually high and completely oblivious of the world. I've heard you need to block shit out when you're a genius, evil or otherwise." She cocks her Nerf gun.

I try not to fixate on what Ziva said. I don't claim to be a genius, but I know what it's like to need the silence.

I sniff and ready my gun, taking a look around and grimacing.

Most of the people on my team look like they've never participated in organized sports a day in their life, let alone shot a Nerf gun. I'm betting they're gamers, though, and that's enough to work with.

I clear my throat. "All right, troops, gather round!"

I see some familiar faces from the welcome ceremony, and I smile encouragingly at Hector and Jillian the psych major as we collect our armbands. Yellow for us. Blue for the Berserkers.

"Raise your hand," I shout, "if you've ever played *Call of Duty*!"

Almost every hand pops up.

"Perfect. Just make sure you have good aim, enough ammo, and help each other if you run out."

I spin toward the right half of our group. "There's a nicely lit trail that most of you use as a shortcut from the dorms. They'll expect us to take it to get to the fountain faster. You have to be like the wind, offensive line. You hear me, Vikings? Run like Hel's hounds are coming for your souls!"

I turn to the middle of our group. "They're going to be hiding in the trees and bushes beyond the trail, using darkness as cover, so our best bet is to draw them into the open field and use the chaos to our advantage. That's where you'll come in, sacrificial distraction people. You, my brave and noble friends, will be our diversion. Some of you might get hit protecting others so they can push through, but just go with it."

I expect enthusiasm, but all I get are blank stares.

I clear my throat, then turn to my left. "You four, you're going to the dining hall. Guard our flag with your lives. Protect it at all costs." I snap my fingers. "Porn star guy, Jameson." He stands a bit straighter. "I'm not saying flash them if they get too close, but you were named that way for a reason. We all have a destiny!"

"Oh my word," Ziva mutters.

I spin to Gaby. "They're coming into your kitchen! You gonna let them take your cupcakes?"

She shakes her head.

"Homestead that shit, Gaby. I want you to go straight-up Amish on their asses."

Eira raises her hand, and I stare her down. "They killed your succulents."

She growls. "Blue Team is going down!"

"That's right. That's right! Okay, team, let's do this! There's no crying in baseball—or capture the flag. You hear me, people? Second place is still losing."

My team cheers.

And then a few seconds later, they're back to milling around.

I eye the scoreboard. Two minutes before we start.

I could've timed that better.

Ziva slow claps next to me. "Good speech. Amish are nonviolent, so, um, you kind of lost me there. I mean, I was totally with you for a little bit, then I got distracted by the idea that actual Vikings like our mascot would show up and lead us into battle in full uniform, but, like, old-school uniforms. Did they wear armor or were they shirtless? Whatever. It's my daydream. Shirtless it is."

All of us are in our respective corners when the timer goes off.

I run toward the trees, Eira and Ziva beside me. We cut past the fitness center and toward the dining hall, where Ziva pulls me behind the big oak tree for cover.

I lean against the bark and duck down—then everything seems to stop around me. I don't see Nerf guns anymore. I don't hear students laughing and cheering.

I see icy spears, red with blood, sticking out of the ground.

Blades covered in ice.

People with runes on their cheeks and blue lines dividing their mouths screaming in horror while the world burns around them—while the forests light up with orange flames.

The cries of sorrow, the stench of death, the destruction of a people.

Find me.

I close my eyes and put my hands over my ears, panicking when the vision suddenly stops. It's like what happened in Aric's room. Is it because I'm close to Mjölnir? It has to be nearby. Only Mjölnir remembers the battles and the bloodshed.

I snap my eyes open again when Eira starts pulling me up.

"Come on, Rey! Ziva is distracting them. Hurry!"

But I can't.

My gaze is glued to the oak tree. Amid initials and heart carvings in the dark bark is a single rune.

Hagalaz.

My lungs seize.

I don't know if it's from the rune or the harrowing vision that consumed me.

What the hell is going on? I can't catch my breath.

"Get your head in the game, soldier!" Ziva whispers, running toward us. She grabs my arm, tugging me behind her. "Let's go."

We join our small shield wall and run across the field, then disperse just like I'd planned. The Berserker team runs into the forest trails as predicted, and I hear laughter as people start getting caught.

"This way," Ziva calls, and Eira follows. A few of our enemies are hiding behind the bushes. I fire off a volley of shots and get two of them, but we're outnumbered. "Go! I'll cover you."

I lay down a peppering spray, mentally counting each dart so I'll know when to reload.

I watch as Aric leads his team toward the dining hall.

Of course he's on the offense. I can't imagine him doing anything else.

Reeve is right next to him, laughing and hollering like a banshee.

I spot Ziva and run ahead to the tree she's standing behind. "I'm going to see if there's anyone over by the building," I say. "It's pretty dark, and the other team could be hiding." It's a lie, but I need to break away from the crowd.

Thunder claps overhead. That can't be good.

"You've got this, Z. Get that flag!"

She salutes me and runs off.

We lost Eira, but I see some of our yellow team trickling out of the trail to run in the direction of the fountain. As they go left, I take a right.

I cut around the admin building toward the service door. Sure enough, it's open. There's an ashtray next to the garbage can and the lingering smell of something stronger than cigarettes.

I glance around quickly, then slip inside.

The directory on the wall spells out the rooms. President's office. Third floor.

I dip into the stairwell and take them as quietly as I can. When I get to the door leading to the third floor, I look behind me to make sure nobody's following me, then quietly set my Nerf gun down on the ground by the door to hold it ajar. Sigurd's office is just up ahead.

I pass all the creepy antlers and lean down to examine the lock I'm about to pick. I grab the doorknob, and suddenly, the door shoves open. That was unexpected.

Everything's blanketed in darkness except for the sliver of moonlight peeking out from the dark curtains lighting up Sigurd's massive mahogany desk. I take a step back. Are those nail marks on the top? Why the hell would he be clawing at his desk?

I peer closer. Six rune paperweights are lined in a perfect circle around his computer. I raise my hand toward the circle, and the shock is enough to have me jerking my hand back.

Damn.

Okay. Well, it's not like I had time to hack into the system anyway. I wonder how he'd explain that to any humans or custodians who came in here. Or maybe there are other wards that would keep people away entirely. I peer at the line of stones.

Raido. Dagaz.

The very runes that appeared with Aric. Both times I was with him.

Coincidence? Not a chance. And yet...the rest of the runes next to them don't match the ones in Laufey's note.

I start opening drawers, quick but careful. If Sigurd's anything like my father, he keeps his sins tucked away in plain sight. And I need leverage. All of it.

Top drawer—pens, ledgers, receipts. The second drawer holds a small black notebook, completely blank. Suspiciously blank, like it's waiting for ink only he can see. My pulse picks up.

I sift deeper. Stacks of student files—color-coded tabs with names I half recognize from orientation. Attendance, grades...and strange annotations in the margins. "Potential?"

Potential for what?

One file is flagged twice. Aric's.

At the very back, shoved under a pile of old syllabi, there's something heavier. A small iron key. I lift it, cold biting into my palm. What does it unlock?

I scan the office again, seeing books, artifacts, and ancient pottery.

But there must be something special here—

"Have you found anything interesting yet?"

Chapter Forty-One

REY

I instantly relax at the sound of Aric's voice, which is absurd. My plan hinges on making him relax around me. Not the other way around.

I don't pull out the knife strapped beneath my shorts, reaching instead for a book. "Yes, well, just catching up on my reading," I lie. Not one of my best, but…I'm committed to it now. I tuck the book under my arm. "If that's all?" I purposefully brush against him as I pass to see if frost appears, if he reacts.

"The book. Now," he grounds out. "Hand it over."

When I turn, the moonlight's sliced across half of his face, bathing it in silver. His brown eyes almost glow. Somewhere in the distance, I hear a clap of thunder.

"Why aren't you outside playing with your brother? Kinda hard to win from in here—"

"Hand over the book, Rey!" His voice thunders in the room, making the chandelier shake above us. Shit. He's terrifying when he's angry. It's almost like he grows a few inches right before my very eyes.

Slowly, I pull the book out.

He tosses it aside and braces his arms on the wall on either side of me, pinning me in. I swear a bit of frost coats his bottom lip where he's just licked it.

He might still be sleeping, but his power definitely isn't.

"Hello? Is someone here?"

A voice picks up from the hallway, and his eyes widen. We both look around, but there's nowhere to hide a six-foot-six man in this tiny space.

An older woman walks into the office. I recognize her right away as Professor Higgins, one of the speakers from Sigurd's welcome ceremony. Her speech then was clipped, rigid, no-nonsense, and she's giving off that same energy now.

Great.

Her sharp eyes find me instantly.

"I—I was with Aric," I blurt, scrambling. Shit, this doesn't look good.

"The president's office is not open to students, even for you, Aric." Professor Higgins crosses her arms.

Aric tenses next to me, and I can feel the anger rolling off him in waves. I wrap an arm around his waist. He's freezing and so tense it's like hugging steel.

He pulls me to his side, steady, his voice even, eyes still wild. "It's true. We were talking and just needed a little privacy."

I grip his shirt, clinging to him. I'm not sure why he's helping me, but the last thing I need is for Sigurd to know I was snooping around.

Professor Higgins's frown deepens. "I knew something was off about you visiting your grandfather earlier, Aric. You never visit. And now this—" She launches into a tirade about the Erikson boys' lack of discipline, the disrespect of desecrating President Sigurd's office, her voice sharp and cutting. Every word grates against Aric's patience. I feel him tense, his anger coiling tighter, the air growing colder. Rain starts pelting the office window.

I grip his hand like it's the only thread tethering him to this reality. To the present. To me.

"Calm down," I whisper.

"Can't," he growls.

It's not just a word. It feels like a dark warning.

His voice carries weight, full of a rage that's just waiting to be unleashed. I don't like it. I don't like the way he's suddenly losing it.

I shove my Aethercall toward him—fast, desperate, forceful.

But it does nothing. It's almost a palpable sensation, like it bounces off him.

Shit.

I yank the Aethercall back and throw it toward Professor Higgins, and she stumbles back like she's been hit. Whoops, maybe I did too much?

I glance over at Aric, and his eyes slam into mine, worried, volatile, and slowly turning whiter by the second. Frost starts to faintly glow on his lips.

"If your parents could see you now," Professor Higgins continues. What the hell is wrong with this woman? "After everything they sacrificed for you, and here you are sneaking around and—"

Nope. Absolutely not. Aric is going to explode.

I grab him by the back of the neck and crush our mouths together. Maybe passion and surprise will take away the anger, at least enough for us to get out of here.

I expect him to freeze.

I do not anticipate his warm tongue.

Or the way his lips mold against mine.

His arms tighten around me, and for one dizzying heartbeat, the world falls away. He tastes like winter and mint. His lips are soft, much softer than I expected, and the stroke of his tongue is so fucking hot I almost lift off my feet. My breath catches, and Aric tightens his arms, hauling me flush against his strong body.

Tension pulses like an erratic heartbeat through the room, lights flicker overhead, and the temperature plummets around us. I sure as hell don't expect myself to react to him so violently that I momentarily forget we have an audience or why I'm kissing him.

I pull back and break the kiss. "We have to go!"

He frowns while I hold up our hands.

Already, ice is forming across his skin.

"Now!" I jerk him toward the door while Professor Higgins is still momentarily stunned and sputtering behind us.

I'll let Aric deal with her later.

For now, we need to get him hidden before he loses complete control.

He's shaking, his grip hard like stone as we run down the stairs and out of the building. It was dark in the room, so there's a chance she didn't see the ice on his skin or his eyes. With the thunder and lightning of the surprise storm, maybe she'd even chalk it up to a trick of the light.

When we make it outside, a jagged line of ice cracks through the sidewalk, disappearing into the grass and nearby forest. I follow it. A few people from capture the flag are running, trying to escape the rain, so it doesn't look strange for us to join in. Careful to get past the majority of the crowd, I tug Aric into the thicker part of the forest, away from the trails.

The wind howls as the sky splits with lightning.

He jerks his hand away from mine and starts punching the tree in front of us.

Over and over and over again.

Silver blood appears, only to re-heal as more ice forms on his knuckles.

His chest heaves, teeth clench like he's trying so hard to hold everything in but break free at the same time. With a roar, he falls to his knees, lightning splintering from the sky and streaming directly into Aric, followed by another strike into the tree closest to me.

Holy shit. Is he okay?

But I don't have the chance to move before his arms are around me. My back hits the ground, his hands moving to protect the back of my head in a gesture that I don't fully understand but makes heat bloom inside me nonetheless.

We roll across the rocks and pine needles, away from the damaged tree. His clothes are ripped, singed by the lightning, and his body shields me while branches burn beside us.

His glowing eyes lock on my mouth before slowly fading back to their normal brown.

There's no way he's still sleeping.

I say nothing.

He's breathing hard, his eyes wild, body rippling with the remnants of his power.

He's beautiful.

I blink up at him and wince. "Thanks for the save."

His chest heaves as he leans over me. "I didn't want you to die without owing me," he says in a gravelly voice.

"Wow, how thoughtful." I lean up on my elbows until our faces are inches apart. "Hey. Are you okay? The lightning—"

"I'm fine," he says. "That wasn't what it looked like. It didn't get me."

That was *exactly* what it looked like, and we both know it. But I *do* owe him, so I let it drop, giving him a small, knowing smile and a nod.

His eyes drop to my mouth.

I smirk. "Sorry about the kiss."

"I might have nightmares about that." He says it jokingly, but it feels off, like his head is still back in that office. Still going over the horrible things Professor Higgins said.

He turns away and rakes a hand through his hair, giving me a clear view of his back through the shredded remains of his shirt.

My breath catches.

Runes.

And this time, there are most definitely two. In the caves, the second looked faded, or like it hadn't taken shape yet, but they're clear as day now, faintly glowing down his spine.

Raido and Dagaz in all their splendor.

They look angry.

They look new.

Chapter Forty-Two

REY

The world goes completely still around me.

My hands shake as I think back on the note.

Raido first. Then Dagaz.

That leaves Hagalaz, Othala, and Thurisaz.

It's time Aric and I had a chat. Laid our cards on the table.

And since we just bled, burned, kissed, and shielded each other in the wreckage of a tree, maybe—just maybe—now's as good a time as any.

"C'mon," he says. "Let's get out of this rain."

As we slowly start making our way back toward campus, I wonder: Does he know what the runes mean? Are these tattoos my path to Mjölnir? I mean, I'm not entirely sure how I activated them, but…

It can't be that easy.

The lack of information from my father makes me think he doesn't have all the answers, either. He probably never did. Doesn't change anything, though—I need the hammer. Aric's the key to finding it. And I have to trust that Laufey's note will guide me.

I lengthen my stride to try and keep pace with the Giant. Aside from the scent of woodsmoke in the air and that faint smell of ozone that comes after a storm, the woods are calm.

The noise increases as we draw closer to campus, though, and I make out whistles and bullhorns, hollers and… Is that music? By the time we make it out to the field, it's like we never left. Students are still screaming and cheering, their wet hair and clothes the only indication they got caught in the same storm as we did.

Reeve's team is celebrating in the middle of the field. Guess they managed to capture the flag. They stop when they see us approach. "Was there another battle we weren't aware of?" he asks.

"Why are you wearing half a shirt?" Eira tilts her head at Aric. "Did you set yourself on fire?"

Everyone laughs.

I join in because, well, kind of?

I probably look just as bad, with dirt and pine needles in my hair. Honestly, I'm surprised Ziva hasn't asked how our romp in the woods went. Save for his shirt, that's exactly what we look like, guilt and all.

Aric's still lightly trembling next to me. I can't tell if he's traumatized, pissed, or both. Eira grabs at Reeve's arm. "Eriksons like it rough, huh?"

Ziva makes a face. "Dude, he looks hurt, read the room."

Aric shrugs, but his eyes are wild, like he's daring anyone to say another word. "We're fine. Looks like we won. Go blue."

Thunder cracks overhead, and lightning streaks across the sky.

Sigurd sounds an airhorn. "Due to the risk of lightning," he shouts, "we need to clear the field. The rest of tonight's festivities are canceled." He shoots a glare at Aric. "Be sure to check your orientation week schedules. And mark your calendars for the Wild Hunt!"

Another rumble of thunder has the crowds of students dispersing.

I chance a glance at Aric.

I can't shake how right it felt to be in his arms. But that's just delusional.

There's no world in which this works out. I know that. He does, too. So why is my heart beating so fast? Why do I want to lean toward him instead of away?

I swallow hard.

Why do I *care* whether or not he's okay?

As our group starts to walk along the path toward the dorms, I fall into step. Reeve is waving his Nerf gun in the air and recounting his great victory like it's one for the ages. Eira is hanging on his every word. Rowen and Ziva just look bored.

As we come toward that creepy basalt arch, the one that blew out my candle, I pause.

We're past the point of pretending. Past the point of retreating to our separate corners.

There's only one way forward.

"Aric," I call out. "Can I talk to you really quick?"

Reeve stops next to him and says something under his breath. Aric shakes his head, then shoves Reeve ahead of him. He turns and crosses his arms as the rest of the group continues on. "You needed something?"

The third rune. A test. It's time to reveal Hagalaz, and I know just the person to recruit.

It's time to risk exposing everything.

"You." I cross my arms. "I need you, and to be more specific, I need a Giant."

Chapter Forty-Three

ARIC

A *Giant.*

I exhale when she says the word. There's power in someone knowing who you are, in someone confirming your truth. A smile curves my lips. "What gave it away? The lightning? The frost? Both?"

Every muscle trembles beneath my skin, my body still recovering from losing control, from the anger and the storm that followed. When I thought I was going to lose it in front of Professor Higgins, it was Rey who reined me in. Her kiss, her voice, everything she did tethered my emotions in a way that kept me present, kept me calm enough to hold it together, at least temporarily.

"Wow." For just a second, her expression shows surprise, but then she grins. "Thank you for the confirmation."

I shrug. Hiding is so fucking exhausting. "It's not really a secret what I am—at least not to you." Then why do I suddenly feel thrilled to be seen? "I mean, maybe to the outside world, but you are Odin's daughter."

Which makes this whole situation so much worse.

I should've let her burn. I should've felt no emotion. But she tried to protect me in my grandfather's office and again when we entered the woods. Most would have let me destroy myself.

When my control broke and lightning struck the tree, my instinct was to protect her. So I did. I just reacted.

I told Sigurd to give me another chance to prove my loyalty to the family, to do what I couldn't two years ago—and first chance I got, I *saved* my enemy.

But seen another way, maybe I *didn't* waffle on my vow. I protected Rey—because she's a means to an end.

My powers are unlocking, and the runes lighting up my back are proof of that. For some reason, she seems to be the key. If I can control it, maybe I can channel it toward Odin and kill him once and for all. Wouldn't that be sweet justice? Using his daughter to ultimately destroy him seems fair to me.

I glance at her. She's hugging her arms around herself. And suddenly, it feels like my heart has cracked in two.

I'm not sure what I've said or done to make her eyes cast down and her lower lip tremble. Not two minutes ago, she was boldly saying she needed me. Well, I guess technically, I did almost kill her, so that might've done it? Delayed response to nearly dying, maybe?

She bites down on her lower lip, and then in the next second, she's composed again. Maybe not dressed in posh clothes with her hair all sleek and makeup on, but even without that, her armor's back in place. I'm almost glad for it.

The thought of Rey Stjerne crying is a terrifyingly sad thing.

Shit.

It would mean she was finally broken.

It would mean I had a part in the breaking. Why does that make my heart clench? Why is hating her getting harder and harder the more time I spend with her?

Other students thread around us on the path. My shirt's torn. She has mud on her clothes and leaves in her hair. We're both a mess. Funny thing, though—no one seems to notice.

"You said you need me, Rey. You planning to elaborate?"

She grabs my arm and pulls me past the library, down the trail, until we're alone again. The wind bites colder here, moonlight bleeding through the trees. But the storm has passed—both the one above us and the one in me. She stops by the old oak near Dallas Hall, the bark covered with carvings of students' initials—all except one that's in the very middle.

Hagalaz—it stands out because it's larger, but also because nobody dares draw anywhere near it.

I don't know why, but I feel drawn to it, like it's familiar to me for some reason.

"What does that one mean?" Rey asks, watching my interest. She points at Hagalaz. "Isn't your grandfather some sort of rune expert?" Her eyes are sharp, searching.

I swallow, jaw tight. "You tell me. You're the one with all the answers, right?"

"Not all of them." She steps closer, lowering her voice. "We need to test it. To see what it does to you."

My laugh is hollow. "Because lightning strikes and burning trees aren't enough experiments for one night?"

"Aric." The seriousness in her voice draws my attention, and our gazes collide. "I need to show you something."

She takes out her phone, goes around to my back.

"Stand still."

I frown. "What's this really about? Why do you need me?"

She's in front of me again, holding up her phone. She doesn't flinch when she says, "I need to know if there's a reason I have a note from the only woman who's ever acted like a parent to me that matches *these.*"

On her phone is a photo of my back. With a new rune tattooed next to the first one.

The blood in my veins turns to ice.

Rey continues. "Before school started, before I was given my assignment by my father, she secretly handed me a note, risking a lot, probably even her life. I need to know if it's connected, and if it is… Are you with me?"

"You're going to have to give me more than that, Rey."

"The thunder." She locks eyes with me. "The lightning storms, the frost, all of it—what if I can tell you it's connected and that I can help. Will you help me?"

The words scrape at me. Because I want it to be that simple—and it isn't. I expected a fight, half-truths made to look like reality. "You want me to *trust* you?"

She nods slowly.

I'd laugh, but nothing about this is funny.

"And does this trust extend both ways?" I eye her carefully.

"It will."

Hmm. "I'll help you," I finally force out. It's the best I can do. "For now. But I need something in return."

Her brow arches. "Nothing's free, Giant." Her smile is unguarded, stunning. I almost stumble backward in disbelief. How can a simple smile unarm me that much?

I look away. "I want answers Sigurd won't outright give. I want to know the real reason behind the runes on my back. I want to know what my parents died for, because no chance in hell was it an accident, and you know it." She says nothing. "I'm changing, becoming something different," I admit. "Before, I could control myself. But it's nearly impossible to keep up now, and with the runes—well, you saw what just happened back at that tree."

Her lips part, then curve into something that looks too much like pity. "Is this where I'm supposed to tell you that you're a special sort of Frost Giant and give you a high five and pat on the ass?"

I bark out a laugh, but it sounds wrong in my own ears. "Work on your bedside manner, doc. And I don't know. Whatever power's inside of me, I just need to understand what it is." I know I'm being vague, but trust isn't something I can just turn on at will.

It'll have to be earned.

I look away, jaw grinding. *Focus*. "And you? What do you want?"

She hesitates, eyes glinting in the moonlight before she finally answers. "My theory? You actually have *five* runes on your back, but only two are unlocked right now, so you can see them. Each one that unlocks wakes up your sleepy-powerful self a little more. Until your power's unleashed fully and you either go boom"—she flicks her hand like an explosion—"or you're finally free."

My heart pounds double-time at her words. It'd either be my end... or my new beginning.

"After that," Rey continues with a nonchalance I know can't be real, "you'll know exactly where to find it—my reward."

My gut knots. "Find what exactly?"

Her arms cross over her chest as she leans against a tree. Calm. Deadly. "The most powerful weapon in the world. Something that was stolen from us. Something I need to get back in order to save the people I love."

I freeze. "The most powerful weapon in the world?"

And she what? Is just going to keep it and never use it? I know she wants my trust, but this is too much.

She nods, eyes sharp. "My weapon. My family's weapon. One that was stolen during a bloody war both of our families were tangled in. Mjölnir's been hidden away, and your runes, I think...they're the map. Except someone locked you down. As long as you stay quiet, controlled, normal, the perfect weapon stays hidden, too."

The words crush me, heavier than the storm still growling above.

"And what if I'm not a weapon?" I whisper. "What if I'm the opposite of everything you need? What if I'm the villain? The monster?"

Rey's composure slips. "Then I guess we face it head-on. Together. Besides, we're all born with a little bit of monster inside us. Who says that's a bad thing? Something has to save us from ourselves."

Her mouth tilts, the faintest hint of a smile appearing on her lips. I like it more than I know I should, how easy and pretty it is, how desperately I suddenly want to be the reason for it.

"And it's not Hyde that does the saving. It's Jekyll."

Her words hang in the air, as dangerous as they are comforting.

And I don't know if the storm inside me is fear...or hope.

Chapter Forty-Four

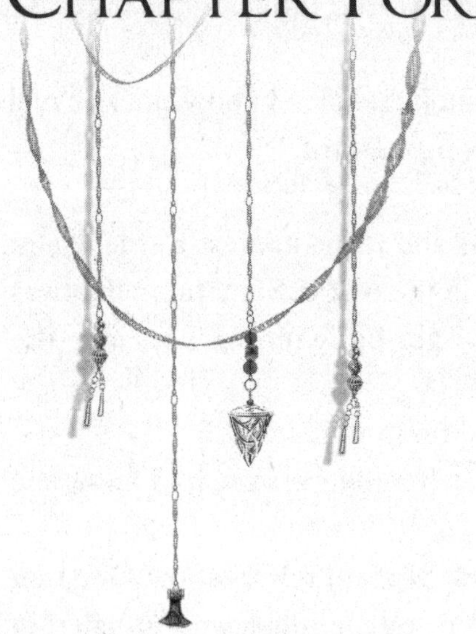

ARIC

I stand in front of the carved rune she says should be the third one, its lines faint in the moonlight. I brace myself, reach out, and brush Hagalaz with my fingertips.

Nothing.

The silence is so complete, it's unnerving. No crackle of power, no storm breaking loose—just the sound of my own breath.

Rey exhales, her voice soft. "It must be terrifying…knowing you can wake up from a dream but not knowing what you're waking up as. It's fitting, I suppose, that Hagalaz is the third rune."

She steps closer, eyes locked on the symbol. "It means awakening, awareness, hope, balance, transformation…" Her words trail off, then harden. "It's the point of no return, Aric. The moment where you either look back and walk away—or move forward."

The bark is rough beneath my hand as I trace the lines again. My throat feels dry. "If everything you're saying is true and I find Mjölnir… can I wield it?"

She says nothing.

I glance down at her. "Can *you*?"

Her teeth catch her lower lip, and she shrugs, hesitation written all over her tight jaw.

Could she wield it? How does a weapon weigh one's worth? Her blood would call to the hammer…

Blood. In the Hall of Ormir, in the Ice Caves.

We bled.

Finally, she shrugs. "A truce for now. We work together until we find it. You have your reasons. I have mine. And once you're fully awake and we find Mjölnir…" She nods, almost to herself. "We go back to our respective sides."

"Back to our own enemy camps," I say to myself.

She turns away, voice quieter now. "I don't think we have a choice. Do you?"

I stare at the rune, at the darkness pressing in all around us. "Something tells me people die either way. I know I'm not supposed to care, but now that I taste this—the thunder, the lightning in my body, the way I can barely control myself without snapping? It's not calming, Rey. It's like standing on the edge of a storm that never ends." I drag in a heavy breath. "Maybe you're right. Maybe you wake a sleeping Giant and the world rights itself. Maybe I kill Odin…and spare you."

She lets out a sharp laugh, though her eyes don't shine with humor. "Straight to murder, huh?"

"To avenge my parents, yes."

"At least you're honest about it."

We both know all bets are off once we find Mjölnir, and we both know nobody walks away innocent in this age-old war. Nobody.

But I nod. Agreement. Truce.

I pull my tactical knife from my pocket, slice open my palm, and press it against the bark, where Hagalaz begins to glow. Blood seeps into the grooves. She doesn't hesitate—taking my knife, she cuts her hand, too, pressing it beside mine against the bark.

The rune flares, blinding white. The tree hums with energy beneath our palms as if it's breathing with us.

And then searing pain rakes down my back.

Chapter Forty-Five

REY

Aric bends forward, heaving, shouting out in pain.

"Aric!" My hands fly to his shoulders, then his back, my gasp tearing through the night.

The sound of a branch snapping jolts us both out of the moment. We whirl toward the noise, my heart hammering, the rune still glowing behind us.

Before either of us can react, though, a figure in all black darts from the shadows, sprinting down the path. Their movements are fluid, fast—too fast. By the time I take a step forward, though, they're already vanishing into the trees.

We don't even bother chasing. We wouldn't catch them.

Dread sinks into my belly. Just how much did that person see? And what were they doing following us?

"Too spry to be Professor Higgins, but still, add another person to the list," I mutter, clutching my bleeding palm.

Aric frowns, breath uneven, seemingly from the pain he's still in. "What list?"

I scan the dark campus. "Of people who don't like our families."

Aric barks out a laugh. "That's gotta be a very long one. To save time, just write down 'everyone.'" Then he sobers and glances across the grounds. I follow his gaze, staring at the silent windows, at the looming halls where shadows watch but never speak. My chest tightens. So many secrets in the still silence, so many unspoken truths. "Even those closest to us."

I shudder, voice barely above a whisper. "*Especially* those closest to us."

The storm rumbles overhead, punctuating the truth neither of us wants to admit.

He glances at my bleeding palm, then covers it with his uninjured hand. A chill runs down my arm at the touch.

And when I pull my hand away, it's healed.

It's obvious he knows so much more about himself, the situation, and my family than I've been led to believe. But I'm focused more on my hand, which still tingles where he healed it, and the fact that when I asked, he didn't lie. He laid his cards on the table and trusted me.

I'm still on edge as we walk back to the dorms. Aric with his tattered shirt on and three runes shining beneath it and me stunned he's agreed to help me find Mjölnir. I should feel relieved.

I can save Laufey and myself, I can finally make my father proud, and yet, am I really grabbing the most powerful weapon in the world for Odin?

And are the Giants who hid it really going to let him give it to me without a fight? Will we even have a choice, or will Mjölnir make it for us?

"So," I say, trying to restart some semblance of the truce we had in the woods, "is this new for you?"

He arches a brow.

"The stalker in the woods. Someone coming after you, watching you?"

He rubs his chin as we finally make it closer to our dorms. "I've had my moments. Do you think they saw anything?"

I shrug. "If they did, we can just say they were drunk. I mean, who would believe them? They saw us slice our hands and cover a rune that then lit up. Would *you* believe them?"

"Yes, but I know what I am."

"Same." I glance around. "According to my father, there are more people like us here, but since the Bifrost is—"

Am I really just spilling secrets now?

He smirks. "Broken. You can say it."

Wow. Okay. I've clearly been misled into thinking he's ignorant of these things. But just how much he knows isn't clear.

"Right. Okay," I say as I process. "So they don't have access to their power or memories, and they just cheerfully exist here, powerless and… happy? I guess?"

"Why wouldn't they be?"

"Is Sigurd? Odin? Happy with their memories, I mean? I'm assuming since you know who you are, Sigurd does, too," I fish. No reaction. Not even a flash of emotion on his face. "Is he happier, though, for it?"

Aric frowns now. "Sometimes I think having tasted true power makes you angrier when it suddenly gets ripped from you."

"Undoubtedly."

We both stare up at the admin building. "History has a tragic way of repeating itself," Aric murmurs. "Do you really think our story will end any differently?"

"I do," I say, and I actually mean it. "Because *I'm* the outlier here. Mjölnir will recognize my blood, and I have something Odin doesn't."

"What's that?" he asks.

"A heart," I whisper.

Chapter Forty-Six

REY

Ever since the third rune appeared on Aric's back, my chest has been hurting. It's deeper than a physical pain, though, more like I'm missing something that even I don't know I ever had. Maybe as his runes awaken, so does my blood?

It's left me with that ever-present ache, combined with a soul-deep sense of loneliness as I sit in my dorm room alone.

I've always been used to being alone, craved it most of the time when living in that house with a monster. But right now, I just want to be held. Which is ridiculous, because when was the last time anyone held me? Ever? I mean, Rowen will hug me sometimes, but this is different.

I'm talking about the soul-crushing sort of holding where you know the person has been searching their entire life for you. That even one second in their arms would be better than never having them at all.

I read a lot about love.

I haven't ever experienced it. Not romantically, at least. One-night stands, either to scratch an itch or to piss off my father, don't count, and both times were so disappointing I cried myself to sleep, wondering if I'd ever find someone who made me feel like I belonged.

Always the outsider.

Always the weapon.

Always the dutiful daughter.

Sleep. I need sleep, and even without a life-or-death quest on my hands, I have a packed day of classes tomorrow and a report on Ice Caves to write.

With Aric.

Yes, thinking of papers and classes and friends and relationships is ridiculous. It's all going to be over soon—more than likely, it's going to be literally *over*. But it's not really about doing the coursework. It's about him, getting close to him. And if I'm enjoying it—if I like pretending these friendships can exist beyond this week—well, sue me.

Would spending a few more days together before a possible tragic ending really be the worst thing?

My father hasn't texted me since this afternoon, so maybe he's having a good day. I can only pray Laufey is keeping his tantrums, his nightmares at bay. Her only power as a Giant is that of healing, both mentally and physically, but I see the toll it takes on her every single time she uses her power on Odin.

It drains her.

It will eventually kill her, compounded by her sickness and my father's abuse. Maybe not for a while, but still, getting Mjölnir is about more than finding a weapon. It's about freedom.

Once it's in my hands, though…then what? Once Laufey is secure, I dread just giving Odin what he wants. A weapon that would make him all-powerful.

I shake my head. I feel like I'm missing something. I pull out the dossier my father gave me and start reading.

Multiple hammers were forged before Mjölnir. The first two nearly split Asgard in half when Thor tried to wield them. The text reads that they weren't tethered, that he was too young, too volatile, that the training to help him control their power only made them more unstable and unpredictable. Interesting. It doesn't seem like the runes are what's making Aric volatile.

And the rune responded to me.

To its identity.

More importantly, it's responding to our blood.

Am I somehow helping stir the storm inside Aric? And what happens if all the memories, his own and the ones of Mjölnir, slam into him at once? Would that kill someone? We haven't talked about it directly, but I suspect part of Aric's powers being dormant may be to protect him.

Then again, the lightning didn't kill him, so maybe he's protected already. How nice for Aric, I think, to have a destiny, a purpose, a clear map of runes to show him the way, and the protection of the ultimate weapon that somehow, out of all the people on this godforsaken planet, chose him.

I've only ever been chosen for death.

I wonder if this is Aric's chance to choose life.

Chapter Forty-Seven

ARIC

The knock is so loud I nearly fall out of bed. A quick glance at the clock tells me it's still the middle of the night. If it's Reeve, drunk and wanting to chat, I'm going to murder him. Heart pounding, I fling the door open.

Rey stands there. Barefoot. Blank-eyed. Vulnerable. Looking like every victim in a crime show right before the other shoe drops.

She's holding a chipped mug that says *Cats Are People, Too*. Without a word, she brushes past me, heads to my sink, fills the mug with water, and chugs it like she's been lost in a desert for a week. It pours down her chin, splashing across her bare legs, which just makes me realize how bare they are.

Legs. Bare legs. Where the hell are her pants?

My gaze jerks upward. She's in nothing but underwear and a silk pajama top that swallows her small frame while simultaneously hugging to every detail. I can see her nipples peeking through the fabric, and my mouth goes dry.

"Rey?" My voice cracks. "Rey, wake up. Seriously. I don't want to die in my sleep, and neither do you. Just…go back to your room."

She doesn't listen. Just pushes at my chest with the mug still in her hand, shoving me back toward the bed. Is this some sort of weird side effect of unlocking the third rune? Before I can react, she crawls in beside me, dragging me with her, pinning me to the wall.

"Rey," I warn. I'd agreed that, for a while at least, we could be on the same side. I didn't mean the same side of the fucking bed.

Don't think about her legs. This is one complication we don't need to add to the mix. "Don't make me carry you—"

She throws a leg over me, anchoring me in place.

And suddenly I'm calm.

So calm.

Just like I was when she kissed me in Sigurd's office, when she tried to get me to stop reacting. Just like I was when we touched the third rune.

What if we just let ourselves?

To rest like this with her.

To drown in the quiet she brings amid the chaos. Her weight against me is steady, grounding, like the storm in my blood is finally silent—not just silent, at peace.

Her breath feathers against my neck. "Just five minutes," she whispers, voice thick with sleep.

And Gods help me, my eyes grow heavy.

Maybe death would be worth whatever sleep follows this.

The last thing I think of is a home I don't even know, with trees so tall they blot out the sun. Branches tangled in silver frost that never melts. Jagged icy mountains rise in the distance with their peaks swallowed up by storm clouds. The air smells like iron and snow, yet beneath it lingers the warmth of pine smoke, like a fire burning just out of reach. Like the warm feeling of the sunrays—like the warm touch of Rey.

I jerk awake when my alarm goes off, and two things happen at once. Rey looks up at me from the bed and screams, while simultaneously punching me in the face.

"Son of a bitch!" I roar. "What the actual fuck, woman. It's too early for this shit! Get out of my room!"

She stumbles out of the bed, collapsing on the ground before getting up and shouting again. "Why am I *in* your room? Your *bed*!" she roars back. Okay, so she was definitely sleepwalking, then.

I rub my sore eye. "Right, it definitely tracks that I just went over to your room, picked your lock, grabbed your feisty little body, careful not to forget the very un-Rey-Stjerne-like cat mug, and decided to use you as a teddy bear. Do I look like I want to sleep with a prickly, knife-wielding cactus?"

She retreats toward the door, opening it slightly to leave, but then turns back. "I happen to *like* that cat mug, thank you very much. And why am I a cactus? And they don't carry knives, Aric! They have...pointy things that, you know— *Shit*, what are their names again? It's early. Why am I here, why am I here with *you*, why am I not—"

"You should wear pants to sleep, Rey. Seriously."

Wrong thing to say. Her eyes immediately darken like she's going to stab me with her knife after all.

She jumps a foot when a knock sounds at the door. Then someone pushes it the rest of the way open.

Reeve waltzes in with a coffee in hand and then stops dead in his tracks, his head swiveling back and forth between us. His mouth opens.

"Say. Nothing," I hiss, voice heavy with sleep and annoyance. Where are the storms now? One would think lightning would strike right between us in this moment.

He holds up his coffee. "I didn't. My breath was bated, but I have the restraint of a much older man. So what, did she crawl out of a coffin to come and murder you, or was this a...planned event?"

I shoot him a glare. "I was sleeping in peace when Stalker Stjerne—"

"Has a nice ring to it." He laughs.

"I thought so, too." I smirk.

"Hey!" Rey yells.

"Anyway," I continue, "this one makes her way over here, drinks my water out of her weird cat mug, then pins me to my bed and... sleeps."

"Oh, she *sleeps*." Reeve winks. "Got it."

"No, that's not code for sex, Reeve. She literally kept me prisoner and slept."

"Please!" Rey grabs one of my sweatshirts and tugs it on. "Like I'm strong enough to pin you to anything. You're a Giant!"

Her face pales like she knows she just called me out, but Reeve doesn't so much as flinch.

He knows I come from a strong bloodline, and that's all Sigurd has trusted him with. My protection at all costs. It's a level of secrecy he's always been fine with, especially since my accident. Reeve isn't really the type to ponder the mysteries of the world.

I frown. "Yeah, I know I'm pretty tall, but you're still scrappy and strong, and I may have also fallen asleep. It was a rough night."

"Unbelievable!" She stomps her foot. "Both of you." She eyes Reeve, then his coffee. "I'll just take that and be on my way."

It's out of his hands before he can do or say anything. The door slams behind her, leaving me feeling guilty for doing...literally nothing.

Reeve leans against the door. "She pinned you? How, again, did she manage that? I'm genuinely curious, because one six-six guy plus one five-foot-nothing girl? The math isn't checking out."

I groan and throw a pillow at him. "She was sleepwalking."

"Sure." He nods, but then all the teasing leaves his face. "You going to be okay today? After last night's storm, I mean." I don't answer. He clears his throat and tries again. "So, runes on your back, hmm?"

I nod, unsure of how much to tell him beyond the bare bones I texted him late last night. "You know I have abilities."

"I know." He crosses his arms. "Does Sigurd know about..." He nods toward the rumpled bed.

"Sigurd knows I'm playing the long game." It's not a total lie. "Sometimes it's better to keep the enemy close, you know?"

Reeve makes a face. "I don't think Sigurd meant naked close, but you do you—and her, apparently."

I glare at him. "It was an accident. But still, what better way to gain the upper hand than get her to trust me with everything—mind, body, soul." I feel dirty, repulsive saying it, but I can't trust anyone. Not even myself.

This is the first time I'm doing something on my own, the first time Sigurd is trusting me with something huge since the broken engagement. I'm not going to mess up. Besides, she's leading me to a very real way to finally kill her father: Mjölnir. We'll trade a life for a life. His blood will be spilled, as it should have been years ago. I'll wipe him from this world—just like he wiped out my parents.

This doesn't go against my truce with Rey. If anything, she should thank me for it.

Reeve sighs and snaps his fingers. "Shirt off. Let's take a look."

"You're not a doctor, and it's not like I have a disease." I keep my shirt firmly on.

One eyebrow arches. "Dude, I'm your brother. Color me curious. Plus, not everyone can say their brother can build a snowman out of his ass."

"I have never once built a snowman out of my ass."

"Pipe dream." Reeve winks. "Seriously, show me."

I sigh, peel off my shirt, and turn. The cold air bites against my skin as I wait.

Silence.

When I glance back at him, his face has gone pale, eyes locked on the runes carved into me like brands. "Interesting mix of runes, Aric. Very interesting mix."

He leans back, studying me as if weighing a choice.

"Hope you know what you're doing with Rey." His voice dips, serious now. "She may seem nice, but the Stjernes killed our parents without hesitation. Have you ever asked yourself why? What they knew that got them slaughtered? We all know it wasn't an accident."

The words land heavy, sharper than I would have expected.

"This isn't child's play, Aric. Odin Stjerne is powerful. Never forget what he controls in this..." He hesitates, just for a second. "City."

I frown. City? Reeve covers it with a smile, but the slip prickles down my spine, his hesitation and sudden amusement making me pause.

"We're safe here," Reeve continues. "Endir's gates protect us. Sigurd sees to that. But be careful with Pandora's box, brother." His eyes focus on my back again. "You can't shut it once you open it. And when you do…" His grin twists, almost eager. "How else do worlds end? Chaos."

The word lingers between us, bitter like he released a curse into the air.

I turn away, tugging my shirt back over my head. I need the second of reprieve so I don't need to look him in the eye. That word reverberates around in my skull. *Chaos…chaos…chaos…*

And I realize that I'm not sure if Reeve is really protecting me—or just waiting to see me burn.

Chapter Forty-Eight

REY

The humidity from the storm last night is lingering, just like the scent of Aric on my skin despite the very cold shower I took the minute I bolted out of his room. Ziva's holding her fan attached to her phone in front of her face and waiting for me in the hall outside my dorm.

"I thought Reeve said maintenance was going to fix the flickering lights. It's like we're on a haunted floor."

I can only focus on one thing at a time, and haunted floors are nothing compared to the utter embarrassment of sleepwalking into enemy territory. What the hell? And why did I have the best night's sleep of my life in a Giant's arms?

It's not like I can share with the class all the reasons why waking up in Aric's arms was the jump scare of my life without sounding like I need to be locked up in a padded room.

"Actually," I finally answer Ziva, "the lights are kind of growing on me. Besides, my money's on Reeve forgetting to tell maintenance whatever they tried didn't work."

"Your faith in me is disappointing," a joking voice suddenly says.

I glare at Ziva. "Could have told me he was in the hall."

"I thought everyone could sense his brand of evil—my bad." She winks.

Reeve ignores both of us as Aric exits his room as well. He's wearing a loose gray T-shirt and even looser jeans that somehow still make him look good enough to eat. He snaps a ball cap over his head and follows Reeve down the hall without as much as glancing in our direction.

"And to think we just slept together," I mutter before thinking.

Ziva slams her hand on the doorframe like I just announced I was betrothed. "I'm sorry, what?"

"No!" I wave at her and grab my key card and phone. "Not like that. I mean, we slept in the same bed, but only because I sleepwalked to his room, invited myself in, and crashed."

The look on Ziva's face doesn't just say *I don't buy it*, it says *I wouldn't buy it even if you* paid *me.* "In his bed," she clarifies as we walk down the hall.

I rub my lips together, then bite down on the bottom one to keep my scream inside my head. "Yeah, in his bed."

"You. And Aric." Does she have to keep processing all the information out loud like I didn't already live through it?

"It would appear so." I hit the down button and get on the elevator.

The doors close, then open again without moving floors. Rowen and Eira walk in. I'm not sure what it is about this girl that bothers me so much, but my hackles rise just seeing her. She's wearing a baggy shirt that covers her ass, dark sunglasses, and she's staring into her coffee cup. Maybe it bothers me that she's taking all of Rowen's time when he could—and should—be helping me? Or at the very least, offering?

"Rough night?" Ziva asks, taking in the scene. "Or rough morning?"

Eira shrugs and elbows Rowen. "This one kept moaning in his sleep."

Well, that's a new development.

Rowen briefly makes eye contact with me before looking at the ground. Is he feeling guilty? I mean, whatever, it's fine if he wants to date, but she doesn't seem like his type, and wouldn't that be an insanely huge conflict of interest?

Once off the elevator, everyone falls into step as we make our way along the trail through the trees to class, with me taking up the rear. The air may be thick with mist, but it smells amazing, fresh. Pine and autumn and fresh rain, and I can almost pretend this is just a normal day in college, headed down the path with my new friends.

Almost.

I'm so lost in my thoughts that I don't notice Rowen beside me until he clears his throat. He's slowed down to my pace like he's waiting for me.

"It was the nightmares. That's why I was sleeping in her room." He says it under his breath. "Really shitty, freaky nightmares. I die every time. I thought maybe I'd sleep better with someone else in the room."

"Err, that doesn't sound pleasant. Do you think you ate something bad? Or"—the look I get is one of pure irritation—"maybe it has to do with your past, with your scars." I hate bringing it up, but I have to believe that at some point, he needs to deal with his trauma. Maybe it's trying to fight through when he sleeps. "You've had it rough. Maybe it would help to talk to someone."

He barks out a laugh. "Yeah, let me get right on that. I can imagine it now. 'You see, doctor, I work for Odin. Yes, that's the one, the ruler of Asgard, about this tall, dark demeanor, not the hero you think, has lots of tattoos, doesn't eat fish, might kill me one day, but it's strange, I just can't seem to close my eyes without dreaming of my death.'"

I wince. "I mean, at least they'd medicate you?"

"Very helpful." He scowls and eyes Eira, who's out of earshot. "Your father can't know. He seems to think he can fix any sort of weakness, and if he can't fix it, he makes whatever reminds him of said weakness disappear. I don't want to be next, Rey."

His voice is desperate, filled with fear. I touch his arm. "I won't let that happen."

"You have enough on your plate dealing with Erikson and finding Mjölnir."

I consider telling him about the runes on Aric's back, but I hesitate. Aric and I struck a truce. We sealed it with blood. I hate to admit it, but it felt good to work with my enemy, and now breaking that enemy's trust feels wrong.

Besides, a small part of me is saying not to tell Rowen everything. He can't help but forward all intel to my dad, which would put him in an impossible situation.

We reach the arts building and walk in. We're side by side, making our way down the hall, since his class with Eira is in the next room over from mine. I see Aric sitting by himself in the same spot as yesterday. I feel different, though—*we're* different. Things have shifted from complete hatred to a weird hot-and-cold game to a possible truce. I'm not sure if crawling into his bed helped or made it worse. Can't wait to find out.

"Hey, Rowen, can I ask you something?" I reach for his arm, forgetting it's his injured one. My fingers come into contact with torn skin, deep scars, pain, but what I feel more than anything is immense heat followed by so much hatred, it takes my breath away.

My Aethercall has never done that before, reversed itself on me and shown me someone else's direct emotions.

I drop my hand. "Sorry."

He flexes his arm and shrugs. "It's fine. You had a question?"

"Yeah, um, I wonder where Thor stored it, you know? I guess I never asked my dad, but do you know, when Mjölnir wasn't being used, where it would chill?"

I smile.

Rowen doesn't.

"It's sentient. It chills wherever it feels most at home, I guess." He shrugs. "I'm sure at one point…before the war, that would have been next to Thor's heart."

Next to Thor's heart. The thought of it sends warmth through me, but the feeling is fleeting. Thor is gone. Mjölnir is in mourning, hidden by the Giants that stole it, until the right person can find it. I hope with everything in me that that person is me. So many lives depend on it.

"Rowen!" Eira calls out.

"It seems I'm being summoned. Keep me updated, though." He stops and puts a comforting hand on my shoulder. "If anyone can do it, Rey, it's you."

If only I believed that.

Chapter Forty-Nine

ARIC

Rey's quiet as we leave the arts building together. We talked in class about finishing up our Ice Caves paper, but both of us knew it was really about making a real plan to find Mjölnir. Neither of us brings up the sleepwalking. I'm pretty sure if we did, I would explode on the spot, and it wouldn't be because of any runes.

My phone suddenly goes off. I look down at the screen.

Reeve: *watch ur back*

Reeve: *dont think with ur dick*

Reeve: *sigurds always watching*

My phone pings again.

Seriously?

Reeve: *dont underestimate him, thats a mistake neither of us can afford to make*

Reeve: *but seriously dont think with ur dick*

I curse under my breath. I know he's not wrong, but I don't want to believe she's capable of fully betraying me in the end. Or that if she is, at least then so am I. Right now, the focus needs to be on unlocking the last two runes. Everything else can wait.

Because I'm tired of feeling numb, I'm tired of feeling like I don't know my true self, and I'm tired of feeling weak against an untouchable enemy. It's time to rise from the ashes of my parents. The reign of the Gods—the reign of Odin—must end. Rey has to know that, even if she won't admit it.

"Something wrong?" Rey asks.

"All good," I lie and shove my phone back in my pocket as we make our way toward the student parking lot.

I click the locks on my SUV and, without speaking, Rey climbs into the passenger seat.

She waits until I pull out of the Endir gates to ask, "Where are we going?"

"Someplace where we can plan our next steps."

"Oh. Right."

Where did she think we were going? On a date?

I glance at her sharply. Is she blushing? Shit, did I say that out loud?

"It would be my first." She blushes harder. "No, I mean, not like my first, not *that* sort of first."

My smile is practically frozen to my face. "A date virgin or a virgin virgin, Rey?"

"Shut up, I'm not that sheltered. I've had my share of hookups despite my dad locking me away. But the only people I ran around with were kids whose parents worked for my father, meaning most either wanted to kidnap me for ransom and force me into marriage"—she stares me down, ouch—"or see what it would feel like to be with the great Odin's daughter. It's not like anybody ever gave me flowers. Ugh, can we not talk about this? I think I'm rambling now."

I refuse to tell her it's cute. "You are, but I kind of like seeing all the little chinks in your armor. I have a mental checklist of all your weaknesses just in case. I'll be sure to add 'dates where all the guy has to do is bring a flower.'"

She rolls her eyes. "Yes, I'm easily impressed."

I finally pull onto the road leading up to the back side of the lake. The forest gets nice and thick as we near an abandoned piece of land.

When I pull off the county road to the wrought iron gates, Rey whistles. "Well, that looks daunting."

"It's supposed to."

Sigurd owns all this land. He doesn't tolerate trespassers.

I park the Defender. Rey gets out of the car, tossing her computer bag into the back seat. As she approaches the tall gates, she glances sharply at me, then leans in and examines the carvings on the decorative finials. Her eyes widen as she takes in the length of balusters, each metal bar bearing a protective rune. "The whole fence is warded?"

"When Sigurd wants something sealed off, he doesn't fuck around. If anyone from the university wandered this way, they'd get a strong urge to turn the hell around and not come back." Feels weirdly nice to talk about this openly with someone. When I touch the gate, the wrought iron shudders and groans, but it opens for me. "This way."

She hesitates for a second, then follows.

The path to the lake is littered with white stone—or things that look like white stone. I always look straight ahead, never to the right or to the left, so as not to acknowledge them. My breath comes out in small pants. I needed privacy for us, but I forgot how much it affected me, being here.

"Wait." Rey stops in front of me and looks around. "Aric, these aren't rocks. They're—"

"Bones," I finish for her. "We call it Hollowood. It's where the majority of the fallen are buried or where the majority of the fallen… fell."

She puts a hand on my arm. I jerk it back on instinct. "The Giants Odin killed."

"Yep. You're surrounded by them. Giants who never got a proper burial, frozen instead in the ground for an eternity. They gave their very bodies to this world, and nobody will ever know the sacrifice."

"People rarely do in war," Rey acknowledges. "I'm sorry. I know it means nothing, but I'm sorry."

"One day, he'll pay for his crimes." I push lightly past her. "And if you're standing by his side, no matter how much I like your smile, you will, too."

Harsh, but then again, so is the reminder of the buried around me.

I brought her here to discuss our plans, but that goal feels secondary now, subdued by the charged energy of this place. We say nothing as we hike along progressively rockier terrain to the edge of the water, where it stretches like a sheet of black glass, as still as the stones rimming the path.

Rey pauses once we get there, staring out at the inky depths. I lean against a smooth, cool wall of black stone and watch her. "I really want to know why the common theme is water in all these places," she says.

"Because water is life," I reply. "It moves through everything. It carves mountains, shapes the earth, grinds even the strongest metals to dust." I shrug. "The Gods feared the Giants for that very power, the power of the ice, water, life itself."

She smiles up at me. "It makes sense."

I like her like this.

Disarmed.

I want to trust her. And then I remember the bodies. Can anyone with Odin's blood truly be trusted?

My mind goes back to Reeve's texts.

The air feels cooler, damp with the mist of a small waterfall trickling down the rock beside me. The water spills into a narrow stream that runs beneath our feet before vanishing into the lake. Rey steps carefully across, running a hand through the spray as she presses her body up against the stone.

She lets out a gasp. "It's beautiful here."

"I think—" My voice cracks. "It's as close to home as I'll ever feel."

She glances up at me then with such a look of understanding, of peace, that it takes my breath away.

And when the wind picks up, twirling her hair around her face, the scent of the earth, heady and strong, slams into me, along with the word. *"Lie."*

In that moment, I don't think. I reach out and take her hand.

She doesn't look at me. We just stand there together. Hand in hand. And I think this may be the most perfect, peaceful moment of my entire life.

Until the moment is broken when heat slams into my palm. The cry coming from Rey tells me she must have felt it, too.

My gaze catches on a light shining from the rock in front of us, an unnatural glow emanating from the waterfall. My heart starts beating double-time as I move a little closer.

"What…what is that?" Rey asks, her voice quiet, reverent.

Carved into the slick rock, half hidden by the rushing water, glows a jagged rune.

Chapter Fifty

REY

My pulse stutters, half from the way he's looking at me, half because I already know this is likely to change everything. That moment just now was intense. New. I liked it…

And it caused a new rune to appear.

Though my heart sinks when I realize it isn't one of the ones on Laufey's note.

"You know," I say, folding my arms, trying to break the sizzling tension between us, "I've heard the lore. Giants, frost, all that. But honestly? Is causing runes to appear your only party trick? I've only seen lame little flecks of frost." I arch a brow. "You misfiring? Shooting blanks?"

For a second, he just stares, silent. Then, in one smooth motion, he pulls me against him. The air leaves my lungs. His breath brushes across my lips, cool and sharp, and they go instantly numb—ice threading across them like glass. I gasp, and his thumb follows, slow, deliberate, warming me again.

"Neat trick," I whisper.

I might die in his arms, right here, in this moment.

"Do it again."

His mouth tilts into something dangerously close to a smile. When he speaks, his voice carries that low resonance I've felt before but never this strong—it vibrates through me, each word landing like a drumbeat in my chest, a cadence that lures me closer even when I know I should run the other way. "I can do more. Much more."

He holds out his hand and flicks his wrist. Snow starts dumping from the sky around us. The flakes are huge. It feels like a fairy tale. I let out a disbelieving laugh.

All thoughts of Mjölnir disappear for one brief moment. It's only Aric and his ice, and I want to exist here, with him in this place, just like this.

"So…you wanna build a snowman?" I ask.

For the first time since I've known him, he laughs. Really laughs. It rumbles through him, deep and raw, and the sound steals my breath more than the ice ever could. "At least you didn't sing it."

Then the sound of branches cracking echoes from behind us.

Are we being followed again?

Even out here? What about the rune wards?

With a sweep of Aric's arm, walls of ice surge up around us, carving a cave from nothing. He pulls me inside, chest heaving, frost clinging to his skin.

We watch and wait as two deer slowly make their way to the frozen lake, looking for water. Aric swears under his breath, eyes glowing. They're white—it's his Giant form truly pushing through. Oh Gods.

"I think they're gone," he mutters, listening. His voice vibrates through the ice itself, the cadence so deep and steady it nearly lulls me into forgetting we're hiding.

I tilt my head up at him, light bouncing off the crystalline walls. "Your eyes."

Our breaths mingle, the air steaming between us. The white in his eyes softens, and he doesn't look like a monster. He's gorgeous, like lightning trapped under ice. I lift my hand, press it against his, and his grip tightens like he can't let go.

"This is the part where I warn you," he says, voice vibrating straight into my bones. "I don't think I can control much beyond this as we unlock more runes. From here on out…"

I shrug, my voice steadier than my heartbeat. "Try not to get in the way, and I won't get killed."

His forehead lowers to mine, heat and cold colliding between us. "Runes are powerful, Rey. They're the only thing keeping the monster asleep. Who knows what I'll become the second they stop suppressing me."

I swallow hard, the truth burning in my throat. "Sometimes I think…I was meant more for the likes of a monster than a man."

His lips part, and I catch the glint in his eyes, something feral wanting to break free. My pulse jumps, but I don't move.

A storm builds behind those eyes.

I lift my face like I want to be trapped in them.

And then I surrender, crashing my mouth to his.

Chapter Fifty-One

ARIC

Frost still hangs in the air when I pull back just enough to see her. Her lips are swollen, her breath ragged, and her eyes—Gods, her eyes—hold me like chains I'll never escape.

And so I give up pretending.

I smash my lips to hers, harder this time. My teeth scrape against her tongue, sharp enough to remind us both what I am. She shudders, and it's all the invitation I need.

My mouth is cold, but somehow, impossibly warm at the same time. Ice spins from me, tiny crystals that catch in her hair, swirling like a snowstorm conjured only for us. They cling to her lashes, her lips, glittering as if even winter itself wants to touch her.

She presses me against the ice wall, her body fierce and unyielding. The frost bites into my back, but I don't care. Nothing exists except the heat of her lips, the burn of her hands pulling me closer.

"I'm not sorry," I rasp against her mouth.

Her whisper brushes my skin. "For what?"

"For kissing you."

She laughs, soft and shaky. "Pretty sure I kissed you first."

Her arms slip around my neck, and I know it's a mistake the moment it happens. A fatal one.

Because I can't stop.

My lips part, desperate, and I clamor for more of her, my entire being vibrating with a need I've never known. Her taste. Her scent. The warmth of her breath against the storm inside me.

Bad idea. Bad idea.

Just a few more minutes. Just a few more stolen kisses. I shouldn't. But the excuses come easy. Anything to keep going.

Each kiss unravels me further as I trail them along her cheek, her throat, lower. Each one steals another thread of control until I know the truth—I'll never forget this. It will haunt me until my last breath.

The taste of her. The weight of her. The impossible dream of this beautiful woman in my arms, our bodies pressed dangerously, deliciously close, and the aching, treacherous thought of a world where she might actually be mine. No past. No uncertain future.

Her mouth is fire and frost all at once. I know I should stop, but her hands are in my hair, her body moving in rhythm with mine, and I'd rather die here than let go.

Then it happens.

My teeth scrape too hard against her neck, and the taste of her floods my mouth—warm, sharp, alive. Blood.

I jerk back, but it's too late. A few drops coat my lips, a copper tang searing down my throat. My body revolts, except no—it craves. Every nerve sings with hunger, with recognition.

Her eyes widen. "Aric—"

I stumble, clutching at the ice wall, my breath ragged. My vision blurs, silver washing to black as if the storm itself has hollowed me out. The world tilts, and when I finally find my voice, it's not my own.

"Blood of Odin."

The whisper scrapes from my throat, guttural, like it's been waiting centuries to be spoken.

My body trembles with equal parts terror and want. My eyes lock on hers, and for the first time…I don't know if the monster in me is waking, or if it's already here.

Chapter Fifty-Two

ARIC

Rey glances back at the edge of my ice, then to me and slowly starts to inch away. I don't blame her. I would, too. I hold up my hands. "Give me a minute."

"I'll give you as many minutes as you want," she rasps. "I'll just be over here."

Her mouth is still swollen, and I can see where I scraped her neck. What the hell is happening to us? To me? "I don't know what came over me. I'm sorry, I didn't think your blood would make me react like that."

I feel like I've been punched in the gut.

"We can blame the runes." She lets out a rough exhale. "Right?"

I try to gather my thoughts, but all I have swimming around my brain is the need to kiss her again, to really taste her. My body hums with the need to possess her. Sure, they used to say the Giants devoured their prey in ancient times, but those were just myths, legends to scare people away. I need a minute. A moment to think clearly. I don't want to be the monster.

My hands are shaking, my head pulsing right along with the runes. I need a distraction. I glance up. She's moved on to fixing her hair like it's offensive that any inch of it would be out of place.

I almost laugh. "You used to not care."

Her head jerks up. "What?"

I grit my teeth. Focus. Get through this conversation. *You aren't losing control—yet.*

"The night of…" I try to power through. "The night of the broken engagement. Your hair was a mess, but you seemed so carefree, and I liked it." I shrug. "I liked you. Kind of."

Her eyes narrow. "Um, thank you? I think? Though apparently you didn't like me enough to say yes."

"I wouldn't have wished a betrothal to appease Odin on my worst enemy."

"Case in point?" She chuckles. "Okay, my turn." She takes a small step toward me. "I hated you then. You were beautiful—"

"Were?" I prod, for my own ego and also to see her smile again.

"Are you going to let me talk, Giant?"

I like this side of her. "Go ahead."

"Anyway." She crosses her arms. "I don't get embarrassed easily. I swear Odin just beat it out of my brain, but I was that day. Not one of my finer moments."

"Because of your hair?" I'm struggling to understand.

Her eyes are unwavering. She may as well be staring right through me. "Because you were this tall, beautiful, powerful person, and I was embarrassed that my father was offering me to you like a sacrifice—a sacrifice that, by all appearances, wasn't even worthy. I don't blame you for taking one look and walking away."

My entire world shifts in that moment.

Does she really see herself that way? "Rey, there was nothing to be embarrassed about. You were perfect. I didn't want to keep you because you weren't mine to take in the first place. And you sure as hell weren't Odin's property to bargain with."

She takes a step toward me, then seems to think twice and spins away. I'm left staring at her back and hearing her make soft sounds as she wipes her eyes.

Is she crying?

"For the record, you're still beautiful. Even if I don't like you."

"You're still tall."

"Wow." I take a soothing breath. "Careful with the compliments. It's never good to overdo it."

"Noted."

I clear my throat and glance away. "Hey, since we have a very temporary ceasefire until we find Mjölnir, and we're actually talking without arguing, can I ask a question?"

She smiles at that and makes herself comfortable on the ground. "Wow, colder than I thought. And sure."

I hesitate and realize the out-of-control feeling is gone.

I slowly walk up to her, then sit on the ground and pull her into my lap.

She shivers against my chest. "Heroic."

"You were cold."

"Sure, that's why you picked me up."

"It's the truth. But okay." I lift her off my lap, but she slings her arms around my neck to stay in place.

The rush of relief has me expelling a breath.

"Okay, hit me with your question. You deserve at least one answer after your heroism." It's physically painful having her in my lap like this, but it's a good kind of pain. She's so warm, smells so good. I ache to press my lips to hers again.

Something shifted between us back there. I don't want to think too much about it. I just want to sink into the feeling.

I clear my throat. "Do you believe in magic? Myths? I mean, beyond what we already know about us and where we come from."

She goes completely still above me. "What do you mean? Like, magic-wand-style magic? Myths like the Roman gods or Hercules?"

"Sure. All of it."

The only sound that fills the air is our breathing and the slow, steady melt of the ice around us as it sloughs off into the lake. It's comforting.

Rey turns in my arms so she can look up at me. Pieces of dark hair are caked to her face. Her lips are still swollen from my mouth, her eyelashes collecting my frost. I feel possessive of it, jealous of myself when I stare down at her.

"Yes," she says.

"That's it?" I ask. "Just a yes?"

She lifts her hand and very slowly cups my face. It's warm. It feels so good, I close my eyes for a moment. "I think there's a lot of truth based in stories about Gods and monsters."

"Gods and monsters," I repeat, pressing my hand against hers to keep it on my cheek. I can't fight the feeling that I'm running out of time. As soon as we have the location of Mjölnir, we'll go our separate ways, burying whatever connection we're sharing now. We'll be enemies again, on the opposite sides of a war we didn't start. "Gods, I can believe in. Not all Gods are bad. And I want to believe in something powerful sent to save the world. But what if you're the monster? What then?"

Her eyes lock on mine. "If the monster knows it's a monster, then it's capable of being something else, don't you think?"

"What if it has a reason for wanting to burn the world? What if it's *necessary*? What then?"

Her lower lip trembles. "Then I guess you already have your answer. Maybe we're all just monsters pretending to be heroes, Aric. Maybe the real heroes *are* the monsters. One thing I do know is that we write our own history. Don't ever let something that feels predetermined make you veer from what you think your path should be."

I reach out and gently pull a few strands of hair away from her face. They're so soft. I drop my hand. "I think that's easier said than done, considering both of our families. The idea of having a choice is a nice fantasy, though, isn't it?"

Tears fill her eyes. "It really is."

I shift my body. "We should get back to the dorms."

"Wait." Rey licks her lips. "I'm not the best at math, but I'm thinking we have at least one minute left of this ceasefire before we have to go back to reality. One minute with both swords on the table? One more minute of pretending?"

"One." I nod. "Sure."

"Okay." She presses both her hands against my cheeks and pulls my face down, meeting my mouth again with hers.

Gods, she shouldn't be trusting me again, not after what happened.

The fact that she is undoes me in a primal way.

It's *everything*.

I moan into her mouth, devouring every part of her. She tastes like home. A home I've never really known but want to. I slide my tongue into her mouth, my hands tangling in her hair. I stop thinking. I stop hoping. I just exist for her taste, for her touch.

Rey slides her arms around my neck and fully pulls herself into my lap. I angle my head a different way and deepen the kiss.

I hate time.

I don't want this to end.

I want more. I *need* more.

Abruptly, she pulls away.

And just like that, her shield is back in place. It's in the angle of her jaw, the stillness in her eyes, the way her shoulders square like she's preparing to land a hit. So I do the only thing I can. I promptly peel my anger back over my own face, the comfortable, familiar rage that's been with me so long, it makes moments like the last ones seem like they were never real in the first place. I let it flame until I no longer want to keep her close.

It's the only way we're going to get through this unscathed.

So easy to believe, the lies I tell myself.

"Minute's over," she whispers.

"Good."

Rey slowly scoots off me. I get to my feet and walk a few steps away.

I feel her step up next to me.

I wave my hand in front of the ice walls, and they melt instantly.

"Fourth rune tonight," I whisper. "What is it? I'll find it and text you."

"Othala."

I don't cringe, but a sickness curls in my gut right along with a bit of satisfaction. "The rune of bloodline. Inheritance." I would laugh if I didn't want to scream into the void. "The fourth rune is one of the most powerful. Sigurd's afraid to even speak it out loud."

Her eyes narrow. "How do you know that?"

"Because it's in his home office." I rub at my neck, heat from the runes building up my back like they're ready for more. "And out of all the stories I grew up memorizing, it's the only one my dad insisted I learn word for word. I think it's paranoia that Sigurd keeps it…"

"Keeps what?"

"The statue that bears the mark." I can't keep the bitterness out of my laugh. "Audhumla. The very cow that allegedly nourished Ymir to life and helped create the Gods. And trust me—it's the most awkward-looking statue in the world."

Her mouth parts like she's about to argue, but then she actually breathes out a sigh of relief.

"It's also at our house," I add, "which means we get to put off rune-hunting for a few more days. Sigurd keeps it locked up tight, but he won't be at the end-of-orientation house party. We'll see it then."

Her shoulders sag like maybe she's relieved. I feel the same way.

I've bought us the perfect excuse to stall.

What's a few more days?

A few more days of lying.

A few more days of believing it's all going to be okay.

A few more days to pretend.

Chapter Fifty-Three

ARIC

I'm still thinking about both my conversation with Rey and our kiss when I get back to my room. I'm not surprised to find Reeve inside, standing in front of the window, looking deep in thought. "Should I be worried?"

Damn, is it really written all over my face?

"About?" I'm exhausted, freaked out about losing control with Rey, and starving. Not in the mood for an interrogation. I toss my phone onto my bed and walk over to him. I can at least play dumb, even though yes, I know what he's asking and yes, he *should* be worried.

Please, universe, let her accidentally sneak into my room again. Even if she brings the mug.

"Rey," Reeve states blandly.

I lean against the windowsill and gaze out at the night sky. "Absolutely not. I know where we stand, and I've firmly drawn the line in the sand. If you think I smell like her, it's only because she could have nearly died in my arms just now. I lost more control than I expected to." I hope it's enough information to satisfy him without wanting more details.

Reeve jerks his head in my direction. "What?" His eyes are wild. "Care to repeat that?"

"We were out by the lake. You know my job is to get close to her." It's a half-truth. "So I created an ice wall and we…argued." *Made out.* "You have nothing to worry about." *Total lie.*

"You went by the water and created some ice walls?" Reeve repeats. "You showed her your power…just decided to bust it out right in front of her?"

"It's not like she doesn't already know." I leave out the part about how intense the kiss really was. "I know what I'm doing." I'm downplaying it, which, by the way he's reacting, is probably a good call on my part. Besides, I barely understand it myself. Reeve may not have any of his own abilities awakened, but he knows how powerful, how dangerous mine can be.

Reeve starts pacing in front of me. "You do realize what that place is, right—or any place near this godforsaken water?"

"A large lake that Sigurd thinks carries the souls of the fallen. Honestly, it really wasn't a big deal at first—"

"Are you serious right now? It's a fucking tomb, you dumbass!"

I slowly lift my head. "The graves, you mean?"

"They call it the *riverbed* of tombs, leading to the lake, remember? You've heard the stories. Or do you just tune everything out if it doesn't interest you?" Reeve runs his hands through his hair. "The river of tombs reflects those who have fallen in honor of the Gods. It's sacred ground. Just like the mirror at the Hall of Omrir reflects the souls of the Gods. The riverbed pathway is what carries souls into the lake, trapping them until Ragnarök."

I almost laugh. "I saw nothing but strong currents and murky water and a stark little reminder of what Odin did to our kind."

"You need to wake the fuck up," Reeve grumbles. "Not the point. The point is, someone like you"—he stops himself—"someone like *her* shouldn't be in a place that powerful, that meaningful. The last thing you want is to trip into the water, have an accident, or Gods forbid have a weak moment and she uses it against you!"

"Hey." I give him a shove. "I'm alive and I'm fine, and so is she, and we're both back in our enemy camps. Nothing happened."

Liar.

Reeve throws his hands up in the air. "If I told you she was sent to kill you, would you listen?"

I bite down on my lower lip. "Listen? Yes. Would it matter in the end? No. We've been heading toward a reckoning for years."

Plus, Rey already admitted as much.

"Not as dumb as he seems," Reeve says under his breath. Then he looks up at the ceiling and groans. "Listen, I'm not going to say anything that'll just mess with your head, but what I will say is this: Rey is not here to be your friend. You need to stay alive at all costs, or every little moment I've spent protecting you will be for nothing." He makes it sound like he's single-handedly kept me out of trouble when, in the end, with the power I have at my fingertips, wouldn't it be me saving him?

My eyes narrow. I touch my chest. It feels like something's pressing against me from the inside out, trying to break free, and then I hear a door shut and shuffling from the other side of the wall. Rey's back.

"Go," I tell Reeve, my voice dripping with disdain. "I'm done talking about this."

Reeve's eyes narrow. Anger crackles off of him like static. But in the next second, his shoulders deflate. "I lost my temper. I'm sorry. I just don't want to lose my brother. We've both seen too much loss."

Yeah. Thinking about our parents guts me. I lean in and give Reeve a hug, the pain between us a living, breathing thing.

"I'm headed to bed." Reeve moves to leave but turns around when he reaches the door. "She's bad news, Aric. She's using you—I know it feels real. I know you're drawn to her. But have you ever asked yourself *why*?"

The door clicks shut behind him.

I walk over to my bed and lie down, staring at the wall between my room and hers.

I can't believe in my soul she would actually kill me now—but why would Reeve lie about something like that? What would he have to gain? And why do just a few words from him have me questioning so much after what Rey and I shared?

My head starts to pound.

I hate this. All of it.

The only way out is to go through the storm. I just wish I knew that we'd survive whatever was on the other side.

I close my eyes and finally fall asleep.

Images of bloodshed fill my vision. I see the archway again, the sparkling pathway, and bodies littered over it.

I hear a voice yell. "It's the only way! You must destroy it!"

"We'll be trapped!" another voice calls.

"So be it!" A roar sounds, and then nothingness.

I jolt awake and look around my room.

It's snowing. *Inside*.

Of course it is.

I slowly get out of bed and stand in the middle of my room as flakes spin around me. I hold out my hand, letting them twirl around my fingertips, and when I glance over my shoulder to look in the mirror, the person staring back at me isn't me.

He looks like me.

But his eyes are a silvery white.

Frost covers his long, braided hair.

I can't breathe.

On his head sits a crown of branches twisted into the shape of an elk's horns.

Chapter Fifty-Four

REY

"Hey!" Ziva knocks on my door. "Open up. Heard you nearly died, need to talk about it. I want details. Leave nothing out. I'm bored."

I jerk open my door. "Good news travels fast, huh? When did I nearly die? I've just been with Aric."

"Yeah. Which means your life is constantly in danger, by my calculations, because unless you've released all that sexual tension, one of you is going to explode." She winks and then points at my door.

The white board hanging there is littered with a few phone numbers, and then scribbled in cursive, *Die, Odin*. With a heart around it.

"Forget Eira—you're the one who needs a bodyguard. No offense. She's the type who'd probably question the kidnapper so much that they'd either give her back or apologize and turn themselves in anyway."

I cover my mouth and laugh. "She's not that bad."

"I have bio with her. Trust me when I say, she's bad. Plus, it's not even like Rowen's really watching her. He's always on his phone or with her at the gym drinking gross-looking green protein shakes. I think she does it to torture him."

My eyes narrow. What? "Gym? Protein shakes?"

"Yeah, word on the street is that Rowen's at the gym a ton, like he's prepping for the Olympics or something. And Eira's always there hovering over him with protein shakes in hand like the world will end if he's not getting his pump on. The weird thing is, though, he doesn't seem annoyed. Maybe she's growing on him."

I chew my lower lip. I thought she annoyed him. Is he just bored? Maybe that's how he's getting rid of all his stress—it would make sense.

"Yeah, I never really pay attention to gossip when it comes to Rowen. People always make up stuff on account of him being alarmingly gorgeous." I shake off the uneasy feeling in my stomach and keep talking. "Anyway, Rowen's probably bored, plus his job as a security guard is to fight off people, so it's not super surprising he'd want to bulk up."

Not completely, but I make a mental note to ask him later. It's tiny details like this that I'm missing out on. He wasn't drinking protein shakes back at home. Is he really trying to put on more muscle? Just how deep has he gotten into Father's business dealings? And why haven't I seen it before?

I hate the feeling that I may not know him as well as I think I do.

We all have our secrets, and I can't sit on my high horse and say I don't have mine. I've left out a lot of details when giving Rowen intel.

We're all just trying to survive, right?

I eye Reeve making his way back down the hall toward Aric's room. Didn't he just leave?

"I don't suppose you feel like being *my* bodyguard tonight, in case that one flies off the rails?" I ask her.

"No can do." Ziva does a little dance in front of me. "I have a date tonight. He's a freshman, a Virgo, likes board games, and plays a mean game of frisbee golf. We might go to a poetry slam, or I might stick my tongue down his throat to forget about all the losers I've already kissed in my life. Oh, hey, Reeve."

He stops in front of my door. "I've been standing here at least five seconds and heard every word, you know."

She shrugs. "Whoops?"

He mimics her innocent stance, then stares me down. "Sorry about the door. Too bad the whole 'die bitch die' thing didn't work out."

Wow, someone's in a mood. What did Aric tell him?

"I bet you are."

"There's always next time, eh?" His eyes flash like he wants to fight me.

I flinch. "That's low, even for an Erikson."

We're chest to chest when Ziva moves between us. "Guys, stop, you're ruining my pre-date buzz."

"Right, sorry." Reeve runs his hands through his hair. "I'm tired. Sorry, Rey." He turns on his heel and starts walking away, lights flickering overhead. "I'll call maintenance again."

Ziva stares after him. "He's acting weirder than usual."

He and Aric fought. I know it.

Guilt assaults me.

It wasn't supposed to be this hard.

Aric was supposed to be so hateful I'd smile while drawing blood—but he's not. The game's changed, and I barely recognize my place in it.

Ziva's checking the time on her phone. "Gotta run. Stay safe, maybe indoors for the rest of the night?"

Message received. "Yeah, I'm tired anyway." I groan, unlock my door, and stumble in.

"You've been busy today." Rowen's voice comes from a corner of the room, causing me to jump about a mile.

"What the hell, Rowen! Did you sneak in here through my window?"

"You know, you really should be more careful with how blatant you are when you leave campus with Aric," he continues, ignoring my question. "That is, unless your plan was for the entire school to think you're dating and have the information reach Odin. Risky, even for you."

I flop onto my bed. "Are you here to remind me that my father's going to kill both me and Laufey if I don't wake up Aric and find the damn hammer, or was there something else? Because I'm not being careless. I'm getting close to the enemy based on *his* instructions."

"Right." Rowen lets out a sigh. "But it's my job to tell him when I think you're in too deep, and I think screwing him for sport probably wasn't on your dad's list of bright ideas."

I jolt up. "Are you kidding me right now? First of all, what right do you have to even assume that? And second of all, even if I was, who cares? It's just a job."

Even I don't believe my own lies anymore.

He sighs. I know he doesn't want to argue any more than I do. "I see the way Aric looks at you, and I can tell he's already partially awake. The guy's terrible at hiding the frost. Plus, I know you well—you know exactly how to finish the job, don't you?"

Two more runes.

I nod my head slowly. "It might kill him. You don't see what happens when I start waking him. It looks like it's painful. Every single time, his eyes turn white, like he can barely control the power bursting from inside of him."

I notice Rowen moving from one foot to the other. He's restless. He wants to fight but can't. Why? A chill runs down my spine.

His cruelty was trained into him. Same as mine.

Rowen prefers to watch his enemies die slowly as the life leaves their bodies—Odin has always said that to watch a life leave for Valhalla is a God's greatest honor. A reminder that true life only comes from one's very breath.

But this is my closest friend in the world. I have no reason not to trust him.

"Look…" Rowen starts, then heaves a sigh. "Aric seems like a nice enough guy right now. I'm sorry he's suffering, but you've got to understand: he's not the only one. Your father…"

Rowen stops himself, looks unsure whether he should continue. But then the words just seem to flow out of him.

"He's losing not just his power, Rey, but his grip on reality. He's your father—and whether you believe he's a monster or not, he's dying here in this realm. He can't afford to wait another year. He needs Mjölnir to go back, to restore his power. Period. The only way for this continuous war between Gods and Giants to end is to get the hammer. The Giants hid it because it's the only thing powerful enough to destroy Odin and they can't figure out how to use it. They broke the Bifrost—trapping who knows how many of us here—and for what? Power? Position?

They say it was to protect the worlds, but at what cost when Odinfather, despite all his faults, the creator of worlds, is here?"

I open my mouth, but it's near impossible to know what to say. "I wish Thor was alive," I try. "He'd know what to do. Because do you really think Odin's only plan is to go back to Asgard and pretend like none of this happened? Do you really think he won't destroy the last Giants, then go after whoever defies him next?"

"So what…if they deserve it," Rowen whispers. "Gods will always reign, and it's your time to decide whose side you're really on." A smile flashes across his face. "I hate Odin as much as you do. I know it's choosing the lesser of two evils, but don't let yourself be distracted." He glances at the wall separating Aric and me. "You know what you need to do. Awaken the Giant. He'll guide you to Mjölnir. The minute he's fully awake, not only will it call to him, but he'll feel compelled to give it to you no matter what."

Could it really be that easy? My heart races. "Why's that?"

"Your blood sings to it. Mjölnir was always meant to be with Thor, with you. It would even respond to Hela if she were in this realm."

I frown. I haven't heard my sister's name in years. I've never met her, nor the birth mother I can't even picture. Sometimes it feels like a distant dream.

"I miss home," Rowen says.

My mouth opens to ask him more about that, but he's already walking toward the door.

"Rowen, wait."

He pauses, and I grab his hand. His scars light up again, burning my fingers. "Have you decided where you stand at the end of this?"

He smiles and grips my hand tighter. "I'm always on your side."

"Even if Odin forces you to choose?"

"Even if I lose the very life he breathed into me." He winks.

I tilt my head. "Oh. So he created you and your family?"

"Bye, Rey." He salutes me and walks off. "Try not to sleep with the Giant tonight."

"It was an accident!" I call after him and lie back down on my bed.

Family. Sacrifice. Betrayal. Love. Impossible choices.

It all swirls around in my brain until I'm tired, suddenly *too* tired. I need to get ready for bed before I crash on top of it.

But instead, I eye my phone. It's Wednesday, which means Laufey's probably out grabbing more flowers for the greenhouse—the one hobby she's allowed.

I don't think. I just dial. I need her.

She picks up on the second ring. "Rey?"

"Hi!" I say it too quickly. "I mean, I'm glad to hear your voice." My own cracks. "Are you doing well?"

"Odin is, of course, treating me as he always does, but he's at the office and I'm in the mansion."

So she's safe for now, albeit under lock and key.

"But…you're okay?" I can't help but ask again.

She's quiet for a moment. "I'm…tired, daughter."

My stomach drops painfully. My grip on the phone is so tight, I have to purposely unclench each finger so I don't shatter the screen.

Daughter. I love it when she says it, but she never calls me that in front of Odin for fear of retribution. It makes my heart ache.

"Now, why are you calling so late?" she asks gently.

It isn't that late. Which can only mean one thing.

They're listening in.

"Just to say I miss you." *I love you. I'm sorry.*

"Oh, sweetie, it's better this way." I can hear the smile in her voice.

"Tell me a story," I blurt, tears in my eyes. "I can't sleep. Silly, right?"

I swipe the tears from my cheeks and suck in a breath to keep from hyperventilating. I didn't realize how much hearing her voice would affect me. I've been so strong for so long.

"A bedtime story? Well, how could I refuse?" She sighs. "Lie down, and when your eyes are heavy, I want you to nod."

I get comfortable, lying on my back, then slowly, I nod, smiling because of course I know she can't see it.

When I was little, my father used to tell me that my voice could conjure monsters. I had no clue he'd made it up to get me to stop talking so much. Back then, he was the center of my universe and I orbited around him, basking in his glow. So of course I believed the story, and it terrified me. So during Laufey's bedtime stories, nodding it was.

The absence of words was my safe space.

"All right, I felt it." She laughs low in her throat. "Good strong nod tonight, Rey."

My throat aches as more tears slip down my cheeks.

"Do you remember the story of the wolf pup?" she asks, her voice steady, melodic. She always has a calming presence, even when the world spins into chaos. It's like she's tucking me in, like I'm seven years old again.

"The pup was small, scraggly," she continues. "He followed the hunters from the village, hungry and limping, hoping for scraps. They laughed at him. Said he was weak. Said he'd never survive the bitter cold of the mountains. But still, he followed. Night after night, step after step.

"And one night, when the fire burned low, the hunters betrayed one another over the last piece of bread. They fought until none was left standing.

"But that little pup? He knew he didn't need to fight. He didn't need to be the strongest or the fastest. He just needed to survive while they fought one another. He was patient and persistent and eventually, they destroyed themselves. And then he licked the crumbs from the snow. He was the last one left to howl while their corpses bled into the ground."

Her breath hitches, just barely, like she's holding back her own tears.

"Courage, Rey, isn't always winning the fight," she whispers. "Sometimes it's staying out of the fight altogether. It's howling."

I cover my mouth with my hand to hold in the sob, but it still breaks free, shaking my whole body. Because even if she never said the words outright, I know. This—her stories, her voice—is her way of loving me.

And it's the one thing my father could never stop.

We hang up in the comfortable silence of family. I turn on my side and stare at the wall I share with Aric.

Blood of Odin. I may be his blood, but I won't let it define me.

I'll be the one who howls.

Chapter Fifty-Five

ARIC

I know it's Rey before the third knock. Is she seriously doing this tonight? She has to be exhausted after today.

I'd be lying if I said I wasn't at least a little happy to see her, though. I yank the door open.

Same routine as last night: she slips in barefoot, clutching her chipped mug like it's sacred; fills it at my sink; drinks it like my water's somehow different from hers. Then she wanders straight to my bed, pats the spot beside her—like I need the reminder—and stretches out as if she owns the place.

I should leave. Go crash on her floor. Anywhere but here.

But temptation sits there staring me down, unapologetic and undeniable.

It means nothing. It means nothing. I keep lying to myself even as I give in, crawl in beside her, and pull her against me.

Because when I say nothing, I mean everything.

She means everything.

I can't explain it, and part of me's afraid that it's just the runes or the monster inside me that wants her—not me. Or maybe it's the situation. I'm not sure.

For now, I'll hold her because I can, and in the morning, I'll push her away because I should.

She nuzzles into my neck, soft and warm, and I bite back the groan that claws its way up my throat.

"You're more tolerable when you don't talk," I rasp, trying to keep the walls up.

Her lips brush my neck. Oh shit. Not expecting that. My body jolts like she just lit a fuse. I force myself to stay still, to breathe, but then her hands slide over my back—slow, searching—until they slip under my shirt.

Her palms press against the runes.

The constant burn beneath my skin—it quiets. It just…rests. Her touch anchors me, drags me under, and I realize how bone-deep tired I really am.

My eyes fall shut before I can stop them.

Sleep swallows me whole.

And that's how it goes for the next two nights.

I wedge a shoe in my door so she doesn't even have to knock. I keep the covers open like a coward, waiting for something I'll never admit I want. I lie there in giddy anticipation like I'm a tween again, listening for the soft pad of her steps down the hall.

And she always comes.

In the morning, we play it off. Pretend she wasn't asleep in the arms of her enemy. Pretend it's just some strange quirk of hers that I tolerate. Pretend so fucking well, it almost feels like our new normal.

Pretend this is okay.

Pretend we aren't losing ourselves to each other.

Maybe pretending is just like hoping—no matter how many times you do it, the end is still the same. Disappointment when reality kicks in.

But for now? The high is worth the fall.

Chapter Fifty-Six

ARIC

"So the party's tonight," Rey says, staring at me in the reflection of the mirror as we brush our teeth.

Translation, we get the fourth rune tonight.

She shoves me to the side and then splashes some water on her face. It's so fucking normal, so domestic, I can't stop myself from grinning.

"Yeah, I was invited to my own house," I confirm. "Apparently I'm back in Reeve's good graces, since I no longer pester you during the day."

No. But we have the nights.

And as long as I hold her all night, I'm calm. I get some sleep. I don't even feel pain. I feel...*normal.*

It's addicting.

I wonder if it affects her in the same way, like we've both been strung so tight for so long that we're finally doing our bodies the great service of calming the hell down.

Not that I'm always calm when she climbs in.

She tugs my hair.

Her lips have met my skin more than a dozen times.

I've touched her ass accidentally. Twice.

She's kneed me in the junk—swear that one was on purpose.

The point is, whatever truce we have is in my bed. But during the day, I see the tension in her. I feel Rowen's anger when they talk, checking up on her constantly. I sense Reeve's anxiety as he watches us, wondering if I've done what has to be done yet.

Rey stares at our reflections in the mirror. I follow her gaze and look down. The water she splashed on her face fell onto my hand and turned to ice.

My nerves build as the ice gets thicker across the back of my hand.

"It seems," she whispers, "it's happening all the time now."

"I don't even think about it anymore around you. It's kind of nice, not having to hide it—"

"Remember the end game." She's suddenly colder than my hands. Like she's made the decision for the two of us and is already closing herself off again. It feels like I just got slapped. Her once warm eyes are distant.

I stare her down in the mirror. She doesn't get to decide shit for me. "Right." My eyes flash with warning. "The end game where I don't kill you."

She punches me in the shoulder. "The end game where I don't kill *you*. Let's just get this over with, yeah?"

Her words slice through the room, shattering the ice I just built, causing my body to boil with anger. "Yeah, good call. It's too weird when we don't hate each other, plus Reeve's been on my ass just like Rowen's on yours."

She looks away. "Yeah, it seems everyone on Team Odin is… stressed."

"Team Odin?" I repeat. "I thought you were Team Middle Ground where you try not to kill or be killed."

I mean, did I expect her to be Team Aric? Absolutely not. So I don't know why I'm suddenly wishing for her to confess it. I need to stop thinking about her as anything but the person I might need to extinguish in order to survive. Maybe this conversation is the reminder I needed.

We aren't friends.

There will never be a world where we coexist without hatred and old wounds dripping on each side.

There will never be peace.

She pulls away from me, physically, emotionally. "See you at the party. Try to stay calm. It's almost over."

"Right." Almost over.

I watch her leave and tell myself it's for the best. I mean, what was I even thinking? Had I really lost my mind there for a minute and hoped? Reeve was right.

The Gods are evil.

Maybe she isn't.

But her family is—and they deserve whatever they get.

I try not to let it bother me while I get ready and make my way to the elevator. Just as I look up and the doors are closing, I see it.

It has a different meaning now.

The stupid comic book picture of Odin fighting off Ymir at the end of the hall.

Odin. Loki. Thor. All standing by his side like heroes.

And an entire realm, Jötunheim, set on fire around them.

They destroy worlds.

How silly to think I had any place in hers.

Chapter Fifty-Seven

ARIC

I'm not in the mood.

If one more person mentions tonight's party, I'm punching them in the face.

Rey's been distant all day—on purpose. Everything she does is surgical. Which means she probably knows where the last rune is and wants to rip the bandage right off despite how much I may bleed.

Class blurs. My notes are a line of slashes that could be runes or a cardiogram but definitely won't help me pass bio. Would be nice if I could get drunk fast and stay there tonight, but my body burns through alcohol like cheap gasoline. I'm an expensive drunk—and that won't fix the actual problem.

Correction: problem*s*.

I round the corner toward the dining hall—and Rowen's posted at the doors like a gargoyle. The guy's been shadowing Rey all week, too smooth, too pretty, the kind of pretty that looks better with blood on it. Scars that say he enjoys collecting them.

I turn on my heel. The last thing I need is him right now.

"Aric." Even his voice irritates me. He talks to me like he has a reason to command me, and it pisses me off.

I sigh and face him. "Yes, asshole?"

He rolls his eyes. "About the party tonight."

"Can I uninvite you?"

"I assume it will be supervised?" he says, ignoring me.

I bark a laugh. He doesn't. "Who died and made you chaperone? Relax. Cameras everywhere, house staff on duty, nobody's dying. Rey can handle herself."

His blue eyes flash a shade colder. "And who watches you? Who controls you when you lose it?"

I glance around the empty corridor—polished tile, trophy case reflecting our shapes. "It's my house, so I plan to exist in it. Drink. Have a good time. Forget for a little while and try to avoid you at all costs. That's my plan."

He steps in, close enough for me to smell his stupid mint gum. "Good. As long as that plan doesn't involve her."

I grin. "You warning me away like she can't make good choices? She's a grown woman—she does nothing she doesn't want to."

His jaw flexes. "Ah. That's the problem. What she wants—"

"Is me." I lean in, lay a cool hand on his shoulder. "Who am I to deny her a taste, Rowen?"

His fist is faster than I expect. It cracks my jaw, rattles my teeth, and drives me a step back into the trophy case. Glass explodes while pain flares all down my back.

Shit. He hits like a truck.

Drops of silvery-red blood run from my nose, and he's already got a fist twisted in my shirt, dragging me close. I let him.

"You're an abomination," he snarls. "You shouldn't exist." His lip curls. "You don't deserve the runes that protect you."

He shoves me and turns away like a little bitch.

"What, you gonna run?" My voice carries down the hall. He stops. "Besides, who made you the judge of who's 'worthy,' huh? I've done nothing wrong in this life. My parents sacrificed everything so I could live on to do something, something important. Can you say the same about yours?"

Something flickers behind his eyes—guilt, rage, both. He lunges.

I slip to the side, grab his shirt collar, and bounce him off the cinderblock. My fist cocks—

And suddenly Reeve is there, wedging himself between us like a human pry bar, palms on my chest.

He shoves me just as his loud laughter fills the room, along with the gasps and whispers of the students starting to gather. "Whoa. Okay, no, Frosty, not today. It's not Christmas." He shoves me a step back and smacks my cold hands, then turns with a sunny smile. I quickly shove them in my pockets. "Rowen, maybe pick a fight you can win? Bro, this is embarrassing."

He throws a glance down the hall at the students congregating before continuing.

"Nothing to see, folks! Too much creatine kills! Stay hydrated! Don't do drugs!"

"I could have beat his ass," I say loud enough for Rowen to hear.

Rowen points at us, breathing hard. "Stay away from her. Both of you. Next time, I won't stop." He stalks off, shoulders stiff, fury tucked back under that guard-dog exterior. I smirk when he shakes his right hand out like it's stinging from hitting my face. I hope it's broken.

I'm wiping blood from my nose when Reeve mutters, almost to himself, "That guy and his temper."

"Rowen? He's just constantly pissed. Wouldn't you be if you had to work for Odin?"

Something flashes in Reeve's eyes. "Hell yeah I'd be pissed. Let's go feed you before you redecorate the hallway with someone's spleen." He claps my shoulder, feels how cold I am, recoils a bit, but doesn't comment on it.

I lift up my shirt, wiping the rest of the blood off my face with the inside of it while Reeve rushes over to the approaching campus security. Two guys who look like they've barely graduated walk up in full uniform, walkie-talkies in hand, concern etched in their eyes.

Reeve grins at them. "I'll let President Erikson know all the gory details, don't worry. Feel free to do your jobs and file a report, though—destruction of property, assault. Oh, and be sure to include that Eira Helian's private security was at fault. You should already have his information on hand."

They talk for a few minutes before Reeve motions for me to follow him. Shattered glass crunches beneath my feet as we pass stunned students and walk back to the dining hall. I don't even care anymore if they see the white of my eyes, the frost just dying to get released.

Fucking Rowen. The rune line down my back throbs in time with my pulse—hot, cold, hot—like it heard the word "Jötunheim" and decided to wake up angry.

"Tea." Reeve suddenly snaps his fingers after shoving me into a chair at an empty table. "Tea always calms the nerves."

"I don't want tea."

"People are staring," Reeve says through clenched teeth. "You'll drink the damn tea and put a nice smile on your face like you don't want to set fire to the school or rip Rowen apart limb by limb and add said limbs to the fire—stop smiling, stop that, it's creepy. I'll be right back with your tea. Think…nonviolent thoughts."

Which means the minute he walks away, I think of Rey. Which leads to thinking about Rowen. Vicious stupid cycle, because now I'm focusing on the way she didn't look back in class, which just tells me she knows where we're going after tonight even if I don't.

I need to accept what's going to happen and, rather than fight it or try to overanalyze everything, open the door and let the storm in.

Chapter Fifty-Eight

REY

Rowen's been driving for maybe ten minutes, and this is the quietest I've ever seen him, let alone Eira and Ziva, who sit silently in the back seat. We're headed to Sigurd's for our end-of-first-week house party. Eira fidgets with her phone behind me, and I've seen Ziva open her mouth at least four times, then seemingly think better of it and close it. Rowen's been stealing uncomfortable glances at me, like he knows I'm pissed.

I *am* fucking pissed. I heard all about the fight, after I already felt bad for pulling away from Aric this morning.

Knowing I hurt him on purpose before he hurt me first was just as awful as seeing the hurt on his face.

But there is no exit clause for us.

No out.

Only through.

I realized too late that I was calm when I was with him, and that me touching him calmed him right back. It was more than just my Aethercall, too. I could feel it in the air when I woke up in his bed. I was drawn to him, and he was drawn to me. It wasn't by accident, which meant it would get harder to keep lying to him the closer we got to unlocking the last two runes.

Selfishly, I want him. Stupidly, I lie to myself and say I can handle all of this—we can handle it. But one thing both Gods and humans have in common is there's no way to prepare for heartbreak. No amount of power can protect us from it.

Eira remains mostly unaware of the tension between Rowen and me. I watch her now as she fixes her lip gloss in the reflection of her phone camera. To be that unbothered about life in general? I can't decide if I'm impressed or annoyed I can't join her.

My phone chooses that moment to go off. With dread, I look at my messages. Father. Again. He's texted me more in this last week than he has in the last few years.

Odinfather: *Rowen is concerned, and he's never concerned. He says you have intel you haven't shared?*

I grip the phone as rage pulses through me. I should never have alluded to Rowen that I knew how to wake Aric up.

Me: *You'll have answers either tonight or tomorrow. Either way, Mjölnir is as good as mine*

I wait for his response, stomach clenched.

Odinfather: *Good. That's good. I knew I could count on you. Once he's awake, he'll know where Mjölnir is, and retrieving it will be all he's able to focus on. Follow his ice and leave everything else to me.*

I think he's done typing when a picture suddenly appears on the screen. It's Laufey, and she's tied to a chair in the living room.

I stifle my gasp in the silent car. But then a video pops up.

I turn the volume off and press play.

My father moves in front of her with his ever-present raven cane. He very slowly pulls it up over his head, then slams it down on her hands over and over and over again until all I see is blood dripping from her knuckles. She passes out. The camera points to my father. His smile is sinister.

He enjoyed it.

I might be sick.

What the hell's going to happen when he has Mjölnir at his disposal?

But this video made one thing extremely clear: I have no choice if I want any hope of saving Laufey's life. Plus, Rowen's here with me. If I screw up, he will be blamed. And Father will make him pay.

I shove my phone in my pocket and try to center myself. My father's video is a harsh reminder that I'm running out of time.

Like I didn't already know.

Rowen parks the car in front of a sprawling three-story lake house, easily 15,000 square feet. The house looms like a bad omen, its sleek tan-and-white exterior standing out against the towering evergreens that surround it.

When we get out, Eira walks ahead while Rowen grabs my hand. "I'm sorry I didn't say anything about fighting with Aric."

I suddenly want to jerk away from him. "Don't keep secrets—not from me. And stop picking fights. I can handle myself."

"You don't understand," he starts to argue. "Your father—"

"Look, I get it. We're in this together, but where's all the hostility coming from? We're on the same side!" But I think I know. Suddenly, his angry outburst in my room makes sense. It's about my father choosing me, isn't it? And me not following through, despite being given the opportunity I think Rowen would kill for.

He bites down on his lip and then runs a hand through his hair. "You're different with him. But you know what he is to us, what we are to him. I just— Do us all a favor and get this shit nailed down, Rey. Before I kill him."

"He's mine," I snap in a voice I don't even recognize as protective rage takes over. "Mine to hunt. Mine to kill."

"Whoa." Rowen takes a step back. "Your eyes. They…" He blinks. "For a minute they just got really terrifying. You sure you aren't all-powerful like Odin?" He's making light of the situation. I'm still mad, but I go along with it.

I finally exhale. "Let's just get this over with, okay? It's a party. We're supposed to have fun."

"I'm sure you'll manage," he snarks.

I bump him with my shoulder while we walk in an attempt to appear normal when my heart is still racing after my own outburst. "Still best friends."

His tone grows serious, and I know he means it when he says, "Until the grave."

Chapter Fifty-Nine

REY

"Tell me you want to intimidate people without actually saying it out loud," I say as we get closer to the house. I look out over a ravine full of trees and statues that leads from the mountainside to the edge of the lake where the house sits. "As cool as this place looks, it's a bit much."

Rowen snorts in quiet agreement.

The wooden walkway leading to the house is almost as impressive as the house itself. It stretches over a rocky canyon that boasts a small stream bordered by rocks and trees. My stomach lurches sickeningly—heights *and* water? Thanks, Sigurd—but I hold my breath and cross. My black cowboy boots click against the walkway as Rowen and I make our way side by side to the front door.

We catch up to Eira, who's already waiting at the door, annoyance plastered across her pretty face.

"No one's answering," she says with an eye roll.

"Weird," I mutter. We're running late, so I'm assuming that the party is already in full swing, meaning people are probably an hour in on making poor life choices.

The door's massive. It's at least twelve feet tall, maybe fifteen. The amount of video doorbells has me almost wanting to joke about them being afraid of intruders. But then again, where there is fear, there is weakness, right?

I sigh in frustration, but just as I raise my hand for a follow-up knock, the door's suddenly jerked open. Aric's jeans look ready to rip off of him in protest against the muscles in his thighs as he leans against the doorframe, arms crossed, wearing a white T-shirt.

"You're late." Several simple chains dangle from his neck, and on his right hand is a ring similar to my father's. I almost smirk. He looks like an angry God. Damn, he's so pretty.

His appreciative yet judging stare is almost too much as he looks me over. I went for a white crop top and a long army jacket I could wrap around my waist later. I loosely braided my hair and put on what I like to call my *going out makeup* so that he'd focus on my eyes.

The only thing missing is my knife, but it's not really a college party accessory.

"Fashionably late," I say, then nod toward the cameras. "Afraid of something?"

He leans down until he's inches from my face. With a deep inhale, he closes his eyes and whispers, "Home," so low that only I can hear. The single word sends my heart hammering in my chest, at least until he pulls back and says something else for our audience. "Or maybe just homeless. I can't decide, but you do smell like something I probably want to forget."

I shove Aric aside and barge in. "Creepy, even for you, Erikson."

He looks over my head as he shuts the door. "Rowen. You made it." His jaw ticks. "And you're wearing another suit. Own anything different, or is it only business for you? Never pleasure?"

"I don't know, do you ever run a brush through that ridiculous hair of yours?" Rowen counters.

"Some might say unkempt, where others might say easier to pull." Aric winks at me.

I feel my face heat.

I have in fact pulled his hair, many times.

I glance away from Rowen's knowing stare.

"Make yourself at home," Aric continues. "The party's down by the water—drinks, food, fireworks, you know the drill."

Eira grabs Rowen's arm. "I need my security detail!" She loops her arm in his, and off they go. I can't decide if I'm annoyed or just curious why Rowen lets her treat him like she owns him.

Aric brings me back to the present by leaning down and brushing his fingers along my cheek. "You look like you're deep in thought *and* you're blushing. Are you thinking impure thoughts about belonging in my arms?"

My breath hitches. "First off, I belong to no one except for my cute cat mug. Second, you guys really need to stop the *my dick is bigger than your dick* competition. He's just…scared for me, I think. Father isn't going to be thrilled about the idea of a party, and Rowen doesn't want to bury me. I don't want to be buried."

"That, I imagine, is an opinion shared by all living things."

"True." Our words hang between us until I shove past him. "You seem happy, despite getting punched in the face today."

"I heal quick. Besides, it's part of my charm. Laughter in the face of danger." He flicks my nose, then leans down like I'm two feet tall. "And just in case you weren't already aware. Be careful tonight. Especially around…" He swallows. "The staff. Okay? Everything we say or do will be reported to Sigurd."

"Well, considering we're always under surveillance in public, I think I can handle it." In private is a completely different story.

He smirks. "I'm not sure I can handle it, not with you looking at me like that."

"Like how?" I ask.

"Like you want to kiss me again," he rasps.

"Maybe that's the way I look at people I want to kill."

He lets out a low groan. "You already sleep with me every night… 'on accident.'" He makes fake quotation marks. "And you're making it harder to stay away while your words and actions point at you doing nothing but retreating."

I ignore how close he is to the truth. "Accidental would be

stumbling drunk into your room. I don't even remember leaving my bed for yours that first night."

His smile's stunning. "But now you remember it, don't you? My bed."

My entire body sizzles with awareness. Oh yes, his bed, his arms, everything forbidden and untouchable wrapped around me like a cocoon. Perfect. Addicting.

There's a staff member watching us from the corner. I can tell because she's been dusting the same spot for our entire conversation. Aric picks up on it and backs away slightly. She walks away, only for another one to come in.

He glances over at us. I stare him down in a challenge, and then I lean in closer to Aric, who grins down at me. He leans in closer, too. Unexpected. His smug smile pushes through, and all I can focus on is his lips, his mouth, the way I know it feels on me, and then I start wondering about the things it can do.

Bad thoughts.

Very bad thoughts.

We're so close, anyone watching would think we're almost kissing, which: more power to 'em. The staff member makes his way into an adjoining room, checks a cabinet, then types back on his phone like he's checking a list or something. He's fooling no one. Well, if he wants a little show of how well we're getting along...

"Oh, I remember your bed," I tease. "I remember how all I want to do is sleep there...and nothing else."

He moves closer to me and shrugs, then leans in and whispers so dangerously close to my mouth, I almost stop breathing. "Maybe that's all we'll ever do. But maybe I want to do something to test *your* self-control. God knows you've been doing it every single night you 'sleepwalk' into my room."

I don't retreat. I get right in his face. His eyes widen with amusement, with lust, and I can almost see them begin to glow. We still have an audience, and I wonder if they felt the shift in the room. The conversation has turned real.

I swear, every single ounce of tension that's built up between us these last few days is about to combust.

I grin. "You're welcome to try me."

He leans over, so close it's almost like he's kissing my neck. "I think I already have."

Chapter Sixty

REY

"God, do you two have to be so annoying all the damn time?" Aric and I practically leap apart from each other at the sound of Reeve's voice.

"I mean really," he continues. "You both need to grab a drink and separate. Your intensity is completely ruining the vibe."

I shoot a glare at Aric, whose eyes flash, but I can see that he's ready to back down.

"Bathroom?" I ask.

Reeve points down the hall, then jabs a finger in my direction. "If you're not back here in five, I'm sending a search party. Or a firing squad. And you." He points that same finger at Aric. "Dibs on chasing this one away if she so much as thinks about giving herself a tour. You shouldn't get to have all the fun."

"To think I'd need to even chase to catch her," Aric says in a dark voice.

Chills run down my spine.

Reeve's eyes narrow, but there's a teasing glint there. "Enough with the innuendos, assholes. Just get out of my house and down to the beach. The sun's setting, there's music, food, and plenty of other people who also can't decide if they want to kill or fuck each other."

I feel my entire body heat. "Why choose?" I ask Arik.

"Couldn't agree more," he says, leaning in, his eyes falling to my mouth. He licks his lips. A warning or a promise? A shiver runs down my spine.

Reeve looks between us and curses. "Bathroom. You. Get the fuck out."

"Right." I nod. "Yes." I was going to try to steal Aric away to put in motion our plan for the party. My eyes fly to his, but he's looking back at Reeve, who's already gotten distracted by a freshman who wandered into the kitchen looking for the keg.

"Reeve!" Ziva's voice sounds from outside. "Get your ass out here now! You have a pet snake!"

Reeve pales, the freshman already forgotten. "Leave Jory alone! He doesn't like loud people, he bites, he's a rescue!" And then he's running off to save his snake, leaving Aric and me laughing out loud at the ridiculousness of his brother.

And then I realize this is how it should be.

This reality right here.

Laughing. Enjoying life.

I decide however short-lived, I'm going to do that—enjoy this moment—because who knows when I'll have anything close to it ever again?

I turn and head in the direction Reeve indicated. Loud footsteps follow, causing me to smile. I know Aric's walk now. This isn't good. I cannot catch feelings. *Will not.*

Already have.

Damn it! Ever since the heart-to-heart by the lake, things feel different, no matter how many times I try to push him away or draw a line.

Could it be fate, then? Our journey? Mjölnir calling to me through him? Or is it something more? What's causing this shift in *me* toward him?

I'll just add those to the list of questions I'll probably never get answers to.

"It's that door," Aric says from behind me. I stop and turn to say thank you, but I pause. In the hallway next to the bathroom are three paintings.

Familiar paintings. "Seems like I'm not the only one who grew up with the happy part of the story," I say.

Aric snorts. "He collects art, and these are interpretations of them."

"Nightfrost," I breathe. "They're stunning."

One shows a beautiful woman with hair down to her feet staring at her hand, where a blue diamond rests. The next is of Thor holding his hammer toward the sky. They're alone, though. Separated.

The other rendition is of the two of them being broken apart by Odin, a ring falling out of her hand the same way Mjölnir falls out of Thor's. I wince. So maybe in the end, they both lost, or maybe it's just a story of forbidden love, betrayal, and all the sad things I shouldn't be focused on when I'm so close to getting Mjölnir.

"It would be nice, though," I whisper. "If love stories like that were real."

Aric leans over until his breath is on my neck. "Too bad they aren't."

"Right." I nod and point at the bathroom. "Well, you should probably get down there so Reeve doesn't flip. We'll just keep up the act until we can safely slip away."

"Don't get lost." He looks like he wants to say more, but instead he turns on his heel and walks back down the hall.

I close the door behind me, as if a simple door could save me from myself. Because the truth is, I don't need a mythical weapon to draw me to Aric.

I've *always* been drawn to him.

"You don't have to be like him," I said on the beach, before our hands touched and the ocean froze and everything was ruined.

"Maybe I don't want to be anything else."

Is that still true? Is Aric really a monster like my father? Does he want to be?

And all I could think at the time—can think now—is that he was just like everyone else. He was given me, and even then he didn't want me.

I shake the thoughts away, looking at myself in the mirror. "Chill, Rey, just chill."

I leave the bathroom and stop at the paintings again.

"It really would be nice, though," I repeat to myself. "If love stories like that were real."

CHAPTER SIXTY-ONE

REY

When I get down to the lake, a game of beer pong is in full swing, distracting me from my usual fear of open water. I laugh when I realize Reeve has teamed up with Eira, then am floored to see their opponents are none other than Aric and Rowen.

Days ago, I would have used this as an opportunity to search the enemy camp without supervision—but days ago, I didn't have a partner in crime. I'm finding that maybe I don't like working alone as much as I thought—plus, it's nice, having someone on your team for once, however short-lived it may be.

"Unlikely alliances," I joke as I sidle up next to Aric.

"Just setting our alibis, like you said," he murmurs. "As soon as I mop the floor with them, we'll go get that rune."

"Reyyyyyyy!" Eira slurs. "Come play with meeeee!" Oh Gods. Looks like she's been losing.

"Care to sub in?" Reeve asks me. "Don't worry, Stjerne. Appearances aren't what they seem. I might look lazy at times, but I never lose."

His eyes lock on mine as if daring me to call him on it. Then, with zero effort, he tosses the ball. Perfect arc. Perfect drop. Right into their cup.

Okay. Game on.

It takes a few throws before I'm realizing this is actually…fun. Rowen and Aric make an unsettlingly good team. Reeve and I trash-talk them all the way to the last cup. His shot.

"Focus!" I smack him on the chest. "Don't let down the team!"

He rubs his chest like I actually hurt him. "Stop hitting me and I will!"

Then he turns around, throws the ball sloppily over his head…and it lands with a satisfying *plop*.

The crowd explodes.

"Victory!" Reeve bellows. And I must admit, this feels pretty great as we high-five.

"Good game," I murmur as I shake Aric's hand. Any moment now, we'll be able to slip away as the next game draws an audience.

But Reeve seems to have other plans. His eyes gleam as he raises his arms, commanding attention. "Before we continue!" People start chattering around us. "It is time to honor an old Endir tradition. Helmet!"

Chants ripple through the crowd until it's an unsettling roar. The lightness that had bubbled into my chest during the game is gone.

Helmet!

Helmet!

Helmet!

Someone emerges from the house with it: a massive, blackened helmet. It takes two people to carry—how heavy is that thing? It's streaked with blue paint and battle scars, dented like it's seen multiple wars and lived to tell the stories. The thing radiates wrongness. The closer it gets, the tighter my chest feels until it hurts to breathe.

The air is permeated with the smell of incense and blood mixed tightly together. The rumbling timbre of Aric's voice carries from his spot next to Rowen. I can't decipher what he's saying, but I feel each word like a hammer against my chest.

No, not a hammer.

A drum.

A war cry.

Reeve hoists it high into the air, voice booming like a priest at some ancient ceremony. "Every new student honors the fallen Gods and Giants. Tonight we welcome Rey Stjerne to do the honors by drinking of Ymir's helmet." He leans down and shakes his head. "Don't worry—it's not really Ymir's helmet. Just some relic dug up in Asia a few hundred years ago. Dude must have been massive, but let us keep our Endir folklore."

He lifts his arms to the crowd once more while I'm having an internal meltdown just hearing him reference Ymir's name. Sigurd would impale him with his sword before letting drunk college students drink from his helmet. "Let's hear it!"

Cheers. Stomping. The ground vibrates under my feet.

My laugh is too sharp. "This kind of feels like hazing."

"No," Reeve purrs, eyes catching the firelight as he shouts. "It's Endir tradition."

I suddenly feel Aric behind me. "Just another ancestral thing from Sigurd. Add it to the list."

I elbow him. "Dug up in Asia, huh? How sanitary is this thing?"

He laughs, and it wraps around me like a warm hug I don't deserve. Genuine. Gods help me, it's beautiful.

Dark hair falling in uneven waves, mahogany eyes sparking even in the shadows, that strong, stubborn jaw catching the glow of the patio lights—he's all sharp edges and impossible perfection, carved from something too ancient and too dangerous to ever belong here, to ever stay hidden or contained.

The crowd pushes me forward, pulling me from my haze. My hands close on the helmet's cold edges, and sorrow punches into my chest so hard I stagger. Justice. Rage. Loss. It's screaming. Can't they hear it?

Aric leans close, whisper warm against my ear. "Skål, little Valkyrie."

Cheers. It means cheers.

Chills run down my spine.

I want his mouth to linger just a little bit longer.

Sadly, he backs away. I turn and look inside. The liquid there reeks of strong alcohol—mead, whiskey, and something metallic, copper-sweet. Blood? I gag at the thought, but the crowd's chanting, and I realize this at least gives me the opportunity to get back into the house and find the rune.

So I tip it back. The mixture burns down my throat, spilling over my chin. The helmet's weight bows my arms, like it wants to crush me to my knees. Wow, how's that for symbolism.

The cheering heightens. Aric steadies me with a hand at my back, sending tiny sparks up my body that should be cold but instead only fuel the heat. My knees nearly buckle from his touch. His eyes lock in on my mouth, his tongue swiping his lower lip like he's imagining it's mine. I may not survive him tonight.

The crowd surges, chanting his name now. Aric groans but lifts the helmet with one hand. He tips it back, grimacing like he's drinking molten glass.

"Delicious," he mutters, wiping his mouth. "Straight from Sigurd's finest collection of horrors."

Nice touch.

"Speaking of," I whisper so only he can hear. Then, louder, "I'm not feeling so well. Beer before liquor and all that. I think I need to go inside." Just for good measure, I push out just enough with my Aethercall that the crowd collectively moves on to more interesting things.

And nobody even seems to notice as we make our way back to the house.

Once inside, though, Aric stops in the living room. "Hey. C'mere," he murmurs. We fall back, him into a chair, me into his lap. His hands catch my hips, grip tight, frost blooming under his fingers. My breath escapes in a gasp, his groan low and guttural.

"Wait," I say. "What about the rune?"

"The rune can fucking wait. This can't." He pulls me more firmly against him and his eyes darken as he groans again, low in his throat. I can't tell if it's a warning or a promise. Part of me hopes it's both. The sounds of the party dissolve completely, the noise, the music, the laughter. It's all meaningless. The only things I register are the iron grip of his hands, the searing heat of his body under mine, and the unmistakable hunger in his eyes as they drag over my mouth like he's already tasting me in his mind, over and over again.

My chest heaves and I resist the urge to squirm as his grip loosens, his fingers trailing slowly and deliberately from my hips, over the bare skin beneath my shirt, sliding across my ribs, and coming to a maddening stop just under my breasts. Heart hammering, I hold my breath as he leans in, exhaling frost across my chest as he snakes his other hand around my neck, digging his fingers into my hair. "Tell me I shouldn't take you right here. Right now."

The demand sends a jolt of thrill straight through me. "Where anyone could walk in?" I taunt, out of breath. "Even your brother?"

"Fuck Reeve. I'll claim you in front of everyone."

He can't possibly mean that. But it's heady. It's so unbelievably tempting to think that he'd choose me above everything else.

With a grin that says *dare me to*, he strokes his thumb in a lazy arc over my breast, just short of my nipple, and I bite back a groan of frustration.

I glance at the door. If anyone sees us, it would for sure get back to Sigurd and Odin. "Should we stop?" I whisper.

His grip in my hair at the nape of my neck tightens. "Don't even think about it. I'm done caring what anyone thinks. I'm tired of fighting this..."

"What?"

"Fighting what I feel for you."

Our foreheads touch. "It's exhausting."

"Agreed," he admits.

"Now can I please...wreck you the way you've been wrecking me every night you climb into my bed and cling to me like I'm the only one in the world who makes your heart beat?"

The distance between us is like a single breath as my lips graze his.

"Is that a yes?" He bites down on my lower lip. "Hmm?" The sound vibrates lightly against my mouth, but I feel it like it's strumming throughout my body. I can barely think straight.

"Don't." I can barely speak. "Stop."

"Stop or don't stop? I've already made up my mind, Rey. And I'm staking my claim. Last chance..."

This time, the warm pad of his thumb strokes over my lacy bra across my aching nipple. I don't even try to fight back my groan. "Yes."

His mouth crashes against mine, and it's everything. *Everything*.

"You taste so good," I manage to breathe out in between searing kisses.

"Eat your fill, then, because when you're done, I'm going to fucking devour you."

All I see is him. A king. A deity.

I'll eat all right. I lick my lips and smile down at him. "Think you can handle the fallout?"

"I look forward to it."

I shake my head and whisper, "Only a Giant would say that."

His hands slide down my body to cup my ass. "No. Say my name."

"Aric." I smile.

"Never forget it."

Chapter Sixty-Two

ARIC

I'm buzzed but not drunk, at least not on alcohol. Which sounds stupid even in my own head, but Rey is sitting on my lap. Pressing into me. I can't get her close enough.

"Room. Now," she says.

"The alcohol—" I start but she shushes me with a finger to my lips.

"I'm completely sober," she assures me. "Reeve did pretty much all of the drinking."

I hear the soft roar of music, people laughing, a new game of beer pong as I lead her down the hall and up the stairs to the back of the house.

"This is your room?" she asks when we get there.

I frown and glance around. "What gave it away?"

"The massive bed and the fact that there's literally nothing in here at all? No decorations, no pictures. Almost like you're afraid to settle down."

I swallow the lump in my throat. "It's not that I don't want to settle down." Slowly, I walk her into my room, shutting the door behind me. "It's that I destroy everything I touch, or for a while, it seemed like that. From the lightning and storms, to the frost, to…my parents. Everything around me eventually dies. Isn't that what ice does? The bitter cold? Takes life?"

She shrugs and wanders closer to the bed, pulling me along by the hand. "Some might say it actually gives life. Doctors use extreme cold all the time to slow people's hearts in order for them to heal. They quite literally put them on ice to slow down death. So maybe you're giving life, not taking it."

I nod. "So what do *you* believe, daughter of Odin?"

"I believe in life. Believe in you." She stands on her tiptoes and, in the blanket of darkness and a sliver of moonlight, my enemy kisses me softly.

With one touch, I don't feel like a monster ready to be unleashed. I feel like a man. Like *myself*. I wrap my arms around her and deepen the kiss. No going back.

And I don't want to.

Her hands slide beneath my shirt, tugging it up and over my head. Our eyes lock, hers blazing, mine—Gods, mine are surely already too far gone. I scoop her up into my arms, walking us back until her bare skin presses against the wood of my bedframe.

She slides down my body, tugging at my jeans. My head drops back as her heat sears into me. My hands are everywhere—her hair, her throat, gripping her ass like I'll never let go.

This is right.

Us.

Together.

My heart slams in a hungry cadence for more. The world itself vibrates in tune with it—like the storm gathering outside is echoing me.

Her hands tangle in my hair, tugging hard enough to hurt, and I groan.

"You did say it was for pulling," she mumbles against my lips.

Her head tips back, laughter spilling out like sunlight, and I kiss down her throat, drinking it in, memorizing the sound.

My lips leave behind a sheen of frost everywhere they touch, like my body's marking her—claiming her—not with chains or force but with everything I am. With the monster she swears can give her life.

With the choice I never thought I had.

I don't choose death.

I don't even choose life.

I choose *her*.

She shudders against me, eyelashes fluttering as ice crystals spark and drift through the air, caught between our breaths. Thunder growls in the distance. I know it's me—my emotions splitting the sky—but I don't care. Let the world hear it. Let it know.

Our mouths crash together, frantic, desperate, a battle neither of us wants to win. She flips me onto my back, her body straddling mine like she's waited lifetimes for this. Her bra goes flying.

I reach for her, my voice hoarse, raw. "You're beautiful."

I seal my mouth over hers, working the rest of her clothes off with so much urgency until it's nothing but fire and ice, thunder and lightning. Her heat. My cold. Our skin colliding in the only way it ever should—without barriers, without hesitation.

She arches into me, and I can't stop touching her—thighs, hips, the curve of her waist, the swell of her breast beneath my palm. Every part of her begs to be memorized. Every shiver she gives me stokes the storm roaring through my veins, begging to be released.

"Aric..." My name falls from her lips like a plea and a prayer, and I don't know if I'll ever recover from the sound of it.

We move together, slowly at first, learning each other, testing the edges of restraint. Her lips part beneath mine, her hands in my hair, tugging me closer, deeper. The ice inside me cracks and melts with every sigh she gives.

Maybe I was meant to break for her all along.

Thunder rolls, rattling the windowpanes, as if the world itself knows what's happening.

I flip us, bracing her beneath me, my forehead pressed to hers as I reach for a condom, slip it on.

"This is right," I whisper, because it feels like the truth. "Us."

Her answer is a kiss so hungry, so affirming, I could come apart right there.

And then her breath is catching as I slide into her, and everything else ceases—no runes, no Gods, no betrayals.

The world could burn, and I'd still choose this.

I'd still choose her.

She moves with me, like the storm's rhythm belongs to us alone. Every kiss I brand down her throat is answered with a shudder and a gasp, her body clenching around me and the thunder outside faltering like even the storm can't keep up with our pace. She claws at my back, running her nails down either side of the runes. With a cry, I sink farther into her, losing myself to the rhythm, feeling her body grow taut, her legs and arms wrapping tighter around me.

When it happens—when we both finally let go—it's not just release. It's annihilation. The house rattles. The lights blow out. Outside, the music cuts off mid-beat. The whole world goes dark because of us and the intense sensations racking my entire body.

Because of our bond.

"That's…not normal." Rey's laugh is breathless, wrecked, beautiful.

"No." I sigh, brushing her damp hair back, pressing a lazy kiss to her temple. "Maybe next time we just start with the lights off."

Her laugh bubbles again, softer this time, as she curls her arms around me. "Yeah. Good call."

But the thunder still shakes the walls. Too loud. Too constant. And I know—I can't control it. I also start to hear voices, lots of them, weaving up from downstairs. The storm's clearly brought the party back inside.

"Bathroom?" she asks finally.

I nod toward the door. "Through there. Connected to my game room, where I keep all the fun stuff."

"Nerd." She slips out of bed and throws on a sweatshirt, giggling when she smacks into the wall before finding the switch. Light spills from the game room, warm and yellow against the dark.

Minutes pass, but she doesn't come back.

"Rey?" I call. My chest tightens when I don't hear her voice. I drag myself out of bed, still raw, still undone, then throw on some boxer briefs and stalk toward the bathroom.

I freeze.

Sitting in the corner of my game room, right next to my shelf of manga like it's always belonged there—like I fucking put it there myself—is the cow. Audhumla. The cosmic cow, Ymir's nurse, carved in stone, her ridiculous horns gleaming beneath the light.

"What the hell—" My throat closes. "That's supposed to be in his office. I didn't bring it here." It's ugly as hell and freaks the shit out of me.

Rey's leaning against the farthest wall, arms crossed. "But that's definitely it, right? Who would have put it in here? This seems too easy."

"You're right," I admit. "But let's not look a gift cow in the mouth. We got what we came here for."

She doesn't look at me. But her whole body is tense. Then suddenly, she thrusts her hand toward me.

"Bite me."

"What?" My stomach lurches.

"Bite me, Giant. I mean that literally. We can't exactly go grab a kitchen knife right now with everyone inside."

Gods. It's like the command itself threads through my blood. I know it's out of necessity, but still. The second her wrist brushes my lips, I'm gone. My teeth sink deep. Her blood floods my mouth—alive, scorching, intoxicating. The monster in me roars awake, clawing for more, hungering for freedom.

She doesn't flinch. Doesn't break eye contact. She pulls her hand away and slaps it against the rune on Audhumla. Her blood.

I want to stop, but it's like whatever she awakened won't be contained. In the next breath, I slice my teeth along my palm and slam it over the rune.

Othala flares.

The burn rips through me, searing down my spine, but it's not just fire this time.

The world blinks out. My vision goes black.

And then—

I'm there.

At the beginning.

"Odinfather," the voice whispers in my ear.

Another battlefield, the hammer flying across a bridge and into a giant fist. A man larger than the people huddled around him praying.

They're covered in frost, and they're moaning, crying out in loss, crying out for the hammer to avenge them.

The moment the weapon hits his hand, five of them die at his side like a sacrifice. His face is blurred, but he turns, and suddenly he's in the basalt archway like he came through a portal.

"I'm sorry. I'm so sorry. It must be done." Several others appear beside him. An infant and a few people in strange costumes, swords and arrows strapped to their backs. Everyone is covered in blood.

"You force its hand, its will." A voice wheezes from a body broken, bloody on the ground, half burned. "Odinfather will have this realm and everyone in it."

"His reign"—the massive Giant raises the hammer—"is over."

Chapter Sixty-Three

REY

Aric's eyes flash white—pure, blinding white—and then he drops. The sound that rips from his chest isn't human. It's a roar, deep and guttural, shaking the walls as he collapses to his knees.

"Aric!"

I stumble forward just as blood—shimmering silver, not red—slides in rivulets down his back. It traces the curve of his spine, pooling at the fresh mark burning into his skin. Othala, the rune of inheritance. My throat closes. It's carving itself into him.

He braces on his hands, shoulders heaving, fingers clawing the floorboards as though holding back something massive, something ancient. His breath frosts in the air between us, white clouds spilling with every ragged exhale.

"Aric, hey. Look at me." My voice breaks, but his eyes are locked somewhere else, not seeing me, not seeing anything but the storm tearing through his body.

I drop to my knees beside him, wrapping my arms around his torso. The ice sliding off his skin stings mine, but I force him upright, half dragging, half carrying him to the bed. He collapses onto it, chest still rising in frantic jerks.

His lips move. Barely. A mumble, broken syllables slurred together.

"Frost..."

I lean closer, my hair falling around us like a curtain.

"Odinfather...frost..."

My stomach twists. He's not dreaming—he's remembering. Gods, what is he seeing?

I pull the blanket over his trembling body and back away, my hands shaking as I grab my clothes off the floor. Every piece I slide on feels mechanical, like I'm dressing someone else, like this moment isn't real.

When I look back, he hasn't woken. He's still caught in whatever vision is clawing at him, silver blood drying like war paint across his skin.

Unsure what to do, I start to inch away from the bed. Aric's hand lashes out and captures mine. He strokes his thumb along my wrist, cooling—and healing—my skin.

"Tired," he croaks from the bed.

"You should rest."

"But the night was going to end so well, with you naked."

I laugh despite being worried. But I don't leave his room. I linger beside his bed.

"It would be easy if I didn't like you," I admit, as if what just happened between us wasn't earth-shattering and world-bending. I can feel him all around me, like I no longer exist on my own.

"Life is rarely easy, and sex complicates everything—even really, *really* good sex with ice, and frost, and shivering—"

I cup a hand over his mouth. "Stop or you'll have an orgasm without me."

He clasps my hand in his. "Impossible. No man left behind."

I laugh again. He cracks an eye and holds the blanket up for me to lie back next to him.

I don't hesitate.

He peels the covers back farther, and I dive in against the golden heat of his skin, the body of a Giant carved from storm and shadow. I gulp.

"I'm not a piece of meat, Rey." His mouth tilts in a lazy grin. "Giants have feelings, too."

My cheeks flame. He catches it, of course.

"Wow," he murmurs, tracing my jaw with his knuckles. "She blushes. Pretty. Where else do you blush?"

Before I can answer, his hand slides lower, cupping my breast, then gliding down my stomach in a slow, deliberate path that makes my pulse stutter.

I gasp as he flips me onto my back.

"Thought you were tired," I breathe.

Shut up, Rey. Not the time to remind the man he's tired.

"Second wind." His palms spread wide over my hips, pinning me. "Don't tell me how to feel. I'm hungry now."

The meaning hits me the moment his head disappears beneath the sheets. A teasing kiss. Then the cool brush of his breath between my legs.

His hands grip my thighs. "Blush," he whispers, icy air fanning heat where I need him most. My body arches in answer.

"Still worried about you," I pant. But we both know that's not true.

"Good." His laugh is dark, wicked. "It'll make me more determined to hear you scream my name."

The rest of his words are lost when his tongue touches me, cool and devastating, each stroke unraveling me further.

"Gods—" I choke out.

He laughs against my skin, the vibration shattering me. "Don't you know? The Gods are sleeping. They won't hear you." His voice is a promise, hungry and sure. "You're stuck with me."

I almost laugh, but it turns into a gasp. "No place I'd rather be."

His head lifts just long enough for his dark eyes to cut into me, sharp and raw. "Same."

And then I'm gone again—lost in the way he tastes me, claims me, makes me forget about heroes and fairy tales. Who needs a savior on a white horse when the storm itself is in your bed?

I clench the sheets in my fists as I lose control. It's lightning.

Chaos. Ruin. I see stars, and in that moment, I know: If this is what love is, then let me fall for the monster. Even if he hasn't been fully unleashed yet.

I have high hopes.

He slides his body back up mine and stares me down, mouth swollen, eyes turning white.

"What happened to no man left behind?" I whisper.

He grins.

Then I push him on his back and sink on top of him.

CHAPTER SIXTY-FOUR

ARIC

The next morning, after a night of rumpled sheets and very little sleep—in a good way, for once—I ask the question that's been burning through me.

"I know it wasn't me," I whisper. "So who moved the statue?"

She looks deep in thought. "Rowen? One of my father's goons? Could be whoever saw us at the oak tree, unlocking rune number three."

"That would make sense. Since they knew specifically which rune to plant in my game room." She nods, silently acknowledging that we're both in the dark.

"We just need to be more careful." I look down at her, hair rumpled, lips swollen from my kisses, and my heart clenches. "*You* need to be careful, to stay safe."

"Teamwork."

I can't help but smirk. "That's all it took for you to be Team Giant?"

"Are we back to that team stuff again?" She rests her head on my chest. "Maybe."

"Speaking of teamwork…" I feel her shift against me. "I bet you already know where the last rune is. Want to share?"

She sighs. "I do know. But it's so public. Right out in the open. I'm... Well, I'm—"

"Scared," I finish for her. "You're afraid that when I'm fully awakened, I'll go berserk and tear down Endir and Everett and everyone in it."

"Or maybe just a building or two," she admits, and I can hear that she's smiling. "We'll need to find a time there aren't people around. Not too easy during orientation."

My heart sinks as I think. "Actually, orientation is the perfect time. Everyone is going to be in one place tonight. It's the Hunt. The perfect time to do something without people around, because they'll all be getting drunk in the stadium or running through the forest, away from campus. It's just..." *Shit.* Sigurd is going to hate this. "The runes will be down," I admit.

"Oh," she whispers. She's silent. "So campus will be unprotected. From everyone. If we awaken you tonight during the Hunt and find Mjölnir, there's nothing stopping my father from taking it."

"Right," I say.

"We can't do it tonight," she declares at the same time I say, "Let's do it tonight."

She pushes herself up on my chest. "What?"

"It's sort of fitting, isn't it?" I ask. "Me and you. Sigurd and Odin. Giants, Gods, all equal players. Everything in balance."

"You're sure?" she asks.

No. I pull her down against me, breathe in the smell of her, the clean air and crushed wildflowers. "I'm sure," I whisper.

I tighten my arms around her, brushing my lips against her forehead before pulling her fully into my arms again.

Her breath hitches. "Will you be angry if you wake up and I'm in your bed again?"

"No." I press my mouth against her neck. "I'll be angry if I wake up and you aren't."

We have one more day of reprieve before we're back in class together, and I wonder how I'll be near her, acting normal, when there's now this massive thing between us. And a road ahead we can't avoid even if we try.

We're still in opposing camps, something we can't ignore. And the fact that someone brought in the fourth rune means our every move up to now has been followed.

If it was Odin, then one would think he'd just call her and say *get it done*.

I groan and get out of bed, then walk over to my game room. The cow's still there. It's ugly, a relic of a past that was best left forgotten.

I feel Rey before I see her. "The last rune," I start. "Which one is it?"

She presses her lips together like she doesn't want to say it, then finally whispers, "Thor's rune." She sighs. "Thurisaz."

The word falls like a stone the instant it's out, sinks into my stomach and just stays there like a curse.

"Thor's rune," I repeat. "The rune of protection and destruction. A weapon and a shield all at once. The thorn that wounds, the hammer that crushes, the force that defends. At least, that's what it's supposed to be, what it was created to do."

My chest feels too tight, like I'm bracing for an impact I can't stop. But she doesn't say anything. She looks at me, like she's studying me and my reaction. I don't know how to feel. Is "disappointed" even the right word?

I want to unlock who I am, but I'm starting to wonder if it will be at the cost of losing the one thing I care about in this world. Will she hate me for what I become?

Rey reaches for my hand and squeezes it. Her eyes are filled with so much emotion, she doesn't have to say the words. I sense them.

And it's the same for me.

"Promise me." I turn fully to her and make sure I have both of her hands. "Promise me that no matter what happens from here on out, you'll still look at me the way you are right now."

"How am I looking at you?"

"Like I matter. Like you're on my side."

Her eyes well with tears. She nods, and then: "I promise. I'll always look at you like this."

It's a beautiful lie.

Chapter Sixty-Five

REY

I wake up with Aric holding me in a cocoon of protectiveness that's so fiercely tight, I can barely move. When did we fall back asleep? What time is it? Did we miss class? And then I remember today is Sunday. My stomach dips as I realize that this little bubble of normalcy—classmates, parties, laughter—they'll really all be done for me when Monday hits.

The thought leaves a bitter taste in my mouth, one I want to wash away.

Aric stirs and pulls me back against him when I try to get up. Okay, I need water.

He's so strong, I can't break out of his hold, so I try to squirm away, and when he still doesn't release me, I go for holding his nose and mouth closed. He jolts awake and falls back off the bed, taking me with him in a tangle of limbs and comforter.

"What the hell, Rey!" he yells through his laughter.

"I! Needed. Water!" I snort through the giggles.

"Then *ask*!"

We're still cracking up when the door opens and Reeve waltzes in. He goes still as Aric and I both look up at him from the floor. Reeve stares us down, expression unreadable, though one thing's for certain: he doesn't look amused.

"Had a good night, did we? Do my eyes deceive me, or am I still drunk?"

"No!" Aric and I yell in unison.

I scramble off him and gesture at myself. "See? Fully clothed. Nothing happened." I hold up my hands. "Can I get some water and a ride back to campus?"

Reeve winks. "Didn't you already get a ri—"

I bare my teeth. "Finish that sentence. I dare you."

He's smiling his ever-present casual grin, but today it doesn't reach his eyes. I follow his gaze. Aric's putting his shirt back on. Reeve focuses on the four runes before snapping his attention back to me. "Water's in the fridge downstairs. Help yourself."

I frown. Normally, Reeve is shoving us in the opposite direction and trying to fuel hate between us. "Is everything okay? You just went really pale."

"Yeah. Uh, yeah." He grabs his phone from his pocket and holds it up. "Need to make a quick call. Be ready in ten." He's already walking away.

"I'll grab two waters," I tell Aric. "You finish getting ready." But when I head out into the hallway, I see Reeve going into what looks like an office. And before the door closes behind him, I catch a glimpse of Sigurd inside. He's impossible to miss—for one, he's tall, even taller than Reeve. And today, he's not in his ever-present school spirit outfit but a full-on black suit that looks a hell of a lot like the armor CEOs and drug lords wear.

I tiptoe over and press my ear against the closed door in order to hear the muffled voices.

"Yes." Reeve sounds different. Angry. "Yes, I'm sure. No, I don't know exactly how it happened. Although I have suspicions. Either way, he needs to be careful—we all do."

Sigurd curses. "We've been careful. And I trust your brother. He knows what he's doing…this time."

This time?

"Clearly not careful enough!" Reeve shouts, followed by the sound of something breaking. "You know what this means!"

"We can prevent it," Sigurd says calmly. "We have so far. Everyone believes the lie, so let them continue to believe it while we keep the truth safe."

"What if we can't keep it safe anymore? What if we can't keep *him* safe?" Reeve swears. "I knew this alliance was a bad idea."

Alliance? Every cell in my body is vibrating. With fear? Anger?

"You've played your part," Sigurd continues. "Now trust your brother—you'll see, all will be well."

"We need to tell—"

"Even if the truth was laid out for all to see, it wouldn't matter, son. Too many moves have already been made."

Footsteps sound, but not near the door. Someone's pacing, or maybe they both are.

They stop talking, and I see the doorknob begin to turn.

I rush downstairs to the kitchen, heart pounding, and quickly pull a water from the fridge, gulping from the bottle in hungry pulls.

Reeve's at my side in an instant. His hand snaps out to grip my wrist. He flips it over and runs his thumb down the veins in my arm.

I laugh. "You really *are* still drunk, aren't you?"

But Reeve isn't here to joke. He grips my wrist harder and presses his thumb against it, like he's trying to count my heartbeat. I've been taught how to calm a racing heart. He'll feel a completely normal pulse.

I shoot him a glare. "If you're trying to feel me up, I don't recommend it. Aric might rip your arm from your body in the process."

"Stop." His whisper is low. "Until now, I haven't been worried. I've ignored signs because he ignored *you*." He releases my hand and tilts my chin toward him. "Enemies on all sides, Rey. I hope you do remember that. We have nothing against a little bloodshed, and I'm convinced you don't, either."

"So." I cross my arms. "Your happy-go-lucky attitude, is it all an act?"

"No." His smile spreads wide. "I was born to be whatever I need to be to whoever needs it in the moment." He snaps his fingers. "It makes people so much easier to manipulate. Something you know all about, right?"

"Is this the part where you want me to tell you what I know?" I ask.

He snorts out a laugh. "Even as a daughter of Odin, you still know nothing, believe me. If you did, you wouldn't be sleeping so soundly at night next to Aric. Now, go find him. I'm sure he's waiting. And watch yourself."

A daughter of Odin. My pulse pounds in my ears. Reeve is awake—maybe more awake than Aric. Why didn't Aric tell me?

"A threat?"

"A promise."

"At least you're honest."

He grips my chin between his thumb and forefinger. "If you so much as breathe evil intent toward my brother, I'll snap your neck myself, and trust me when I say I'll feel no remorse."

I laugh, but it sounds hollow to my ears. "You think I'm that easy to kill?"

He lightly shoves me back. "Of course. How is the family, by the way? Laufey still have her garden?"

For the first time, I feel true fear around Reeve, hot and sharp in my chest. "Leave her out of this!" What the hell does he know?

He takes a step toward me just as Aric rounds the corner. He has Reeve in a chokehold before the guy can even attempt to defend himself.

Good. I hope he bleeds.

"You touch her and I break your fingers one by one." Ice has full-on descended around the kitchen like a fog, Aric's breath coming out in puffs. "Apologize."

Reeve's green eyes are wild as he chokes out, "You'll have to let me go first, brother."

Aric shoves him against the fridge, causing it to shudder. The sound of things falling on the inside is like a bomb going off in the kitchen.

Reeve cracks his neck. "You see her naked once and suddenly you're—"

Aric lunges, and this time he slams his fist against Reeve's nose so hard, I hear bones break.

I wince. *Shit.*

"Fuck!" Reeve rolls on the ground. "You know I don't heal as fast, you piece of shit!" He groans and gets to his feet. "Heal me."

I'm frozen in place.

"No." Aric walks over to me, completely ignoring Reeve. "Are you okay?" Eyes full of concern, he starts checking my neck and arms.

"Yeah, I'm fine. Reeve's just being his typical asshole self." I reach for his hand and squeeze it. "Really, I'm fine. I can handle myself."

Aric's eyes soften slightly. But he's still breathing hard. Jeez, the fourth rune is not messing around with his emotions.

"Okay?" I ask him.

His eyes are wild, like he still wants to pick a fight. At least Reeve hopefully learned his lesson—don't piss off a Giant in love.

No.

Wait.

Not love.

I mean…

Did I really just think that?

Aric tilts his head. "You're blushing again."

"Am I?" I touch my cheeks with the backs of my hands. "Just kind of hot."

He holds out his hand. I grab it immediately.

"It's fine, I'm fine, not bleeding to death over here," Reeve grumbles. "Shit, can nobody take a joke anymore?"

"No," we say in unison.

I start tugging Aric toward the door. "Let's head back."

"Yeah." Reeve lets out a rough exhale. "You guys go, just leave me here to fix my face. Shit, this is going to mess with my costume for the fun tonight."

"Costume?" I ask. "Fun?"

"Yes, fun. The Wild Hunt," Reeve clarifies. "Cosplay. Though now I'm thinking Aric should have gone as a boxer. Shit, that hurt."

Aric ignores him and groans. "I forgot about the costumes."

"Biggest event of the year," Reeve continues. "How could you forget the costumes?" He turns back to me. "It's a party and feast with rich alumni, parents, and lots of hidden alcohol. What's not to love? Plus, you know how Sigurd looks forward to releasing the fucking ravens."

My entire body goes numb. This is new information. "Sigurd releases ravens?"

The Release of the Ravens. If it's anything like Odin's Wild Hunt, that would be a total death wish. *Odin* releases the ravens. *Odin* started the Hunt, and now Sigurd is shitting all over it.

It all clicks. This is why Father gave me a week to find Mjölnir. The runes will be down—he'll be able to walk right onto campus and claim the weapon in the most dramatic, devastating way possible, reclaiming the Wild Hunt—and the Nine Realms—as his own.

He's been planning this since he learned where the Eriksons were keeping Mjölnir a year ago. And I'm just a pawn on his board.

"Ah, Rey." Footsteps echo as the man in question makes his way into the kitchen. I feel Aric tense next to me. "Parents are, of course, always welcome at our Hunt. I do hope Odin stops by to say hello. It's been what? Two years since the broken engagement?"

He does a double take at Reeve and then glares at Aric. "You boys get in a fight?"

"A fight means it's evenly matched." Aric rolls his eyes. "Weaker link over there can barely take a punch."

Sigurd smirks. "Yes, well, he's more of a talker than a fighter."

Reeve's eyes narrow.

I'm too focused on the Hunt to be amused.

In fact, I think I'm going to be sick.

"So." He nods at me. "Your father?"

"He's pretty busy these days." The lie falls so flat, I want to disappear into the ground. "And yeah, about two years since you two connected." My hands are in fists at my side.

"Yes." Sigurd's glare intensifies. "Water under the bridge and all that. Did you decide on your costume yet?"

"I didn't really bring anything, so…"

"Nonsense, it's tradition!" He claps Aric on the back. Aric doesn't so much as flinch, even though it had to have hurt. "Be sure to let the staff know to grab an extra costume for Rey. I'm thinking…" He tilts his head. "Valkyrie. After all, weren't they soldiers for Odin?"

Chapter Sixty-Six

REY

When I get back from Aric's, I knock on Ziva's door to make sure she got home safely last night, only to be greeted with an empty coffee mug and a glare. "Do not come back unless you fill this." The door slams in my face.

"Glad you're alive!" I call and decide maybe I need coffee, too. Coffee, and to think, and maybe a miracle. I chew my bottom lip and finally make the call I don't want to make. Better I tell Father first so I have time to plan.

He picks up on the first ring.

"Daughter." His voice is deep. "Do you have good news for me?"

It's honestly no use lying. "He'll be awakened tonight, like I promised."

I wish I didn't have to tell Odin, that we didn't have to do this at all, but we don't have a choice. We need to finish this, no matter what may happen. I need to hope for the best.

There's that stupid word again. *Hope*.

"Good." His voice is clipped. "Then I won't have to kill Laufey. I do enjoy her company. It would be useless and tragic to spill her blood solely because you took too long."

I stare out at campus as a chill washes down my spine. "What do you plan on doing first?"

"Where are you?"

Weird question. "In my dorm."

"Go outside. I'll wait."

I don't hesitate. I take the stairs down to the main lobby and walk outside. "Okay, now what?"

"Do you see the basalt arch?"

"Yes."

"Imagine a bridge protruding from it, leading to a different realm, a *perfect* realm without war or pain, with ultimate power, where there is no more fighting, where I'm not forced to use people you love against you. My plan, daughter, is to regain what is owed us and then pay back those who dared steal from us."

"Why—" My voice cracks. "Why did they steal the hammer in the first place if such a utopia existed?"

I think of the paintings, of Laufey's stories. Of Aric's.

"Did Thor betray the Giants?" I ask.

He is quiet.

"Father, did Thor betray them first?"

"Believe me when I say he had no choice. And leave it at that."

Oh my Gods, did *we* start the war?

"Get Mjölnir before I lose patience. I'll see you tonight for the Wild Hunt. Insulting that he would attempt to steal my party, so I should at least make an appearance. Besides, Laufey loves a party. She misses you so much; rarely does she sleep without crying. Her soul breaks knowing you're in danger, but don't worry, I tell her daily—you'd do anything to save her. Right?"

Tears clog my throat. "Right."

"See you this evening. I think I'll dress…like a God."

I turn and walk back in the building. Of course, Reeve's at the front door to witness my mental breakdown. I can't handle any more stress.

I force a smile. I'm sure it looks as fake as it feels, but I can't be good at everything, can I?

"Good phone call?" Reeve asks.

Gods, I want to punch him. "Lovely, thank you."

"Delighted to hear it."

We walk through the lobby and into the elevator together. *Please don't press the emergency stop button, please don't press the—*

He presses the emergency stop button.

"I really need this to not be our thing." I go to my corner of the elevator, and he goes to his. "What do you need to tell me that you can't say in the dorm or at the party or in front of Aric or your little snake?"

"Cute." Reeve folds his arms, looking at me with a serious expression. "Hunt's in a few hours," he adds.

"Yeah. So?" I ask. "Not exactly a reason to kidnap me in an elevator. What's going on, Reeve?"

"I know what you did," he growls in a low voice. "And now you'll know what I can do."

Something's not right, not with the way his voice suddenly sounds gravelly, not with the gleam in his eyes. I lunge for the button to open the doors, but at the same moment, Reeve is shoving me up against the side wall. Heart pounding, I heave forward to get him off me, then kick him backward. He stumbles and then faces me.

"Is that all?" He laughs. "I expected more from the daughter of Odin."

I throw my right fist. He spins out of the way, dodging me completely, and grabs me by the throat. His fingers tighten.

I knee him in the groin, and he immediately goes down, releasing my neck. There's no time to regain my breath. I shove my palm against his chest and use my other arm to cut off his air.

"Don't pick fights with someone stronger than you," I say. "It's embarrassing."

"Stronger than me?" He laughs again. In the next breath, he vanishes.

What the fuck?

He reappears, standing on the other side of the elevator, arms crossed, leaning back arrogantly.

I blink and blink. Did I really just see that?

"Let's try this again, shall we, Rey?" The air cracks and hums around us, and then his eyes flash a bright white as he whispers with a grin, "I'm Loki. Nice to meet you."

Chapter Sixty-Seven

REY

Loki? Giant of Jötunheim Loki? I thought Loki died in the wars, too. This is bad, so very bad.

And yet, it also makes so much sense. I can't believe I didn't see it sooner. Reeve has always been the jokester. Leading all the fun and games on campus. Never taking anything too seriously.

Of course he'd be the God of Mischief.

By the time the elevator hits the second floor, he's dropped two more bombs. One: No, Aric doesn't know, and two: If I breathe a word to anyone, he'll kill me.

Then he's gone.

I clench my fists in the middle of the hallway. I'm too in shock to even open the door and enter my room. Not about the *him threatening my life* part—my life has been on the line here from day one. But not telling his brother… Aric would be gutted.

Did Reeve—Loki—always know? Or is he just remembering now?

My father said "they" were asleep, that the ones stuck here didn't have memories of the war, that he used the last of his power to wipe them all—a *kindness*, he said, to keep them from remembering the suffering. Since his power is waning, could that mean their memories are coming back? And that their powers are returning, too?

Reeve vanished in that elevator like it was nothing.

And that's when realization dawns. *That's* the urgency. The war between the Gods and Giants has been on pause on our end—but only until Odin finds Mjölnir…or Sigurd hits play.

Reality comes crashing down. Are some of the students around us awake to who they are? Are the Gods and Giants just biding their time, waiting to start another war, while it feels like the old one hasn't even ended?

This is bigger than my brain can handle right now.

Suddenly, it feels like someone's behind me. *Reeve?* I turn around and land a punch before I realize who's standing there. My hand aches like I just hit steel, but Aric doesn't even take a step back.

It's really not a good sign that the man didn't even flinch.

I make a face. "I panicked."

He towers over me, pieces of his hair falling across his face, but his eyes aren't as cold. They have life, and they're so solely focused on me, my heart skips a few beats. "You look pissed."

"I'm usually pissed." I grit my teeth. "Listen, I think we need a better plan. What if everyone around us—" I pause. "Can I come in really quick?"

His eyes search mine. "Sure."

I want to blurt out everything I just learned about Reeve—or better yet, demand that Aric come with me to unlock Thurisaz right away, innocent bystanders be damned—but as soon as he closes his door behind us, Aric drops a single question that steals the breath right out of me.

"Will I forget you?" he asks.

I stop in my tracks. He means with the last rune unlocking.

"It feels like with the visions, they're going to take over. That I'll become someone else—some*thing* else."

I swallow the lump in my throat, force my lungs to work, my lips to move. "I—I don't think that will happen."

"But you don't know for sure," he says, more to himself than to me. "No one knows. My parents didn't. My grandfather doesn't—or if he does, he won't tell."

"You know who you are, Aric."

"But what if I forget who I am? Forget about us."

That cracks something open inside me. He isn't afraid of the power burning through him. He isn't afraid of losing himself to it. He's afraid of losing *us.*

I take his hand. "You'll remember. I'll make sure of it."

"Then it'll be okay." He wraps his arms around me. It takes a minute, but his humor returns. "You know, if I was a romantic, I'd say this is some real *Romeo and Juliet* kind of shit, warring families, bloodshed, revenge."

I laugh against his chest, the sound muffled by the steady beat of his heart. "Let's not comp to Shakespeare. Most of his stories didn't end so well."

His lips brush my forehead, the featherlight kiss so soft it feels like a promise, when days ago I would have seen it as a threat.

I tilt my head up, nerves tangling with want, with a need to explore this further before everything goes to hell.

Aric's arms wind tighter around me until our breaths are mingling, until the space between us disappears into nothing. His mouth descends slowly, like he's giving me a chance to run. He presses the faintest kiss to my lips. It's nothing but a tease of everything I want and more.

He exhales a cool breath across my lower lip. I feel the frost first, the chill seeping into me—then the heat of his tongue follows, melting me all over again. Making me want to lose control.

I should step away and tell him about his brother. He deserves to know.

But he's clearly in a vulnerable place already, and I think he needs me right now. To feel safe and loved and not like everything he thought he knew has been pulled out from under him. Again.

A tremor rolls through me. I know he can probably see it, feel it. The talking can wait. Everything else can wait. Right now, I need to show him just how loved he is.

Before our time together runs out.

Chapter Sixty-Eight

REY

When I get back from the dining hall later, Aric is gone. But he tucked a handwritten note underneath my door.

Sigurd has me helping set up for the Hunt. Be back as soon as I can.

I shoot him a quick text.

Me: *Hope it's going well*

Giant Asshole: *I'm forced to work alongside a clown who keeps juggling hammers. My brother's an idiot.*

My stomach clenches.

Me: *That he is. See you soon?*

I debate saying more. It doesn't seem fair to deliver the kind of news I need to via text.

Giant Asshole: *Yeah, got your costume, I'll bring it over later.*

Me: *Cool*

I want to type *I love you.* I don't. Instead I just stare at my terrible "Cool" response and let out a groan.

I glance at the clock beside my bed. Almost two p.m. The Hunt doesn't begin until sundown, but I feel like I'm running out of time. This is it.

Tonight...it ends.

There's a sharp knock at my door, and I open it to find Rowen there. His hair's a mess, and his ever-present suit jacket is gone. He still wears a dress shirt, but a few buttons are open at the top and his sleeves are rolled up.

"Hey," he starts, lingering in the hallway.

"You obviously came here for a reason, Rowen. You might as well come in."

His face says it all—*I'm angry, I'm sorry, I don't know what to say.*

Yeah. Same.

Though I'm not really angry with him. He's just another victim in this war. Same as me. Another pawn in Odin's game.

Rowen comes in and closes my door. He's carrying a small red gift bag.

"Where's Eira?" I ask.

"Getting ready for the Hunt. Something about smoky makeup and a proper blowout. She's been at it for hours." He shrugs. "At least she ignores me enough that I can do what I prefer doing when I'm on campus."

"What's that?"

His eyes flicker to mine. "Watch you. Protect you. Keep my only friend safe." His smile's warm. "Take your pick."

I walk toward him, and he envelops me in a hug that I can tell we both sorely need.

"I'll always be here for you," he whispers. "You can trust me."

I want to believe that.

I frown and stare down at his arm. The pain there radiates off his skin and into mine. The anger is there, too, only dimmer now, the rage seemingly replaced by a new, crushing emotion: regret.

He shifts in my hold, and it's almost like the scars falter and shimmer. I do a double take. For the first time since I've known him, it almost looks like two runes intertwined. How have I never noticed it before? Or is it because he's never let me look this close?

"Your scars," I murmur, and he goes still. "They almost look like a combination of Laguz and Berkano, the ones you have on your door back home." I smile. "I guess I never noticed before?"

Rowen slowly pulls his sleeves down. "You know your father—he thinks using the power of runes is beneath him, but these serve our purpose. You're part God, so you see me clearly. But these runes…they make me look different to the outside world."

He rakes back the strands of hair that fell out of his bun. "Speaking of runes, though." Rowen shifts away and lifts the bag. "I was going to give you this on your birthday," he says quietly. "Then everything happened, and it just…" His eyes flick to mine. "Now feels right."

When I don't immediately grab it, maybe because I'm surprised and not used to gifts, he digs in and pulls out a thin chain, the silver catching the dim light in the room. Dangling from the chain is a small carved rune.

"Tiwaz," he explains, pressing it into my palm. "The warrior's rune. It means honor, sacrifice, victory bought with blood. Tyr's rune. I figured you'd appreciate that—fighting battles you didn't ask for, carrying more than anyone should."

My throat tightens. It's in the shape of an upward arrow. The metal is cool against my skin. "I don't get gifts a lot." He knows that.

"You've felt alone," he continues, "but you're not. Not anymore. I'll be by your side, Rey—always. Even if it means watching you hold hands with a Giant."

A burst of laughter escapes me. "Dramatic much?"

"Maybe," he admits with a small smile. He clasps the chain behind my neck, fingers brushing the back of my skin. "But you deserve someone who doesn't walk away. Not ever."

I think of Aric. "Thank you."

He nods. "Maybe I'll see you for dinner. Keep it on. It makes me feel better. Runes are powerful, and tonight, the ones at Endir will be down."

"Right." I nod. "All the wards are gone tonight."

"Except yours." He smiles. "So basically, don't die."

I give him another small hug. "I'll do my best."

Chapter Sixty-Nine

ARIC

It took longer than I thought it would, setting up for the Wild Hunt. Between the buffet tables, candles, and chopping wood for all the mini bonfires, I'm exhausted.

Reeve left Rey's costume with me and bounced on account that he had to meet the DJ in the stadium. I call bullshit. He just got tired of stacking firewood. What is with the guy and physical labor?

It's not like I wanted to leave Rey, but I still answered Sigurd's call. He and Reeve are the only family I have left. I chalk it up to loyalty, maybe a sense of obligation, but the truth is I also needed a minute to myself.

So much is at stake tonight, and it's impossible to focus with Rey in my arms. When I'm with her, all I can think about is touching her. And one touch is never enough.

A few girls pass me in the dorm lobby. They're already dressed up in silver fairy costumes, the guys trailing behind them wearing horned helmets and leather vests. Some people like to dress early and hit the local pubs and restaurants to pregame before the Hunt. The fraternities on the other side of campus have been at it since breakfast. Any excuse to party, I guess.

I hope Rey's going to be okay with hers having so many layers. I peeked inside the garment bag because it was heavier than I expected. It looks like Sigurd had it commissioned specifically, which makes me wonder just how long Sigurd's had this planned. And does he actually know what an authentic Valkyrie used to dress like? Did he fight them? He holds vast memories of the war and our people, but he seldom shares his stories with me. My parents didn't like to talk about the past, either. I think it pained them too much.

Sigurd isn't as sentimental. He's just selfish.

But for once, the pain my family has caused me doesn't sting to think about. Because Rey's my future now. If we can just get through tonight...maybe we can truly be together.

I jog the stairs and shoulder open the door to our floor, then head straight to her room. I've just lifted my hand to knock when I hear muffled voices inside. Is she with someone? I press my ear to the door.

"You can't just pop into my room unannounced!" she growls. Now that my powers are almost completely awakened, my hearing is so good it sounds like she's right beside me.

"Get over it."

I jerk my head away from the door. Reeve is here. Not at the stadium. Something dark edges along my spine. I press against the door again.

"I want Mjölnir, Rey."

"You and everybody else." She laughs darkly. "Why didn't you just steal it from your *other* brother, huh?"

Other brother? What is she talking about?

"This isn't gossip hour," Reeve tells her. "The last thing I want is to revisit Thor's death and my part in it."

Rey gasps. "Your part in it?"

"Who else do you think killed him, the Easter Bunny? It was war, Rey. All's fair."

"You're a fucking monster, Loki!"

I freeze.

My entire body goes cold.

Loki?

As in...*the* Loki. Adopted by Odin and raised as a brother to Thor.

I stumble back, completely numb. Then I jerk the door open so hard the electronic lock breaks.

Reeve throws up his hands and curses.

Rey freezes on the spot.

Betrayal washes through me so hard and fast, I can't catch my breath. My brother. My brother who was supposed to be protecting me, warning me away from her, the whole time was lying to me about who he is and what he really wants.

And she knew?

Rey *knew*.

Was it all bullshit? Needing me? Protecting me? Was it all for show?

Of course it was. It always was.

Both of them.

Fuck.

What else hasn't she told me?

And *him*...his betrayal churns from the depths of my heart, shredding what little bit of home I had left. My hands ball into fists, ice rising and crackling off my skin. Thunder rumbles so hard overhead, the room rattles with it.

The monster within me roars for release, icy claws tearing beneath my skin so viciously, it's a wonder I don't rip apart. I force it down. Swallow hard.

"Loki," I whisper. "Right."

Reeve shakes his head. "Aric, no, it's not what you think. I have no skin in the game. She's the one—"

"Are you kidding me right now!" Rey shouts.

But she's not innocent, either. That much is obvious. "You knew. And you didn't tell me."

"I was going to, Aric! You have to believe me."

I shake my head. "I don't know what to believe right now other than you're both fucking liars willing to gamble with my life. And for what? For a weapon. Nobody cares if I burn the world, turn into a monster, lose my fucking soul—you all just want power."

I level Rey with a glare. "I think it's safe to say that this little ceasefire is over. And we"—I shake my head at Reeve—"aren't brothers."

They both start yelling at once.

But I hear nothing.

I toss the costume into her room, then turn and leave the hall, the dorm, the campus. As storm clouds gather, darkening the sky with the fury of a hurricane, my vision blurs. My chest aches.

I've always walked the line between being the man I hoped to be and the monster I knew lived inside. But with Rey, I started to believe things could be different. Now a cold emptiness unfurls in my heart...

And I welcome it.

I guess I have my answer, then. I'll turn into the monster.

Because nobody wanted the man anyway.

Chapter Seventy

REY

"Aric!" I'm still yelling his name. Reeve shoves me back into the room, his hand clapping over my mouth.

"Stop," he hisses. "He's pissed, so let him be pissed. You have bigger problems right now. Like how the fuck you're going to unlock Thurisaz without his blood."

My entire body freezes.

He knows.

Reeve knows how to unlock the runes.

His grin is cruel, spiteful. Then in a blink, he's gone.

"I am never going to get used to that," I mutter, then pace the room for a while. Reeve was right about the rune issue, but I barely care about that right now. What I care about is the devastated look on Aric's face. It was like he didn't recognize me, like the woman he knew—maybe even was falling for—no longer existed.

It broke my heart.

Maybe a few hours go by, maybe a few minutes, but when I next look up, it's to see the wall between my and Aric's rooms completely frozen solid. Like he's purposefully, literally freezing me out.

My stomach hurts, but at least it means he's there.

I suddenly see my own breath in front of my face. If he doesn't watch it, he's going to freeze the entire floor.

A crack flashes outside. A rumble follows.

The world will hear it as thunder.

But I know the truth—it's the sound of a giant's heart breaking.

And I'm the one who did it.

I stare down at my costume lying haphazardly on my bed and try calling Aric again. First on his phone. Then leaning against the wall that divides us. He doesn't answer.

So I go to his room and knock three times on his door. No answer. Four more times, a bit more aggressively, pushing my Aethercall even though I know it's pointless.

"Leave!"

"I'm not leaving until you open up and talk to me."

"I mean it, Rey!" he yells. "I don't want to see you right now."

I hesitate. We don't have time, and he needs to know where I stand—where we stand. "Aric, I'm going to keep knocking, so you may as well open up now." I knock for the next two minutes, until my knuckles are sore. "I'm not leaving." I knock again, then jerk my hand back. "Ouch."

Suddenly, he's there, dragging me in by the shirt and slamming the door behind me. At first he looks like he's going to yell, but when he speaks, it's in a low growl.

Somehow, that's even scarier.

"How long have you known?"

I swallow hard. "Only since this morning. Reeve—*Loki* cornered me in the elevator."

The silence between us is so thick, I'm now definitely wishing he'd yell.

"You should have told me," he finally says.

"You're right. I wanted to." I could launch into some excuse about bad timing, how he was vulnerable enough already, or how I didn't want to be the one to hurt him. Or how we were, you know, distracted by mind-blowing sex. But he's right. I should've just blurted it out. He deserved to know.

"I'm sorry."

Aric's jaw tightens. His voice drops, low and dangerous. "You think saying 'sorry' erases anything?" He shakes his head. "This is what your family does, Rey. Odin imprisoned Laufey. Thor betrayed Alvaldi. You…broke me." He sighs. "Should've seen it coming a mile away."

"No! Aric, please—"

"History's just repeating itself."

"We're *not* them."

But he's stopped listening. "Lure the Giant with love and then take what you want, destroying everything."

"Stop. Please. I don't want to fight. I don't want to lose you—"

"Lose me?" He laughs, sharp and humorless. "That's rich. You don't give a shit about how this would affect me, only how it could help you."

"That's not true. I just panicked because every single moment I'm with you, I fall harder, and I realize I may not be able to do it, Aric! I may not be able to save everyone, and for once I want to be really selfish. I can't live in a world where you don't exist!"

His face falls just briefly before he glares. "Well, there's a replacement Giant on the table now, so—"

His words land like perfect little punches. I move before I think, shoving him hard enough that the icy plaster at his shoulder spiderwebs and a chunk falls away from the wall. He stares down at the pieces, then at me. "Are you kidding me right now?"

He doesn't care about the plaster. He cares about the lie.

"My turn," he breathes. In one fluid motion, he reverses our positions, lifting me into the air and pinning me against the icy division. The cold digs into my skin with a sweet, sharp sting.

"That all you've got?" I ask with an arched brow.

My hands are on his shoulders, my feet off the ground so we're eye to eye.

One heartbeat. Another.

I wrap my legs around his waist.

Then his mouth finds mine.

It's hungry and fierce—all the anger funneled into a kiss that robs me of breath. He bruises and claims, and I can taste the fury on his lips, the pain on his tongue. I claw at his back, fingers finding skin that sparks under my touch. With each press of my hand against a rune, his body hums to life, begging to be set free.

"Still mad?" I gasp when his mouth scorches a trail to my neck.

Aric answers with a series of kisses down my throat, each one more insistent than the last until the urgency becomes undeniable. He moves with me and against me—and before I know what's happening, our hands are everywhere, ripping, fumbling, clothes sliding to a heap on the floor. Shoes scatter along the way. I'm not looking at the mess. I'm watching his eyes.

They flare white as lightning as we become one. The runes along his spine pulse against my palms, small constellations of light that walk up his back. I feel the hum under my hands, the way the air tastes metallic and sweet, like the edge of something monumental. The edge of an awakening.

It's not pretty, this surrender.

It's jagged, fraught with anger and pain and uncertainty.

We slam into walls, ice and plaster crumbling, then slide and crawl and roll across the floor, scattering papers and shattering what's left of our self-control. The desk groans beneath us, then the bed until we land again on the floor.

My nails rake down his back, desperate to hold on, to keep him here with me in this moment. His thrusts are merciless, feverish, each one strumming my body higher. Tighter. A deep growl rumbles from his chest to mine, undeniable pleasure coiling so tight that I almost can't take it anymore. I cry out, and then his mouth finds mine, drowning out the noise with his lips.

Everything I can't put to words is in my kiss.

I need you. I want you.

I love you.

I'm sorry.

Aric drags himself back. *"Rey."* My name falls from his lips like a plea.

I'm not alone in this storm.

Tears sting my eyes as I cling to him.

But he isn't done. He takes me harder. Deeper. His huge body shuddering. I come apart again with a cry that feels ripped from my soul, my body clenching around his as the world tilts. His answering roar pounds through me. His release drags me under again.

And then it's just us in our own wreckage of sweat, frost, and ruin.

We break apart in a hot, sweaty tangle. He rests his head against mine, and the world goes quiet and still. All I hear is his heart racing; all I feel is mine responding.

Not yet.

Don't let it be over yet.

This—*us*—is everything.

And yet nothing has changed.

After a few minutes, he whispers, "What happens now?"

"I wish I knew."

I rise and fumble for my clothes. Aric slowly dresses, too. He watches me with an expression so bare it hurts.

Then he turns and finally takes my hand.

He grins, and that little smile is everything.

Chapter Seventy-One

ARIC

I'm so pissed, I can't see straight.

Reeve's—Loki's—betrayal. Rey's misguided attempts at protecting me. Granted, I hold so much of myself in when I'm around her, she has no concept of what I'm capable of, but still…I'm not the one who needs protecting.

I left her back at the dorms to get ready for the Hunt, and as I closed the door, I thought: *If only we could run away. Leave this all behind. Just you and me, together.*

But running from problems doesn't solve them, and this is bigger than either of us.

Tonight, we finish it.

But first…

I nearly take off the door to the admin building, barely keeping my rage in check as I stomp up the stairs. Sigurd's door's open, like he's waiting for me.

I storm in, and he smiles.

"I do hope we can make this quick, Aric. We have a busy evening ahead."

He opens the blinds at his window and stares out. Catering trucks are unloading food, and tons of cars are starting to pile up along the main drive, waiting for the event coordinators and valets hired for the evening.

He lets the blinds drop back into place as I approach him. "So," he murmurs. "Have you figured it out yet?"

"Figured what out?"

"Your awakening. I had my suspicions, though I never really imagined they would have sealed their power into you. Yet in a strange way, it does make sense." He sighs. "It all makes sense now, doesn't it? Why they were so weak in the end, why they…perished so easily. What a pity."

"What?" I begin. "What the hell are you talking about?"

"Your parents, Aric. The very power oozing from your body comes from them, you know. You were born a Giant, but even with your powers suppressed, even with that side of you sleeping under the protection of the runes, you're dying to break free. You hold the power of three. Your parents and yourself.

"Isn't this a lovely twist," he mumbles, more to himself than me. "Have you planned to let her finish awakening you, then?" He glances at his Patek Philippe wristwatch like he's about to schedule it if I haven't yet.

For the last few years, he's kept me locked down, isolated, medicated, always telling me to have control. To never let my Giant free.

"It's time to break out of the shell your parents put you in," Sigurd says. "Maybe then we can finally defeat Odin."

"Without Mjölnir?"

His head whips in my direction. "She told you? Splendid. You've done well, befriending and seducing your enemy, Aric. I'm proud of you." Why the fuck is he so calm about all of this? He used me. He used *her*! And he looks seconds away from popping off for a quick lunch followed by a massage.

My stomach clenches, but I keep my expression even.

"You can find it. Your true self knows where it is. You *will* find it. And let her claim it. The moment she possesses the hammer, though, we strike. We can avenge your parents' deaths." He sighs like he's at peace.

"She won't even see you coming for a death blow instead of a kiss."

That's fucked up. Even if Rey had remained my enemy, if I'd never felt her warmth or tasted her lips...I wouldn't be able to kill her like that in cold blood.

Sigurd tilts his head. "You're not falling for your enemy, are you, Aric? In this war, sacrifices have to be made."

My mind goes to the sacrifices that my parents made for me. Why did they give me their power?

"How did they die again?" I cross my arms. "My parents. You said they gave their power to me and that's why they perished so easily. How do you perish easily in a car wreck?"

Sigurd goes very still. "It's in the past. Focus on the task at hand, Aric. Be stronger than they were."

His words don't sit right with me. But a horn sounds across campus, the long, haunting note that only comes from real bone.

Sigurd smiles. "The festivities will start soon, and then it will all be up to you."

"Do you really think you can convince Rey to use it for your own purposes?" I ask.

"Me?" He laughs. "Absolutely not. *You?* Yes. The time of the Gods is over, Aric. The rise of the Giants has just begun. You're either for everything your family built—or against it. Pick a side."

I almost laugh. "Both sides have chosen to eliminate each other. Is there no peace? No middle ground?"

Sigurd slams his hand down onto his desk so violently that it cracks right down the middle.

I jump back, shocked at the gesture and the strength—the anger—behind it. If he's trying to remind me that he's the first Giant, he's doing a great job.

"Do you want to see me dead?" Sigurd demands. "Odin plans to break my body and rebuild his world with it. He will stop at nothing to take over realm after realm in his name. This is the man who burned Jötunheim to the ground. He's responsible for your parents' deaths. If that isn't enough motivation, then maybe you never loved them at all—or me, or Loki."

I snort out a laugh. "So you've always known, then."

"Just like you, he was forced to choose. You chose poorly two years ago." With a swish of his hand, the cracked desk splits in two, the halves slamming into the walls. Books fall from the shelves, and pottery crashes and shatters.

Sigurd steps over the pieces toward me.

He's stronger, more vicious. I see it, the look in his eyes. He'll kill me. Right here, right now, in this very room if he finds my will lacking.

And I may be strong, but I'm not yet awakened. I can't defeat him as I am now, just like I can't defeat Odin.

I need access to my power even if it kills me.

"I won't fail, Grandfather." I meet his stare and hold it. "I'll bring you Thor's hammer. And then I'll bring you Odin's head."

Chapter Seventy-Two

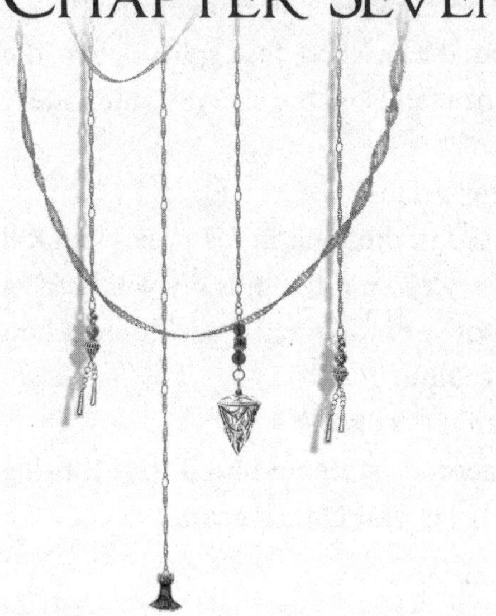

REY

I'm dressed as a Valkyrie.

I'll admit, this wasn't what I would have picked for myself to ride into battle. But whoever did pick it for me knew their stuff. Long white-sleeved shirt with a matching corset fitted tight against my body. Sewn-in patterns of gold make a design of wings on the front, while the shoulder armor is made of golden feathers jutting out at sharp angles. The long white cape flows out from the shoulders and rests against my calves.

Embroidered runes on the skirt catch the light when I move. A gold belt cinches around my waist, a perfect place for weaponry. A raven's head clicks into place as the buckle.

And finally, a small, crown-like helmet rests on my hair, leaving the top of my head exposed. There are nine tiny spikes that protrude out of the top, maybe resembling the Nine Realms? I'm not sure.

I braid my hair back and look in the mirror.

I feel like I'm being mocked.

The daughter of Odin.

Who can't even protect her stepmother or save the world from her own father. How poetic that I should be dressed up for the occasion.

Still, though. I have to admit: I look like a warrior.

I just wish I felt like one.

I mentally slap myself and reach for Laufey's note, tucking it into my corset, then grab my very real knives, situating them in the hidden compartment of my skirt.

Finally, I grab my phone, which feels oddly out of place, and head into the hallway, letting my door close behind me. The lock doesn't work anymore, but it's not like I'm planning on coming back here after tonight anyway.

Aric's standing there, waiting for me.

I completely stop breathing.

He's shirtless.

My eyes lock on the mask covering his face—half a white skull, stark and merciless, and half painted in shades of blue with lilacs growing across the bone like something both sacred and savage. Horns twist upward from the crown like a fallen ancient king.

His cape—a heavy royal blue—falls in thick folds to the floor, sweeping past the dark brown leather of his pants and the laced boots wrapped tightly around his calves. He's leaving nothing to the imagination. Smooth muscle basically smacks me upside the head—arms, abs, chest. He looks every inch the Giant he is. My pulse pumps against my ribs in an uncontrollable cadence. I just don't know if it's telling me to run or stay.

His icy expression doesn't waver.

My head feels too heavy, my body too weak under the weight of him and the costume I'm wearing—maybe the moment, too. "You look good."

His gaze rakes over me slowly, deliberately, and though he doesn't speak, the hunger in his eyes says everything. Even behind the mask, it's there—in the way his eyes hood, the way his stare pins me in place and dares me to move.

Desire doesn't pick sides.

It simply wants.

He gives me his back like that's it, that's the pep talk. We walk in silence to the elevator and of course, because it's Reeve, he's already there leaning against the wall, waiting for us.

He also has a cape, but his is green. He grins. "Thought it would be funny."

"It's not," Aric snaps.

Okay, so maybe I'm losing my mind, but I do crack a smile, earning a little wink from the bastard who threatened me earlier. Well, at least the myths are right about one thing—Loki is truly every inch a confusing little dick. One minute I want to strangle him, the next I'm trying not to laugh, then the next I'm like, okay, but the supervillain cape and black crown are working for him.

College is confusing.

His crown is smaller than Aric's. It rests around his head like mine and has four spikes that twist into black antlers with bloodred tips. He's wearing an all-black leather chest plate with a silver snake sewn into it and matching black leather pants. Black armored gloves cover his hands, and on the tips of his fingers are long, razor-sharp black nails that make noise every time he clenches his fists.

He looks intimidating as hell.

We all pile into the elevator. "This is cozy," Reeve pipes up.

"Shut your goddamn mouth." Aric glances up as if praying for patience.

Reeve looks between us. "Listen, I think if we all talk things through and come up with a really good plan so I don't have to kill people I like, then things will work out."

Aric and I are both silent.

"Or have it your way, I guess." He rocks back on his heels and sniffs the air. The elevator hits the lobby level. "I remember this fitting better."

"That's what happens when you get old, Loki," I say sweetly. "Your body just isn't what it used to be."

"Don't knock it till you try it." He winks.

Aric lets out a growl.

"Naturally, after his untimely death," he adds like that's somehow helpful.

We walk out into the lobby, where everyone else is gathered. I sent a text to Ziva earlier, asking for them to wait for me. I didn't expect Aric or Reeve to show.

Eira looks like death itself. Not in the sloppy, last-minute-Halloween way—in the way that makes your stomach twist and your skin crawl. Her usually polished features are hollowed out, her eyes ringed in dark shadow that sinks them deep into her face, making her cheerful smile look like a mask she borrowed from a corpse. Her hair falls in a glowing sheet from the top of her head, but with strategic strands sticking out like the fractured halo of something fallen wrapped around her head like a crown.

She leans on a staff—slick, black, and gnarled at the top—and every inch of her skin-tight leather ensemble screams predatory. The outfit is sculpted in sharp angles and ridges, leaving little to the imagination. Bloodstains streak down from her torso, dripping over her thighs, painted across her arms like she's just walked out of a massacre.

She wasn't kidding when she said she was dressing up as Hela, and I'm not completely convinced this isn't the real deal. Please, Gods, no more surprises.

"Death does devour us all." She winks. The words are playful. The delivery isn't.

Ziva shudders. Her contrast couldn't be sharper—she's draped in a simple white dress that flutters with every step, a delicate harp tucked under her arm. She looks like she wandered out of some pastoral painting. "Judge not," she huffs. "I went Greek last-minute. Or…Roman?"

I frown. "What are you?"

"Cupid." Her grin is wicked.

Reeve groans. "Of course you are."

I glance at Rowen. He's the simplest of all, just a sharp black suit that fits too perfectly to be casual. It's his eyes, though, that make me do a double take. They're brighter tonight, edged with something that flickers with determination. I grip my necklace. At least I have his protection tonight.

He looks over at Aric and then me. "Let's get this over with."

"Yay, party." Reeve's sarcasm cuts through as he slouches forward.

And just like that, we fall into step, costumes brushing against each other, headed down toward the football field, where the Hunt and the feast wait like a trap ready to be sprung.

Campus sprawls in front of us like a kingdom preparing for war. It doesn't look like the same place I've been hiking through between classes. Tonight, the gates are open—really open. Alumni have pulled up in polished black SUVs, glossy limos, and sports cars with engines that make so much noise, I'm annoyed. The air reeks of money and power.

And at the center of it all: the massive stadium and the Endir Vikings, all lined up in full cosplay. They have helmets with iron horns, and I'm pretty sure the fur draped across their pads was bought from IKEA in rug form, then cut up and glued. They're marching around in formation, chanting, yelling about shield walls, and laughing. A few of them are so drunk, they trip over their own swords. Safe to say Endir's more known for its academics than its sports.

An outdoor buffet stretches the length of the football field. A completely gaudy feast fit for a king with candles of every shape and size lit down the table. Whole roasted boars glisten on saucers next to bread piled like multiple armies are about to pillage. Platters of carrots, leeks, and onions. Dozens of golden pitchers filled with what I hope is mead or something strong.

It also feels a bit like home.

Reeve's the first to speak up. "Old world meets new. They've been running this since forever. Nothing like an ancient tradition dressed up as a frat party."

Aric doesn't respond. His eyes flick briefly to the lake as we pass. It's turbulent, slapping against the shore. The sky is clear, no wind. The violence in it doesn't make sense.

"How many feasts are we having?" I mumble, mostly to myself.

Reeve rubs his hands together. "Thought you'd never ask. The Hunt happens in three diabolical stages. Phase one—" He points to the middle of the field. "Behold, drink and be merry." He holds up two fingers. "Two is usually when you have a significant other who's agreed to go with you."

Reeve turns a judgmental stare my way.

"Assuming they don't dump you before the big event, you sit

together and feed each other. Showing true trust in food is directly related to trust for the actual Hunt, which is phase three. This is basically your excuse to run through the forest. There are games set up on different trails, but the only part that's mandatory is that whatever trail or adventure you stumble upon, you have to finish and cross the creek that feeds the lake at the end. The water is the final ceremonial cleansing of your sins in front of the Gods and everyone. Afterward, we end up back where we started for the bonfires and fireworks to officially kick off the school year—and, of course, to feast!"

I snort. "And here I thought it was just a myth about Odin releasing ravens."

"It's that, too," Aric says quickly. "You know Sigurd. He likes to honor old traditions and mix in the new."

At least a hundred students mill about, all in elaborate masks and costumes. The air feels thick, charged, like the entire campus knows what's coming.

I spot a group outside the student union holding torches, thrusting them high as if summoning something. The flames illuminate carved masks, the distorted faces of wolves, stags, and ravens everyone seems to be wearing.

"The professors," Reeve says casually. "Tradition."

Tradition. They love that word around here.

And I'm a bit surprised Endir's professors are shouting around a fire.

"We aren't actually hunting anything, right?" I ask. "It's just a party? A play on words?"

"Spirits. Ghosts. Trolls. And men who deserve worse," Aric answers. "At least that's what the Hunt used to be about. *Right*, Reeve?"

Reeve snaps to attention. "Yes, its original intent was exactly that."

The tension among the three of us is suffocating.

Ziva elbows me. "You okay?"

I let out a rough exhale. "Fine."

She raises her hand to pat me on the shoulder, then thinks twice about it. "Too pointy."

"Cool, right?"

Eira lets out a snort. "When do we get to party?"

"After the ceremony," Reeve says. "And after all the alumni and parents have arrived." He turns to face us and starts walking backward. "Everyone needs to relax. Think of it as a game. A race through the forest. Get to the other side, and you win. Get caught, you pay a price." He smirks. "Has anyone ever even looked up Odin's Wild Hunt?"

Odin. He was a good hunter.

And then he trained me to be better.

I open my mouth. "Odin would lead the charge into the forests with his ravens chasing after spirits. Most humans disappeared or didn't survive the night."

"Survival is always key," Aric adds.

The crowd goes silent around us when we arrive. At first I think it's because we're dressed so extravagantly, but they're looking behind us, awe on their faces.

When I turn, I no longer have to wonder about what's captured their attention, because Odinfather has arrived.

And he looks every inch the God he is.

Chapter Seventy-Three

REY

The whispers grow louder, and I know why. Father rarely attends events unless he's the one hosting. He's notorious for being secretive. I might be sick before the night ends.

Odin is in tall, polished boots that glint like obsidian, a tailored black suit that drapes like heavy armor, and a thick gold chain worked with runes across the front. His coat falls to his calves. It's lined with fur, blood still splattered on parts of it, and I just know—he hunted down his own costume on purpose as a taunt to Sigurd himself. The runes may be turned off tonight, but even if they weren't, they couldn't hold Odin.

Every inch of him screams power. His hair is slicked back, and from his white beard dangle several intricate silver beads. One stands out among the rest, right in the middle, holding the lower part of his braided beard together.

A silver Mjölnir replica.

He's dressed like the type of man who could whisper into the void and it would come across like a scream.

Mafia.

Norse God.

Predator.

And my father.

"Old friend." Sigurd's voice resonates as he steps out of the crowd to greet my father. People divide like the Red freaking Sea as Sigurd walks.

He's wearing the head of an elk. Its skull is massive, the antlers stretching wide enough that they scrape against the tops of his shoulders and threaten to hook the torches lining the pathway from the parking lot to the field. Hollow sockets leer above his own eyes, the bone bleached and cracked with age. Every ridge is etched with runes that seem to pulse faintly in the torchlight.

You'd think he was afraid Father was going to dismember him. I shouldn't smile, but I do. You can take the hunter out of the Hunt, but you can't take the Hunt out of the hunter.

Some things are bred into you.

Beneath the crown of antlers, Sigurd's face is streaked with ash and white paint, crisp lines drawn down his jaw to sharpen the edges of his already brutally handsome features.

The sheer weight of their presence presses down on the crowd. Both look like they're not playing dress-up for some student ritual. They look like the men who started it themselves and lived to tell the tale.

When Sigurd lowers his head, the antlers cut a stark silhouette against the firelit sky. I feel the sudden heavy need to bow my head. It's strange, because I've never once felt like this before in his presence. Maybe it's because tonight, I can't help but acknowledge that Ymir was first.

"Ymir is formidable when he draws his own power in," murmurs Reeve. Right. The runes being down tonight benefits him, too.

"The wind," Reeve continues under his breath. "Nature cannot help but recognize its creator—it is more unnatural to stay still than it is to fall to your knees in worship of Ymir."

Aric overhears Reeve. I can tell by the way his shoulders tense.

I don't think the others do, though; I think they're too entranced, like everyone else. Slowly, the music picks up again. My father and Sigurd walk together.

Mortal enemies.

Both of them killers.

They reach the front of the football field, where the rest of the alumni and parents are sitting at round tables arrayed before a massive stage. If it wasn't for the scoreboard and the sponsor banners hanging along the stands, I'd think we were assembling in an ancient stadium.

My father sits to the right of the stage while Sigurd takes the stairs and moves to the podium.

"Oh, shit," Reeve mumbles. "Another microphone."

But this isn't the quirky professor or the bumbling college president who addresses the crowd. His voice is deep, somber.

He lifts up his hands. "In days of old, the Wild Hunt was more than a chase; it was a reckoning. It represented death and rebirth, the passage of one age to another." Everyone goes silent. "Warriors offered themselves to the Hunt so their courage may be judged, their souls carried by Odin's majestic riders into the next life.

"Here at Endir, we hunt not for death, but new beginnings and fresh starts. Tonight, we seek new bonds with one another and ask for courage to face what lies ahead." I swear his eyes lock on mine as he continues. "And the wisdom to let go of what is weighing us down. So let us join together and call on our courage this school year! Let us release the ravens, our messengers of transformation, and begin this year's Hunt!"

He holds out a hand to Professor Higgins. She walks up with a box covered with a black cloth.

Sigurd holds his hands wide and then makes a motion in front of his face, two fingers against his nose, one touching his chin and neck. "Join with me, please."

Everyone mimics the ancient motion meant to honor the Gods and Giants.

Goose bumps race up my arms.

This feels like some very ritualistic shit's about to go down. Father doesn't lift a finger, but of course, I don't expect him to. Sigurd's mocking a tradition my father started.

"Be blessed in the Hunt," Sigurd calls out. He tosses the cloth and opens the box. "Release the ravens!" He holds his hands to the sky. The stadium rumbles with applause as the ravens disperse into the air.

"Now, please take your seats," Sigurd says. "The official dance soon begins."

I steal a glance at Aric.

He frowns as if this isn't something he was expecting.

Moments later, the band begins to play and conversation sparks up. People start to gather around their tables for appetizers and drinks. It's then I notice that those who aren't wearing costumes are wearing red masks. They look creepy as hell.

I glance around casually, calmly. At least half the campus is in red masks.

Chills run down my spine.

"Curious..." Reeve taps his chin. "Why certain ones are marked to wear the masks."

Bile rises in my throat when Eira approaches in her creepy costume, one of the red masks on her face. "I'll be presenting the dance of the Lure for you tonight. In ancient tradition, it's a sensual dance presented to the Gods as a sacrifice for humans who gave their lives in service."

She doesn't wait for us to say anything. But like it's been practiced for centuries, the people in red masks move around each table as music blasts through the outdoor stereo system. It sounds primal, ancient, full of pipes and horns and a steady, driving beat of drums. With each circle around the tables, they turn and face Sigurd, bow, and then do a movement with their hands above their heads like they are transfixed by the sky as it presses down onto them. They all bend backward, then twirl into a chaotic flurry, hands over heads. They all stop and let out a scream as the drums end.

The movements are addicting to watch. "Did they volunteer?"

"Handpicked." Rowen suddenly pipes up. "Right? By Sigurd himself?"

"Clever." Reeve winks at me. "And yes, they just have something about them. Can't you feel it?"

My mouth drops open. "Are they—"

"I can answer that," Reeve interrupts. I'd really prefer he didn't.

"They're chosen, important, special, though they just think it's a program for the gifted. Soon they'll all remember, and soon they'll have the power to do a lot more. At least that's the hope."

Sigurd clears his throat into the mic. "Beautifully done, students. Now, if you'll look to the tables, you'll each find a rune, or what we like to call party favors from the Gods. Before the Hunt begins, choose yours carefully. Hold it close, whisper your wish, kiss the stone, and toss it into any of the surrounding bonfires. That fire represents your vow, your promise, your beginning here at Endir. A journey you and only you can take."

The crowd quiets as flames from the surrounding bonfires leap skyward, sparks scattering like stars. Father hasn't moved a muscle still, but I do see his jaw tense. Maybe because years ago, he did this for his people, for Asgard, for humanity, and Sigurd has hijacked it.

"From there, the tradition is simple. You'll go together in groups or pairs—never wander alone, not tonight—and follow the marked trails into the forest. Which path you choose is up to you, but each holds its own challenge. Some of you will find feasts laid out along the way; some will stumble into games you must complete to keep going; others, perhaps, into shadows that don't belong to the living. Ghosts, demons, spirits of the fallen—consider them part of the fun. Survive them, laugh at them, scream if you have to—but make it through." He shrugs. "We do ask that no flash photography takes place. Let's keep things as authentic as possible."

"Don't die!" some idiot yells.

A ripple of nervous laughter spreads through the students.

Father actually smirks at that and looks down. I wonder what it was like…before his obsession for knowledge made him into this. Before he was bound by it, controlled, owned. Was he ever free?

Sigurd pauses and looks around the campus. I wonder if he genuinely likes the way people adore him, hang on his every word. His grin is sharp as firelight dances in his eyes.

The torches blaze higher, drums resume their beat, and the cheers rise again.

"Let the Wild Hunt begin!"

Chapter Seventy-Four

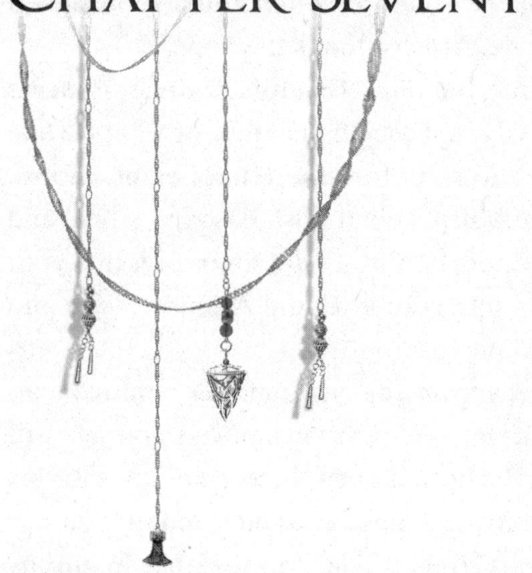

REY

"Respectfully." Ziva clears her throat, then points up at my father while we all find a circular table to sit at near one of the bonfires. "And I mean respectfullyyyyyy." She draws out the word. "Daddy Odin is hot."

"Nope!" I hold up my hands while Reeve makes a gagging noise and Rowen chokes on a laugh. Aric puts a hand on my thigh and squeezes, holding me in place. He knows me too well. I want to run in circles and then tell her all the reasons she shouldn't think that.

"What?" Ziva shrugs. "I'm just saying, the guy has this aura, and he has really intense eyes like he's seen things, controlled things—how does he feel about younger women?"

"How do you feel about death?" Reeve asks cheerfully. "Because he's more likely the type to kidnap you and leave you on the side of the road for sport."

"I can handle myself." Ziva grins.

And just like I've conjured up the devil himself, my father comes walking toward us. It was different when he was texting me, when he was out of sight, out of mind. Now, it's harrowing.

I don't feel so brave anymore.

I feel less than clever.

I'm small.

I'm just a girl wishing her dad said he was proud, a girl trying to prove herself to a man who will never approve of her or love her. A man who hurts her instead.

I keep my eyes focused on him, my posture straight.

Don't break. Please, Gods, don't break. Not now.

I can do this.

"Ahh." He suddenly smiles and looks over my head. "There she is."

Laufey is approaching us, her hands hidden beneath black bandages. Her jet-black hair runs in smooth braids down her back, her beautiful brown skin shimmering in the moonlight.

Her eyes meet mine. "Rey."

I get up and walk over, pulling her in for a quick hug and even quicker kiss on each cheek. When I face my father, I do the same, and I feel like puking.

"Are you enjoying your evening?" He's not just asking me.

"Yes, sir." Reeve salutes him. "My favorite part was when Sigurd released the ravens. What about you?"

Father's eye twitches. "Had he done it right, I might have been impressed."

Reeve grins. "It looked right to me, but memory's kind of fuzzy when it comes to ancient texts. Not much of a reader, anyway, plus Odin was way too emotionally attached to those birds."

"Who are you again?" Father asks. He nods as several men in suits make their way over to him. A few glare at Reeve but do nothing. "Do enjoy your evening. I'm sure I'll see you later, Rey."

"Yes." I can barely find my voice as I sit back down between Aric and Ziva.

"Come," he commands Laufey. She puts a hand on my shoulder and squeezes once before obeying.

The moment he walks off, everyone looks at me like I've just grown three heads.

Rowen is the first to speak. "You okay?"

"I need some air." I shove back from the table and walk a few feet away, a panic attack imminent. I can feel it. I know we're outside, but I need to walk. I take off, heading away from the bonfires.

Suddenly, someone's rubbing my back. When I look over my shoulder, I find that it's Rowen, staring straight ahead. "Everything will go just like we planned, Rey."

He followed me. What plan? What is he talking about?

"I'll distract as many as I can while you run off. Eira's going to help and—"

I jerk my head toward him. "Since when?"

"What?"

"Since when did you ask Eira for help?"

He reels back. "Um, since I figured a hot girl throwing herself at Reeve might actually distract him enough not to shadow your every move."

My stomach sinks. "What did you tell her?"

"That Odin's a God," he says with a smirk. "Relax. I told her I needed her help and that I would really appreciate it, and she said okay."

"Sexual favors?"

"No. But I did promise I'd help her pass bio. Are you done interrogating me now? We have more important things to worry about, like unlocking the last rune, setting a Giant into the wild, and hoping he leads you to Mjölnir, all without anyone finding out."

"Right." I huff out an exhale. "You're right."

"You're making the best choice."

I am. He just doesn't know that my choice has nothing to do with giving my father Mjölnir and everything to do with trusting Aric.

I glance over at Odin.

Mjölnir is rightfully his—ours—but he doesn't deserve it. "Did he really burn the entirety of Jötunheim to the ground, Rowen?"

"Yes."

"And worlds before it?"

"He only killed those who wouldn't bow."

I smile. "I thought the Giants were peaceful?"

He scowls. "I thought Gods were good?"

Touché.

People start getting up from their tables. I slowly make my way back toward Aric, pushing the crowd with my Aethercall for good measure. "Now's as good a time as any," I say quietly when I reach him.

"Agreed," he says gruffly.

As the others run ahead of us, we fall into step together, shoulders brushing. The drums fade as the forest closes around us, shadows thickening, the air colder.

The minute the canopy swallows the torches, I tug at Aric's sleeve. I dart my eyes once toward the others, then back to him. Without a word, I pull him sideways, shuffling us into a group of revelers before yanking him deeper into the trees.

The crowd's noise muffles, fading into the distance until all that's left is the sound of our breathing and the crunch of frost beneath our boots.

We run. Away from the laughter. Away from the bonfires. Straight into the kind of darkness that feels like it was waiting for us.

Chapter Seventy-Five

REY

"So," I say once we're out of earshot. "I'm going to need you to create a protected spot for us before we start so you don't go boom and attract attention."

"And you with me," he whispers. "You do realize if I can't control myself, you're in the direct line of fire."

"Yeah," I say. "I do. But I'm not leaving you." I grab his hand and lead him away from the noise. I know people are watching us, but I also know that by the time we make it to where we need to go, he can protect us.

Plus, if we go farther into the forest down their path, we'll miss the location of the rune.

I squeeze Aric's hand.

He looks down at where our palms meet as if thinking the same thing I am—*will I ever hold you again?*

"It's not too late to change our minds," I joke as the sound of an airplane flying overhead makes me pause. How easy would it be? Abandon everything, escape together.

I stop for a second, pulling on his hand so he stops, too.

"Would you?" I whisper as a breeze tousles my hair. "Would you run away with me, knowing that the world would eventually end? Knowing that the world would *burn*?"

I hug my arms around myself, shivering, suddenly lonely. Aric's breath fogs in front of him, reminding me of everything he's capable of.

"You're hesitating," I choke out.

His dark gaze holds mine.

"I can't promise you," he finally says. "Not until we end this." My whole body deflates.

"So that's it, then? We're doing this." I'm blushing, but I can't help it.

His tongue slides across his bottom lip, then his jaw tightens, but his eyes remain locked on mine as a few flakes of snow catch my vision.

I shake my head. "I don't need the cold," I say. "I don't want it."

"But I still need your warmth." His voice is deep, gravelly, and I know he means it.

Snow dusts his broad shoulders, which are now hunched over with pain.

"One of us is going to die." I finally say the words out loud.

And deep in my soul, I know.

It's going to be me.

Thunder rumbles in the distance. We start walking again, and I finally stop when I'm in front of the trail by our dorm. Where it all began.

Aric spreads his arms wide. "Why are we here?"

"Because." I stare up at our dorm the same way I did my first day here. "It ends where it started. With a simple misstep." I reach down and grab the cobblestone I tripped on the first day I arrived. It was a sign. "This was right here all along." I swipe my hand over the stone. "The universe knew even before we did."

Aric stares at the rock in my hand with the rune Thurisaz etched on it. "One of the most powerful runes, hidden in plain sight."

"Powerful things often are," I whisper, giving him a meaningful look and holding it out to him.

Aric takes both the rock and my hand. He guides me away from the dorms, angling us toward the water. "Let's go to the other side of the lake."

I try not to freak out, but my heart is pounding. This is it. The last rune.

"It's going to be fine," Aric says. "I promise."

Points for trying to make me feel better. We move quickly away from the festivities, past the admin building, where a macabre game of Pin the Tail on the Donkey is happening, freshmen blindfolded and searching in the dark. Nope, not it. I shudder as we continue down the path, the air getting heavier, chillier with each step, until my breath starts to come out in quick white puffs that look like smoke.

Once we're at the lake, Aric holds out his hands, and the water bubbles at the lake's surface before freezing, A straight line of ice continues, bluish white against the dark water, bridging us to the opposite shore. "It won't last long. We need to hurry."

He grabs my hand, and we move quickly across the ice bridge. Over halfway across, I make the mistake of glancing over my shoulder. Choppy waves splash over the ice, melting and reclaiming it. My stomach drops through my feet, but I hold my breath and keep walking.

Within moments of reaching the shore, the ice bridge dissolves completely, like it was never there at all.

From the far shore, we can see all of Endir. The stadium where the feast is celebrated, the buildings and dorms, the basalt arch. Torches light the path for the Hunt. The smoke from the bonfires swirls toward the sky as music and laughter carry across the water. Will we ever go back to those people? To the school? Or is this it?

Aric squeezes my hand. "Come on, there's a cave just up here."

We walk another thirty feet and reach the mouth of a massive cave that's part of one of the rocky hills that surround the lake.

I let out a shaky breath as Aric pulls the runestone from his pocket. "Wait."

He curses. "What? What's wrong?"

The once-clear skies are now covered with rainclouds. I swallow the lump in my throat. "I'm afraid."

Aric covers my hand with his.

"What? No saying it's all going to be okay or that you'll save me?"

His grin already has me at ease. "First off, you're perfectly capable of saving your own ass, though it is nice to be needed. And second…I won't lie to you. Ever. If we burn—we burn together."

"You mean it?" A tear slides down my cheek.

"With all of my soul." He nods. "Until the last breath leaves my body—and even after that."

I hug him close, my hands drawing small circles along his bare back. "I…never expected this," I start. "Never trusted anyone's feelings because of my Aethercall. But with you…" Our eyes meet. "It's real."

He kisses my head, then steps away. We reach for our knives, make the shallow cuts on our palms, then press the blood onto the Thurisaz rune.

The stone crumbles.

The world around us freezes.

There's no scream, no pain coming from his mouth.

There's…nothing.

Nothing but pieces of icy crystals frozen in time around us and a very calm Aric staring me down, holding my hand.

It's quiet. Too quiet.

Suddenly, the runes illuminate one by one down his back, like a key's just been turned, like something has opened. His eyes widen and completely white out. An earsplitting roar escapes his lips as he crashes to his hands and knees.

And then lightning zaps directly from the sky into his back.

My mouth opens in a silent scream.

The lightning doesn't leave, though. It stays there, trapping Aric in place like he's a bug caught under a scientist's pin. But somehow, he's not stuck. He slowly takes a deep breath and leans back on his haunches, then cautiously, methodically raises both hands, pressing them together like he's reining in the power.

Thunder booms. I reach out a hand, wanting to help Aric, to protect him, but before I can get close enough, the sound of an explosion fills the air. I'm thrown back so violently, my vision blurs and my ears ring.

And then there's nothing but silence.

The ringing is gone.

The crickets chirping, water lapping on the shore, the sounds of the Hunt—it all just stops.

Chest heaving, I look up and see Aric covering me with his body. And when I peek out from his frame, I gasp.

He just leveled acres of forest.

Gone as if it never existed.

I pick up the rocks at my feet, and immediately they turn to sand in my hands.

"Aric." I test his name on my lips and slowly gaze up at him. His eyes are pure white, his hair has lengthened, and tiny ice crystals twist their way through the strands, creating a sort of crown on his head. His arms are covered in blue-and-white etchings, runes all the way down to his fingertips. A blue line divides his lips the same way it did for his costume mask, like he somehow knew that it was his natural state. It's majestic, beautiful.

He looks like he's ice himself.

A king.

He finally opens his mouth and whispers so low that I feel the rumble in my chest. "Home. He burned our home, destroyed world after world."

My stomach clenches.

"You were next."

Tears burn the backs of my eyes.

"Give him the hammer, and he'll stop at nothing. Give it to Sigurd, and he'll get revenge. Take it yourself…"

"And Laufey dies."

"Is one life worth more than a world?" he asks, his gaze piercing. "What would Laufey want?"

I know in my gut exactly what she would want. She gave me the note. Spelled out exactly what to do. I kept thinking it was too easy… because it was.

Find Mjölnir.

Save the world from Odin's rule.

Forfeit everyone else—me included.

The note wasn't a clue.

It was her final goodbye.

Her last gift to a daughter she failed to protect—so I could do what she couldn't. So I could be brave.

"I kept getting visions of frost," Aric rumbles out, his voice growing deeper by the second. He starts to clench his teeth like he's in pain, then arches his back. The rune, it's doing something, and he's trying to hold it at bay. "Frost is the key."

"What do you mean? The key to what?"

But he can only hold out a shaking hand. "The note—do you have the note?"

"I have it." I reach into the bodice of my costume and hand it over to him.

"Frost," he repeats. "The Giants would communicate with frost on what looked like normal letters, but only a Giant—" He clenches his teeth again, then starts to cough. "Only a Giant's frost can unlock it." He breathes over the note, and ink appears between the runes. "Trust in Aric," he reads. "You are safe. Giants will rise. Gods will fall. Do. Not. Fail."

Chapter Seventy-Six

ARIC

My back aches, my mind races, and the frost begs to be unleashed underneath my fingertips. Visions are coming so hard and fast, I can barely organize them in my mind.

But one vision stands out among them all.

A simple note being passed from my father to my mother.

And finally, in secret, to Laufey.

They entrusted her with this message.

And in the end, Laufey entrusted me with Rey.

Power builds and snaps within me, constantly pushing against my restraints. I have to keep Rey safe—I have to control my emotions and figure out a way to get these new abilities calm.

The runes on my back now pulse in my head, repeating their names like a chant over and over again. My blood sings out the location of Mjölnir. It's like now that the power is free, it's screaming too much information all at once.

Will the ancients' whispers inside my head stop once she finds Mjölnir? Would I want them to? I'm overwhelmed, drowning under the weight of so many memories, so many possible future paths, but at the same time, *they're* there. My heart strains at seeing them once again.

My parents.

They're talking at the edge of a body of water. They stand still, holding each other, staring into water with trepidation, and it takes everything in me not to race over and pull them into my arms. I know this is just a memory, a vision. But it feels so real.

Slowly, they hold out their hands and squeeze drops of blood into the water. I can tell that there's more, and I try to stay grounded in it, but my head aches, and I can't calm the hum of power long enough to focus.

Suddenly, my vision clears. I know where we're going next.

The mirror hitting Rey in the head was no accident. My blood sings the location like an ancient hymn on repeat. The Hall of Omrir—the water.

The lake.

Down.

Down.

Where the souls rest.

"Rey." My voice echoes through the forest. "The Hall of Omrir, the water. It's at the bottom."

My eyes burn as my body remembers them. My parents' last goodbye, their tears of sorrow and rage. It's all Odin's fault.

My mind screams for revenge.

I drop to my knees as anger starts to wrap itself around me, the power all-consuming. How easy it would be to kill Odin. Right now, right here.

The runes are disabled. He's vulnerable.

I need to kill him.

Strength howls alive beneath my skin, demanding to be seen—to be used.

No. I press my hands to my temples, gritting my teeth as a roar escapes my mouth. The air around us shakes while the ground itself moans, and my body shudders under the weight of it all.

"Aric." Rey's voice is barely above a whisper. "I have to swim?"

Her fear nearly fills the area surrounding us; it's thick with it. I can sense it, taste it. She doesn't want to go into the water.

She's never been more scared than this moment.

I reach for her, then snap my hand back. I can barely control my power, and the last thing I want to do is hurt her when I'm trying to comfort her. "You can do this."

My body burns with awareness of the power surging inside it. I'm running out of time.

"Rey," I warn. "You have to hurry." I start to get up, but my legs suddenly give out underneath me. My head spins. "It's too much all at once. I'll be behind you—just run. You need to get it or we can't save everyone. It's up to you now."

Her eyes widen as she takes me in. I have no idea how I look, but I do know that every muscle feels taut, my heart beating a scattered rhythm behind my eyes.

"Rey," I warn again. "Go. Now."

"I can wait with you—"

"RUN!" My entire body shakes with tethered power as I hold out my hand, and ice immediately builds across the lake. I'm stunned for a moment. I barely thought it and there it is, sturdy, beautiful.

Rey starts making her way around me while I attempt to stand. I still smell her fear. But she can do this. I know she can. I stumble after her, trying to get my power under control. She's already on the bridge. Good.

Sweat pours down my temples.

Something feels wrong.

My heart's beating too fast.

My eyes burn.

I hear her short breaths as she runs across the ice. I need her. I miss her, feel weaker without her. What's going on?

With a roar, I lunge after her, only to have someone block my way. Dizziness washes over me as chains come flying at me from all directions. They burn when they collapse onto my skin like they weigh a thousand pounds each.

I try to lift them, but it's nearly impossible.

"A runed trap," a familiar voice says. "Asgardian chains etched with the very runes meant to cripple a Giant. Sigurd does know his stuff."

I blink through the haze and look up.

My heart sinks like a stone.

I barely feel the rueful smile on my own lips as I nod and say, "I should have known."

We've already lost before we even really began.

"Yes," he hisses. "You should have."

"The seventh circle of hell is reserved for people like you."

Suddenly, pain radiates out in unbelievable waves from my stomach. Looking down, I see a spear has been shoved through my back. Someone else is behind me?

Blood pours out in thick rivulets from where the spear pierced straight through my abdomen. My vision wavers.

He leans down. "Be sure to say hi, then, when I send you there."

And then he winks.

It's the last thing I see before everything goes dark.

Chapter Seventy-Seven

REY

I wake up to the heady smell of water and incense, my eyes blurring as I glance around me. I'm in the Hall of Omrir. What the hell happened? I was running across the ice bridge Aric made, and something grabbed me. Or some*one*?

Ice covers the floor, shard-like daggers impaling the walls, like a glacier detonated. Torches glow from stone corbels, casting shadows among the high wooden arches of the temple.

My head aches and my stomach hurts, but I fight to stay conscious.

I realize I'm lying on my side on the icy ground. My shoulder armor, cape, and knives have been removed, and my legs and arms are bound with some kind of iron. The drip, drip, drip of ice melting is interspersed with a groaning sound. Wait, is that me?

"Ah, she awakens!" My father's voice echoes against the rafters. "Bring her," he orders.

Two suited guards in black uniforms with silver-threaded ravens embroidered at the collars—the mark of Odin—grab my arms. Their faces are hidden behind half-carrion masks of bone, hollow-eyed and emotionless, terrifying. They lift me up and spin me around, dragging me toward my father. When they release my arms, I lock my legs to stand. But they kick the backs of my legs, forcing me to kneel.

Someone nearby releases an inhuman growl.

Aric?

He looks like he's already been through war. His face is streaked with both red and silver blood. It mats in his hair all the way along his temples. His arms and chest are still bare, but blood is caked on his abdomen like he suffered a horrific wound there.

He's chained and beaten, bleeding and broken.

He's losing blood, so much blood. It pools beneath him, running in a steady beat toward that cursed obsidian mirror and those deep black waters. The sight of the pool still fills me with dread, but I try to tamp it down. I need to save Aric.

Why can't he heal? He's even more powerful than before—he shouldn't be losing this much blood.

I want to call out his name, to comfort him in some way.

But to show even a flicker of emotion toward my "enemy" right now would seal Aric's fate. So I bury the pain, the fear, and stare down my father.

"Ah, daughter. Is this not everything we planned?" The way the word "daughter" rolls off his tongue makes my stomach roil. I may be of his blood, but I was never anything more than a means to an end.

From the corner of my eye, I see that Aric doesn't as much as flinch. Though broken, he doesn't bend. His eyes blaze white, unyielding. Between his fingers, faint flickers of lightning spark as he rubs his thumb and forefinger together over and over again. He never blinks. He simply stares at my father, his silence speaking volumes.

Odin snaps his fingers. "Rowen!"

Rowen appears, and though I know he sees me, he doesn't look my way.

He's in his black suit and has a similar mask on to the men in my father's employ, only his is pitch-black. My stomach drops. I know Rowen goes along with everything because he has no choice, but I wish for once, he would choose himself.

I used to respect Rowen for his strength, but now I see it for what it really is: misplaced loyalty to a man who would kill him without a thought. He talks a big game about hating Odin, but it means nothing. Why? What did my father ever do for Rowen? To him? I know it has to do with his scars, but until this moment, I don't think I realized just how deep that loyalty went—deeper than our friendship, clearly, if he's just standing there ignoring me while I'm chained up.

Eyes wildly searching, I look at his hands. He's free. He's safe. He's part of this.

He's under my father's control, so what else is new?

I shake my head at him. "I expected more."

"He's doing his job," Father snaps. "One of you is, at least."

"I'm sorry," Rowen rasps next to me. I look up again. Tears fill his eyes, but he blinks them away and stares straight ahead at Odin.

"I'm going to kill you," Aric speaks up. "Slowly."

"Pathetic." Father slams his cane against the ground. "I knew you wouldn't bring Aric to me like you promised—"

I almost roll my eyes. "He's here, isn't he?"

He scoffs. "No matter. I brought you a reminder of what's at stake." A masked guard brings someone out of the shadows. Laufey. Like Aric and me, she's chained. Shaking. Bloodied.

Odin shoves Laufey forward, then pulls a gun out of its holster at his waist. *Fuck.*

He points the gun at Aric's head. "Tell us where Mjölnir is. And think very carefully how to proceed, because it's not just your life on the line, is it? But Aric's, Laufey's, Rowen's." Next to him, Rowen lets out a small gasp, but he doesn't waver. Odin continues. "Don't think I won't take everything from you until we're the last two people on this planet. Is it really worth all of their lives?"

Past me would have said he was right, but current me knows Aric too well. The cost would be too great. My lips part, but it's Rowen who grabs my hand and squeezes it. Tears fill my eyes, threatening to break free again. "I need you."

"I promised I'd always be by your side." He nods, then speaks louder. "Tell him, Rey. I know the Giant told you." He's calling Aric "the Giant" now? I search his eyes.

The room is quiet except for Aric's moans and the lapping of water against the steps.

It was supposed to be so easy.

"Unchain him," I demand, my heart pounding erratically at what I know I need to do. "I'll get it."

I glance back at Aric. His eyes are full of so much pain, I wonder if he even recognizes me anymore, recognizes the fact that each time he exhales, tiny particles of ice follow into the air, creating a path toward me—a path that the ice will never reach.

He can't save himself.

Or me.

We can only hope that I have enough time when I find Mjölnir to use it against Odin. I start to toe off my boots.

The door to the Hall of Omrir creaks open.

"Ah, right on time." Father seems genuinely pleased to see whoever is walking in.

I turn around. I should be surprised.

I'm not.

Chapter Seventy-Eight

REY

All smiles, Reeve sidles up next to Father, tossing the Thurisaz cobblestone in the air. What I wouldn't give to smash that grin off his smug little face. Preferably with that rock. Repeatedly.

He tosses the stone up and down, up and down.

If he's holding it, does that mean he's the one who hurt Aric?

He winks at me.

There isn't enough ice in the world to cool the rage burning underneath my skin.

He stops in front of my father. "See? I told you I was right about the last two runes. But no, you still needed me to prove it." He smiles at me. "Was the cow too obvious? Drastic times call for drastic measures and all that. Bonus: I got to see you half naked."

I strain against my chains. I will kill this man if it's the last thing I do.

"Enough!" Rowen shouts. "Odin, release Rey. She's— "

My father holds up his hand. "Reeve, for your service, my offer does still stand, but you have to show your loyalty. I won't tolerate anything less."

"Not a problem."

I lunge for him again, but Rowen holds me back. "You selfish coward," he grits out, eyes trained on Reeve. "Odin's going to murder you after he gets what he wants—surely you know that? Though why am I not surprised? You're a dumbass."

Reeve laughs and then shoots me a wink. "Gods, you're so dramatic all the time." Then he walks over to Odin and grabs his cane. "To prove my loyalty."

Does he have a death wish?

Father never even lets *me* near it.

Odin holds up his hand to his men. "I'll allow it."

Reeve pulls out the sword from inside and makes his way over to where Aric is on his knees. He pulls his brother's head up by the hair, then lifts the sword to his neck. Excruciatingly slowly, he draws the edge lightly along Aric's skin.

Silver blood starts to eke out. Just drops for now, but the intent is clear.

No.

Reeve holds the blade steady at Aric's neck. "Tick, tock, little goddess."

Aric's eyes plead with mine. "Don't be…afraid."

My body trembles, my teeth chattering. "Aric." Tears fall. I don't think I can do this.

"I believe." His smile is calm. "In you. You know where it is. Do what he's asking. Get Mjölnir."

"Yes," Odin agrees. "Listen to him. Hurry now. The Giant doesn't want to die. Bring me the hammer and I will lift his chains, allow him to heal."

Aric's gaze is steady on mine. His beautiful mouth curves for a second.

This isn't about me saving him.

Aric knows my father will never lift those chains. Will never spare him or set him free.

He's telling me to find the hammer. Because he wants me to fight.

Because he believes in me.

"Swim into the storm, Rey." Aric's eyes lock onto mine. "Finish this with me."

He means swimming by myself into the dark. He means doing this without him, without anyone but myself.

He said I could save myself.

I want to believe him.

I want to believe that heroes exist and that I can be my own.

But when faced with certain death, I only feel weak.

"Untie her!" Father commands.

Aric clenches his jaw and nods one more time. "I believe in you."

Runes light up and down his body as he flicks his wrist, creating an icy path from him all the way to the stairs and down into the water. He's using his power to light the way. "I'll be right by your side."

Ice suddenly wraps itself around my hand.

I know with each use of his power, he loses more.

With each loss, he draws closer to death.

And still he chooses to hold my hand as I walk into the unknown.

I open my hand to his cold. I embrace it. I breathe it in.

"Destiny awaits, daughter of Odin." Reeve grins as Rowen releases my chains. He leans closer, sword still held taut, and whispers, "Swim fast."

"I hate you."

His foot comes out, kicking me hard in the knee, and I buckle.

I hit the icy path with a thud. Reeve laughs, and the rest of the men join in as Rowen curses. But while I'm on the ground, my eye catches on something. It's glowing faintly. The rune of the serpent, etched into a stone smaller than my palm. As I lift myself back to my feet, I grab it.

"If I were you?" Father nods at me. "I'd hurry."

Chapter Seventy-Nine

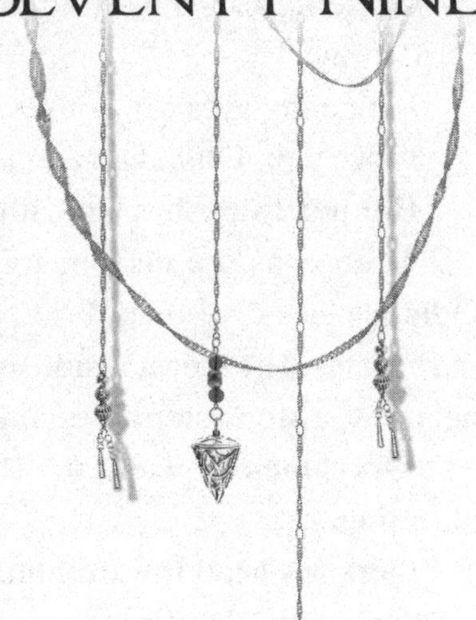

ARIC

I can't see straight. Everything blurs. The only thing I feel is the burn of the runes, pounding through my back like a second, broken heartbeat, and the cold of the steel Reeve holds to my neck.

I never imagined it would be my own brother who would betray us. But he isn't truly my brother, is he? I suck in another labored breath. It's getting harder and harder to breathe. The cold is keeping me alive, slowing my heart just like Rey talked about what feels like a lifetime ago, but the chains are keeping me from truly healing.

I will get free somehow. And when I do, I'm going to use my hands to rip Odin limb from limb.

We were hoping the Hunt was distraction enough to buy us some time once we found Mjölnir—but we were wrong.

The important thing now is to get myself free so I can help Rey. She's the only thing left that matters to me. I weigh my options as more silver blood spews from the purposeful slices across my arms and legs. I might need to take them all on. I might also die trying.

If they thought I was done fighting, they're dead wrong.

My chest seizes as Rey takes the first step into the dark pool at the end of the hall, then the second. Her body shakes. When she hits the third, she looks over her shoulder at me one last time.

Gutted, I can only hold her gaze, my heart in my throat as she turns away.

I hope my eyes can convey everything my voice can't.

I love you. I believe in you. I'm sorry.

Her head vanishes beneath the water.

As soon as she disappears, Reeve drops the sword at my throat. Odin glances over once, brief, calculating, before turning back to the dark water. The storm inside me breaks loose outside, waves crashing against the stone steps, freezing into jagged sheets of ice.

"Only one can wield it," Reeve whispers under his breath, eyes glittering.

I jerk my head toward him. "What?"

"Only one." He enunciates every syllable. "It calls to the blood of Odin, but only those of worth can lift it."

My heart warms for just a second. If Rey finds the hammer, I know she can wield it, even without her blood. She's worthy.

My breaths come shorter, thinner, every second dragging me closer to the edge. Every second she doesn't surface. Every second she's under, looking for Mjölnir, I realize I've lost everything that ever mattered.

I close my eyes and envision the ice. I send light down through it, the last of what I can feel snapping between my fingers. I only hope it's enough light for her to find her way home.

To me.

Chapter Eighty

REY

My lungs scream as I fight the current, chest tightening with every stroke. The water is surprisingly warm, ink-dark, except for the faint blue light shimmering from the ice trail Aric created. I dive deeper, deeper than I'd ever dare, heart pounding and vision tunneling as the glow sharpens into shape. Ten feet more, maybe less.

Something waits at the bottom.

The current claws at me, whipping at my skirts, trying to drag me away. I've never been a strong swimmer, obviously never delighted in practicing. I don't know what dark sources feed this pool or where these deadly currents lure their prey. But the thought is tearing at my brain, making me desperate to stop, to turn back.

But I keep going. Aric needs me.

Ears popping and lungs straining, I kick deeper into the murky depths. The darkness is nearly absolute now, past the point Aric's light can reach, and I can barely force down my panic—but I suddenly notice a sickly green glow emanating from my palm.

No, from the stone. From the rune of the serpent.

Light seems to drift from it like smoke, leading me toward...

There, at the bottom. A raised square shape. I'm almost there. I can do this.

The current pulls me away, and then it shifts, almost like it recognizes me. With a violent shove, it slams me against the floor, anchoring me in place.

I wrap my hand around the hammer, hold tight. My chest convulses with the need to breathe, to let panic take over in the all-consuming water, but I try not to listen. I've got it. I'm nearly there.

But when I push off the muddy bottom, I don't move.

The water refuses. It pins me, iron-heavy.

I kick again, terror flaring as my throat tightens, desperate for air.

Mjölnir let me pick it up. Why isn't it letting me escape?

Dark edges start closing in around my vision, the warm water growing even warmer. Visions flash: Laufey planting in her garden, telling me a story. Ziva and me, laughing together over steaming cups of to-go coffee. Aric. Teasing me. Loving me. Protecting me.

I know it's the end, and I should feel alone. But I'm not alone. They're all here with me.

That's when I see a murky shape swimming toward me. I can barely make it out, but I know it's him.

Rowen.

He came for me.

I grab his outstretched arm with my free hand, grip so tight that my nails dig into his skin. Together we launch upward, the current slicing past us as though it's suddenly letting go. We break the surface in a burst of spray, gasping, and collapse against the stone steps.

My teeth chatter, my lungs burn raw, my vision blurred from lack of oxygen. Body trembling, I drag myself across the floor, eyes immediately searching for Aric. He's still where I left him, but at least Reeve's no longer got him at sword point.

Rowen stands.

"Thank you," I rasp, every breath jagged, pulling the strings on my corset loose to breathe easier. "For saving me."

Father's laugh rolls across the chamber like thunder. "Do you really think it's about you?"

Rowen cuts him a glare. "Keep your word."

Odin's eyes gleam, too bright, too hungry. "Your time starts now."

Time? Time for what? I don't understand.

Rowen lifts me, his grip ironclad, and sets me on my unsteady feet. He pries the box from my hand.

When he flicks it open, my world splinters.

It isn't Mjölnir.

It's not Thor's hammer.

I failed.

Chapter Eighty-One

REY

I stare for a few seconds in disbelief.

Then a scream, raw and blood-soaked, tears out of me before I even realize it's mine. "No. No, no—" My voice breaks. "This is wrong! You said it would lead to the hammer!" I yell at my father. "You promised if I did this one thing..."

I can't fight without Mjölnir.

My father is too powerful. Without the hammer, I've failed.

My gaze turns to Aric. Tears stream down my cheeks. "I'm sorry, Aric. I'm so sorry." My knees buckle.

Rowen holds the object up and examines it, a small smile on his face.

It's an artifact all right. Just the wrong one.

I recognize it as the lost Nightfrost diamond, the one given to the Giant Alvaldi by Thor himself. Mjölnir's counterpart, the only relic in the universe that is the hammer's equal. The legend from Laufey's stories, from the paintings in the Eriksons' home—it shouldn't be here, now, in the real world.

It's a simple band crowned with a diamond as blue as the deepest ice.

I stare, shaking. "Why would it lead me to Nightfrost?" My body trembles. "I didn't know. I swear!"

Rowen's eyes suddenly lock on mine, full of a grief I'm trying to understand. "I'm sorry, Rey. I really am."

For what? What is he sorry for?

He slides the ring onto his finger.

The air splits with a jarring scream from the sky.

The moment the diamond touches his finger, the Rowen I know vanishes—and in his place stands a figure ripped from my nightmares. Black armor. Black cape. A shattered red hammer painted across his chest in blood. Eyes glowing with an unnatural blue fire and a smile that screams evil.

Rowen.

My Rowen.

What's happening?

Odin rises to his feet, triumphant. "Son. Welcome back."

Son.

The word echoes in my skull until it breaks.

Thor.

The runes over his door. The glamour.

Reeve is cursing up a storm, glaring at Rowen. "Are you fucking kidding me? I killed you!"

Rowen—Thor—ignores him. Reeve turns to Odin instead.

"We had a deal, Odin! These two for the location of Nightfrost."

Odin flicks a hand, and Reeve goes flying into the wall.

As if held by an invisible force, Reeve is pinned, thrashing. "Should have seen that coming a mile away, and yet I trusted you—fuck you very much."

With another flick, Odin slams Reeve's head against the wall and he drops, unconscious.

My *brother* ignores Reeve. He strides to Aric, bleeding and broken, tilts his head up with the finger wearing that cursed ring, and whispers, low in his throat, "By the time I'm finished with you, Giant, you're going to wish you were dead. Now…try not to become a corpse before I get my weapon free."

Then he moves around to face Aric's back and slams his hand into it, right where the runes burned themselves down his spine. The next thing I know, he's trying to grip something massive buried under Aric's skin. Gold glints in the light.

Rowen pulls.

And I can see it, the world tearing open as the handle of Mjölnir becomes visible under Aric's skin.

Aric knew the location of Nightfrost.

And Nightfrost knew the location of Mjölnir.

Hidden in plain sight, under the power of runes and three Giants.

The greatest weapon in the world wasn't just being protected by Aric.

It's a part of him.

Chapter Eighty-Two

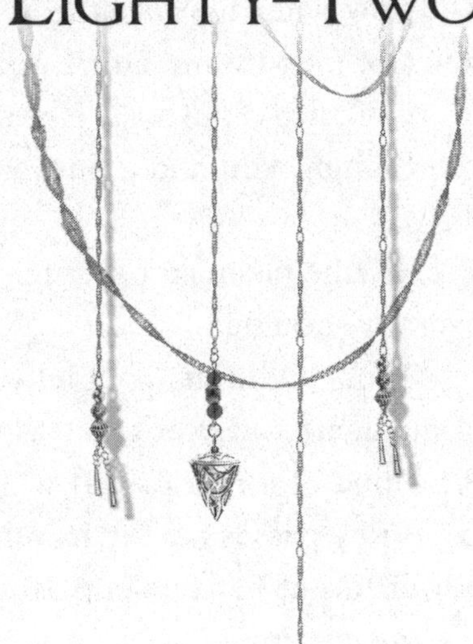

REY

I'm too stunned to move.

Rowen. The one I trusted, the one I leaned on. All those nights I complained to him, the way he joked with me when I was breaking, the stories we would tell about Thor—about the God he could never be. And all along, he was sitting there, smiling at me, lying to me.

My chest tightens. Tears burn hot and blur everything, but not enough to erase the sight of him in that armor, not enough to silence Aric's cries echoing like a dirge through the chamber.

Hiding in plain sight. Thor. God of Thunder.

The ground crunches beneath my boots, shards of frost cracked and shattered from someone's fury—Aric's fury. His rage is etched into every surface: walls clawed with jagged ice, pillars fractured where the frost exploded outward.

Rowen steps away, empty-handed. What happened? Did he not set Mjölnir free?

Men shove me forward, rough, causing me to fall to the hard ground in front of my father.

Odin's still holding his pistol—sleek, black, merciless like his eyes. He levels the weapon at my chest.

"All I ever needed," he says softly, almost lovingly, "was your blood. And now, when we have the hammer in our hands, I can regenerate as much of it as I want. Don't worry, you won't be awake for it. After all, everyone has a purpose. I've always found it entertaining how often you thought you had a purpose outside of existing simply so he can thrive."

He tilts his head past me, eyes cutting to the figure standing just over my shoulder.

"Thor," Odin snaps. "I let you try on your own out of the kindness of my heart, but you know as well as I do that it will not respond to the blood of a betrayer. It will not choose you as worthy any longer. Once Rey passes me the hammer, I'll restore the Bifrost, then use my power to put her to sleep. If you ever cared for her, you'll show her this one kindness."

"And if I refuse?"

"Everyone dies." Odin shrugs. "Your friends, Laufey, your precious Giantess…one by one, I'll kill every soul at this school. Is that what you want?"

"I can pull it!" Thor yells. "It's my birthright!"

"And it will be your downfall," Father snaps, then shoves me toward Rowen.

Thunder rumbles overhead as Father continues talking.

"Destroying Jötunheim needed to be done, but Mjölnir refuses to see it. The hammer will no longer respond to our tainted blood, yet hers has never seen war. It will only recognize her."

This is it.

I'll pull Mjölnir and save Aric, shield him with my body, and hope it gives him enough time to heal so he can enact his revenge.

And if I die in the process?

Worth it to save the world.

Slowly, I stand, aware of my father's gun still pointed at me, and walk toward Thor, desperately trying to push both of them with my Aethercall, knowing we're well past that. My last steps. I think about my moments with Aric. At least I had them. At least I had friends. At least, for just a fraction of a second, I experienced life.

And it was everything.

The chamber cracks with tension as lightning snaps through the ceiling onto the ground. Sparks erupt. I almost smile as Aric keeps his head bowed and body taut. I trust him. I trust him.

He's too pissed to quit. And this time, I don't care if he has to blow up the place with me in it—I *want* him to lose all control.

"Do it," I yell.

Aric snaps his head in my direction. "Let their world burn, Rey. The way they burned yours."

Chapter Eighty-Three

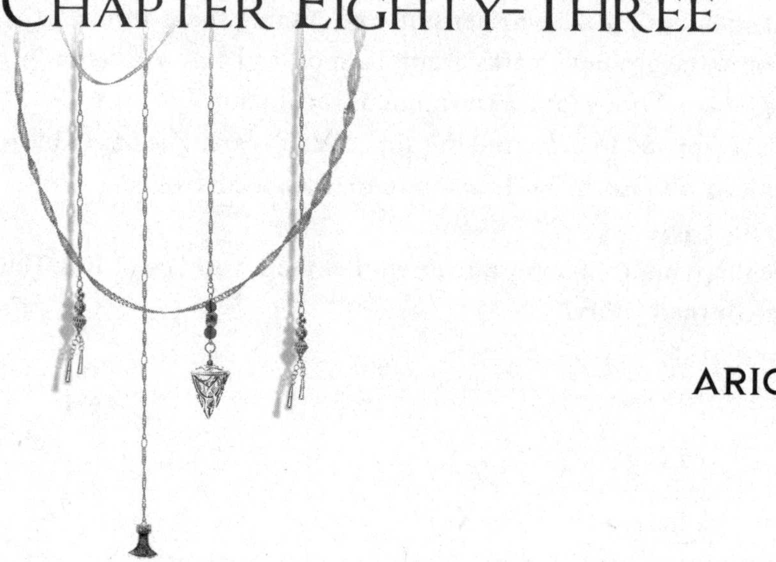

ARIC

The chains burning around my wrists must be special. Every time I move, they dig deeper into my skin, making the pain severe. I may not be able to break free, but that doesn't mean I can't cause a little chaos.

After all, they haven't broken me yet. The ultimate weapon still lives under my skin.

I latch onto the distant storm in the sky, the power of the lightning, the sensation of thunder, and exhale. I smirk. They want to make her bleed? I'll make them pay.

"You can't do it," I hiss under my breath to Rowen. Not Rowen—Thor. Maybe he and Reeve are more alike than I thought, both of them lying, pretending to be who we needed them to be.

Thor's jaw clenches, but his right hand, the one with the scars that suddenly fucking make sense, burns against my spine like the metal is trying to unlock the very bones beneath my skin. It feels like any minute my spine is going to snap. Mjölnir's inside of me. I know that now. It makes so much sense—why I control the lightning, the storms themselves. Not only did Mjölnir have the map to the Nightfrost, but the ring could find Mjölnir. They're a pair, a powerful pair.

Odin didn't just want one. His plan all along was both.

I suck in a shaky breath and stare across at Rey. Her head's lifted high, her eyes focused on Odin like she's still thinking of ways to win. She's perfect.

"You aren't, but I am," I finally whisper. "Worthy." I hiss as his hand digs deeper into my spine. "I'd die for her. Would you? Or do you only care about past glory?" His hand pushes harder as a frustrated scream erupts from his lips. "Even now, it won't recognize the great Thor."

"Shut up!" Rowen screams. "It's mine, created for me. I am a *God*!"

The hammer embedded in my back thrums, faint golden light gleaming all around me.

Does it hurt? Like a motherfucker.

This asshole is trying to rip out by force an archaic weapon that's anchored and buried beneath my skin.

And Mjölnir isn't budging.

"The Gods failed for a reason, Rowen. They destroyed themselves because they were serving themselves." I raise my head. It burns to meet Rowen's gaze. Voice shaking, I whisper, "Mjölnir, you know me. My parents chose me the way you chose them. I'm not Rey. But I know who I am now. I'm the only Giant born in this realm sworn to protect you at all costs."

The walls crack around us. Ice shatters, cascading like glass around Odin and Rey.

Tears stream down Rey's face. "Aric, the lightning, the thunder—" She doesn't want me to get hurt. I'm still bound by these cursed chains. The more I push, the more the chains pull.

But in the end, it's not what I'm fighting against—it's who I'm fighting for.

Decision made.

I close my eyes and summon all the strength of the storms, the chaos, the uncontrollable power that could easily undo me, and I cling to it.

I grit my teeth as pain erupts down my spine. "Choose me."

Pain rips through my body, so hot that I can't breathe. Lightning tears open the sky, pouring into me until I'm shoved against the ground in a dazzling arc.

Mjölnir erupts from my back, the gold colliding with the chains binding my hands and breaking them open in the lightning storm surrounding me. I grip the weapon, and in an instant, the wars, the bloodshed, my memories with Rey—my parents sealing Mjölnir into my body—all of them slam into me like a tidal wave.

And Odin?

It seems Mjölnir and I agree on one thing.

He's about to die.

Chapter Eighty-Four

REY

With a battle cry, Aric surges to his feet. His clothes burn under the heat of the lightning, and suddenly he transforms right in front of me. His body stretches to his full height, muscles surging beneath silver armor. His skin is pale as frost, hair jet-black, with pieces of ice clinging to the ends like adornments.

Odin stumbles back, true fear flashing in his eyes. "Impossible... You're a Giant without any birthright—and Mjölnir is mine!"

Aric snarls, voice no longer just human but layered with undercurrents of thunder, the soft thrum I always felt but could never quite place. "Did you forget? I was only sleeping. And now—" He hefts the hammer, lightning spiraling around it like a never-ending charge. "You're fucked for waking me up."

He hurls Mjölnir. Odin barely raises a hand before Rowen leaps in front, deflecting the blow as the Nightfrost ring spirals out into a blue shield. The clash detonates in an explosion of light and frost.

I'm thrown backward, my ears ringing, the taste of blood sharp on my tongue.

Aric's completely healed now—and the man is pissed as hell. Mjölnir returns to his hand, and he holds it high over his head, then bellows as he throws it down to the ground. Crackling fire erupts from where it hits, then snakes out directly to the men near my father, narrowly avoiding the unconscious Reeve but searing the guards alive. Then, just as quickly, a wall of ice appears, so frigid it freezes their skeletons in place before they can even fall to the ground.

"Thor!" Father yells, slamming his hands together, creating a loud screech that has me covering my ears. Ravens pour into the hall, surrounding all of us while he pulls Laufey to his side.

Rowen staggers, but Odin shoves him forward, fury carving his features. "Take Rey!"

"No!" I scream. I'm done being used.

I am the blood of Odin, daughter of Asgard.

I woke a fucking Giant.

And I'm worthy.

My gaze flickers to Aric as he smashes Mjölnir onto the icy ground again, causing a spiderweb of lightning to crack toward Odin and Rowen. Without hesitation, I hold out my hand.

Aric has only a second to smile at me before the hammer slams into my palm. "Awaken," I whisper, then hold it high toward the ceiling. The sound of ice splitting fills the room.

Odin staggers back, eyes wide, and for the first time, I don't just see fear on his face. I taste it.

And it's the sweetest thing I've ever savored.

I keep my hand raised, ready to throw Mjölnir and end this once and for all. But first: "Release Laufey."

She's still behind Odin, still chained, still looking terrified. I'm not leaving without her.

At the mention of my stepmother, Odin's gaze turns assessing, shrewd. Like he knows he still has one card left to play. But in my world, it's already game over.

"Thor. Now—" he starts in a low voice, but I heave Mjölnir above my head, putting every ounce of anger, fear, and retribution I have into the throw. Odin's eyes widen in horror as the strongest weapon of the Gods hits him square in the chest.

"Father!" Rowen screams, pulling him to his side as blood spews from Odin's mouth. He holds Odin tight, and then, just like Reeve did in the elevator, they both disappear into thin air.

He's gone.

But he left someone behind.

Rowen has Nightfrost and a very wounded Odin, but we have Mjölnir. And we have Laufey.

I rush over to her. Her blue eyes lock onto mine as she slowly raises her shaking, bandaged hands and cups my face. "You did good, daughter."

Tears well in my eyes. "Daughter?"

The fact that she can say it freely now makes me want to burst into tears. I throw my arms around her and hold her tight.

"Everything is going to be okay." Laufey pats my face. "For now, rest. Tomorrow, you can decide what to do with that weapon with your… new friend." She smiles up at Aric. "I've heard a lot about you. Odin positively hates you."

Aric bursts out laughing.

"And your parents," she says, sobering, "were some of the best friends I had in my entire miserable life here in Midgard—Earth."

Aric reaches for her hand. "That means a lot."

"What now?" I ask, looking around at the damage.

"We wait," Sigurd's voice says from the door. How long has he been standing there? "I'll take Laufey and get her checked out." He shares a look with us, then notices Reeve still unconscious on the floor and all the dead bodies frozen around the chamber. "The wound to Odin is likely fatal. Thor will stop at nothing to try to heal him, though." He presses his wrists together, then twists his hands in a counterclockwise motion. I hear an audible click. "The runes are back on." He walks over to Laufey and gently grabs her hand, addressing me one last time. "I hope you know what you just did."

"What?" I ask.

"They're waking up." He shakes his head. "All over campus."

The other fallen Gods and sleeping Giants.

Good, I think. *They deserve to know. To have* all *their memories, the good and the bad.*

"And the Bifrost?" Aric asks.

"I'll send for cleanup. Join the bonfire. If anyone asks, the storm caught a few things on fire. Don't call on the hammer. For now."

He leaves like we didn't just take out Odin, probably for good.

I rush to Aric's side. He pulls me in for a hug before I can make it. Then he kisses down my neck. "Are you hurt?"

The hammer's back in my hand. I press it against him, and it sinks underneath his skin like a lock clicking into place, the runes doing their jobs. "It was you the whole time."

"More like us."

Reeve starts coughing. "Hi, still here, conscious again. Please don't have sex next to the dead people, it's weird. And good job on surviving, sorry for what I did."

"Why shouldn't we kill you right now?" Aric growls, thunder still in his voice, the hammer sparking down his back.

Reeve arches a brow. "Because I gave Rey that rune. Helped you out, didn't I? And if you kill me, who would explain what happens next? I'm known to be a very good storyteller, you know."

Before Aric can retort, Mjölnir groans. The sound is alive—hungry. Sparks shoot from it, not toward Aric, but toward me.

I freeze and then hold out my hand. The hammer wrenches itself from Aric and floats to me, then sends a series of fiery sparks down my legs and arms. My wounds quickly heal, the warm feeling putting me at peace.

Mjölnir drifts into my hand, and the shaft lights up with runes beneath my palm.

Mine, I think.

Aric stares. I stare back, the weight of it settling between us. The hammer belongs to both of us.

The realization is sharp.

By birth, it's mine.

By worthiness, it's his.

The weapon shimmers once more.

Aric holds up his hand. It leaves me just like that. He doesn't use it, though, merely lifts it into the air. It presses against his back and locks into place again. His body jolts with the impact, breath ripping free from his mouth like the hammer is truly a part of him.

He's not using it; he's protecting it.

For now.

For one breathless moment, the cavern is silent. Balanced.

Then Reeve grins, whistling low. "See? You're going to need me. Who else can teach you how to survive Ragnarök? Gods have fallen. Giants have risen. Did you really think this was the end?" He spreads his arms wide, mocking and theatrical. "Guys, the party's just getting started."

EPILOGUE

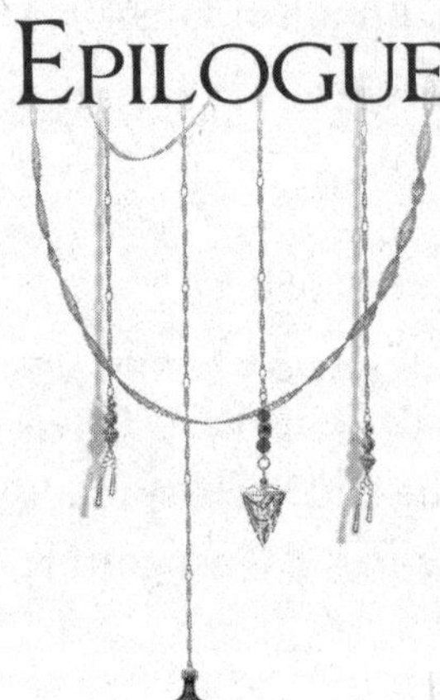

REY

TWO DAYS LATER

The lake looks like glass. Silver frost stretches across its surface in a perfect sheet. I grin as the moonlight seems to scatter diamonds over the frozen water. Some girls get dinner and a movie. I get an ice-covered lake under the blanket of the stars.

We slip our way across, my boots skidding until Aric's hand clamps down on my elbow. His laugh is low, rough from exhaustion, as he pulls me flush with his chest. "Keeping your enemies close?"

"Something like that." My breath plumes white in the air. "Though if you wanted me dead, you'd have killed me last night after I snuck into your room again. Sorry not sorry."

"I should watch my back," he murmurs with a sexy grin. "I hear you're a hair puller." His grip tightens on my elbow as he leads me across the lake toward the dark shape of the tree line.

A cabin pokes out from the trees ahead. Old, weather-worn, and small, with antlers nailed above the door like some ancient ward. Once we get to the water's icy edge, we take the trail up to the door. He pushes it open, and warmth greets me in a rush—firelight, cedar smoke, and...

My breath catches.

Flowers.

Everywhere.

The table, the floor, even the rough shelves are crowded with blooms—wildflowers in jars, roses clumsily jammed into mugs, daisies spilling from a chipped vase by the window. A hunter's cabin turned into something soft, something beautiful. Something just for me.

I turn in the doorway, blinking hard against the tears burning in my eyes. "What is this?"

He shrugs, jaw flexing like he's embarrassed. "Because every girl should be asked out on a date and given a flower. Even the blood of Odin."

The words break something in me. He remembered. My eyes sting, and a tear slides free before I can stop it.

Aric catches it with one finger, lifts it to his lips, and blows. Frost sparks from his breath, the tear freezing midair into a tiny crystal that floats before us. He sighs. "Also, I was just trying to get laid."

I choke out a laugh. It's ridiculous and so perfect.

I launch myself at him. He catches me easily and spins me around. It's freeing, being in my enemy's arms.

We stop spinning, my body slowly sliding down his. My feet almost touch the ground before he lifts me back up and crushes his mouth against mine.

It's different now, his kiss. Fiercer. Hungrier. His hands trace my back, and when my palms slide down the runes etched into his skin, they spark under my touch—tiny bolts of lightning dancing between us.

When we finally break apart, we're both out of breath. I rest my forehead against his chest. "Any word from Sigurd?"

Aric exhales slowly, his eyes going from silver back to brown. "I did exactly as planned. Told him *we* control Mjölnir."

My chest tightens. "We."

"Yeah." His thumb brushes my jaw. "We. And that it's up to you to decide what to do with it."

I swallow hard and tilt my head into his palm. "We open the Bifrost, and they get their power back. All of them, including the ones who're already regaining their memories on campus. Each of them deserves it."

"They do." Aric's sigh is heavier than the storm outside. "But that means Odin also gets his power back. And you know he'll keep trying to use Laufey against you. Rowen, too."

It's a risk I'm going to have to take. One way or another, this war has to end.

I change the subject slightly. "I wonder if Odin has more allies or enemies waiting on the other side."

Aric stares down at me, something dark and steady in his eyes. "Only one way to find out."

"First things first." I force a shrug. "We eliminate the threats here."

"Tomorrow," he says, a ghost of a smile pulling at his lips.

I tug at his shirt, grinning despite myself. "At least Reeve's good for something."

His face clouds. "Other than being annoying and manipulative? Yes."

I laugh. "What? We wouldn't have Mjölnir if he hadn't helped me. Plus, he's good at distracting and confusing Sigurd, though I still think Sigurd knew what was going on that night. He just banked on Reeve getting the ring."

Aric nods reluctantly, mouth twisting. "Yeah, I don't know. He won't ever give us a straight answer. For now, let's just focus on tonight. We deserve at least that."

The fire pops, the frost crystal spins once before dissolving into the air, and for the first time all day, I let myself breathe, then finally rest in my Giant's arms.

His visions have gotten more vivid now. Sometimes I see war in them; other times, I see the edges of Asgard shining out from the deep blue sea that surrounds it, like a castle among the stars.

Other days, it's Jötunheim before it was destroyed.

It's snowing. I blink and open my eyes. I'm in another one of his visions, but this one is beautiful. We're standing out in a field, staring at the snow, a blank canvas.

For a moment, it feels hopeful. *Peaceful.*

The word echoes in my chest as Aric's hand closes over mine, bringing me back to the present. Ice sparks where our fingers meet. The lake groans outside, the storm simmers between us, and for one fleeting heartbeat, it feels like the world is holding its breath right alongside us. Allowing this moment.

But the silence won't last.

It never does.

Acknowledgments

First off, I have to thank God. Though this book was *truly* one of the most challenging experiences of my life, it was also a labor of love. I could not have done it without my family, from my amazing husband, who was there twenty-four seven when I needed backup and a shoulder to cry on, to my dad, who I'd text late at night and ask questions. He's a solid research partner and would always come back with an answer. My favorite was when we were at the end of edits and my agent texted: *ask your dad!*

Which brings me to Nicole Resciniti. Oh man, the best agent in the world. We were in the trenches with this one. You are a rock star for fighting for me, for this book, and for working so hard on it. You sacrificed sanity, sleep—we both did. And it was worth it. Thank you.

To Stacy Abrams for jumping in there at the end, bless you! Amy Pierpont, thank you for not panicking over the panicked texts when we needed a quick edit or cleanup. You would drop everything. Thank you! *Liz Pelletier*, my goodness, thank you for believing in this book and hyping me up when I needed it, giving me the confidence to keep going.

Angie, Krista, Denise, Kristin, and Sophie, your beta reading and availability and just helping with feedback were so valuable to me. Tijan, your check-ins were everything. (I KNOW I am forgetting people!) Mai, ha-ha, I won't forget you! You talked me off many cliffs during this process. To everyone in Rockin Readers and on Insta, thank you for being patient as I quite literally put all of my other projects and series on hold for this. Jill, I know you're smiling from heaven.

To all the Entangled people who I either met via email or never met at all and who worked so hard behind the scenes, you guys are so amazing, I wanted to give you a special shoutout. I appreciate you so much! In art: LJ, Elizabeth, Bree, Liz. In production: Curtis, Brittany, Molly, Justine, and Beth. In editorial: Mary, Rae, Hannah, and Jessica. And in marketing/publicity: Victoria, Erin, Cai, Meredith, Heather, Melanie, Hannah, and Lindsey.

It takes more than a village, as you can see, so to my readers, thank you so much for supporting me and being there for me. I hope you all enjoyed the journey.

HUGS

RVD

She's a barmaid who doesn't believe in fairy tales.

He's a prince cursed to live one.

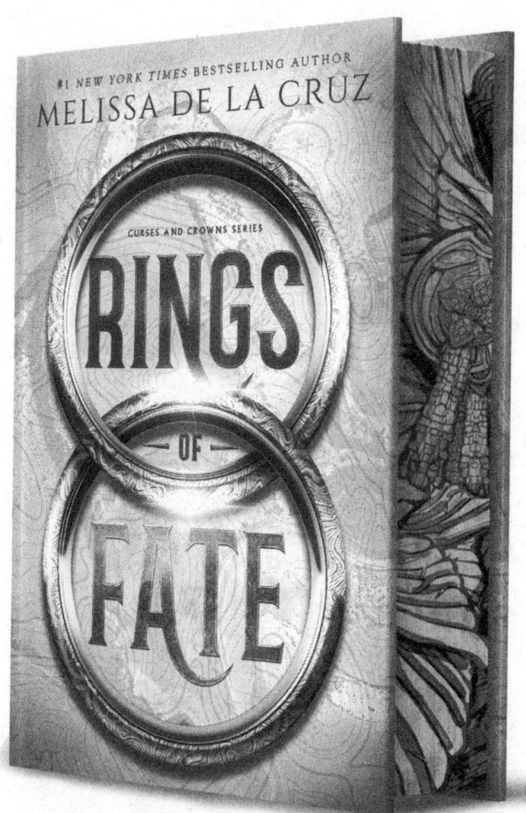

A sweeping romantasy of sharp-tongued heroines, cursed princes, and the kind of love worth defying fate for.